THEY ARE EVERYWHERE...

IN BRITAIN...Doris lay back when she had sampled the breakfast Marigold brought. The alien was tunneling into the decaying storehouse of her memories—perhaps making better sense of them than she could, the old woman reflected.

"Is it with you, Mother?" Marigold asked.

"Death it likes," Doris said faintly. "It's excited. I feel that it's excited by my..." After a while she said, "Perhaps where it comes from, they don't die."

IN AUSTRALIA...I must confess that in our true forms on either of our home worlds we should never have dreamed of close physical contact. What could a steely carapaced being, all jaws and claws, do to a blob of sentient jelly—except eat her, of course.

IN THAILAND...In the middle of the act I became aware that someone else was there with us. I mean, I was used to the way Mary moved, the delicious abandon with which she made her whole body shudder. I thought, The alien's here too! Well, I'm really going to show it how a Thai can drive. Here we go!

The next morning I said, "How was it?"

She said, "It was a fascinating activity, but frankly I prefer mitosis."

CREATED BY

FREDERIK POHL
AND ELIZABETH ANNE HULL

TALES FROM THE
PLANET EARTH

ST. MARTIN'S PRESS/NEW YORK

Armer, Karl Michael, "On the Inside Track." Copyright 1986 by Karl Michael Armer. Originally published in *Entropie*, edited by Wolfgang Jeschke, 1986.

Harrison, Harry, "The View From the Top of the Tower." Copyright 1986 by Harry Harrison. Originally published in *The Magazine of Fantasy and Science Fiction*, May 1986.

Nesvadba, Josef, "The Divided Carla." Copyright 1985 by Josef Nesvadba. Originally published in *Literarni Mesicnik*, June 1985.

Pohl, Frederik, "Sitting Around the Pool, Soaking Up Some Rays." Copyright 1984 by Frederik Pohl. Originally published in *The Magazine of Fantasy and Science Fiction*, June 1984.

Sucharitkul, Somtow, "Fiddling for Water Buffaloes." Copyright 1986 by Somtow Sucharitkul. Originally published in *Analog*, April 1986.

Yano, Tetsu, "The Legend of the Paper Spaceship." Copyright 1983 by Tetsu Yano. Originally published in *SF-Magazine*, 1983.

(Remaining stories have not been previously published.)

Library of Congress Catalog Card Number: 86-13832

ISBN: 0-312-90779-6   Can. ISBN: 0-312-90781-8

Printed in the United States of America

First St. Martin's Press mass market edition/November 1987

10 9 8 7 6 5 4 3 2 1

For A. Bertram Chandler and Janusz A. Zajdel,
who are greatly missed and affectionately remembered.
Their loss impoverishes us all.

CONTENTS

Report From
the Planet Earth

When I first began reading science fiction, the practice came under the heading of "a solitary vice." A fair number of people did it, but they kept it as quiet as they could.

It did not occur to me at that time, half a century ago and more, that a day would come when college professors taught it, doctoral candidates wrote their dissertations on it, the best-seller lists were saturated with it, and the movie screens would have to go dark without it. I certainly never suspected then that it would be a worldwide phenomenon, with people deeply committed to it in places as diverse as Uruguay, Sweden, and the People's Republic of China.

If I were first encountering science fiction today in America, it's pretty likely that I still might not suspect its global nature. For the average science-fiction reader in America, there are few signs that it happens anywhere outside the English-speaking countries. There are around a thousand science-fiction books published each year in the United States, and it is a banner year when more than half a dozen of them originate in any other language. English-language science fiction is read in every country of the world, but we are far less hospitable to the return flow.

It was not always so.

The first science-fiction magazine was *Amazing Stories*,

founded in 1926. It was certainly an American magazine, but its editor, Hugo Gernsback, was born in Luxembourg, and for its first decade it made considerable use of translations from other languages. Readers of the 1920s and early 1930s became almost as familiar with people like Henrik Dahl Juve and Otto Willi Gail as with Ray Cummings and Harl Vincent (to say nothing of such staples of the early *Amazing Stories* as Jules Verne and H. G. Wells).

It is true that Gernsback's policies were at least partly dictated by economics: He could pick up European stories and publish them, even after counting in the cost of translation, cheaper than he could buy new ones from American writers. But there were at least two other reasons that motivated Gernsback. One was that there simply weren't enough American writers of science fiction around (and wouldn't be, until the magazine had begun to generate its own stable of contributors). And the other was that Gernsback thought the non-American writers had something special to offer—a different point of view; a distinctive flavor; a kind of story-telling that grew out of other influences in other societies.

In this I think Hugo Gernsback was absolutely right.

I've thought so for several decades, in fact. As a result, I've tried now and then, while employed as an editor for one publishing house or another, to introduce some of these writers to American audiences.

My principal effort in this direction was in the 1960s, while I was editor of the *Galaxy* chain of science-fiction magazines. I persuaded the publisher to launch a new magazine composed entirely of stories from other countries. We chose the not very original title of *International Science Fiction*, and did in fact get it published.

It was not a success. It lasted two issues, and the only reason it got that far was that we didn't have sales figures on the first issue before the second was already irrevocably in print.

Well, I think I know now what we did wrong. We dumped it on the market with no preparation (advertising, publicity, all those huckstering things that make a new magazine an instant seller); the format was wrong; there should have been certain features that we didn't have the opportunity (or the inspiration) to create. If we had it to do over again, I think it would work—in spite of some pretty tough problems.

The toughest of problems is finding the right translators. It takes very special people to do the job.

Translating is always a major headache; there is an Italian saying, *"Traduttore, traditore,"* which means, roughly, "To translate is to betray." A translation need not *always* be some sort of betrayal of the original author's intentions, but to avoid that sin takes great skill. Particularly in the translation of science fiction, where the translator must be wholly fluent in not two languages but three— the language of the original; the language of the translation; and the special vocabulary and mind-set of the language of science fiction itself.

People with those qualities are rare—in some cases, particularly in the more arcane languages, almost nonexistent. They are very nearly impossible to find through the regular publishing channels.

But there are treasures to be found. . . .

Over the past few decades I've been lucky enough to visit some forty or fifty countries of the planet Earth (much depends on what you call a country). In most of them I've found science-fiction readers and writers.

I'm not sure just how many science-fiction writers there are in the world (much depends on what you call a science-fiction writer). My best guess is maybe about two thousand. Of these, a little more than a quarter are in the United States. Another couple hundred are in the other English-speaking countries. There are perhaps a hundred or so each in Japan and the Soviet Union, several hundred in the other countries of Western Europe, the rest scattered from Singapore to Reykjavik and in points along the way. I doubt that there is a country in the world capable of supporting any publishing industry at all which does not have at least one or two local writers of science fiction. Years ago, when I was a magazine editor, I received a manuscript from a man who described himself as "the second-best science-fiction writer in Iran"—thus implying there were at least two. Unfortunately, for reasons one can only surmise, nothing has been heard of either of them lately.

Such is the geographical distribution of science-fiction writers. For science-fiction *readers,* and especially for those quintessential readers, the science-fiction *fans,* the distribution is equally global and numerically a whole lot larger.

Science-fiction fans are unlike any other kind of reader the world has ever known. The reading of science fiction is no longer solely a private vice. It is practiced in public, in large numbers, at "sf cons." An sf con is a conference, convention, or gathering devoted to talking about science fiction, and unless you have had some experience you would not *believe* how many of them go on all the time, all over. In the United States alone there are half a dozen every weekend of the year, large and small—some five hundred American cons a year, and probably around the same number elsewhere in the world.

The very first con of all, half a century ago, involved only about a dozen people—six fans from New York who took the train to Philadelphia to meet with six or seven locals. It would have been little remarked and less remembered if the idea hadn't caught on. Within a few months the second, slightly larger and drawing on more localities, took place in England; now they usually attract some hundreds of attendees, and many have registrations in the thousands. There is the "Worldcon"—the annual World Science Fiction Convention—which is ordinarily held in the United States, or at least in an English-speaking convention. There are national conventions in at least twenty countries, and regionals and locals beyond tabulating. Most of them are, almost totally, fan gatherings, with a sprinkling of authors and artists to bask in praise. Some are more specialized, as the academics' annual Science Fiction Research Association convention.

And then there is World SF.

A decade ago Harry Harrison issued a proclamation to the world's science-fiction writers saying, roughly, that although we all loved fan cons and attended lots of them, there should be at least one international meeting for *professionals;* and, he said, he was sponsoring one in Dublin, Ireland.

It was a great success, although not actually the first such international meeting of pros—there had been one in Rio de Janeiro in 1969, and another in Japan (a traveling show, with stops in Tokyo, Osaka, and elsewhere) a year later. The Dublin meeting, though, was both larger and more serious-minded. More than a hundred of us were there, and we found the international exchange of views so rewarding that we decide to institutionalize the event by forming an international organization of science-fiction professionals that would remain in being all year round; and we called it World SF.

World SF began with mostly writers. At once it began attracting critics, editors, agents, bibliographers, artists, filmmakers, teachers, musicians, librarians, publishers—anyone who works at any aspect of science fiction professionally. It now has members in thirty-odd countries. Its World General Meetings have been held in almost a dozen—past or current sites including Dublin, Ireland; Brighton, England; Fanano, Italy; Stockholm, Sweden; Rotterdam, the Netherlands; Linz, Austria; Zagreb, Yugoslavia; Vancouver, Canada; and Budapest, Hungary.

It was at the 1982 World General Meeting, in Rotterdam, that the chain of events which culminated in this book began. Krsto Mazuranic, one of our Yugoslavian members, proposed a World SF anthology of stories from all the countries of the world where we had membership.

This is not exactly that book. (That book, edited by Sam Lundwall and Brian Aldiss, is currently in preparation.) This is a second-generation derivative of it, based on a later idea of Betty Anne Hull's and my own.

I had written a short story called "Sitting Around the Pool, Soaking Up the Rays," which had to do with people from elsewhere in the galaxy taking over human beings for their own purposes. (It is in this volume, in a substantially altered form.) We had also recently seen a short story by our friend Tetsu Yano, "The Legend of the Paper Spaceship," which was on a similar theme. After I had shown my story to Betty Anne, we looked at each other and said, "Why don't we get other science-fiction writers to create stories on that theme for their own countries?" And we took the half-formed proposal to Tom Dunne, our editor at St. Martin's Press, and he agreed to publish it.

Easy to decide—hard to do! Several years and hundreds of working hours later, Betty Anne and I finally completed this volume. (Along the way we decided to get married. This did nothing to speed up the preparation of the book, but it made it a good deal more enjoyable.)

So what you have here is a book, originally inspired by a Yugoslavian in the Netherlands, edited and assembled by Americans (both while in the United States and while traveling in twenty-odd other countries), containing stories from Ireland, Sweden, England, Australia, Thailand, Japan, Canada, Uruguay, Italy, West Germany, Poland, Bulgaria, Brazil, Czechoslovakia, Norway, and the People's Republic of China—two from the last-named because, after all, it contains more people than all of the others combined. This isn't exactly an anthology. It is, we think, essentially a novel with nineteen authors; and it is indeed internationally created "Tales From the Planet Earth."

We hope you'll enjoy it.

—Frederik Pohl

The Last Word

A novel with nineteen authors, indeed! Who are we kidding? Like the proverbial blind men with the elephant, we can look at this collection of stories and clearly see that no two parts are quite a match.

Another image seems more appropriate, though some would think it more pretentious. Like the Judeo-Christian Bible, we've collected here a series of stories that complement each other, even as they contradict each other. They vary in tone from light to bleak, in style from stark to baroque, in apparent purpose from didactic to cryptic. Yet these stories together create a whole that is greater than the parts.

They do share one special quality—they're all good tales. What makes them good is their humanness. To be human means to be unique, to be born alone (even twins enter the world one after the other, not simultaneously), to inhabit a particular body occupying a point in time and space that is physically shared with no one. Surely no other species anywhere could cherish its own uniqueness more than we do. Paradoxically, to be human also means to be a social animal. Born helpless, we "imprint" on others while we're still non-rational, preverbal. To ignore either our basic individuality or our social selves is to diminish the possibilities of human potential. Because these stories focus on the union of humans with aliens, they get at the heart of the human condition, longing to join with others, afraid of losing autonomy.

Two witnesses can watch the same automobile accident and sincerely differ about the details, who was at fault, the order in which events occurred, who had the right of way. Writers are witnesses of human nature who have the talent for observing the world, reshaping events, and telling us what happens in such a way that the rest of us enjoy being the judge and jury.

I've come to realize that even when I don't agree with another's vision, it's valuable to learn the way the world looks from a different angle. Who holds the truest vision of humanity? I have my own favorites, but I suspect they will not exactly coincide with anyone else's. I invite you to sit with me and see the world as these nineteen imaginative writers have seen it.

—Elizabeth Anne Hull

Sitting Around the Pool, Soaking Up the Rays

BY FREDERIK POHL

I had no way of telling how well the conference was going. None of us did. We didn't understand much of what was being said, and anyway we didn't really know what the issues were in the first place, so the way I tried to judge it was by the amount of yelling. There had been a lot. My head hurt. From that, and from not being allowed even a drink of water for three and a half straight hours, and from a lot of other things, too. So I came out of the Liliuokalani Ballroom feeling poorly and looking worse, lifting each foot in turn in that circular Howdy-Doody prance my boss favors, and that Maui sun hit me right in the face. I blinked. I stumbled. And all of a sudden the boss whispered, "Later," and left me on my own. That's the way it always was, take over without warning and without warning take off.

So I had some slack time. The first thing I did, of course, was pee. You do that when you can, whenever you get a chance; you learn that right away. Then I headed for the pool. Marc Socul was coming toward me. If I have a real friend among the bunch at the Makele Motel—male friend, anyway—Marc is it. But he went by me without a word, slithering along like a mime doing serpents; there was no point in talking to him and I didn't try.

It was hot in the sun. There were a hundred and forty of us at the motel, but you'd never know it from the skimpy showing around the pool. When we're not working we tend to run and hide somewhere, at least for the first few weeks. The Makele Motel is built on the side of a hill, in the shape of a U, with big staggered rooms going down toward the ocean and the wings of the building surrounding the palm trees and the pool and the sun deck and the winding carp stream and the kerosene flares they still light up with torches every sundown, beating out time on a drum as the beach boys race from flare to flare. Pretty much it's the way it was in civilian days, when tourists paid a hundred and sixty dollars a day for the rooms and lanais, and more than that in the bar. Doesn't cost us a thing. Especially the bar doesn't, since they closed it down. I was hoping to find Lois around the pool, but she was probably busy—or at least absent—so I sat down on a beach chair and threw my terrycloth robe off to catch some sun. The one thing I definitely expected to gain out of this was a tan.

Alice leaned over in her predatory way and said, "How about it, Ben, you want to play some bridge?" Alice is a nice enough old lady, but she's over seventy and she didn't really look good in a deep-cut one-piece bathing suit. She is also someone I don't really want to play cards with. She's a professional card hustler—or was— took her retirement from the math department at Georgia Tech and went out to beat the blackjack dealers in Vegas. She did it very well, too, until she got recruited. So I turned her down, as she expected I would. She settled for backgammon with sad, sorry little Elsa McKee, our newest recruit and unhappiest.

A shadow fell over me from behind.

I jumped up and turned around and yelled, "Don't do that!" It wasn't anyone to worry about. It was just Arnold, who is one of our doctors. All he wanted was to check me out, but he should have known better than to startle me.

"Sorry," he said. He probably was. "Just hold still." He stethoscoped me and pulsed me and pulled down one eyelid to look at the broken veins. "How are you feeling, Ben?" he asked.

"Hungry," I said at random, and he nodded and snapped his fingers for a poolside waiter and told me I was all right. Shows how much he knows. Arnold doesn't really like us much. Neither do the waiters or the maids or the guards—when you come right down to it, I wouldn't even say we like ourselves a whole bunch—but of course they're afraid to let anything go wrong with us. When the waiter rushed up to offer me the menu, the poor son of a bitch was trembling.

The menu was about a yard tall and printed on what felt like plush. I tried to hold it so the sun glare didn't make me squint while I studied every item. It all looked very good.

The thing I've noticed about my life is that I almost always get everything I want, but only when I either can't take advantage of it or don't want it anymore. This was a case of Category A. Before I was recruited, I was a tech-manual compiler for an electronics company in Redondo Beach. Twenty-two thousand dollars a year when I was working, which wasn't always, and a ninety-thousand-dollar mortgage to pay off. A big Saturday night date for me was Alaska king crab legs at the nearest Red Lobster. And here the beach boy was handing me Mr. Lucullus's personal menu, pressed duck and mahimahi and Chateaubriand, and all of it free—*free!* We live like kings, we servants of the stars, only I didn't know if I'd get a chance to eat it if I ordered it. So I asked what was ready right that minute.

"Roast beef, mashed potatoes, salad," he said without looking me in the eye. Afraid of what he might see. He was prepared to go on but I said that would do, with a lot of fresh orange juice. The doctor looked up from tapping Elsa's sweet, skinny little knee and nodded approval. Arnold is always after us about vitamins. He convinced me he was right when Jack Marcantonio fell over right in the middle of a screaming session with another delegate in the Sandalwood Room. They had to take him away. Arnold told us later that he had been D.O.A. at the hospital. Jack had been getting most of his calories from bourbon, and right after that they closed the Whaler Bar.

I dialed Lois's room on the poolside phone; no answer, so I leaned back to work on my tan, sort of hoping I would fall asleep, but across the pool Walter and Felice were keeping me awake. Not Walter. Felice. They were stretched out on canvas mats, face down and lips almost touching, and Felice had a blue bikini on. Wherever

I looked I saw her bottom, and it kept me looking up every minute to see if Lois was coming, so we could take a quick dip in the pool and then go up to one of our rooms and forget what we were doing with our lives. One of the soldiers from the machine-gun nest was staring at Felice, too. When he looked away and caught my eye he glared at me. As though he were jealous of us pampered proxies. Jealous of us! He was a new man. By the end of the week he wouldn't be jealous anymore. If he lasted that long. He wasn't supposed to be looking our way. He was supposed to be guarding us against any evil-intentioned Earth patriots or guerrillas who might be trying to sneak in to interrupt our deliberations, and if the lieutenant caught him gazing at the girls he would have been in trouble of his own.

The funny thing was that the machine-gunner wasn't looking at Elsa, who was a lot closer and just about as naked. I guess a weeping woman was not the right kind of sex object. "Pay attention to your game," Alice scolded, but Elsa was not capable of that. You couldn't blame her. She had been on her honeymoon when she was recruited and they wouldn't let her new husband come with her. Elsa is short, slim, pretty, very, very, young. Her hair is short, too, muddy brown streaked with gold, and it flops around her head when she moves. I would bet that represented a seventy-five-dollar investment at the beauty parlor to get ready for the wedding, and now it was wasted on us. "Hell with it," said Alice, tipping the backgammon board so all the pieces slid to the end and turning to me. "Ben? Do you know what you were talking about today?"

"The same thing. Minerals. Radionuclides and rare earths, mostly—they're apeshit for rare earths."

She nodded as though it meant something to her. Perhaps it did, but not to me. In those wheeling and dealing sessions I understand only part of what is being said, even when it comes out of my own mouth. What do I know about beneficiating ores of the lanthanum series? This may be just as well. Sometimes I think the Earth patriots have the right idea, and if I really knew what the deals were about in the Liliuokalani Ballroom I would be grabbing a gun and trying to storm the Makele Motel myself. If the boss let me, of course—which, of course, he wouldn't.

Elsa had stopped sobbing long enough to gaze mistily at the

lobby door. "What's that?" she asked, the object of her question being five dilapidated people in clothes meant for Boston or Chicago, gaping apprehensively at the pool and the armed guards. The assistant manager of the motel was trying to soothe them, but not succeeding.

"Congratulations, Elsa," I said, "you're now a senior member. That's what we all looked like when we got here. There's a new generation of recruits."

It would have been an act of kindness to go up to them and welcome them and try to make them feel less trapped and hopeless. But why should I lie? Anyway, my lunch was arriving. And there were two members of our happy family walking toward them already, except that their errand was not welcoming. They were occupied. They were walking along together, clutching each other's hands and shouting in each other's ears. Alice scowled because they were making so much noise, and the waiter, coming toward me with my dinner, switched and took the long way around to avoid them. Their names were Greg and Julio. I said they were "walking," but actually Greg was bouncy-hopping like Peter Cottontail and Julio was slinking like a two-legged cat. Or like Groucho Marx. They were heading directly for one of those palm trees that looks like a green fright wig growing out of the top of an artichoke and, as they were not looking where they were going, Julio plowed right into it. Head on. Still talking; and he kept right on talking while Greg jerked him back on his feet and they walked on, although Julio was beginning to bleed fairly heavily around the cheekbone. The new arrivals scattered despairingly, and then disappeared back in the lobby.

But I had my lunch to attend to. The orange juice was fresh and fine. The roast beef was good, too, although as the pool waiter was serving it Alice suddenly jumped up, kicked over the backgammon board, and left for one of the motel meeting rooms at a dead run, arms and legs windmilling wildly. The waiter dodged out of the way, his face blanching. Elsa gaped after her and then lifted her face and howled, big tears sliding down her face. Then Elsa turned and ran in the opposite direction, back to her room. But there was nothing queer about her gait. It was Elsa doing it herself, just scared sick and despairing. And there I was, all alone by the million-dollar pool, eating my fifty-dollar meal outside my two-hundred-dollar-a-day motel room and wondering if, after all, there was really anything wrong with suicide.

It was a thought that had crossed my mind before. It had occurred to me, in fact, about every other minute since that minute when I turned off the eleven o'clock news, got into my pajamas, brushed my teeth in front of the bathroom mirror . . . and then, in an instant, saw that something else was looking out of my sleepy eyes. It was something I neither recognized nor knew what to do about, but I didn't have any choice. What I did for the next little while was not my own doing. I dialed an 800 number I hadn't known I knew. I put a coat on over the pajamas and waited about five minutes, not more, until a Long Beach ambulance pulled up at my door and a jittery driver took me to a helicopter pad, then to LAX, then by jet to Hawaii, then here. I left a whole life back in Orange County. Three girls I was dating. Folk dancing every Thursday night. Car payments, mortgage, an unfinished manual on a new pocket calculator, and the Sunday crossword puzzle left undone. I didn't even get a chance to say good-by. So my thoughts are often gloomy, but the brightener is Lois. I was fiddling with the last of the roast beef when I heard her call my name.

I jumped up, and she ran into my arms. Lois is not anything like any of the three women back in Orange County. I don't think I would have dated her there, not so much because she is black as because she is skinny, at least ten years older than me, and not really all that pretty. But here on beautiful Maui she had one big thing going for her. That was that when we made love, *after* we made love, she was the one with whom I could hold tight while we admitted to each other how bad we really felt. "Are you hungry?" I asked her. She gave me the answer just by the way she looked up at me, grinning, and I said, "Your place or mine?" I didn't have to ask that. I knew the answer. The answer was "the nearest." With my free hand I grabbed a couple of rolls for Lois in case she really was hungry, and we started off, arms around each other's waist.

And then the boss whispered, "Now."

That was that. I dropped the rolls. I stepped on them as I

turned. I felt my knuckles bounce off Lois's elbow when she didn't get out of the way fast enough, but I didn't look at her. I was looking where I was heading, in that fast and spastic marionette hustle, all the way to the Liliuokalani Ballroom.

There is a book about a little boy named Curdie. I read it as a little kid. Curdie spent his time in the deep mines in, I guess, Germany or somewhere, being chased by weird-looking kobolds and gnomes and creepy, awful creatures of all kinds. The book scared me into five-year-old nightmares. I did not, at that time, think I would ever be one of the gnomes.

But that is what we all were. Crawly and spastic. Berserk or just bizarre. We moved the way our bosses moved. We writhed and wriggled, and we hissed at each other or screamed. I looked at my colleagues in the ballroom or the meeting rooms, when we were settling the interstellar trade balance or whatever it was we were doing, and they were awful. And so was I. I cannot tell you how grossly violated this makes you feel, when some far-off boss takes over the body your mother lovingly hatched for you and the mind you've filled with a million memories and the mouth you have used to speak your heart. It isn't your mouth that's speaking now. It is someone else's, or something else's, and most likely it is something that doesn't even have a heart back where it comes from, but turns out to be a cluster of heavy-metal polyps on the slushy bottom of an ammonia sea, or a halogen jelly in some poison swamp. The other night, while Lois was having her once-a-day hysterics, she whimpered that it was like being raped by the Fifth Armored Division, tanks and all. It isn't, though. It's worse.

I suppose that in its time the Liliuokalani Ballroom has had its share of weddings and corporate planning sessions and bar mitzvahs, or whatever they have on Maui that's like a bar mitzvah, and I bet every one of them was more fun than the bargaining sessions. You'd see the hotel people sneaking around, trying not to attract attention while they dusted off the tables and picked up the trash—and the worse than trash—because the sessions went on nonstop. All day, every day. It was about three in the afternoon when I bounced back in, heading right for the rare-earths group, but you would have seen the same forty or fifty bargainers at midnight. I plunged right in. That's how the boss does it, no introductions, just all of a sudden you're battling fiercely over which planet gets which shipment of the scandium, or who is willing to give up a batch of yttrium if he can have a load of spent fuel from nuclear generating stations. As if any of it was theirs to begin with!

They say the spent fuel is actually a kindness on their part, because we've been worrying so much about how to get rid of it. They're going to ship it to Borneo. Why Borneo? Because Borneo is on the Equator, and that's where they're building their launch catapult, which will throw the cargoes into low-Earth orbit, whereupon they will be packed into photon-sail ships, and sooner or later it will get to where somebody wants it. Maybe it will take a thousand years, because they say photon-sail ships are very slow. They don't care. They have plenty of time. And they tell us that by the time the cargoes start arriving we pitiful human beings will be educated right up to their standard. Then we can join the galactic club. Then the trade will be two-way. Then they'll send us just shiploads and shiploads of the most marvelous technological gadgets. . . . I imagine that's what Captain Bligh told the Tahitians when he swiped their breadfruit.

They're not the only ones to feed us that stuff. Our own governments say that this is an honor. They tell us how important we are. You don't feel very important when you're trying to emphasize a point by shaking or waving and uncoiling a member you don't have, although you'd be surprised how close you can come. But they say we do big work. They say that because the travel times are so long there's no way at all for these starborn creatures to come in person to our miserable little out-of-the-way planet. So if we want poor primitive Earth to play any part at all in the great galactic congeries of cultures, they have to do it the only way they can. Telepathically. Not exactly telepathically, but by thought, beefed up by some sort of amplifying technology that lets them reach out millions of times faster than light, into the minds of such handy appliances as Lois and Elsa and me, so that we can be their eyes and arms and voices. The word is "possessed." There really are demons, only they come from places like Fomalhaut and Alpha Centauri. And they don't

want our souls. All they want is our rare earths and our radionuclides
. . . and the frail and frantic bodies of people like me to puppet so
they can squawk and scream at each other as they confer to divide
up the loot.

So they say we matter, we miserable puppets on Hawaii's
golden island. They say we're so terribly important that they have
to protect us. They surround us with machine guns and patrol the
air above us with F-15s and Foxbats, so that no wild-eyed Earth
patriot can break in to interrupt our galactic deliberations. They say
that we few are the only ones in all the human race who can, through
some biochemical fluke, receive the transmitted minds from the
distant stars and be host to their originators. Big deal! Oh, biggest
of all deals ever! I do not deserve such an honor. I've got my faults.
But that wicked, never!

And all over the world the recruitment continues. . . .

The Thursday Events

BY YE YONGLIE
Translated by Dingbo Wu

On that Thursday in the great seaside city of Shanghai, things occurred in succession, like the beads in an abacus.

First, there was the recital in a music hall, where a soprano sang the wonderful "Love Song" poem by the celebrated Guo Moruo, with its enchanting music by He Luting:

> *My love is as cold as spring ice.*
> *My heart is as warm as spring breeze.*
> *Ice no sooner falls into the bosom of the breeze*
> *Than it melts into spring water.*

The woman sang beautifully, with so much emotion that the audience cheered her off the stage. It was a fine concert, all decided, but there was no time for encores because the next performer was already stepping forward. The announcer gave her name: "A violin solo performed by Gao Lili."

The violinist was a slim girl with a slender waist and narrow shoulders. She was dressed all in white—white dress and white high-heeled shoes—with an eye-catching ruby brooch on her chest. It was a great challenge to follow the singer, and the audience could see a glistening bead of sweat on the tip of her nose.

Then she took up her violin. The audience fell so deeply silent that a single muffled cough from the rear sounded through the whole auditorium.

But what was she playing? It was not Mozart, nor Liszt, nor Tchaikovsky. It certainly was not Debussy's *La Mer*. Could it have been "The Buffalo Boy's Flute," by that same He Luting, or perhaps the old folk melody called "Liang Shanbo and Zhu Yingtai"? No! It was none of those. It was something new and wondrous; it sounded sometimes like howling wind, sometimes like gurgling water, sometimes like the gallop of horses, and sometimes like the whispers of two lovers in the dusk.

Entranced, the audience glanced at each other in delight and astonishment. No such artistry had been expected here, at a perfectly ordinary practice performance by the students of the Shanghai Conservatory. Certainly no music that was now as fervent fire, now as icy frost, now as pelting rain or still night. When the violinist reached a crescendo and stopped, the audience leaped to its feet, in thunderous applause. "Encore! Encore!" the shouts rolled around the auditorium; but there was no encore. The performer fled the stage, for she was as astonished as the audience.

Backstage, the faculty members of the Conservatory were clustering around the exhausted girl. What was the name of that composition? But Gao Lili could not say. Well, who wrote it? She shrugged helplessly; it had just come to her as she was playing. Nor was there any record of it. The stage manager had not expected much, so he had not arranged any recording; not even any student in the audience had thought to switch on his cassette machine; they were all too wrapped up in the glorious sounds. Minutes later a silver-gray sedan appeared at the stage door and whisked Gao Lili, along with as many of the professors as could squeeze in, to the Shanghai television center. She was hurried to a studio, her beloved violin still in her hand. The door was closed. A row of sofas covered in claret velvet faced her as she stood before a battery of microphones and cameras. The lights went on, glaring at her. From the seats a voice called, "Just play it again, please."

The girl's eyes glistened with crystal tears. "I'm awfully sorry," she whispered. "I can't. I don't remember it at all."

That same day there was an amazing event at the sports meeting of the Shanghai No. 9 Middle School. The No. 9 school was in no way special; it was quite average among the several hundred like it in the city. The meeting, too, was merely a routine exhibition for the students. Most of the interest was in the tug-of-war, where boisterous teams took the ends of a rope with a red flag in the middle; whichever team succeeded in pulling the flag across the line would win. The physical-education teachers who served as referees had all clustered around the tug-of-war pit. None had bothered to observe the corner of the stadium where the high-jumpers were at work.

There were only eight contestants, the crossbar set only at one and a half meters. Seven of them had cleared the bar without incident. The eighth was a roly-poly boy whose chest bore the cloth No. 93. The other seven boys watched him worriedly as he ran toward the bar.

Then No. 93's gait straightened and he launched into a spring. What a wonder! He did not merely clear the 1.5-meter bar. He sailed effortlessly far above it—four or five meters at least—a jump that even an Olympic athlete would have envied!

A shout went up from the few people watching, almost drowning out a yell from No. 93 himself, as he fell heavily into the pit and cried out in pain.

The teachers rushed toward the high-jump area, spectators hurrying after. The words exchanged grew excited, the newcomers denying that such a great jump was possible for a dumpy little boy like No. 93, those who saw it maintaining that their eyes had not deceived them. The boy himself, whose name was Cao Jiajia, was oblivious to it all; he was moaning in pain. When a medic from the Red Cross ambulance that was standing by arrived, he announced that Cao Jiajia had a fracture in the bones of both feet.

That evening the newspaper *Xinmin* carried a short report of the event. It said that when sports authorities had asked Cao Jiajia how he could jump so high, the boy had wailed, "But I can't!"

The next bead strung on the abacus took place in Shanghai No. 1 Hospital, and it involved the celebrated orthopedist Dr. Wang. That was the doctor's name, but to the staff, and even many of the patients of the hospital, he was better known as "the Chimney," so called because he smoked like one. Wang came from North China, where children learn to smoke at an early age; he was fifty-three, and had had forty years of life with a cigarette always hanging from a corner of his mouth. His ashtray was always full. His fingers were stained brown. Being a doctor, he knew that smoking was harmful to health; but being a confirmed smoker, he did not give it up.

That is, he did not until the afternoon of that astonishing day. Then the nurses and orderlies whispered among each other, for the Chimney was emitting no fumes. Even when he finished treating a patient and the patient offered him a cigarette, Dr. Wang started to stretch out his hand, then withdrew it. He looked puzzled as he said, "Thank you, but I don't smoke."

The patient looked puzzledly at the doctor's fingers, as brown as though stained with iodine. "You don't?" he asked.

The Chimney said firmly, "I did at one time, but I don't now."

The nurses whispered among themselves, rejoicing and chuckling. But their pleasure was premature. An hour later Dr. Wang returned to the ward, a cigarette once more dangling from his lips. And when another doctor on the staff politely said, "I thought you didn't smoke anymore, Dr. Wang," Wang replied: "I didn't. But now I do again."

The other doctor was astonished to hear this. He would have been even more astonished if he had known what had become of the patient.

For the patient was the well-known artist Xu Danqin, and he did not only give up smoking as he left the hospital. He did not even stop for some of the Chinese yellow rice wine which was his favorite beverage. He hurried home, nursing the right arm Dr. Wang had set.

Xu Danqin drew pictures on Xuan paper all day long. When he was away from his paintbrush, he missed it. His specialty was landscapes, and his wonderful pictures "The Great Wall," "Lushan Mountain in Fog," "The Changjiang, Yangtze, River Bridge," and "Roaring Waves on the East China Sea" were praised all over China. When he reached his home, his wife was not surprised to see that he hurried at once to his easel, although it saddened her to see that, with his right arm in a cast, he was trying to paint with his left hand.

Still, the picture that emerged on the Xuan paper was something wonderful! It was a landscape, with a dark velvet sky containing a silvery sun. Bathing in its light were orange-colored hills, light-yellow streams, purple fields.

"Oh, how beautiful!" his wife whispered from behind him. "Where is it?"

The artist shook his head. "I don't know. But it is a real landscape, I have seen it."

"That doesn't matter. It is as good as anything by Da Vinci or Picasso. Let me take it right away to be photographed and mounted, so that we can keep it forever!" And as soon as it was dry, the wife rolled it up and hurried to the bus.

The bus was full, but the conductor, a pretty young girl who was a regular on the run, recognized the woman. "What have you got there?" she asked in a friendly way. "Is that another marvelous painting by your husband?"

"Let me show you," cried the wife, unrolling it. The conductor exclaimed in wonder and pleasure, and the other passengers crowded around to see the beautiful piece of art. Even the driver looked back longingly.

And then, as they were crossing a bridge, a sudden gust of wind caught the paper and whisked it out of her hand. It flew high, and dropped into the lake.

"My painting! Oh, it's a masterpiece! Help me get it back!" Xu's wife cried.

The driver at once stopped the bus. Remembering the Chinese saying "If one is in need, all render help; when difficulties arise in one place, aid comes from everywhere," all of the passengers, and even the driver and the conductor, jumped out to help. The younger passengers took off their outer clothing and plunged into the lake, in pursuit of the masterpiece. But it was not the young ones who found it. The one who triumphed was a medium-statured man of about forty, obviously a first-rate swimmer. He was something more than that. His name was Jin Ming, and he was the head of the investigations section of the Shanghai Public Security Bureau.

Jin climbed up the bank, bearing the smeared and tattered

painting. "Thank you," the artist's wife said in dismay, gazing at the ruined painting.

"I'm sorry it was damaged," said the policeman, putting on his blue trousers and white uniform coat again. "Perhaps your husband can paint it again?"

But when the woman got back and showed the mess to her husband, the artist said despondently, "I can't paint it again. I don't remember it anymore."

The policeman was the last bead on the abacus, though he did not know that. What he knew was that he found himself especially excited and strangely high-spirited. "Please hurry," he called to the driver as the bus began its trip again. The driver looked at him strangely, but did not answer. It was only a short time, though, until it pulled up at the stop near the Public Security Bureau and Jin Ming got off. He hurried at once to the office of the chief of the bureau, and opened his mouth to say, "I have something to report."

However, to Jin's surprise, those were not the words that came out. What he heard himself saying was, "I must apologize for causing embarrassment, loss of property, and even injury to some of your people."

The chief of the bureau stared at his valued subordinate. "What are you talking about, Jin?" he demanded.

And Jin heard his own voice say, "I am not Jin. I have merely taken possession of Jin's body for a time, as I have with several other of your citizens. I meant well, but in fact I caused a painting to be lost, and a young child to be hurt. I meant you Earth people no harm, and so I must apologize before I leave you."

"Earth people?" the head of the bureau said, not comprehending. "But what, then, are you?"

"Oh," said Jin's voice, "I am an extraterrestrial."

For the next hour Jin Ming was the center of attention in a way that he had never experienced before, and did not much like. The first question the head of the bureau asked was whether Jin had been drinking. Jin had to admit that it was a fair question, for he himself could not understand what was happening to him; yet he knew that he had not touched anything of that sort.

It was not until Jin's voice, speaking for the being who called himself an extraterrestrial, had described the ways in which he had temporarily taken control of the violinist, the artist, the small boy at No. 9 Middle School, and others, that he began to be believed. By that time Jin's audience had grown—three more police officials, two representatives of the municipal government, even several scientists called in urgently from their posts at the Shanghai Museum of Science and various research establishments. And, as the evidence piled up, the people there began to believe.

"You are very welcome here," said one of the scientists, Professor Guo. "You are a distinguished guest, and so we would like to invite you to stay with us at our new and luxurious guest house, the Longbo Hotel."

"No, no," said the voice from Jin's mouth. "I wish to leave, although I thank you all. I love Shanghai and the People's Republic of China, but, to be truthful, I love my mother planet more."

Disappointed, Professor Guo said courteously, "Of course, we will understand. But before you leave, can you do us one favor?"

"What is that?" asked the alien.

"Please let us give you a title of honor—to show our appreciation and friendship, since you are the first extraterrestrial ever to have visited Shanghai. We would like to make you an Honorary Citizen of Shanghai!"

The alien laughed—at first, with the ordinary laughter of Jin Ming himself, then exploding into clackings and twitterings such as none of the Earth people had ever heard. When it was in control of itself again, it said:

"I thank you very much. I accept; and now, good-by."

Professor Guo gazed anxiously into Jin Ming's face. "Are you —I mean, is he still here?" he asked.

Jin Ming said hesitantly, "No, it is just me again."

The professor scowled in regret. "I had so much to ask him!" he complained. "Well, never mind. Perhaps he will come back again."

But Jin Ming, rubbing his throat, which was sore from trying to reproduce the sounds the alien used for laughter, said only, "If he does, I hope he chooses someone else to inhabit!"

FROM CANADA:

User Friendly

BY SPIDER ROBINSON

When he saw the small weather-beaten sign which read "Welcome to Calais, Maine," Sam Waterford smiled. It hurt his mouth, so he stopped.

He was tired and wired and as stiff as IRS penalties; he had been driving for . . . how long? He did not really know. There had been at least one entire night; he vividly remembered a succession of headlight beams coring his eyeballs at some time in the distant past. Another night was near, the sun low in the sky. It did not matter. In a few more minutes he would have reached an important point in his journey: the longest undefended border in the world. Once past it, he would start being safe again. . . .

He retained enough of the man he had once been to stop when he saw the Duty-Free Store. Reflex politeness: A guest, especially an unexpected one, brings a gift. But the store was closed. It occurred to him distantly that in his half-dozen trips through these parts, no matter what time he arrived, that store had always been closed. The one on the Canadian side, on the other hand, was almost always open. Too weary to wonder why, he got back into his Imperial and drove on.

He had vaguely expected to find a long lineup at the border crossing, but there was none. The guards on the American side ignored him as he drove across the short bridge, and the guards on the Canadian side waved him through. He was too weary to wonder at that, too—and distracted by the mild surge of elation that came from leaving American soil, leaving the danger zone.

It was purely subjective, of course. As he drove slowly through the streets of St. Stephen, New Brunswick, the only external reminders that he was in Canada were the speed limit signs marked in metric and the very occasional bilingual sign (French, rather than the Spanish he was used to in New York). Nonetheless, he felt as though the invisible band around his skull had been loosened a few notches. He found a Liquor Commission outlet and bought a bottle of Old Bushmill's for Greg and Alice. A Burger King next door reminded him that he had not eaten for . . . however long the trip had lasted so far, so he bought something squishy and ate it and threw most of it up again a few miles later.

He drove all the rest of that evening, and long into the night, through endless miles of tree-lined highway interrupted only seldom by a village speed trap, and once by the purely nominal border between the provinces of New Brunswick and Nova Scotia, and he reached the city of Halifax as the sun was coming up on his left. Dimly, he realized that he would shortly be drinking Old Bushmill's and talking, and he expected both to be equally devastating to his system, so he took the trouble to find the only all-night restaurant in Halifax and tried eating again, and this time it worked. He'd had no chance to change his money, but of course the waitress was more than happy to accept Yankee currency: Even allowing him a 130 percent exchange rate, she was making thirty-seven cents' profit on each dollar. The food lifted his spirits just enough that he was able to idly admire Halifax as he drove through it, straining to remember his way. It had been many years since any city in America had looked this pleasant—the smog was barely noticeable, and the worst wino he saw had bathed this year. As he drove past Citadel Hill he could see the Harbour, saw pleasure craft dancing on the water (along with a couple of toothless Canadian Forces destroyers and a sleek black American nuclear sub), saw birds riding the morning updrafts and heard their raucous calls. He was *not*, of course, in a good mood as he parked in front of Greg and Alice's house, but he was willing to concede, in theory, that the trick was possible.

He was still quite groggy; for some reason it seemed tremendously important to knock on the precise geometrical center of Greg's door, and maddeningly difficult to do so. When the door opened anyway, it startled him. His plans stopped here; he had no idea what to do or say next.

"Sammy!" His old college buddy grinned and frowned simultaneously. "Jesus, man, it's good to see you—or it would be if you didn't look like death on a soda cracker! What the hell are you doing here, why didn't you—"

"They got her, Greg. They took *Marian.* There's nothing I—"

Suddenly, Greg and the front of his house were gone, replaced by a ceiling, and Sam discovered that he was indoors and horizontal. "—can do," he finished reflexively, and then realized that he must have fainted. He reached for his head, probed for soft places.

"It's okay, Sam: I caught you as you went down. Relax."

Sam had forgotten what the last word meant; it came through as noise. He sat up, worked his arms and legs as if by remote control. The arms hurt worse than the legs. "Got a cigarette? I ran out"—he thought for a moment—"yesterday, I think."

Greg handed him a twenty-five pack of Export A. "Fill your boots. Have you eaten more recently than that?"

"Yeah. Funny—I actually forgot I smoked. Now, that's weird." He fumbled the pack open and lit a cigarette; his first puff turned half an inch to ash and stained the filter. "Did I drop the bottle?"

"You left it in the car." Greg left the room, returned with two glasses of Irish whiskey. "You don't have to talk until you're ready."

Sam restrained the urge to gulp. If you got too drunk, you had *less* control of your thoughts sometimes. "They took her. The aliens —you must have read about them up here. They *appropriated* her, like losing your home to municipal construction. Sorry, railroad's coming through, we need your universe. No, not even that polite— I didn't even get the usual ten percent of market value and a token apology."

"Christ, Sam, I'm sorrier than I know how to say. Is she . . . I mean, how is she taking it?"

"Better than I would. She's still alive."

Greg's face took on the expression of a man who is not sure he should be saying what he is saying, but feels compelled to anyway. "Knowing you, the way you feel about such things, I'm surprised *you* didn't kill her yourself."

"I tried. I couldn't. You know, that may just be the worst part."

"Ah, Sam, Sam—"

"She begged me to. *And I couldn't!*"

They waited together until he could speak again. "Damn," he said finally, "it's good to see you." And it would be even better to see Alice. She must be at work, designing new software to deadline.

Greg looked like he'd been missing some sleep himself. Novelists often did. "You might as well get it all out," he said. "How did it happen?"

Sam nodded slowly, reluctantly. "Get it over with. Not a lot to tell. We were lying in bed together, watching TV. We'd . . . we'd just finished making love. Funny, it was better than usual. I was feeling blessed. Maybe that should have warned me or something. All of a sudden, in the middle of David Letterman's show—do you get him up here?"

"We get all the American shows; these days, it's about all we get. Go on."

"Right in the middle of Stupid Pet Tricks, she just got up and left the room. I asked her to bring me back some ice water. She didn't say anything. A few moments later I heard the front door open and close. I didn't attach any significance to it. After five or ten minutes I called to her. I assumed she was peeing or something. When she didn't answer I got up and went to make sure she was all right. I couldn't find her.

"I could *not* figure it out. You know how it is when something just does not make sense? She wasn't anywhere in the apartment. I'd heard the door, but she *couldn't* have gone out—she was naked, barefoot, her coat and boots were still in the hall closet. I couldn't imagine her unlocking the door for anyone we didn't know, certainly not for someone who could snatch her out the door in two seconds without the slightest sound or struggle. I actually found myself looking under chairs for her.

"So eventually I phoned the police, and got all the satisfaction you'd expect, and called everyone we knew with no success at all, and finally I fell asleep at four A.M. hoping to God it was some kind of monstrous joke she was playing on me.

"Two government guys in suits came that night. They told me what had happened to her. 'Sir, your wife has been requisitioned by aliens. Quite a few people's husbands and wives have been. And we wouldn't do anything about it if we could, which we can't. . . .' They were good; I never laid a hand on them. When I calmed down enough, they took me to the hospital to see her. She was in pretty good shape, all things considered. Her feet were a mess, of course, from walking the streets barefoot. Exposure, fatigue. After the aliens turned her loose, she was raped by four or five people before the police found her. You remember New York at night. But they didn't cut her up or anything, just screwed her. She told me she almost didn't mind that. She said it was a relief to be only physically raped. To be able to struggle if she wanted, even if it didn't help. To at least have the power to protest." He stubbed his cigarette out and finished his drink. "Strange. She was just as naked while she was possessed, but no human tried to touch her until afterward. Like, *occupado*, you know?"

Greg gave him his own, untouched drink. "Go on."

"Well, God, we talked. You know, tried to talk. Mostly we cried. And then in the middle of a snuffle she chopped off short and got up out of the hospital bed and left the room. I was so mixed up it took me a good five seconds to catch on. When I did I went nuts. I tried to chase after her and catch her, and the two government guys stopped me. I broke the nose of one of them, and they wrestled me into somebody's room and gave me a shot. As it was taking hold I turned and looked sideways out the window, just in time to catch a glimpse of her, three flights down, walking through the parking lot. Silly little hospital gown, open at the back, paper slippers. Nobody got in her way. A doctor was walking in the same direction; he was a zombie too. Masked and gloved, blood on his gloves; I hope he finished his operation first. . . .

"She came home the next day, and we had about six hours. Long enough to say everything there was to say five times, and a bunch of other things that maybe should never have been said. This time when she left, she left dressed, with an empty bladder and money to get home with when they let her go. We had accepted it, taken the first step in starting to plan around it. Only practical, right?" He shook his head, hearing his neck crack, and finished off the second drink. It had no more effect than had the first.

"What happened then?"

"I got in the car and drove here."

For the first time, Greg looked deeply shocked. "You *left* her there, to deal with it *alone?*"

Someone grasped Sam's heart in impersonal hands and wrung it out. Greg must have seen the pain, and some of the accusatory tone left his voice. "Jesus wept, Sam! Look, I know you. You've written three entire books on brainwashing and mind control, 'the ultimate obscenity,' you call it: I know how uniquely horrible the whole thing must be to you, and for you. But you've been married to Marian for *ten years,* as long as I've been married to Alice—how could you possibly have left her?"

The words came out like projectile vomit. "I *had* to, God damn it: I was *scared!*"

"Scared? Of what?"

"Of *them,* for Christ's sake, what's the matter with you? Scared that the thing would look out of her eyes and notice *me*—and decide that I looked . . . *usable.*" He began to shudder, and found it extremely hard to stop. He lit another cigarette with shaking hands.

"Sam, it doesn't work that way—"

"I know, I know, they told me. Who said fear has to be logical?"

Greg sat back and sighed deeply, a mournful sound. There was a silence then, which lasted for ten seconds or more. The worst was said, and there was nothing else to say.

Finally, Sam tried to distract himself with mundane trivia. "Listen, I saw the 'No Parking' sign where I parked, I just didn't give a damn. If I give you my keys, will you move it for me? I don't think I can."

"Can't do it," Greg said absently. "I don't dare. They could fine me four hundred bucks if I get caught behind the wheel of an American-registered car, you know that."

The subject had come up on Sam's last visit, back in 1982. Marian had been with him, then. "Sorry. I forgot."

"Sam, what made you decide to come *here?*"

He discovered that he did not know. He tried to analyze it. "Well, part of it is that I needed to tell somebody the whole thing, and you and Alice are the only people on Earth that love me enough. But there wasn't even that much logic to it. I was just terrified, and I needed to get to someplace safe, and Canada was the nearest place."

Greg burst out laughing.

Sam stared at him, scandalized. "What's so funny?"

It took Greg quite a while to stop laughing, but when he did —despite the smile that remained on his face—Sam could see that he was very angry.

"Americans, no shit. You're amazing. I should be used to it by now, I guess."

"What are you talking about?"

"About you, you smug, arrogant bastard. There are nasty old aliens in the States, taking people over and using them to walk around and talk with, for mysterious purposes of their own—so what do you do? Take off for Canada, where it'll be safe. You just *assume,* totally unconsciously, that the aliens will think like you. That they'd never bother with a quaint, backward, jerkwater country like Canada, The Retarded Giant on Your Doorstep! Don't you read the papers?"

"I don't—"

"Excuse me. Stupid of me: It probably wouldn't make the Stateside papers, would it? You simple jackass, there are *three times* more Canadians hag-ridden than Americans! Even though you've got ten times the population. They came here *first.*"

"First? No, that can't be, I'd have heard—"

"Why? We barely heard about it ourselves, with two out of the sixteen channels Canadian-originated. It ain't news unless and until it happens in the friggin' United Snakes of America!" He had more to say, but suddenly he tilted his head as if he heard something. "Shit. Stay there." He got up and left the room hastily, muttering to himself.

Sam sat there, stunned by his old friend's inexplicable anger. He finished his cigarette and lit another while he tried to understand it. He heard a murmur of voices elsewhere in the house, and recognized the one that wasn't Greg's. Alice was home from work. Perhaps she would be more sympathetic. He got up and followed the sound of the voices, and it wasn't until he actually saw her that he remembered. Alice hadn't worked night shift in over a year—and she had a home terminal now anyway. . . .

She was in pretty fair shape. Face drawn with fatigue, of course, and her hair in rats. She was fully dressed except for pants and panties; there was an oil or grease stain on the side of her blouse. She tried to smile when she saw Sam.

"He caught me sitting on the john," she said. "Hi, Sam." She burst into tears, still trying to smile.

He thought for a crazy second that she meant her husband. But no, of course, the "he" she referred to was not Greg, but her—

Her *rider*. Her User . . .

"Oh, my dear God," he said softly, still not quite believing. He had been so sure, so unthinkingly convinced that it would be safe here.

"Naturally, the Users came here first," Greg said with cold, bitter anger, handing his wife the slacks she had kicked off on her way out the door some hours before. "We were meant for each other, them and Canadians. Strong, superior parasites from the sky? Who just move right in and take over without asking or apologizing?" His voice began to rise in pitch and volume. "Arrogant puppetmasters who show up and start pulling your strings for you, dump you like a stolen car when they're done with you, too powerful to fight and indifferent to your rage and shame? And your own government breaks its neck to help 'em do whatever they want, sells out without even stopping to ask the price in case it might offend 'em?" He was shouting at the top of his lungs. "Hell, man, we almost didn't even notice the Users. *We took 'em for Americans.*"

Alice was dressed again now. Her voice was soft and hoarse; someone had been doing a lot of talking with her vocal cords recently. "Greg, shut up."

"Well, dammit all, he—"

She put a hand over his mouth. "Please, my very beloved, shut your face. I can't talk louder than you this time, my throat hurts."

He shut up at once, put his own hand over hers and held it

tightly against his face, screwing his eyes shut. She leaned against him and they put their free arms around each other; the sight made Sam want to weep like a child.

"Greg," she said huskily, "I love you; part of me wants to cheer what you just said; many Canadians would. But you're wrong to say it."

"I know, baby, I know *exactly* the pain Sam's going through, don't I? That's why I got mad at him, thinking his pain was bigger 'cause it was American. I'm sorry, Sam—"

"That's only part of why you're wrong. This is more important than our friendship with Sam and Marian, my love. Pay attention: *You would never have said what you said if there'd been an Inuit in the room.* Or a MicMac, or a French Canadian, or a Pakistani. You'd never have said it if we were standing in North Preston, talking to someone who used to live in Africville till they moved all the darkies out to build a bridge approach. Don't you see, darling, *everybody is a Canadian now.* Everybody on Earth is now a Native People; a Frog; a Wog; a Paki; a Nigger—gradations of Niggerhood just don't seem all that important anymore.

"Gregory, some of the Users wear a human body as though it ought to have flippers, or extra legs, or wings—I saw one try to make an arm work like a tentacle, and break it. There are a *lot* of different races and species and genuses of User—one of the things they seem to be using Earth for is a conference table at which to work out their own hierarchy of power and intelligence and wealth. I've heard a lot of the palaver; they don't bother to turn my ears off because they don't care if I hear or not. Most of it I don't understand even though they do use English a lot, but a few things I've noticed.

"If two neighboring races discover that one is vastly superior to the other in resources or wisdom or aggressiveness, they don't spend a lot of time whining about the inequity of it all. They figure out where it looks like the water is going to wind up when it's finished flowing downhill, and then they start looking for ways to live with that.

"I've never heard a User say the words 'It's not fair.' Apparently, if you can form that thought, you don't reach the stars. The whole universe is a hierarchy of Users and Used, from the race that developed the long-distance telepathy that brought them all here, down to the cute little microorganisms that are ruthlessly butchered every day by a baby seal. We're part of that chain, and if we can't live with that, we'll die."

The three were silent for a time. Finally, Sam cleared his throat. "If you two will excuse me," he said softly, "I have to be getting back home to my wife now."

Alice turned to him, and gave him a smile so sad and so brave that he thought his heart might break. "Sam," she said, "that's a storybook ending. I hope it works out that way for you. But don't blow your brains out if it doesn't, okay? Or hers. You write about mind control and the institution of slavery because subversion of the human free will, loss of control, holds a special horror for you. You're the kind that dies fighting instead. Marian isn't. I'm not. Most humans aren't, even though they like to feel they would be if it came to it. Maybe that's why the Users came here.

"It may be that you and Marian can't live together anymore; I don't know. I do know that you need twelve hours' sleep and a couple of good meals before it's safe to let you back on the highway —and Greg and I badly need someone to talk to. My User won't be back for another ten hours or so. What would you say to some eggs and back bacon?"

Sam closed his eyes and took a deep breath. "I guess I'd say, 'Hello there—do you mind if I use you for twelve hours or so?" *And turn you into shit in the process,* he thought, but he found that he was ashamed of the thought, and that was something, at least. "Can I use your phone?"

"Only if you reverse the charges, you cheap Yankee son of a bitch," Greg said at once, and came and hugged him hard.

FROM BRAZIL:

Life as an Ant

BY ANDRÉ CARNEIRO
Translated by Joe F. Randolph

Three months after his divorce, things were looking good for Fabian. It was true that his wife had succeeded in getting custody of their two children, and Fabian got to see them only twice a week. That rankled. But he had found and furnished an apartment, all in good taste, with works of art on the wall—some of them by his own hand —and his job with one of the best advertising agencies in São Paulo had always been good, and suddenly got better. Their biggest account, a huge multinational pharmaceutical firm, was in the process of introducing a new tranquilizer called Calmox, and that morning Fabian had been given the account.

When Fabian let himself into his apartment he had a thick sheaf of reports in his dispatch case, and a sample bottle of the new product in his pocket. Fortunately for him, Fabian was a fast reader. He was expecting company at eight; by a quarter to, he had skimmed the reports and was holding the attractive package of Calmox in his hand.

All the formal reports were very, very good. Calmox calmed. It didn't harm. There was some suggestion that there might be euphoria from taking it sometimes—not a bad thing, Fabian reflected— and there was a rumor of an office boy who had appropriated some Calmox and got high on it.

It was necessary, Fabian told himself, to make a personal experiment. He popped the top of the vial of pills with his thumbnail, and a single tablet fell out. Very good, he thought with pleasure; nice dispensing cap design; it would be difficult for anyone to overdose accidentally.

The trouble with taking a tranquilizer to test its effects, Fabian realized, was that he felt really good already. To counteract that, he gazed at the picture of his children, reminding himself of the scenes that had led to his divorce, the custody struggle, the bitter financial aspects. Then he swallowed the pill and went into his bedroom to straighten his bed, since one never knew what might come of his engagement for the evening. As he was finishing, the doorbell rang. Whistling, Fabian went to the door to let his guest in.

The name of the guest was Vivian, and she worked in the art department of the same advertising agency. She was a little strange, Fabian thought—a feminist, who enjoyed getting into verbal duels with the macho types at the agency—but she was also a looker. "How wonderful you look, Vivian," he cried as she appeared in a see-through dress that revealed a pretty brassiere over an even prettier bust. "What've you got there, pizza?"

"I thought there was no sense in going out to a restaurant," she smiled, "so I brought something we can eat here. I don't eat much dinner anyway."

"That's why you have such a perfect figure," said Fabian gallantly, and Vivian smiled again at the expected flattery.

"I'll put the pizza in the oven to keep it warm," she said, "while you fix us a drink."

"Right away," said Fabian. He opened a bottle of wine, took out some hard liquor for later on, and wondered if Vivian smoked pot. He glanced at the bedroom door, open just a crack; the bed was visible there, with the soft lights he had left on around it.

When he put a drink in her hand Vivian did not sit down at once, but wandered about the apartment, gazing at the paintings and decorative knickknacks. He could see that she liked the reproductions of Picasso nudes, and that she had noticed the inviting bedroom. As they sat down to devour the pizza, Fabian was feeling quite content. "You're quiet," Vivian observed. "How's your new campaign coming along?"

"Oh, fine," he said. "I just took a Calmox to see what would happen."

"Has anything?"

"I feel good," he said, "but then I was feeling good already." He hesitated, frowning. "Well, not so good in some ways," he admitted. "I've spent some pretty unhappy days in this place. Alone. The divorce was very difficult—"

He paused in mid-sentence. Vivian, watching him curiously, said, "Is something the matter?"

Fabian didn't answer. He got up abruptly and went into the bathroom. There he stood for a long time, gazing into the mirror at his own face, with the look of a man studying an unfamiliar object.

"Fabian?" called the girl. He didn't answer. "Fabian, don't you feel well?" she asked.

The door opened and Fabian came out. He was smiling with great self-possession, glancing around the room in curiosity and then, with the same eagerly expectant look, "Why, this is very strange," he declared. "I'm a man. You're a woman. In order to effect reproduction I would have to enter you."

Vivian's expression froze. "What?" she demanded. And then, as he started to repeat what he had said, "No, no! I heard what you said, but I don't understand the joke. It's a little crude, isn't it?"

He didn't answer, but simply gave her a bright smile. Then he looked away, walking around the room curiously, pulling drawers out to glance inside, peering inquisitively into the bedroom. He opened the window and leaned far out to study the city of São Paulo, stretching out before him. Then he turned back to the girl, who was sitting on the couch staring at him. He sat down beside her and began to talk.

"It is all quite strange," he said delightedly. "But what is most interesting is reproduction. I know about viruses, microbes, amphibians, invertebrates, insects . . . all fascinating; but this—" He shook his head wonderingly, staring at Vivian's breasts under the flimsy garment. "I am very interested in love on a fifty-fifty basis," he announced.

The girl looked at him in bafflement, then suddenly chuckled.

She took his hand in hers. "Ah, Fabian," she said, shaking her head, "you had a few before I got here, didn't you?"

He stared at her in puzzlement. "Had a few?" Then his expression cleared. "Oh, of course, you mean alcoholic beverages. No, I haven't ingested any, but I certainly intend to try that."

Shaking her head, Vivian excused herself and headed for the bathroom. As she closed the door, she saw that Fabian was following her with an expression of friendly curiosity. Startled, she shut the door in his face.

When she came out a little later he was standing by the window with his back to her, absorbed in something. As she got closer, she saw that he had opened his belt and sucked his stomach in, gazing down into his pulled-out undershorts.

"Fabian!" she cried.

The man turned to look at her. "Have I done something wrong?" he asked in perplexity. "Oh, yes, I remember—one does not look at one's own genitalia in the presence of others. What a queer custom! But, really, they're very interesting." He smiled and shrugged. "Anyway," he said happily, "I think you will be pleased with them. Shall we begin?" And he hugged her forcefully, kissing her over and over on the lips, on the face, on the neck.

"Now, slow down!" Vivian ordered, freeing herself. "You're acting like a horny teenager. What's the matter?"

"But it's wonderful to kiss!" he said enthusiastically. "Would it be better if we went into the other room? I know there is a very comfortable mattress there—"

"Whoa," she said firmly. "You're a very charming man, Fabian, but this isn't going right. Fabian? Didn't you tell me you'd taken one of those pills?"

"Calmox," he agreed. "Yes. One tablet."

"Well, maybe that's what makes you so . . . strange. Listen, dear. I'm going now. You get some rest, and we'll talk tomorrow." She gave him a demure kiss on the cheek. Then she giggled, patted his face, and left.

Because both were busy at the agency the next day they didn't really have much chance to talk with each other. But Vivian noticed that Fabian was performing beautifully, heading up the new campaign. He was decisive, fast, creative; he gave orders and approved copy, art, commercials, and everything else that went into the drive to sell Calmox, making suggestions that always were better than the subordinates' own work.

Vivian was not the only one to observe that Fabian seemed even more competent than usual. More than that, he seemed far more authoritative, making decisions on his own that normally one of the higher-ups would have had to approve.

This worried Vivian, because, to be truthful with herself, she had to admit that she was very nearly in love with him. She had seen how painful the divorce had been for him and it was she who had first suggested that they have dinner together. And it was she who, a day or two later, when the campaign was actually launched, called him on the office phone and made another date.

When he let her into his apartment that night he seemed euphoric. "Ah, Vivian! Here again, and as nice-looking as ever!" he cried. Then he said, "I must apologize for my behavior the other night. I won't make any more faux pas, I promise."

Vivian smiled and kissed him quickly to show that she had forgiven him. But as he poured wine and set out the pizza she had brought he seemed abstracted, even agitated, and when they sat down she observed beads of sweat on his forehead.

"Fabian," she said, "do you have a fever? Are you coming down with something?"

He looked at her strangely for a moment, then reached out and gripped her hands so forcefully that she shrank back. "A fever," he moaned. "If it were only that!" He leaned across the table, gazing into her eyes, and spoke rapidly and nervously:

"Please, Vivian, I need help. Right now I'm myself, do you understand?"

"But of course you're yourself," Vivian began, and Fabian shouted:

"No! It is not 'of course'! Don't you remember how different I was the other night? It wasn't me! It was—I don't know—a *thing*. A creature. Another person, who took control of me. There was no warning. I could do nothing about it. I knew I was somebody else, and I said what this other person wanted, did what it ordered. And it wasn't even of this Earth."

Vivian opened her mouth to speak, but Fabian cut her off. "Please, listen! I have to talk now, while it has left me alone for a moment. It can control me again, and I know it's from somewhere beyond the Earth. Don't look at me like that! I'm perfectly sane. Don't get the idea that I'm hallucinating or my judgment is impaired—after all, you noticed the difference, didn't you? And the worst part—"

He stopped in mid-sentence. The anguish in his expression faded away. He released Vivian's hands and sat back, almost smiling. And then, without a word, he stood up and walked away, to the window.

Vivian gazed after him in total confusion. "Fabian?" she called.

"Yes, my dear?" he said over his shoulder.

"Well—aren't you going to tell me the rest of your story?"

He turned, smiling. "Oh, that," he said. "That's what it was, Vivian. A story. I was thinking about introducing something new into the Calmox campaign, a sort of fantastic drama about creatures from another planet. Did I convince you?"

The girl looked at him with her mouth open. Although she was fond of Fabian and not at all unwilling to become closer, even a great deal closer, she could not help feeling both astonishment and some indignation. "Fabian," she said, getting up, "I'm sorry, but I think I have a migraine. I'd better go now." And she left—hurriedly—trying to ignore Fabian standing behind her at his door and calling to her agitatedly to come back.

The next day did not start well for Vivian. Fabian greeted her genially enough but seemed uninterested in discussing the night before—or indeed anything at all significant. She sat at her drawing table, with a blank sheet of paper in front of her, and stared into space, thinking. There was no question that Fabian's changes of behavior were out of the normal. Why? She could not answer. Perhaps it was the Calmox. Perhaps it was—she hesitated even to think it—some sudden mental disorder, like schizophrenia. Vivian realized that she didn't know enough about the subject to even guess at whether that might be true.

Just as she was forming the resolve to go to the library and read up on the subject, her phone rang.

"It's Robert," said the voice on the other end. "Fabian's brother. Do you remember me?"

"Of course," said Vivian, though in fact she had only the vaguest recollection of a chance introduction as she and the brothers were getting into an elevator, weeks before. All she remembered about Robert, really, was that he was a psychiatrist, or something of the sort.

But that was enough to make her agree at once when he said, "I'd like to see you, to talk about Fabian. Could you possibly come to my office?"

"Of course," said Vivian, already getting up. "I'll come right away." In the taxi on her way to Robert she tried to remember more about him. A well-known figure, that she was sure of. She had heard that he was somewhat eclectic in his ideas and therapies, but definitely an authority in many areas—had even written a book on the famous French psychiatrist Jacques Lacan. Although there was a patient waiting in Robert's anteroom, the nurse was obviously expecting Vivian. She showed her in at once.

"Thank you for coming," said Robert, waving her to a seat. "I'll come right to the subject. I got a very strange letter from Fabian this morning. It mentions you in quite apologetic terms—Fabian seems to care about how you feel, and to think that he has offended you. But it also says some quite peculiar things." He pulled out a sheet of paper from his desk drawer and glanced at it, frowning.

"Is it that he claims some being from another planet has taken over his body?" Vivian guessed.

"Yes, exactly," said Robert. He scowled at the letter. "He says it happened without warning, and that only from time to time does this creature—or whatever it is—release him so that he can be himself. The rest of the time he is completely under its domination. Is that what he told you?"

"I think that's what he was trying to say," Vivian said slowly. "He was pretty hard to understand."

"I don't doubt that," said Robert gloomily. "He's asking me to notify the Federal authorities and international organizations. He's afraid that these—these beings—are intending to take over the world. It's all very telegraphic and confused," said Robert, "but he says that's because he has only time to write quickly and dash to a mailbox, because he might be taken over again at any moment."

Vivian said worriedly, "I think that's what he wants me to believe, too. I thought he was joking—or, I don't know, just nervous about, well, about having a date with a woman after his divorce. But the things he did . . ." She hesitated, then gave a full description of everything that had happened between them. "What does it all mean?" she begged when she was through.

Fabian's brother stared down at the letter for a while, thinking hard. Then he raised his eyes to hers. "Scientifically speaking," he said, "I would have to consider a diagnosis of paranoid schizophrenia, though with some rare aspects. It isn't just the letter. It is the way he behaved over the phone this morning, when I called him as soon as I'd received his letter. He simply denied ever writing it— quite coldly, even in a hostile way. And yet I'm sure he did send it; it's his handwriting."

"So you think he's insane?" Vivian demanded.

The doctor paused to choose his words carefully. "I think," he said at last, "that there are puzzling aspects to this. I have a patient who seems to share the same—I was about to say 'delusion,' but perhaps I should—" He stopped and shook his head. "My patient was mildly neurotic, no more than that. He was responding well to therapy. Then, just a few weeks ago, he changed. It's almost as if —well, as if he were taking on another personality. I could make no sense of what was going on. I even consulted other experts. Then last week—you understand, all this is quite confidential," he interrupted himself. "Even though I don't give you the patient's name, there's still a question of ethics. Understood? Well, last week my patient came in, without notice, without any appointment, demanding to see me. And he told me the same story as Fabian."

"That he was taken over by some alien creature?" Vivian demanded.

Robert nodded. "I tried to calm him," he said. "I even gave him a mild sedative and had him lie down for a while, in one of the private rooms. Then, while I was seeing another patient, he put his head in at the door. He was laughing. 'What a joke I played on you!'

he said. 'Never mind, I'll just go home and forget it.' His whole demeanor was different. And he didn't show up for his next appointment. In fact, I haven't heard from him at all, except that two nights ago I had a telephone call from someone who seemed to have great difficulty in speaking, and finally hung up abruptly. I am not sure, but I think it was my patient."

Vivian said sincerely, "I don't understand any of this. Can you clear it up for me?"

"I wish I could," said Robert dejectedly.

Vivian stayed on for a quarter of an hour, but there was nothing more to say. And finally she left to return to work, more puzzled than ever, and beginning to be afraid.

Vivian was a sensible woman. She hadn't taken Calmox because she mistrusted all pharmaceutical claims; she smiled ironically when friends told her about their astrological readings, had no superstitions, relied as far as she could only on the evidence of her senses and what she knew of natural law.

But where was natural law in this case? What was really happening with Fabian?

To find out, she made a date with him for a Sunday's outing, hoping that away from his own apartment his behavior would be less peculiar. They went for a drive up to Pico do Jaraguá, then to the beginning of the old Santos road. The scenery was fantastic and wonderful. Columns of chemical smoke rose from the Cubatão oil refineries; it invaded the virgin forest and perhaps changed it. The trees seemed to be dying. Strange creepers took over the dry branches, surrounding them like a skeleton being taken over by another possessive being.

While Fabian was fondling her, Vivian was busy in one part of her mind trying to understand what was going on. She liked what he was doing. She liked him. But she liked him in different ways at different times—almost as though he were indeed two men, or two creatures, with quite different traits.

In his apartment that night Vivian did not resist his advances. There was a rare, even a unique, flavor to being loved by two men at once, she thought. . . .

And wondered if she, too, were losing touch with reality, to accept this situation so easily.

Sílvio Mantos was famous throughout the country for his TV game show. His cash prizes were big; his way of joking with the contestants and the audience was entertaining; all in all, he was an idol of the lower middle classes.

On the air, a young man who had demonstrated a remarkable knowledge of the prophecies of Nostradamus was pondering a question. He had already answered enough to have accumulated a lot of money, and this was his last round. If he got the answer right he would win a house. Sílvio Mantos repeated the question, beaming with the smile that had endeared him to the nation's TV viewers. The young man hesitated, then gave a confident nod and cleared his throat. He stepped forward to answer. . . .

Then his entire demeanor changed. His expression froze in panic and worry. He grabbed the microphone and shouted:

"This wasn't me! There are beings who want to subjugate everybody on Earth, and one of them has taken control of my body! It has let go for a moment, but I'm sure it will come back and I want to warn everyone, all the authorities, to watch out, be careful, be on the alert—"

The beaming smile of Sílvio Mantos stayed on his face, but for once the famous television star seemed at a loss for words. Inside, his mind was churning: What should he do? Try to respond to this strange declaration? Simply declare that that was the wrong answer and send the young man away? His producer, high in the control room, saw that Mantos was in trouble and quickly ordered a cut to commercials. What an unlucky break, thought the producer as he watched the monitor switch to a pretty face informing the world that there was, really, only one detergent she would entrust with her family's wash.

And when the cameras returned to the studio the young man's expression was once again confident. "I hope you will forgive my little joke," he said, smiling at Sílvio Mantos. "I was merely giving a dramatization of one of Nostradamus's predictions as a joke. Now I will answer your question."

And so he did, correctly and completely. There was wild applause from the studio audience, although for some time after that there were jokes about space invaders all over the country.

The joke penetrated even to Brasilia, where a Congressman got up out of his chair and tapped a fellow legislator on the shoulder to ask for the floor. The other legislator agreed in surprise, though he was in the middle of a speech, whereupon the Congressman shouted that he was not responsible for the things he would be saying and doing, since for a week he had been inhabited by a spirit that directed his every act. In the galleries the whisper was *umbanda— umbanda,* the African rite of spiritualism, with millions of followers throughout the country.

Umbanda and possession by aliens from the stars competed for headlines in the nation's tabloids, with smaller articles in the back pages from derisive scientists, who compared the present fad with flying-saucer hysteria and other examples of mass hallucination.

Yet the cases multiplied. In Brasilia the political scene changed from moment to moment, as leaders of opposing parties joined together in complicated programs. Senator Paulo Saluf rose dramatically to propose doubling the minimum wage; although it was resisted by the most powerful elements in business and the administration, the measure passed instantly. But the following day the Senator took the floor once more to declare emotionally that the legislation had not been his idea; that he opposed it completely, and had voted for it only because some entity had taken over his mind. It was a dramatic speech, made even more dramatic a moment later, in the anteroom, where a television cameraman recorded the same Senator stating, with full self-possession, that he certainly did favor the raising of the minimum wage, and must have been hypnotized by a member of the opposition to speak as he had just done.

Then he left for the airport and booked passage to the State of Bahia, on the coast. He was not alone. There was quite a flood of visitors to that state, and all of them seemed headed for a luxurious resort on the beach. The Senator was there, with a number of his colleagues. So was the winner of the game show. So was Fabian. And for a week and more they stayed there, conferring in closed sessions. Their idle hours were not tedious. Secretaries and swimming instructors, dance teachers and other very decorative young people of both sexes were there to keep single men and women company. The food was fine. The accommodations were superb. They were enjoyed by military people, executives, leaders in various fields—some of them very rich—but not a single journalist.

The reporters were kept at bay outside the resort. Not a single word of the deliberations leaked out.

When Fabian came back to São Paulo he was suntanned and, it seemed to Vivian, quite different. They were in his apartment, talking in the way that lovers talk and doing what lovers do, when he suddenly drew back and looked her in the eye. "My mission has ended," he said gravely. "This country is very poor. Many are abandoning it."

"Many what?" asked Vivian, but she thought she knew the answer. Fabian's remark had been a total change of subject—she had just been in the middle of admitting she was in love with him—and she had a good idea of what the abrupt change meant. "What mission are you talking about?" she added, but Fabian did not reply. He stared at her in a strange way, wordlessly.

Vivian, feeling very strange, reached out and took his hands into hers. She felt that she was talking to—to *it,* whatever "it" was —and directly. Not to the real Fabian. Not even to the "it" pretending to be Fabian. But to the being itself, whatever it was.

The voice from Fabian's mouth said at last, "I don't want to tell you what you want to know. I don't want to describe what I really look like in the place I come from. You would be astonished. I don't think you could understand, for we are very different. Imagine, if you can, that I am living in the body of an ant, or a butterfly."

"That is not so repulsive," breathed Vivian, trying to keep control.

"No," admitted the voice. "But perhaps you would not think so kindly of our real form. Oh, this is so hard! This articulated language that you people speak is very poor. Can we not simply understand each other in an intuitive way? My mission is over. I will return to my own place."

Fabian's eyes were sad as he spoke. Vivian burst into tears and embraced him.

"No, no! I don't want you to go. I love you! I—" She hesitated, then laughed wildly. "I love both of you! I want you both, like this —together! Don't leave me, please. . . ."

For her as well as the inhabitant of Fabian's body, language was not enough to express what she felt. The two of them turned to that "intuitive" language of lovers. They fell on the sofa, pulling off their clothes with buttons popping. When they made love it was desperately, between sobs and screams, and Vivian hung onto the body of Fabian as if the strength of her hands could keep that alien soul inside it forever.

Indeed, Vivian was in turmoil, for she loved two men—two beings, at least—even though they both inhabited the same double-souled body. Whatever the being was that had become Fabian's tenant—ant, butterfly, or bee—she loved it. She also loved Fabian himself, the quiet, sad man heartbroken over his divorce and the loss of his children; and she loved, very much loved, the body they both inhabited. In the Western world it is customary to speak of the soul as separate from the body, as something that exists outside the flesh, giving orders for the body to obey. To love someone "body and soul" is to express the fullest of love.

But in Vivian's case she loved Fabian not only body and soul, but body and souls.

When she could stand it no longer she came to Fabian and said: "Which are you?"

"Which am I? Why, I'm Fabian, of course." Fabian smiled.

"Yes, but it isn't Fabian I want to talk to. I want to talk to the ant. The butterfly. The real person behind the imitation Fabian."

Fabian was silent. To Vivian's astonishment, she saw tears in his eyes. "Is it you, the old Fabian?" she demanded.

He said, almost sobbing, "Yes, it's me. What a strange world I live in now! And you there with me, while everything is topsy-turvy. I see you. I touch you. I kiss you, make love to you. And all the time—*it* is inside me. It tells me strange things—some I don't agree with, some I accept. Now and then I can appear in my own body, speak myself with my own voice. . . ." He hesitated, then went on, "But don't worry, Vivian. It's not as serious as all that. I'm fine. You can rest easy. We don't want you to suffer—"

Vivian threw herself at him, clawing at his face, pounding his chest with her fist. "You didn't let him finish!" she cried. "It's you now, the other one. You pushed him out!"

Fabian sat back, running his fingers over his face. One of Vivian's fingernails had left a red streak on his chin, but he said calmly, "You said it was me you wanted to speak to. And he was very nervous. He might have said something quite silly."

"Oh, Fabian," she said dismally, weeping.

Things were not getting better. There were, she realized, three Fabians. The old one; the one that play-acted being the human Fabian; and this most recent one, the extraterrestrial who admitted his identity.

And she loved them all.

"Don't be frightened," his voice soothed. "It's only natural. You people are terrified of what comes from beyond. But you shouldn't be, for even your own religions sometimes teach that the soul will live on in another body when this one dies. Do you not know that some of the geniuses who have changed the history of human-kind really came from—outside?" The voice stopped, then began again. "Vivian? It's me who's talking again, the human Fabian. I'm learning how to separate myself, to enjoy the pleasures of my body without fear or question, to feel the pressure of my fingers on your skin without knowing whether they're going down to your thighs or up to your breasts. I feel pleasure as if I was not the one who was caressing you—but it's your body that moves under my fingers—"

Vivian flung herself into his arms. It was frightening, but it was also wonderful to hear three voices talking to her out of the one mouth she loved.

And she knew that she gave pleasure back to all of them, for living in the body of a caterpillar or a butterfly had its own primitive beauty.

So she loved and lived with her lover, Fabian—with all of her loves in the body of Fabian. The present was what mattered. She felt happy. . . .

And did not allow herself to think of a tomorrow.

Fiddling for Water Buffaloes

BY SOMTOW SUCHARITKUL

When my brother Lek and I were children we were only allowed to go to Prasongburi once a week. That was the day our mothers went to the marketplace and to make merit at the temple. Our grandmother, our mother's mother, spent the days chewing betel nut and fashioning intricate mobiles out of dried palm leaves; not just the usual fish shapes, dozens of tiny baby fish swinging from a big mother fish lacquered in bright red or orange, but also more elaborate shapes: lions and tigers and mythical beasts, nagas that swallowed their own tails. It was our job to sell them to the *thaokae* who owned the only souvenir shop in the town . . . the only store with one of those aluminum gratings that you pull shut to lock up at night, just like the ones in Bangkok.

It was always difficult to get him to take the ones that weren't fish. Once we took in a mobile made entirely of spaceships, which our grandmother had copied from one of the American TV shows. (In view of our later experiences, this proved particularly prophetic.) "Everyone knows," the *thaokae* said (that was the time he admitted us to his inner sanctum, where he would smoke opium from an impressive *bong* and puff it in our faces), "that a *plataphien* mobile has fish in it. Everyone wants sweet little fishies to hang over their baby's cradle. I mean, those spaceships are a tribute to your grandmother's skill at weaving dried palm leaves, but as far as the tourists are concerned, it's just fiddling for water buffaloes." He meant there was no point in doing such fine work because it would be wasted on his customers.

We ended up with maybe ten baht apiece for my grandmother's labors, and we'd carefully tuck away two of the little blue banknotes (this was in the year 2504 B.E., long before they debased the baht into a mere coin) so that we could go to the movies. The American ones were funniest—especially the James Bond ones—because the dubbers had the most outrageous ad libs. I remember that in *Goldfinger* the dubbers kept putting in jokes about the fairy tale of Jao Ngo, which is about a hideous monster who falls into a tank of gold paint and becomes very handsome. The audience became so wild with laughter that they actually stormed the dubbers' booth and started improvising their own puns. I particularly remember that day because we were waiting for the monsoon to burst, and the heat had been making everyone crazy.

Seconds after we left the theater it came all at once, and the way home was so impassable we had to stay at the village before our village, and then we had to go home by boat, rowing frantically by the side of the drowned road. The fish were so thick you could pull them from the water in handfuls.

That was when my brother Lek said to me, "You know, Noi, I think it would be grand to be a movie dubber."

"That's silly, Phii Lek," I said. "Someone has to herd the water buffaloes and sell the mobiles and—"

"That's what we both should do. So we don't have to work on the farm anymore." Our mothers, who were rowing the boat, pricked up their ears at that. Something to report back to our father, perhaps. "We could live in the town. I love that town."

"It's not so great," my mother said.

My senior mother (Phii Lek's mother) agreed. "We went to Chiangmai once, for the beauty contest. Now there was a town. Streets that wind on and on . . . and air conditioning in almost every public building!"

"We didn't win the beauty contest, though," my mother said sadly. She didn't say it, but she implied that that was how they'd both ended up marrying my father. "Our stars were bad. Maybe in my next life—"

"I'm not waiting till my next life," my brother said. "When I'm grown up they'll have air conditioning in Prasongburi, and I'll be dubbing movies every night."

The sun was beating down, blinding, sizzling. We threw off our clothes and dived from the boat. The water was cool, mud-flecked; we pushed our way through the reeds.

The storm had blown the village's TV antenna out into the paddy field. We watched *Star Trek* at the headsman's house, our arms clutching the railings on his porch, our feet dangling, slipping against the stilts that were still soaked with rain. It was fuzzy and the sound was off, so Phii Lek put on a magnificent performance, putting discreet obscenities into the mouths of Kirk and Spock while the old men laughed and the coils of mosquito incense smoked through the humid evening. At night, when we were both tucked in under our mosquito netting, I dreamed about going into space and finding my grandmother's palm-leaf mobiles hanging from the points of the stars.

Ten years later they built a highway from Bangkok to Chiang-mai, and there were no more casual tourists in Prasongburi. Some American archaeologists started digging at the site of an old Khmer city nearby. The movie theater never got air conditioning, but my grandmother did become involved in faking antiques; it turned out to be infinitely more lucrative than fish mobiles, and when the *thaokae* died, she and my two mothers were actually able to buy the place from his intransigent nephew. The three of them turned it into an "antique" place (fakes in the front, the few genuine pieces carefully hoarded in the air-conditioned back room), and our father set about looking for a third wife as befit his improved station in life.

My family was also able to buy a half-interest in the movie theater, and that was how my brother and I ended up in the dubbing booth after all. Now, the fact of the matter was, sound projection systems in theaters had become prevalent all over the country by then, and Lek and I both knew that live movie dubbing was a dying art. Only the fact that the highway didn't come anywhere near

Prasongburi prevented its citizens from positively demanding talkies. But we were young and, relatively speaking, wealthy; we wanted to have a bit of fun before the drudgery of marriage and earning a real living was thrust upon us. Lek did most of the dubbing—he was astonishingly convincing at female voices as well as male—while I contributed the sound effects and played background music from the library of scratched records we'd inherited from the previous regime.

Since we two were the only purveyors of, well, foreign culture in the town, you'd think we would be the ones best equipped to deal with an alien invasion.

Apparently, the aliens thought so too.

Aliens were farthest from my mind the day it happened, though. I was putting in some time at the shop and trying to pacify my three honored parents, who were going at it like cats and dogs in the back.

"If you dare bring that bitch into our house," Elder Mother was saying, fanning herself feverishly with a plastic fan—for our air conditioning had broken down, as usual—"I'll leave."

"Well," Younger Mother (my own) said, "I don't mind as long as you make sure she's a servant. But if you marry her—"

"Well, *I* mind, I'm telling you!" my other mother shouted. "If the two of us aren't enough for you, I've three more cousins up north, decent, hardworking girls who'll bring in money, not use it up."

"Anyway, if you simply *have* to spend money," Younger Mother said, "what's wrong with a new pickup truck?"

"I'm not dealing with that usurious *thaokae* in Ban Kraduk," my father said, taking another swig of his *Mekong* whiskey, and "and there's no other way of coming up with a down payment . . . and besides, I happen to be a very horny man."

"All of you shut up," my grandmother said from somewhere out back, where she had been meticulously aging some pots into a semblance of twelfth-century Sawankhalok ware. "All this chatter disturbs my work."

"Yes, *khun mae,*" the three of them chorused back respectfully.

My Elder Mother hissed, "But watch out, my dear husband.

I read a story in *Siam Rath* about a woman who castrated her unfaithful husband and fed his eggs to the ducks!"

My father sucked in his breath and took a comforting gulp of whiskey as I went to the front to answer a customer.

She was one of those archaeologists or anthropologists or something. She was tall and smelly, as all *farangs* are (they have very active sweat glands); she wore a sort of safari outfit, and she had long hair, stringy from her digging and the humidity. She was scrutinizing the spaceship mobile my grandmother had made ten years ago—it still had not sold, and we had kept it as a memento of hard times —and muttering to herself words that sounded like, "Warp factor five!"

My brother and I know some English, and I was preparing to embarrass myself by exercising that ungrateful, toneless tongue, when she addressed me in Thai.

"Greetings to you, honored sir," she said, and brought her palms together in a clumsy but heartfelt *wai.* I couldn't suppress a laugh. "Why, didn't I do that right?" she demanded.

"You did it remarkably well," I said. "But you shouldn't go to such lengths. I'm only a shopkeeper, and you're not supposed to *wai* first. But I suppose I should give you 'E for effort' "—I said this phrase in her language, having learned it from another archaeologist the previous year—"since few would even try as hard as you."

"Oh, but I'm doing my Ph.D. in Southeast Asian aesthetics at UCLA," she said. "By all means, correct me." She started to pull out a notebook.

I had never, as we say, "arrived" in America, though my sexual adventures had recently included an aging, overwhelmingly odoriferous Frenchwoman and the daughter of the Indian *babu* who sold cloth in the next town, and the prospect suddenly seemed rather inviting. Emboldened, I said, "But to really study our culture, you might consider—" and eyed her with undisguised interest.

She laughed. *Farang* women are exceptional, in that one need not make overtures to them subtly, but may approach the matter in a no-nonsense fashion, as a plumber might regard a sewage pipe. "Jesus," she said in English, "I think he's asking me for a date!"

"I understood that," I said.

"Where will we go?" she said in Thai, giggling. "I've got the day off. And the night, I might add. Oh, that's not correct, is it? You should send a go-between to my father, or something."

"Only if the liaison is intended to be permanent," I said quickly, lest anthropology get the better of lust. "Well, we could go to a movie."

"What's showing?" she said. "Why, this is just like back home, and me a teenager again." She bent down, anxious to please, and started to deliver a sloppy kiss to my forehead. I recoiled. "Oh, I forgot," she said. "You people frown on public displays."

"*Star Wars,*" I said.

"Oh, but I've seen that twenty times."

"Ah, but have you seen it—dubbed *live,* in a provincial Thai theater without air conditioning? Think of the glorious field notes you could write."

"You Thai men are all alike," she said, intimating that she had had a vast experience of them. "Very well. What time? By the way, my name is Mary, Mary Mason."

We were an hour late getting the show started, which was pretty normal, and the audience was getting so restless that some of them had started an impromptu bawdy-rhyming contest in the front rows. My brother and I had manned the booth and were studying the script. He would do all the main characters, and I would do such meaty roles as the Second Storm Trooper.

"Let's begin," Phii Lek said. "She won't come anyway."

Mary turned up just as we were lowering the house lights. She had bathed (my brother sniffed appreciatively as she entered the dubbing booth) and wore a clean *sarong,* which did not look too bad on her.

"Can I do Princess Leia?" she said, *wai-* ing to Phii Lek, as though she were already his younger sibling by virtue of her as-yet-unconsummated association with me.

"You can *read* Thai?" Phii Lek said in astonishment.

"I have my master's in Siamese from Michigan U," she said huffily, "and studied under Bill Gedney." We shrugged.

"Yes, but you can't improvise," my brother said.

She agreed, pulled out her notebook, and sat down in a corner. My brother started to put on a wild performance, while I ran hither and thither putting on records and creating sound effects out of my box of props. We began the opening chase scene with Tchaikovsky's Piano Concerto, which kept skipping; at last the needle got stuck and I turned the volume down hastily just as my brother (in the tones of the heroic Princess Leia) was supposed to murmur, "Help me, Obiwan Kenobi. You're my only hope." Instead, he began to moan like a harlot in heat, screeching out, "Oh, I need a man, I do, I do! These robots are no good in bed!"

At that point Mary became hysterical with laughter. She fell out of her chair and collided with the shoe rack. I hastened to rescue her from the indignity of having her face next to a stack of filthy flipflops, and could not prevent myself from grabbing her. She put her arms around my waist and indecorously refused to let go, while my brother, warming to the audience reaction, began to ad-lib ever more outrageously.

It was only after the movie, when I had put on the 45 of the Royal Anthem and everyone had stood up to pay homage to the Sacred Majesty of the King, that I noticed something wrong with my brother. For one thing, he did not rise in respect, even though he was ordinarily the most devout of people. He sat bunched up in a corner of the dubbing booth, with his eyes darting from side to side like window wipers.

I watched him anxiously but dared not move until the Royal Anthem had finished playing.

Then, tentatively, I tapped him on the shoulder. "Phii Lek," I said, "it's time we went home."

He turned on me and snarled . . . then he fell on the floor and began dragging himself forward in a very strange manner, propelling himself with his chin and elbows along the woven-rush matting at our feet.

Mary said, "Is *that* something worth reporting on?" and began scribbling wildly in her notebook.

"Phii Lek," I said to my brother in terms of utmost respect, for I thought he might be punishing me for some imagined grievance, "are you ill?" Suddenly, I thought I had it figured out. "If you're playing 'putting on the anthropologists,' Elder Sibling, I don't think this one's going to be taken in."

"You are part of a rebel alliance, and a traitor!" my brother intoned—in English—in a harsh, unearthly voice. "Take her away!"

"That's . . . my God, that's James Earl Jones's voice," Mary said, forgetting in her confusion to speak Thai. "That's from the movie we just saw."

"What are we going to do?" I said, panicking. My older brother was crawling around at my feet, making me feel distinctly uncomfortable, because of the elevation of my head over the head of a person of higher status, so I dropped down on my hands and knees so as to maintain my head at the properly respectful level. Meanwhile, he was wriggling around on his belly.

Amid all this, Mary's notebook and pens clattered to the floor and she began to scream.

At that moment, my grandmother entered the booth and stared about wildly. I attempted, from my prone position, to perform the appropriate *wai*, but Phii Lek was rolling around and making peculiar hissing noises. Mary started to stutter, "*Khun yaai*, I don't what happened, they just suddenly started acting this way—"

"Don't you *khun yaai* me," my grandmother snapped. "I'm no kin to any foreigners, thank you!" She surveyed the spectacle before her with mounting horror. "Oh, my terrible karma!" she cried. "Demons have transformed my grandsons into dogs!"

On the street, there were crowds everywhere. I could hear people babbling about mysterious lights in the sky . . . portents and celestial signs. Someone said something about the spectacle outside being more impressive than the *Star Wars* effects inside the theater. Apparently, the main pagoda of the temple had seemed on fire for a few minutes and they'd called in a fire-fighting squad from the next town. "Who'd have thought of it?" my grandmother was complaining. "A demon visits Prasongburi—and makes straight for my own grandson!"

When we got to the shop—Mary still tagging behind and furiously taking notes on our social customs—the situation was even worse. The skirmish between my father and mothers had crescendoed to an all-out war.

"That's why I came to fetch you, children," my grandmother said. "Maybe you can referee this boxing match." A hefty celadon pot came whistling through the air and shattered on the overhead electric fan. We scurried for cover, all except my brother, who obliviously crawled about on his hands and knees, occasionally spouting lines from *Star Wars*.

Shrieking, Mary ran after the potsherds. "My god, that's thing's eight hundred years old—"

"Bah! I faked it last week," my grandmother said, forcing the *farang* woman to gape in mingled horror and admiration.

"All right, all right," my father said, fleeing from the back room with my mothers in hot pursuit. "I won't marry her . . . but I want a little more kindness out of the two of you . . . oh, my terrible karma."

He tripped over my brother and went sprawling to the floor. "What's wrong with him?"

"You fool!" my grandmother said. "Your own son has become possessed by demons . . . and it's all because of your sexual excesses."

My father stopped and stared at my brother. Then, murmuring a brief prayer to the Lord Buddha, he retired, cowering behind the shop counter. "What must I do?"

His wives came marching out behind him. Elder Mother hastened to succor Phii Lek. Younger Mother took in the situation and said, "I haven't seen anyone this possessed since my cousin Phii Daeng spent the night in a graveyard trying to get a vision of a winning lottery ticket number."

"It's all your fault," Phii Lek's mother said, turning wrathfully on my father. "You're all too eager to douse your staff of passion, and now my son has been turned into a monster!" The logic of this accusation escaped me, but my father seemed convinced.

"I'll go and *buat phra* for three months," he said, affecting a tone of deep piety. "I'll cut my hair off tomorrow and enter the nearest monastery. That ought to do the trick. Oh, my son, my son, what have I done?"

"Well," my grandmother said, "a little abstinence should do you good. I always thought you were unwise not to enter the monkhood at twenty like an obedient son should . . . cursing me to be reborn on earth instead of spending my next life in heaven as I ought, considering how I've worked my fingers to the bone for you! It's about time, that's what I say. A twenty-year-old belongs in a temple, not in the village scouts killing communists. Time for that when you've done your filial duty . . . well, twenty-five years late is better than nothing."

Seeing himself trapped between several painful alternatives, my father bowed his head, raised his palms in a gesture of respect, and said, "All right, *khun mae yaai,* if that's what you want."

When my father and the elder females of the family had gone to pack his things, I was left with my older brother and the bizarre American woman, in the antique shop in the middle of the night. They had taken the truck back to the village (which now boasted a good half-dozen motor vehicles, one of them ours) and we were stranded. In the heat of their argument and my father's repentance, they seemed to have forgotten all about us.

It was at that moment that my brother chose to snap out of whatever it was that possessed him.

Calmly, he rose from the floor, wiped a few foam flecks from his mouth with his sleeve, and sat down on the stool behind the counter. It took him a minute or two to recognize us, and then he said, "Well, well, Ai Noi! I gave the family quite a scare, didn't I?"

I was even more frightened now than I had been before. I knew very well that night is the time of spirits, and I was completely convinced that some spirit or another had taken hold of Phii Lek, though I was unsure of the part about my father being punished for his roving eyes and hands. I said, "Yes, *Khun Phii,* it was the most astonishing performance I've ever seen. Indeed, a bit too astonishing, if you don't mind your Humble Younger Sibling saying so. I mean, do you think they really appreciated it? If you ask me, you were just fiddling for water buffaloes."

"The most amazing thing is this . . . they weren't even after me!" He pointed at Mary. "They're in the wrong brain! It was her they wanted. But we all look alike to them. And I was imitating a woman's voice when they were trying to get a fix on the psychic transference. So they made an error of a few decimal places, and— poof!—here I am!"

"Pen baa pai laew!" I whispered to Mary Mason.

"I heard that!" my brother riposted. "But I am not mad. I am quite, quite sane, and I have been taken over by a *manus tang dao.*"

"What's that?" Mary asked me.

"A being from another star."

"Far frigging out! An extraterrestrial!" she said in English. I didn't understand a word of it; I thought it must be some kind of anthropology jargon.

"Look, I can't talk long, but . . . you see, they're after Mary. One of them is trying to send a message to America . . . something to do with the Khmer ruins . . . some kind of artifact . . . to another of these creatures who is walking around in the body of a professor at UCLA. This *farang* woman seemed ideal; she could journey back without causing any suspicion. But, you see, we all look alike to them, and—"

"Well, can't you tell whatever it is to stop inhabiting your body and transfer itself to—?"

"Hell, no!" Mary said, and started to back away. "Native customs are all very well, but this is a bit more than I bargained for."

"Psychic transference too difficult . . . additional expenditure of energy impractical at present stage . . . but message must get through . . ." Suddenly, he clawed at his throat for a few moments, and then fell writhing to the floor in another fit. "Can't get used to this gravity," he moaned. "Legs instead of pseudopods—and the contents of the stomach make me sick—there's at least fifty whole undigested chilies down here—oh, I'm going to puke—"

"By Buddha, Dharma and Sangkha!" I cried. "Quick, Mary, help me with him. Give me something to catch his vomit."

"Will this do?" she said, pulling down something from the shelf. Distractedly, I motioned her to put it up to his mouth.

Only when he had begun regurgitating into the bowl did I realize what she'd done. "You imbecile!" I said. "That's a genuine Ming spittoon!"

"I thought they were all fakes," she said, holding up my brother as he slowly turned green.

"We do have some *genuine* items here," I said disdainfully, "for those who can tell the difference."

"You mean, for *Thai* collectors," she said, hurt.

"Well, what can you expect?" I said, becoming furious. "You come here, you dig up all our ancient treasures, violate the chastity of our women—"

"Look who's talking!" Mary said gently. "Male chauvinist pig," she added in English.

"Let's not fight," I said. "He seems better now. . . . What are we going to do with him?"

"Here. Help me drag him to the back room."

We lifted him up and laid him down on the couch.

We looked at each other in the close, humid, mosquito-infested room. Suddenly, providentially almost, the air conditioning kicked on. "I've been trying to get it to work all day," I whispered.

"Does this mean—"

"Yes! Soon it will cool enough to—"

She kissed me on the lips. By morning I had "arrived" in America several delicious times, and Mary was telephoning the hotel in Ban Kraduk so she could get her things moved into my father's house.

The next morning, over dinner, I tried to explain it all to my elders. On the one hand there was this *farang* woman sitting on the floor, clumsily rolling rice balls with one hand and attempting to address my mothers as *khun mae,* much to their discomfiture; on the other there was the mystery of my brother, who was now confined to his room and refused to eat anything with any chilies in it.

"It's your weird western ways," my grandmother said, eyeing my latest conquest critically. "No chilies indeed! He'll be demanding hamburgers next."

"It's nothing to do with western ways," I said.

"It's a *manus tang dao,*" Mary said, proudly displaying her latest lexical gem, "and it's trying to get a message to America, and there's some kind of artifact in the ruins that they need, and they travel by some kind of psychic transference—"

"You Americans are crazy!" my grandmother said, spitting out her betel nut so she could take a few mouthfuls of curried fish. "Any fool can see the boy's possessed. I remember my great-uncle had fits

like this when he promised a donation of five hundred baht to the
Sacred Pillar of the City and then reneged on his offer. My parents
had to pay off the Brahmins—with interest!—before the curse was
lifted. Oh, my karma, my karma!"

"Shouldn't we call in some scientists, or something? A psychiatrist?" Mary said.

"Nothing of the sort!" said my grandmother. "If we can't take
care of this in the home, we'll not take care of it at all. No one's going
to say my grandson is crazy. Possessed, maybe . . . everyone can
sympathize with that . . . but crazy, never! The family honor is at
stake."

"Well, what should we do?" I said helplessly. As the junior
member of the family, I had no say in the matter at all. I was
annoyed at Mary for mentioning psychiatrists, but I reminded myself that she was, after all, a barbarian, even though she could speak
a human tongue after a fashion.

"We'll wait," my grandmother said, "and see whether your
father's penance will do the trick. If not . . . well, our stars are bad,
that's all."

During the weeks to come, my brother became increasingly
odd. He would enter the house without even removing his sandals,
let alone washing his feet. When my Uncle Eed came to dinner one
night, my brother actually pointed his left foot at our honored
uncle's head. I would be most surprised if Uncle Eed ever came to
dinner again after such unforgivable rudeness. I was forced to go into
town every evening to dub the movies, which I did in so lackluster
a manner that our usual audience began walking the two hours to
Ban Kraduk for their entertainment. My heart sank when a passing
visitor to the shop told me that the Ban Kraduk cinema had actually
installed a projection sound system and could show talkies, not only
the foreign films, with sound and subtitles, but the new domestic
talkies . . . so you could actually find out what great actors like Mitr
and Petchara sounded like! I knew we'd never compete with that.
I knew the days of live movie dubbing were numbered. Maybe I
could go to Bangkok and get a job with Channel Seven, dubbing
Leave it to Beaver and *Charlie's Angels*. But Bangkok was just about

as distant as another galaxy, and I could imagine the fun those city people would have with my hick northern accent.

One night about two weeks later, Mary and I were awakened by my brother, moaning from the mosquito net next to ours. I went across.

"Oh, there you are," Phii Lek said. "I've been trying to attract your attention for hours."

"I was busy," I said, and my brother leered knowingly. "Are you all right? Are you recovered?"

"Not exactly," he said. "But I'm, well, off-duty. The alien'll come back any minute, though, so I can't talk long." He paused. "Maybe that girlfriend of yours should hear this," he said. At that moment Mary crept in beside us, and we crouched together under the netting. The electric fan made the nets billow like ghosts.

"You have to take me to that archaeological dig of yours," he said. "There's an artifact . . . it's got some kind of encoded information . . . you have to take it back to Professor Übermuth at UCLA—"

"I've heard of him!" Mary whispered. "He's in a loony bin. Apparently, he became convinced he was an extraterre—oh, Jesus!" she said in English.

"He *is* one," Phii Lek said. "So am I. There are hundreds of us on this planet. But my controlling alien's resting right now. Look, Ai Noi, I want you to go down to the kitchen and get me as many chili peppers as you can find. On the *manus tang dao's* home planet the food is about as bland as rice soup."

I hurried to obey. When I got back, he wolfed down the peppers until he started weeping from the influx of spiciness. Suspiciously, I said, "If you're really an alien, what about spaceships?"

"Spaceships . . . we do have them, but they are drones, taking millennia to reach the center of the galaxy. We ourselves travel by tachyon psychic transference. But the device is being sent by drone."

"Device?"

"From the excavation! Haven't you been listening? It's got to be dug up and secretly taken to America and . . . I'm not sure what or why, but I get the feeling there's danger if we don't make our rendezvous. Something to do with upsetting the tachyon fields."

"I see," I said, humoring him.

"You know what I look like on the home planet, up there? I look like a giant *mangdaa.*"

"What's that?" said Mary.

"It's sort of a giant cockroach," I said. "We use its wings to flavor some kinds of curry."

"Yech!" she squealed. "Eating insects. Gross!"

"What do you mean? You've been enjoying it all week, and you've never complained about eating insects," I said. She started to turn slightly bluish. A *farang's* complexion, when he or she is about to be sick, is one of the few truly indescribable hues on the face of this earth.

"Help me. . . ." Phii Lek said. "The sooner this artifact is unearthed and loaded onto the drone, the sooner I'll be released from this—oh, no, it's coming back!" Frantically, he gobbled down several more chilies. But it was too late. They came right back up again, and he was scampering around the room on all fours and emitting pigeonlike cooing noises.

"Come to think of it," I said, "he *is* acting rather like a cockroach, isn't he?"

A week later our home was invaded by nine monks. My mothers had been cooking all the previous day, and when I came into the main living room they had already been chanting for about an hour, their bass voices droning from behind huge prayer fans. The house was fragrant with jasmine and incense.

I prostrated myself along with the other members of the family. My brother was there too, wriggling around on his belly; his hands were tied up with a sacred rope which ran all the way around the house and through the folded palms of each of the monks. Among them was my father, who looked rather self-conscious and didn't seem to know all the words of the chants yet . . . now and then he seemed to be opening his mouth at random, like a goldfish.

"This isn't going to work," I whispered to my grandmother, who was kneeling in the *phraphrieb* position with her palms folded, her face frozen in an expression of beatific piety. "Mary and I have found out what the problem is, and it's not possession."

"*Buddhang samang gacchami,*" the monks intoned in unison.

"What are they talking about?" Mary said. She was properly prostrate, but seemed distracted. She was probably uncomfortable without her trusty notebook.

"I haven't the faintest idea. It's all in Pali or Sanskrit or something," I said.

"*Namodasa phrakhavato arahato—*" the monks continued inexorably.

At length, they laid their prayer fans down and the chief *luangphoh* doused a spray of twigs in a silver dipper of lustral water and began to sprinkle Phii Lek liberally.

"It's got to be over soon," I said to Mary. "It's getting toward noon, and you know monks are not allowed to eat after twelve o'clock."

As the odor of incense wafted over me and the chanting continued, I fell into a sort of trance. These were familiar feelings, sacred feelings. Maybe my brother *was* in the grip of some supernatural force that could be driven out by the proper application of Buddha, Dharma, and Sangkha. However, as the *luangphoh* became ever more frantic, waving the twigs energetically over my writhing brother to no avail, I began to lose hope.

Presently, the monks took a break for their one meal of the day, and we took turns presenting them with trays of delicacies. After securing my brother carefully to the wall with the sacred twine, I went to the kitchen, where my grandmother was grinding fresh betel nut with a mortar and pestle. To my surprise, my father was there too. It was rather a shock to see him wearing a saffron robe and bald, when I was so used to seeing him barechested with a *phakhoma* loosely wrapped about his loins, and with a whiskey bottle rather than a begging bowl in his arms. I did not know whether to treat him as father or monk. To be on the safe side, I fell on my knees and placed my folded palms reverently at his feet.

My father was complaining animatedly to my grandmother in a weird mixture of normal talk and priestly talk. Sometimes he'd remember to refer to himself as *atma*, but at other times he'd speak like anyone off the street. He was saying, "But mother, *atma* is miserable, they only feed you once a day, and I'm hornier than ever! It's obviously not going to work, so why don't I just come home?"

My grandmother continued to pound vigorously at her betel nut.

"Anyway, *atma* thinks that it's time for more serious measures. I mean, calling in a professional exorcist."

At this, my grandmother looked up. "Perhaps you're right, holy one," she said. I could see that it galled her to have to address her wayward son-in-law in terms of such respect. "But can we afford it?"

"Phra Boddhisatphalo, *atma*'s guru, is an astrologer on the side, and he's says that the stars for the movie theater are exceptionally bad. Well, *atma* was thinking, why not perform an act of merit while simultaneously ridding ourselves of a potential financial liability? I say sell out the half-share of the cinema and use the proceeds to hire a really competent exorcist. Besides," he added slyly, "with the rest of the cash I could probably obtain me one of those nieces of yours, the ones whose beauty your daughters are always bragging about."

"You despicable cad," my grandmother began, and then added, "holy one," to be on the safe side of the karmic balance.

"Honored father and grandmother," I ventured, "have you not considered the notion that Phii Lek's body might indeed be inhabited by an extraterrestrial being?"

"I fail to see the difference," my father said, "between a being from another planet and one from another spiritual plane. It is purely a matter of attitude. You and your brother, whose wits have been addled by exposure to too many American movies, think in terms of visitations from the stars; your grandmother and I, being older and wiser, know that 'alien' is merely another word for spirit. Earthly or unearthly, we are all spokes in the wheel of karma, no? Exorcism ought to work on both."

I didn't like my father's new approach at all; I thought his drunkenness far more palatable than his piety. But of course this would have been an unconscionably disrespectful thing to say, so I merely *wai*-ed in obeisance and waited for the ordeal to end.

My grandmother said, "Well, son-in-law, I can see a certain progress in you after all." My father turned around and winked at me. "Very well," she said, sighing heavily, "perhaps your mentor can find us a decent exorcist. But none of those foreigners, mind you," she added pointedly as Mary entered the kitchen to fetch another tray of comestibles for the monks' feast.

The interview with the spirit doctor was set for the following week. By that time the wonder of my brother's possession had attracted tourists from a radius of some ten kilometers; his performances were so spectacular as to outdraw even the talking cinema in Ban Kraduk.

It turned out to be a Brahmin, tall, dark, white-robed, with a long white beard that trailed all the way down to the floor. He wore a necklace of bones—they looked suspiciously human—and several flower wreaths over his uncut, wispy hair; moreover he had an elaborate third eye painted in the middle of his forehead.

"Narayana, Narayana," he said, with the portentousness of a paunchy deva in one of those Indian historical movies. This, I realized, was a sham to impress the credulous populace, who were swarming around the stilts of our house. One or two children were peering from behind the horns of water buffaloes, and one was even peeping from a huge rainwater jar. The Brahmin had an accolyte just for the purpose of removing his sandals and splashing his feet from the foot-washing trough, an occupation of such ignominy that I was surprised even a boy would stoop to it. He surveyed my family (which had been suddenly expanded by visiting cousins, aunts, uncles, and several other grandmothers junior to my own) and inquired haughtily, "And which of you is the possessed one?"

"He can't even tell?" my grandmother whispered to me. Then she pointed at Phii Lek, who was crawling around the front porch moaning "tachyon, tachyon."

"Ah," said the exorcist. "A classic case of possession by a *phii krasue*. Dire measures are indicated, I'm afraid."

At the mention of the dreaded *phii krasue*, the entire family recoiled as a single entity. For the *phii krasue* is, as everyone knows, a spirit who looks like a normal enough creature in the daytime, but at night detaches its head from its body and, dragging its entrails behind it, propels itself forward by its tongue. It also lives on human excrement. It is, in short, one of the most loathsome and feared of spirits. The idea that we might have been harboring one in our very house sent chills of terror through me.

Presently, I heard dissenting voices. "But a *phii krasue* can't act this way in the daytime!" one said. "Anyway, where's the trail of guts?" said another. "This fellow's obviously a quack . . . never trust a Brahmin exorcist, I tell you." "Well, let's give him the benefit. See if he comes up with anything."

The Brahmin spirit doctor took a good look at us, clearly appraising our finances. "Can he be cured?" Elder Mother asked him.

"Given your very secure monetary standing," the Brahmin said, "I see no reason why not. You can take him inside now; I shall discuss the—ah, your merit-making donation—with the head of the household."

My grandmother came forward, her palms uplifted in supplication. "Fetch him a drink," she muttered to my mothers.

My mother said, "Does the *than mo phii* want a glass of water? Or would he prefer Coca-Cola?"

"A glass of Mekong whiskey," said the spirit doctor firmly. "Better yet, bring the whole bottle. We'll probably be haggling all night."

Since Phii Lek was no longer the center of attention, Mary and I obeyed the spirit doctor and brought him inside. He chose that moment to snap back into a state of relative sanity. We knew he had come to because he immediately began demanding chili peppers.

"All right," he said at last. "I've been authorized to tell you a few more things, since it seems to be the only hope."

"What about that monstrous charlatan out there?" Mary said. "He's only going to delay your plans, isn't he?"

"Not necessarily. I want you to insist that he perform the exorcism *at* the archaeological dig. Once there, I'll be able to home in on the device and get rid of the giant cockroach at the same time. You know, that exorcist wasn't far wrong when he said I'd been possessed by a *phii krasue*. Would you be interested in knowing what my alien overlords like for dinner?"

"I take it they're scavengers?" Mary said.

"Exactly," said my brother. "But no more of this excremental subject. You have to convince that exorcist of yours. Unless the device is returned, there will be awful consequences. You see, the aliens were here once before, about eight hundred years ago. They planted a number of these devices as . . . well, tachyon calibration beacons. Well, this one is going dangerously out of synch, and some of the aliens aren't ending up in the bodies they were destined for. I mean, this psychic transference business is expensive, and the military ruler of nine star systems doesn't want to get thrust into the body of a leprous janitor from Milwaukee. That is precisely what happened last week, and the diplomatic consequences happen to be rippling through the entire galaxy at this very minute. Anyway, if the beacon is sent back posthaste for deactivation, guess who gets it?"

"You?" I said.

"Worse. They call it a preventative measure. They randomize the solar system."

"I think that's a euphemism for—" Mary began.

"That's right, Beloved Younger Siblings! No more planet Earth."

"Can they really do that?" I said.

"They do it all the time." My brother reverted for a moment to cockroachlike behavior, then jerked back into a human pose with great effort. "They might not, though. All the xenobiologists, primitive cult fetishists, and so on are up in arms. So it might happen today . . . it might happen in a couple of years . . . it might never happen. Who knows? But Galactic Central thinks that no world, no matter how puny or insignificant, should be randomized without due process. But . . . I don't think we should risk it, do you?"

"Maybe not," I said. The theory that my brother had contracted one of those American mental diseases, like schizophrenia, was becoming more and more attractive to me. But I had to do what he said. To be on the safe side.

Mary and I left Phii Lek and went out to the porch, where the spirit doctor had consumed half the whiskey and they had lit the anti-mosquito tapers, whose smoke perfumed the dense night air.

"Excuse me, honored grandmother," I said, trying to sound as unassuming as I could, "but Phii Lek says he wants the exorcism done at Mary's archaeological dig."

"Ha!" the exorcist said. "One must always do the opposite of what a possessed person said, for the evil spirit in him strives always to delude us!" His sentiments were expressed with such resounding ferocity that there was a burst of applause from the crowd downstairs. "Besides," he added, "there's probably a whole arm of *phii krasue* out there, just waiting to swallow us up. It's a trap, I tell you! This possession is merely the vanguard of a wholesale demonic invasion!"

I looked despairingly at Mary. "Now what'll we do?" I said. "Sit around waiting for the Earth to disappear?"

It was Mary who came to the rescue . . . and I realized how much she had absorbed by quietly observing us and taking all those notes. She said, speaking in a Thai far more heavily accented than she normally used, "But please, honored spirit doctor, the field study group would be most interested in seeing a real live exorcism!"

The spirit doctor looked decidedly uncertain at being addressed in Thai by a *farang*. I could tell the questions racing through his mind: What status should the woman be accorded? She wasn't related to any of these people, nor was her social position immediately obvious. How could he respond without accidentally using the wrong pronoun, and giving her too much or little status—and perhaps rendering himself the laughingstock of these potential clients?

Taking advantage of his confusion, Mary pursued relentlessly. "Or does the honored spirit doctor perhaps *klua phii?*"

"Of course I'm not afraid of spirits!" the exorcist said.

"Then why would a few extra ones bother the honored spirit doctor?" Mary contrived to speak in so unprepossessing an accent that it was impossible to tell whether her polite words were ingenuous or insulting.

"Bah!" said the spirit doctor. "A few *phii krasue* are nothing. It's just a matter of convenience, that's all. . . ."

"I'm sure that the foundation that's sponsoring our field research here would be more than happy to make a small donation toward ameliorating the inconvenience. . . ."

"Since you put it that way," the exorcist said, defeated.

"Hmpf!" my grandmother said, triumphantly yanking the half-bottle of whiskey away and sending my mother back to the kitchen with it. "These *farangs* might be some use after all. They're as ugly as elephants, of course—and albino elephants at that—but who knows? One day their race may yet amount to something."

The whole street opera of an exorcism was in full swing by the time my brother, Mary, and I parked her official Landrover about a half-hour's walk away from the site. It had taken a week to make the preparations, with my brother's moments of lucidity getting briefer and his eschatological claims wilder each time.

By the time we had trudged through fields of young rice, squishing knee deep in mud, several hundred people had gathered to watch. A good hundred or so were relatives of mine. Mary introduced me to some colleagues of hers, professors and such like, and they eyed me with curiosity as I fumbled around in their intractable language.

Four broken pagodas were silhouetted in the sunset. A water buffalo nuzzled at the pediment of an enormous stone Buddha, to whom I instinctively raised my palms in respect. Here and there, erupting from the brilliant green of the fields of young rice, were fragments of fortifications and walls topped with complex friezes that depicted grim, barbaric gods and garlanded, singing *apsaras*. A row of trunkless stucco elephants guarded a gateway to another paddy field.

Every part of the ruined city had been girded round with a *saisin*, a sacred rope that had been strung up along the walls and along the stumps of the elephant trunks and through the stone portals and finally into the folded palms of the spirit doctor himself, who sat in the lotus position on a woven rush mat, surrounded by a cloud of incense.

"You're late," he said angrily as we hastened to seat ourselves within the protected circle. "Get inside, inside. Or do you want to be swallowed up by spirits?"

If I had thought Phii Lek's actions bizarre before, his performance now shifted into an even more hyperbolic gear. He groaned. He danced about, his body coiling and coiling like a serpent.

I heard my grandmother cry out, *"Ui ta then!* Nuns dropping in the basement!" It was the strongest language I'd ever heard her use.

Mary clutched my hand. Some of my relatives stared disapprovingly at the impropriety, but I decided that they were just jealous.

"And now we'll see which it is to be," Mary said. "Science fiction or fantasy."

"He's mumbling himself into a trance now," I said, pointing to the exorcist, who had closed his eyes and from whose lips a strange buzzing issued.

"Are you sure he's not snoring?" one of my mothers said maliciously.

"What tranquility! What perfect *samadhi!*" my other mother said admiringly, for the spirit doctor hadn't moved a muscle in some ten minutes.

Phii Lek's contortions became positively unnerving. He darted about the sacred circle, now and then flapping his arms as though to fly. Suddenly, a bellow—like the cry of an angry water buffalo—burst from his lips. He flapped again and again—and then rose into the air!

"Be still, I command thee!" the exorcist's voice thundered, and he waved a rattle at my levitating brother and made mysterious passes. "I tell thee, be still!"

A ray of light shot upward from the earth, dazzlingly bright. The pagodas were lit up eerily. The ground opened up under Phii Lek as he hovered. There he was, brilliantly lit up in the pillar of radiance, with an iridescent aura around him whose outlines vaguely resembled an enormous cockroach.

The crowd was going wild now. They clamored, they cheered; some of the children were disobeying the sacred cord and having to be restrained by their elders. My brother was sitting, in lotus position, in the middle of the air with his palms folded, looking just like a postcard of the Emerald Buddha in Bangkok.

The flaming apparition that had been my brother descended into the pit. We all rushed to the edge. The light from the abyss burned our eyes; we were blinded. Mary took advantage of the confusion to embrace me tightly; I was too overwhelmed to castigate her.

We waited.

The Earth rumbled.

At last a figure crawled out. He was covered in mud and filth. He was clutching something under his arm . . . something very much like a Ming spittoon.

"Phii Lek!" I cried out, overcome with relief that he was still alive.

"The tachyon calibrator—" he gasped, holding aloft the spittoon and waving it dramatically in the air. "You must get it to . . ."

He fainted, still clasping the alien device firmly to his bosom.

The light shifted . . . the ghostly, rainbow-fringed giant cockroach seemed to drift slowly across the field, toward the unmoving figure of the exorcist . . . it danced grotesquely above his head, and he began to twitch and foam at the mouth. . . .

"I'll be dead!" my grandmother shouted. "The spirit is transferring itself into the body of the exorcist!"

In a moment the exorcist too fainted, and the sacred cord fell from his hands. The circle was broken. Whatever was done was done.

I rushed to the side of my brother, still lying prone by the side of the abyss.

"Wake up!" I said, shaking him. "Please wake up!"

He got up and grinned. Applause broke out. The exorcist, too, seemed to be recovering from his ordeal.

"And now," my brother said, holding out the alien artifact, "I can return this thing to the person who was sent to fetch it."

A small, white, palpitating hand was stretched forward to receive it. I turned to see who it was. "Oh, no," I said softly.

For it was Mary who had taken the artifact . . . and Mary who was now gyrating about the paddy field in a most unfeminine, most cockroachlike manner.

Later that night, Phii Lek and I sat on the floor of our room, waiting for Mary to snap out of her extraterrestrial seizure so we could find out what had happened.

Toward dawn the alien gave her her first break. "I can talk now," she said suddenly, calmly.

"Do you need chilies?" I said.

"I think a good hamburger would be more my style," she said.

"We can probably fake it," my brother said, "if you don't mind having it on rice instead of a bun."

"Well," she said, when my brother had finished clattering about the kitchen, fixing this unorthodox meal, and she was sitting cross-legged on my bedding, munching furiously, "I suppose I should tell you what I'm allowed to tell you."

"Take your time," I said, not meaning it.

"Okay. Well, as you know, the exorcist is a total fake, a charlatan, a mountebank. But he does enter a passable state of *samadhi*, and apparently this was close enough to the psychic null state necessary for psychic transference to enable a mindswap to occur over a short distance. His blank mind was a sort of catalyst, if you will, through which, under the influence of the tachyon calibrator, I could leave Phii Lek's mind and enter Mary's."

"So you'll be taking the spittoon back to America?" I said.

"Right on schedule. And it's not a spittoon. That happens to be a very clever disguise."

"So . . ." It suddenly occurred to me that she would soon be leaving. I was irritated at that. I didn't know why. I should have been pleased, because, after all, I had essentially traded her for my brother, and family always comes first.

"Look," she said, noticing my unease, "do you think . . . maybe . . . one last time?" She caressed my arm.

"But you're a giant cockroach!" I said.

She kissed me.

"You've been bragging to your friends all month about 'arriving' in America," she said. "How'd you like to 'arrive' on another planet?"

In the middle of the act I became aware that someone else was there with us. I mean, I was used to the way Mary moved, the delicious abandon with which she made her whole body shudder. I thought, "The alien's here too! Well, I'm really going to show it how a Thai can drive. Here we go!"

The next morning I said, "How was it?"

She said, "It was a fascinating activity, but frankly I prefer mitosis."

Fiddling for water buffaloes.

In a day or so I saw her off; I went back to the antique store; I found my grandmother hard at work in her antique-faking studio. A perfect Ming spittoon lay beside her where she squatted. She saw me, spat out her betel nut, and motioned me to sit.

"Why, Grandmother," I said, "That's a perfect copy of whatever it was the alien took to America."

"Look again, my grandson," she said, and chuckled to herself as she rocked back and forth kneading clay.

I picked it up. The morning light shone on it through the window. I had an inkling that . . . no. Surely not. "You didn't!" I said.

She didn't answer.

"Grandmother . . ."

No answer.

"But the solar system is at stake!" I blurted out. "If they find out that they've got the wrong tachyon calibrator. . . ."

"Maybe, maybe not," said my grandmother. "The way I think is this: It's obviously very important to someone, and anything that valuable is worth faking. You say these interstellar diplomats will be arguing the question for years, perhaps. Well, as the years go by, the price will undoubtedly go up."

"But *khun yaai*, how can you possibly play games with the destiny of the entire human race like this?"

"Oh, come, come. I'm just an old woman looking out for her family. The movie house has been sold, and we've lost maybe fifty thousand baht on the exorcism and the feast. Besides, your father will insist on another wife, I'm afraid, and after all this brouhaha I can't blame him. We'll be out one hundred thousand baht by the time we're through. I have a perfect right to some kind of recompense. Hopefully, by the time they come looking for this thing, we'll be able to get enough for it to open a whole antique factory . . . who knows, move to Bangkok . . . buy up Channel Seven so your brother can dub movies to his heart's content."

"But couldn't the alien tell?" I said.

"Of course not. How many experts on disguised tachyon calibrators do you think there are, anyway?" My grandmother paused to turn the electric fan so that it blew exclusively on herself. The air conditioning, as usual, was off. "Anyway, *manus tang dao* are only another kind of foreigner, and anyone can tell you that all foreigners are suckers."

I heard the bell ring in the front.

"Go on!" she said. "There's a customer!"

"But what if—" I got up with some trepidation. At the partition I hesitated.

"Courage!" she whispered. "Be a *luk phuchai!*"

I remembered that I had the family honor to think of. Boldly, I marched out to meet the next customer.

FROM ITALY:

S Is for Snake

BY LINO ALDANI
Translated by Joe F. Randolph

> Dr. Fabio Cali&tri
> Chief Archivi&t
> The National Library
> Rome
> July 26, 1998

Profe&&or Aurelio Buonaiuti
Chancellor
College of Education
Florence

Dear Profe&&or:

   Aware of the &cholarly and brilliant pre&entation you gave in Rome two year& ago at the International Exobiology Convention (on that occa&ion I acted a& &ecretary for the Italian contingent), I am writing to you &ince I con&ider you, becau&e of your &pecific area of experti&e and your univer&ally recognized merit&, the per-&on mo&t qualified to receive my account. It i& ab&olutely true and written with my mental facultie& fully re&tored.

   You will notice that in this typewritten letter the &eventeenth letter of the Italian alphabet ha& been &y&tematically replaced with the amper&and (&). The rea&on& for thi& &ub&titution,

which for the time being may &eem &trange and eccentric to you, will be explained later on if you have the patience to continue reading my account.

Two year& ago you cau&ed quite a &tir at the convention by a&&erting with ingeniou& intuition that extraterre&trial intelligence& could communicate with u& via mental projection. The light-year barrier &eparating u& from them could in&tantaneou&ly be bridged in &pite of Ein&tein'& po&tulate& or maybe in &pite of their confirmation, &ince the mind circumvent& the law& that matter mu&t obey. You were ab&olutely right, my dear profe&&or. Let me add that not only i& communication po&&ible, but al&o genuine p&ychic tran&fer& them&elve&. For one long month, I my&elf have been the fle&h-and-blood receptacle playing ho&t, again&t my will, to the annoying pre&ence of an alien entity from a world hundred& and hundred& of par&ec& away. Plea&e do not tear up my letter, but ju&t keep reading. It i& a true account even though it &ometime& come& di&gui&ed a& ab&urdity.

It all began a month ago, right on &unday morning, June 28, 1998 A.D. It wa& 11 A.M., and a& on every &unday I wa& to be found on the terrace in &t. Peter'& Cathedral in Vatican City. A long time ago Rome became a beguiling but unlivable city, a jumble of gridlocked car& where the average &peed, in the be&t of ca&e&, did not exceed two kilometer& an hour.

There wa& alway& a mob of touri&t& up there on the terrace in the &hadow of the dome. But, generally &peaking, people were quiet, German&, American&, Japane&e, all orderly, lined up and accompanied by their guide, all toting binocular& and movie camera&. They did not bother me becau&e at tho&e moment& I wa& too ab&orbed in &tudying from a high vantage point my city, finally all mine; one &ingle look captured the whole panorama.

Well, on &unday, June 28, I wa& &tanding there a& u&ual leaning again&t the &outhern parapet, my eye& glued to the di&tant architectural profile&, familiar to me by now—the Janiculum, the Forum, the Eur &ky&craper&, and the ba&ilica dome& &tanding out again&t a cloudle&& azure-blue &ky. All of a &udden, perhap& preceded by a &hort &en&ation of emptine&&, I noticed a zinging &ound a& when a taut metal cable i& cut. At that &ame

moment, &omething bur&t in my brain. I fell back again&t the
balu&trade and then &ank to the &lab floor of the terrace.

When I opened my eye&, I wa& &urrounded by a fore&t of
leg&. &omeone had given me &melling &alt&. There were &everal
people bent over me and &peaking in loud, confu&ed voice&. "Der
&onne&tich," an elderly German woman propo&ed her diag-
no&i&. "It'& a dizzy &pell," a young man with an unmi&takable
American accent tried to correct her. But both were wrong. It wa&
neither a &un&troke nor a dizzy &pell. There wa& &omething
really unu&ual in&ide me. For the fir&t time in my life, I felt a&
if my brain were being fitted in&ide my &kull. I noticed it& phy&i-
cal, material, almo&t-tangible pre&ence.

A policeman came into the crowd and helped me to my feet.
"Do you feel all right, &ir?"

I nodded ye& like a groggy boxer.

"I'll go with you," the policeman &aid.

He took me by an arm and led me to the elevator. But once
I got down in the middle of the nave, my trembling leg& notwith-
&tanding, I told him I did not need hi& help anymore. The policeman &hrugged and turned on hi& heel.

I pa&&ed by Bernini'& baldachin. And there another di&con-
certing thing happened in me. I have alway& hated the baroque
&tyle, maybe more than gothic, fond a& I am of the uncluttered
line& of the Romane&que form. Well, tho&e four column& ri&ing
in &piral&, ma&&ive, gaudy, and weighty like four mon&trou&
anaconda&, at that moment &eemed to me the quinte&&ence of
perfection, beauty executed in the mo&t &ublime and harmoniou&
form&. Engro&&ed in e&thetic delight, I would have &tayed in
front of the baldachin for the re&t of my day& had not a &udden
internal pre&&ure propelled me toward the exit.

The piazza, ringed by a double row of column&, wa& flooded
with &unlight. I lived behind the &t. Angelo Ca&tle, ju&t a kilome-
ter away, a &tretch of &treet I u&ually covered on foot. But that
day, to get back to my place, I thought it wi&er to take a cab. When
my wife Livia &aw me appear on the door&tep, &he wa& unable
to hold back a cry of a&toni&hment.

"What happened to you, Fabio? Your face i& a& white a& a
&heet."

A& on every &unday, Livia had fixed an excellent dinner. But that day I did not touch the food. I felt my eye& burning with fever and went to bed right away. My head felt like a beehive. I could count the convolution& on my brain one by one, or rather, &ome-one el&e in&ide wa& doing the counting for me, &earching every nook and cranny, even the mo&t &ecret rece&&e&, the limitle&& maze& I had not &u&pected the exi&tence of until then.

After an hour, I fell into a deep coma.

I woke up in the ho&pital after three day&. The fever wa& gone almo&t a& &uddenly a& it had come. I had pretty well recovered, ju&t a little weak, my head di&oriented becau&e of that &trange beehive &till in my brain. The doctor& wanted to keep me in order to &ubject me to God know& what te&t&, but I &igned a relea&e ab&olving them of any re&pon&ibility, and I went back home.

That very evening in my clo&ed &tudy, I &uddenly &tarted to act according to the dictate& of the alien that had infiltrated my brain. At fir&t, I could &till delude my&elf about being in control of my action& and deci&ion&. I had taken the fir&t volume of the *Enciclopedia Treccani* and had &tarted thumbing through it me-thodically, beginning with the fir&t page. For year& I had been toying with the idea of writing an e&&ay entitled "Etymology and Cu&tom&." &o, at fir&t, while thumbing through the volume, I could &till believe I wa& engaged in a &y&tematic &earch of the mo&t intere&ting etymon&, in view of the work that I had &et out for my&elf &ome time ago. There were word& and word& that held no etymological intere&t for me and that therefore I would have willingly bypa&&ed quickly. But the alien wa& of quite another mind, ab&orbing word after word with the care of a neophyte, who even noted marginal information and lingered where he thought it appropriate to do &o.

He read and retained at the average rate of ninety page& an hour. Every now and then I felt, in&ide, a vibration of plea&ure, &omething re&embling a hi&&. And I had a &plitting headache, but by now I wa& re&igned to it, only paying attention to the recurrent pre&&ure under my neck that the alien u&ed to alert me that it wa& time to turn the page.

The next day—the alien'& order wa& peremptory—I called

the director of the library to tell him my decision to take my vacation a month early. My wife—unaware of anything—did not quite agree, got sour, and was miffed at me for several days. Half the hotels in Viareggio had already been booked, all the arrangements made with friends and relatives we vacationed with every summer. And so, you know, my decision had nothing to do with a change of date, it meant cancellation of the vacation.

"Damn you and your book," Livia cursed.

Nevertheless, she patiently fixed my meals and never bothered me during my frantic work that occupied me from early morning until late at night.

I think I already said that the alien was a methodical type. In a space of ten days he assimilated thirty-eight volumes of the *Enciclopedia Treccani* plus the bibliographic appendices and the yearbooks.

"That's enough for now." I tried to tell him that I was dizzy by then. "I'm beat. I need some rest and diversion."

In my mind I felt a long, drawn-out hiss that I took to mean a sign of approval. Then I poured myself a big glass of brandy, took a tape of Mahler's first symphony out of its case, and slipped it into the stereo.

That evening I discovered that the alien could not tolerate alcohol. In addition, I found out that music calmed him by taking away his power and aggressiveness. The sound of the violins hypnotized him—if I can put it that way. The oboe weakened him, and the flute made him as tame as a puppy.

"Who are you?" I asked, suddenly taking advantage of his momentary debility. "Where are you from? How did you get into my mind?"

"Take it easy, archivist. Take it easy!"

I turned up the stereo.

"Who are you?" I pressed after taking another long sip of brandy.

"Just call me Ophis," the alien said. The voice inside seemed to me to be the drawling voice of a drunkard in a confiding mood. "I'm a snake, and I'm from far, far away. At this very moment, a thousand members of my species are joined together and are concentrating mentally to allow me, the cho&en one, to make the fir&t contact with your civilization—"

"But where're you from, I'm a&king."

"From a long way away. From the &tar you people call Rigel. My &nake body i& there in &u&pended animation, but my mind i& here, enclo&ed in your&."

"And how did you get here?"

"I told you, archivi&t. By mental projection. The experiment'& a &ucce&&. But right now don't try to pump me for information about my world and our &cience. Even if I wanted to furni&h you with it, you wouldn't be in any po&ition to gra&p it& &ignificance. You people are a bit backward."

I took a minute or two to &ip my brandy. Then I a&ked, "Why me in particular? Ye&, indeed. Why did you pick me for your experiment?"

"That'& exactly the point. I could ju&t a& well have wound up in an Au&tralian Aborigine'& brain. I thought—what a wa&te of time! With you, we've been extremely fortunate. You're a &ufficient epitome of your &pecie&, cultured to boot. My mi&&ion ha& been made a lot ea&ier."

"What do you want from u&?"

"Nothing, archivi&t. Nothing dangerou& to you human&. We ju&t want to &ati&fy our curio&ity—"

"You drained my brain while I wa& in a coma, then you gobble up a whole library. I&n't that enough for you?"

"Huh. No. There are other thing& we want to know. Thing& written in book& that aren't here in your hou&e. But you, a& chief archivi&t, have unlimited acce&& to the Central Library. Tomorrow you'll take me back into the &tack&—"

"Tomorrow'& &unday. The library'& clo&ed."

At that moment, my wife came into the &tudy. &he &tared at the gla&& of brandy with a di&approval-laden expre&&ion and rai&ed her eyebrow to give me to under&tand that the &tereo wa& too loud and wa& di&turbing her.

"I wa& ju&t talking to my &i&ter," &he &aid matter-of-factly. "&he'd appreciate it if you'd take Filippo to the zoo tomorrow afternoon. You promi&ed to &ome time ago."

I wa& on the verge of telling her to go to hell. But Ophi&'& voice in&ide coun&eled me to be quiet. Evidently, the alien wa& intere&ted in vi&iting the zoo.

"OK," I wa& &urpri&ed to hear my&elf &ay, almo&t without being aware of it. "I'll take the boy to the zoo tomorrow."

My wife ca&t another hard look at the bottle of brandy. "What are you doing? Aren't you going to bed?"

I nodded ye&. Ophi& did not gain&ay me. On the contrary, that evening he &eemed &trangely intere&ted in . . . In &hort, he wa& the one to urge me on with hi& half-&ubtle trick&. I drank another half gla&& and &taggered into the bedroom to join my wife.

I wa& drunk. That i&, we were drunk, the alien and I. Every pet name, &tupid and meaningle&& word&, I had ever called my wife came to mind. And then I &aid to her, "Come clo&er." I wanted to add, *I wanna &queeze you in my arm&*, but, in&tead, hone&t to God, I hi&&ed, "I wanna wrap my coil& around you."

In &hort, that damned alien wa& &tealing my wife from me, or at lea&t he wa& having a good time, too, without my being able to &top him.

The next day I took my nephew Fillipo, a little nine-year-old boy who already knew all about even the mo&t exotic animal&, to the zoo.

I am bringing up detail& about the zoo trip ju&t to under&core the inten&e intere&t the alien &howed when we went into the reptile hou&e, an intere&t, however, returned by cobra& and python& when face to face with me. A& I pa&&ed by, it wa& a& if an electric &hock had all at once rou&ed them from their torpor. They ro&e up on their tail&, and their forked tongue& &hot out very excitedly.

When we got near the mu&talid cage&, I broke out in a cold &weat. I had no intention of going any farther. Even the alien in&ide rolled up, a victim of panic. But my nephew wanted to &ee the mongoo&e& up clo&e.

All hell broke loo&e. A& &oon a& I unwillingly approached, the two &pecimen& of *Herpe&te& edward&i* furiou&ly threw them&elve& at the protective barrier. They had it in for me,

&quealing and baring their teeth at me, rolling their viciou&
blood&hot eye&.

"Get away! Get away!" the alien commanded. "&tay away
from tho&e brute&."

We all calmed down after I put two hundred meter& between
u& in front of the &wan pond. &itting on a bench, I wiped the
&weat away while my nephew wa& bu&y with hi& ice cream.

The next day, Monday, Ophi& dragged me to the library. He
dictated the book title& that he needed—by now he wa& highly
learned—and I ha&tened to take them down from the &helve& or
waited for a hard-working clerk to bring them to me. Then, I patiently flipped through them from the fir&t to la&t page.

Many of the book& the alien wanted to con&ult were all
unknown to me. Other& were cla&&ic&, the billion& of building
block& of our cultural evolution. He lingered for a long time over
Uli&&e Aldrovandi'& naturali&t treati&e&, and, obviou&ly, he
went over the &ection& dealing with reptile& in minute detail.
Then he wanted to look at the &eventeen volume& of Diderot'&
eighteenth-century *Encyclopédie*, then the late&t edition of *La-
rou&&e*, then the work& of Freud, then the treati&e& of Adam
&mith, David Ricardo, Karl Marx, and a dozen other economi&t&.
He hardly touched any literature, but wa& greatly intere&ted in
&ampling a few page& of Lovecraft and &ome of Garcia Lorca'&
and Emily Dickin&on'& poetry. On the other hand, our &tudie&
of parap&ychology made him &mile—I would not know how to
define in any other way the feeling of patient annoyance that he
knew how to communicate to me automatically.

"In thi& field," he whi&pered, amu&ed, "you're &till in the
ABC'&. It'& natural. You people wanted to develop the art& in-
&tead of the brain. A minimum of ten centurie&, or perhap& a
hundred, will have to pa&& before you will be able to accompli&h
in&tantaneou& projection and thereby duplicate our vi&it."

Meanwhile, another ten day& went by, and by now I felt a&
if I were at my wit&' end. And yet—Ophi& in the interim had
learned Engli&h—I had to put the entire *Encyclopedia Britannica*
at hi& di&po&al. Of cour&e, he had also learned &pani&h, German, and who know& how many other language&, but by then it

wa& almo&t time for him to go back. Ophi&'& mi&&ion wa& drawing to a clo&e, and there wa& not enough time for him to memorize the 72 volume& of *E⊙pa⊙a Calpe* or the 167 volume& of the *Allgemeine Enzyklopädie.* But he did not give up reading the Bible in it& numerou& ver&ion&. Then he wanted A&&yrian-Babylonian text&, the Ave&ta, Vedic literature, Buddha'& &uttapikata, the Analect& of Confuciu&, the Koran, and a dozen other treati&e& on hi&tory and religion. Finally, he wanted an overview of the vi&ual art& from every period, and &o I wa& compelled to fulfill hi& wi&h to look at thou&and& and thou&and& of photoreproduction& and color &lide&, beginning with Phidia& and Praxitele&, Pompeian fre&coe&, Cretan pottery painting, and late Helleni&m.

Laocoön'& vi&ion with it& tangle of enraged &nake& ju&t about made him faint, a little like what happened three week& earlier in &t. Peter'& before Bernini'& baldachin. He merely glanced at Giotto, Raphael, and the Renai&&ance painter&, but Bruegel and Bo&ch cau&ed him to writhe painfully. He &tudied the French Impre&&ioni&t& with indifference, almo&t went to &leep over Braque, Mati&&e, and Pica&&o, but he wa& rou&ed by Modigliani, Kandin&ky, Mondrian, and Diego Rivera, Pollock'& action painting, and Andy Warhol'& and Rau&chenberg'& pop art.

&tanding in front of Pou&&in'& *Land⊙cape with ⊙nake,* the alien &tarted crying. In other word&, he wa& moved.

"Thi& &ublime painting," he explained, "pay& me back for all your people'& na&tine&&. Here, in contra&t to the ordinary, the &nake play& a balanced role in the harmony of nature. Your& i& an ophidiophobic culture. For you, the &nake, with rare exception&, i& alway& depicted a& a &ymbol of evil, &omething to be &qua&hed and removed. 'Upon thy belly &halt thou go,' your holy &cripture& &ay. 'The woman will come who will cru&h your head,' and &o forth. It'll be very difficult, even in the far future, for u& Rigel &erpent& and you human& to get along."

I tried in vain to pre&ent a defen&e. "On our drug&tore window&," I told him, "we have the caduceu&, two &nake& intertwined—"

"That'& enough, archivi&t. You're just like all the other&, a mongoo&e eager to &ink it& teeth into my brain."

The alien wa& getting ready to leave. "By now I know enough about it," he &aid. "At any moment I can make the leap and be back home."

"Now I'm free!" I exclaimed, pouring my&elf a big gla&& of brandy. For an in&tant I leaned out the window. In the noonday light, the Tiber flowed like a &ilver ribbon right below the ma&& of the &t. Angelo Ca&tle and again&t the background of the Janiculum. From the &treet& ro&e whiff& of burning rubber and car exhau&t, and a cacophony of blaring horn&.

I ru&hed to clo&e it.

"I'd like to write Profe&&or Buonaiuti right away and tell him about what'& been happening to me. May I?"

Ophi& &hrugged. At lea&t, that i& the way I interpreted the &light contraction& that made my brain throb for a moment.

And &o, two hour& ago I &at down in front of the typewriter, an ancient Olivetti who&e key& I had to pound on in order to get a barely legible image. The ribbon wa& al&o dried up, and I had not changed it yet.

And that i& when my agony began. Ye&, becau&e a& &oon a& I hit that certain letter of the alphabet that &ounded like a &nake, the alien flew into a rage.

"You have no re&pect for me," my brain &creamed with a jolt. "You hit that key in a na&ty and hateful manner, in total &corn for my image, for the &ymbol that i& ba&ed on my phy&ical &tructure. I forbid you to u&e that key!"

I put in another &heet and &erved my&elf another brandy. By now Ophi& was looped, but thi& time the alcohol wa& turning him viciou&.

"Write, ju&t write your report," he kept repeating, "but &teer clear of that key, or el&e I'll kill you."

"All right already," I &aid, complying. "In place of that letter, I'll u&e the amper&and (&). No matter if it turn& out to be rather annoying to read."

"Fine with me, archivi&t. The &ymbol you &ugge&ted u&ing bring& to mind our ophi&aurian cou&in& from Betelgeu&e that I don't get along too well with merely becau&e of tho&e two little leg& that make them irredeemably inferior. I have nothing again&t your beating on them with your foul finger. And now hear thi&,

archivi&t. I &hould project my&elf right away, but I'm curiou& to read the non&en&e you'll be writing in your account. But make &ure you don't &lip. If you ever touch the key I have pro&cribed, I'll &queeze your coronary arterie& and leave you a corp&e on your typewriter. Watch it! I'm not kidding."

Here I am, my dear profe&&or. For two hour& now, after devoting my full attention to it, I have been writing my account and I am ju&t about fini&hed, in the hope& that, notwith&tanding the letter I have been denied, it will neverthele&& be both clear and under&tandable. It will be up to you to decide whether or not to inform the academic world about the up&etting experience I have been going through. Keep in mind that for any further detail& or explanation& I will be available any time.

Very truly your&,
Fabio Calis

Rome
July 28, 1998

Dear Professor Buonaiuti,
I am Livia Bonfoco, widow of Fabio Calistri, Chief Archivist at the National Library. My husband had a heart attack three days ago while in his study finishing the letter addressed to you that I have enclosed solely to carry out what seems to me to be my late husband's last wish.

I do not intend to dwell on the contents of this letter. It will strike you—as it has me—as eccentric and bizarre, the product of a disturbed mind.

I make no bones about the fact that my husband has recently been suffering from a nervous breakdown. I therefore feel I should inform you that several facts, as he described them in his letter, are, as far as I know, absolutely in keeping with the truth. I refer to his stay in the hospital, the visit to the zoo with his nephew Fillipo, the almost-month-long seclusion while he feverishly consulted books and encyclopedias as well as, please believe me, the intimate incident one night when he was exercising his husband's rights and got the words *arms* and *coils* mixed up.

The last page of the letter to you was still in the typewriter. The typed signature ends with an *s*. It must have gotten by him, I think, because he was tired after a long period of concentration, and he left it off.

Pure coincidence, of course. But the fact that my husband was struck right at that exact instant leaves me puzzled and distressed.

A true happenstance? Fate? Or else the ridiculous and absurd revenge of a drunk snake?

Sincerely yours,
Livia Bonfoco

FROM CZECHOSLOVAKIA:

The Divided Carla

BY JOSEF NESVADBA

It is now ten years, it may be twenty, since I retired from my post at the Psychiatric Clinic and retreated to a small town near the western border of Bohemia, in what we call the Precious Ore Mountains. My purpose was to complete a book; however, I did not wish to abandon my work in psychiatry entirely, and so I settled down in apartments in a large and nearly empty psychiatric hospital in the town of Usti. (It is pronounced almost like the American city of Houston, but it had nothing to do with any space program—or so I thought when I moved in.) The hospital complex was built in the last century in the style then popular; it contains ten buildings, looking more or less like villas, surrounding a church, the whole set in a large park. The reason it is nearly empty is, of course, because of the introduction of the new pharmacotherapy in the 1950s. Many patients could be discharged, and so now only two of the buildings are in use and the others remain empty. The town itself dates back to medieval times. It was a flourishing center up to the time of the Thirty Years War. Silver and other precious metals were mined on a large scale in the mountains nearby (thus giving the range its name). It was not very far from here, in the town of Joachimstal— "Tal" for short—that silver Thalers were minted in the sixteenth century, thus providing a name for the "dollars" of some of the world's present currency.

Writing my book and looking after the few remaining hospitalized patients does not consume all of my time, of course. I have therefore developed a counseling service for those who need it in the places nearby. Since I believe that prevention is the right approach, I spend a good deal of time traveling to give lectures. My general working title is, "How to Live Reasonably and Avoid Mental Problems." I particularly like to speak in schools. The young need this kind of counseling, with their habit of forgetting reason to "fall in love," taking their dreams as reality and so on. And it was in this way that I became acquainted with the principal of the Usti Grammar School, Mr. Kork.

Mr. Kork is about my own age—which is to say, not much short of retirement—and, like me, he lives alone. Or generally does, at least. His wife, a very beautiful woman to whom he was devoted, died two years ago, leaving poor Kork greatly affected. I was rather sorry for him, in fact, and made it a point to see him from time to time to discuss our mental health campaign. I knew that there was a young girl who spent the summers with him for some sort of health reasons—a daughter, I supposed, or perhaps a cousin—but I did not know the young woman.

I did, however, think I knew Kork, and so I was thoroughly surprised when he woke me in the early hours one morning. He had the young girl with him, and she was trembling.

I don't know exactly what I said to him—some vaguely polite remark about being pleased to meet his cousin, I suppose. I was only in my dressing gown, and not at all prepared for visitors. He cut me off agitatedly.

"She is not my cousin," he said. "To begin with, I have no cousin. Carla is my second wife. We married in secret—and, oh, you must examine her at once!"

I was beginning to be more awake. As I brought them into my study, I saw that she had to be more than twenty years younger than Kork and she did, indeed, seem overcome with emotion of some kind. Before I could ask questions, Kork was rattling on:

"Carla is the daughter of an old friend—simply, he sent her here because the climate is better than in the cities and the air purer. But she suffered an accident while driving a car. She was unconscious for four days. She needed someone to look after her, and I was alone—" I tried to stop him, as I do not like to hear people's secrets revealed under stress, but it was no use. "So we married. She was much better. We live happily together, and she has become quite healthy—you have seen that for yourself, have you not?" Kork demanded.

I made some sort of sound of agreement. It was true. I remembered seeing the young lady in shorts, riding a bicycle around the neighborhood. She had been a feast for one's eyes, actually, and certainly had given every appearance of health.

"Healthy she was," Kork repeated. "Until tonight! All of a sudden, while I was sleeping, she crept out of bed, went to the local post office, woke up the telephone operator, and demanded to be put through at once to a number in Geneva!"

"In Geneva?" I repeated.

"Exactly, in Geneva! This would be extraordinary enough, but there was more. She was not speaking with her usual voice. The operator thought it more like the voice of a man. She thought the whole affair quite odd and—as she was of course one of my former pupils from the grammar school—did not call Geneva, but me. I ran down there at once"—Kork opened his long leather coat, and I saw that he still wore his pajamas underneath it—"but when I got to the post office Carla was her usual self again. However, she was trembling and frightened."

Indeed, she still was. As Kork was describing this adventure, tears appeared on his wife's face. She made no attempt to stop them or wipe them off, but whispered, "I must know what is happening! Such a thing has never occurred before. I have no friends in Geneva; I have never even visited there in my life. I can only think that I was commanded to do this thing!"

"A voice commanded you?" I asked, since many psychotics claim to hear voice.

"Oh, no, I don't think so," she said doubtfully. "I don't remember an actual voice. And I don't hear anything now."

Her husband was watching her apprehensively. Then he turned to me and asked eagerly, "Will you admit her to your hospital?"

"My dear Mr. Kork," I said, frowning, "that is certainly the last resort in a case of this kind. No, no. I shall give you some pills to help you both sleep better and ask you to return to your home. All of this could be a mere consequence of her accident and prolonged unconsciousness—and I am sure you don't wish to have everyone learn about your secret marriage in this way, do you?"

The school director didn't seem convinced. "There are worse troubles than public scandals," he proclaimed. "You must treat her!"

"Of course I shall treat her," I assured him. "In the proper way. We can meet tomorrow afternoon and have a chat, that will be the best way to start."

Kork looked frustrated but accepted my decision without argument. As they left I thought they both looked quite disturbed, and wondered if I were to have one patient or two.

In my work at the institute I have a youthful assistant, a very willing and quite intelligent young man, though perhaps not quite suited to this sort of work. His first interest after receiving his diploma was in sports medicine, and in fact he was himself an active weight lifter. Unfortunately, he damaged his spine in a too-daring attempt at heavyweight lifting and had to leave his own institute to seek a quieter and less physically demanding job here. He remained quite daring, and indeed very muscular. But as he gave up his training he began to grow fat. Following me on our morning rounds to the patients, he resembled a dynamic, round ball.

I had been aware of a certain interest in Carla on his part; indeed, I had often seen him, as we walked from building to building and she occasionally appeared through the fence, gazing after her bicycling behind. He would perhaps have been a more suitable partner for her, at least in terms of age, but as far as I knew they never spoke. That was, I am sure, because of Mr. Kork's temperament. It was said in the town that he was a jealous man.

I had paid no attention to such gossip, not least because I thought him a man devoted to reason, while jealousy is an extremely unreasonable passion. Yet it was true that Kork had kept his wife away from the townspeople. He even went shopping by himself, and had no visitors in his home. In short, he took no risks of anything that might ultimately lead to an affair on the part of his wife.

Remembering all this, I thought it probable that we should try to get at the roots of this aberration of his at our afternoon session.

However, events did not work out that way. I had to wait a long time for the couple. I drank two cups of tea, and finally decided not to wait any longer in my little office in the attic of the first building. But as soon as I stepped out of the door I saw a very nervous Kork, pacing agitatedly around his obsolete black Ford, casting glances toward my building helplessly.

"Oh, at last you are here!" he cried—totally unjustifiably, of course. But before I could reprove him he pointed to the rear of the car.

There Carla was sitting in a tweed traveling costume. Suitcases were piled beside her. She had dark glasses on, looking exactly like someone who is starting on a long trip. "She has changed again," Kork sobbed. "She wants to go to Geneva now, and she won't discuss anything else. You must speak to her! Get her inside—use force if you have to!"

I gave him a look to quiet him and marched up to the car, rapping on a window. Carla turned toward me. She rolled the window down and said, quite calmly, "I suppose you think this is extraordinary. However, it is of great importance. I am on a diplomatic mission, and it is your duty to support me in it. You will be rewarded, naturally, provided you make that old rascal drive me directly to Geneva, and at once."

I must say, I was taken aback. Her voice was low, slow and precise, not in the least like the voice I had heard from her in the middle of the night. But then I rallied. It all became clear to me. A case of split personality! Very rare in our profession, to be sure, but nevertheless one which could be diagnosed and even treated.

I gave Kork a satisfied glance and said persuasively to his wife, "Yes, but this old wreck will never make it as far as Geneva. It is thirty years old at least. Come inside and I will order a better car for you. I presume you have your passport in order and so on?" I continued, opening the door and watching her carefully. This was an experiment, of course. I was trying to ascertain to what extent her logical functions were operating, since of course it is no simple matter to cross the border between two social systems.

"That is quite all right," said the contralto Carla, but she followed me peaceably enough toward our third building. Although it has scarcely been in use for thirty years, it still remains equipped with the paraphernalia of pre-chemical psychiatry, including a complete armorarium of what we call "restriction" equipment.

Without suspicion, she entered the cell I led her to. It had been designed for psychotics from rich or influential families; it had rubber walls and floor, nets before the windows and a special open shower in one corner, where patients were calmed or cleansed with hot or cold water—in restraints, of course—until they gave up their hallucinations or stopped shouting their protests and threats. A pillow was fixed firmly to the floor. She sat on it calmly, and asked, "When will the taxi arrive? My business is of the utmost importance."

"Yes, of course," I said, studying her through the door. There was something decidedly odd about her appearance. She seemed to undulate. Her costume was rather loosely cut, and she moved rather like the saints in our old baroque churches, almost as though wanting to fly.

I bid her a polite au revoir and locked her in. Then I called in the male duty nurse from the main building. He was an experienced man, and listened attentively to my instructions: He was only to wait and observe her, nothing else.

Back in my office, I explained the situation to director Kork. "I saw my last case of a personality split some fifteen years ago. It is rare, yes. But the prognosis is quite good."

"Fine, fine," he said, eager to be relieved, and to be convinced that science would cure his young wife. He even went so far as to offer me a cash gift. That is quite forbidden, as doctors are employed by the state. Annoyed, I ignored his attempt and went on to tell him more:

"That last case was a middle-aged man who split his personality as "Jan" and "Johann." Jan lived in Prague, Johann in Vienna. Both had families, with very attractive wives, blondes, rather similar to each other. He was a hysteric. His case had a utilitarian function for him, as it was only that which let him escape prosecution for bigamy. Of course, that was unintentional. Such symptoms always are in our profession; otherwise our patients would be mere frauds."

"Yes, yes," he said, not listening. "You will help her? You will cure her?" Kork almost embraced me in his enthusiasm, but I backed away. "You are a true friend! I should have told you all about my marriage years ago," he sighed and, not a moment too soon for my taste, took his departure.

Obviously, he was confident that curing his wife would be easy, given the present level of rationalism and science. I had not said that. I had only said it was possible; and in a moment, as my assistant entered, I began to wonder about that.

"I have seen your new patient," he declared. "She says she comes from the planet of a distant star, and that she is an ambassador on her way to Geneva so that she can then go on to some island in the Pacific."

I brought him up sharply. "Since when do you believe in the hallucinations of a hysteric? The woman will give up her symptoms only when she understands they are of no use to her."

"She is very attractive," he said wistfully.

"She is very ill!" I corrected.

"But," he said, "perhaps there are such galactic empires, after all—"

"Only in stories!" I said sharply. The day had tired me, and he was tiring me even more.

He was obstinate. "Space travel was once considered a fantasy," he pointed out. "So were ecological dangers, not to mention nuclear weapons. At least I suggest she should be observed in more normal conditions, not in a restraining cell. Even if it is a case of split personality, is that so serious? Isn't everyone who, for example, writes in his scrapbook while talking on a long, tiresome telephone call equally 'splitting' himself?"

I shook my head. "One may write automatically without doing so in a different language, or experiencing different lives. No. You can observe her if you like, but only in the rubber cell, with the male nurse present."

I turned my back on him in some discomfort. His generation is the first one that is foreign to me. He is romantic, hectic, inclined to superstition and Eternal Love—everything we have been trying to extirpate for our whole lives.

Besides, I had not eaten yet.

For some time, eating had been something less than a pleasurable experience for me. Not to put too fine a point on it, my teeth were bad. One may wonder why a man of science like myself should neglect such matters until they became unpleasant. The reason is not entirely rational, though perhaps it can be understood: For many years I had been married to a dentist. In any case I ate rather little, and almost always in private. It was the custom for my head nurse to cook supper for me and leave it in the little fridge in my room.

On this evening she had provided me with some grilled chicken with salad and a potato. I had not realized I was so hungry; I ate the whole thing, standing, and found it exquisite. I finished with tomato juice right out of the can and, as I was swallowing the last of it, my telephone rang.

Evening calls always mean trouble. The interruption spoiled my good temper, as I had wanted to devote this time to my book, and I answered it in no good mood.

My feelings were not improved by the voice on the other end of the line. "I have received your new X rays today," said my wife, calling long distance from our flat in the capital. "They are much worse than I even suspected. I think you should take a leave and come over here for surgery at once. I spoke to my boss about it. He's ready to do the work himself, and there isn't a better dental surgeon in the whole state."

I did not answer at once. There is not a great deal left of our marriage. I visit her twice a month, to hear the news from our married daughter, who works in Africa, and to talk about the repairs and improvements for our flat that always seem necessary and that must be financed jointly. We drink a bottle of red wine together, and next morning we part again. However, on the last visit my wife had prepared a turkey and observed I had some difficulty in chewing it. She is ten years younger than I, in the middle of her career in dentistry, and quite convinced of the importance of her work; she would like to repair the teeth of everyone she meets. To save argument I had agreed to have some X rays taken the next morning.

But I no longer felt any pain. "I have no problems at all with my teeth," I told her. "I've just successfully devoured most of a chicken. Can you hear me?"—and I clicked my teeth over the telephone, like a skeleton's jaw at an anatomical display.

"That would have to be a miracle," said my wife. "Please don't be obstinate. Come home and have your treatment."

I understood her at once. It was not my teeth she was concerned about; she was trying to lure me back to our flat and disturb my work on my book; she never gave up hope of getting me to come back again.

"I don't feel any pain at all," I repeated. "Good night."

But even after the call was over I could not concentrate on my work. Something was ringing in my mind. Hadn't split Carla promised I would be "rewarded"? And what exactly had she meant?

I gazed out of my window. The house of my neighbor had lighted windows. As I thought, I went to the fridge again and took out a big apple. I bit into it without the help of a knife, using only the front incisors which I knew had been in a hopeless state.

There was again no pain. They sliced the fruit as easily as a rabbit crops lettuce. The apple juice trickled pleasantly over my lips.

It seemed to me that I needed to ask some questions, so I put out my light and went down the stairs.

My neighbor's house was one of the oldest in town, and it was called the Sorcerer's Nest—a silly old notion of the villagers, of course. One of the reasons Kork had chosen it when he came to our town was that he felt it would be proper for a campaigner for Reason to inhabit a house that had curious stories told about it. No one knew when the stories started, because in all the village only the church and the town hall, constructed in the gothic style of the fourteenth century, were equally old, and the stories seemed as old as the house. That was the time when the fame of the nearby silver mines was spreading and, although the rumors were vague and unlikely, they seemed to concern a sorceress who dwelt there. She was said to have been tortured and, thus compelled, confessed her conspiracy with the Devil himself. Until this day, townspeople show off to visitors the place before our church where she is said to have been burned alive. Of course, it should properly have been called the Sorceress's

House if those stories were true, but no doubt that was too hard to pronounce over the years.

My neighbor opened the door at once. He seemed tense and worried, and spoke freely at once. "Of course," he said, "I should have told you everything years ago. That would have been much better for my poor wife than shutting her in this house. You could have helped her, I'm sure." He led me into the big room where his dead wife had dwelt—a room I had never been in until this evening.

I said, "What is it you feel you should have told me?"

"Everything!" cried Kork. "For she suffered the same symptoms that Carla does! If I were not a rationalist, I would say this house is cursed. My late wife began to speak in just that commanding way, in the same deep contralto, five years ago. The episodes came at irregular times, first once a year, then sometimes as often as once a month. Just before she died, she no longer spoke in her natural voice at all."

"But I knew nothing of any of this!" I exclaimed.

"Of course not. I could not bring myself to let anyone know, and it was much worse even than I have said. She insisted I believe in what she told me, even follow her instructions—and what instructions! She demanded that I raise an army to March on Tal and conquer it—liberate it, she said. She demanded to be taken to our church—as though she didn't know the way herself—and to be introduced to the believers. Well, of course there are very few believers left around, after all our campaigns, and those who do still want to attend services simply take the bus to Tal on Sundays. So, in order to make people come to the church, she insisted on playing the organ, very loudly—very well, too, as a matter of fact. It didn't attract any believers. Everyone watches television these days; they only complained she was interfering with their listening to the programs. And then one day, when she had played for an hour and no one came, she jumped over the railing of the organ loft and fell to the floor. She was killed instantly."

"How terrible," I said, watching him intently. He told the story so well that it was almost as though he had rehearsed it, or told it many times before—but the latter was impossible, since he had kept all this secret from everyone.

"Yes, terrible," he agreed, bobbing his head. "A great tragedy, and of my own making. I should not have pretended to be an ordinary jealous husband. I should have come to you honestly and asked your help. But I was weak. I was ashamed to have people know my wife was a crazy woman."

"Yes, yes," I murmured, looking around. Whether or not my neighbor's wife was crazy, my neighbor himself, it seemed, was at least quite strange. There was a single picture reproduced on every wall of this room. It is called "The Assumption," and it is the very painting that hangs over the altar in our deserted church. It shows a saint . . . and it struck me then that there was a close resemblance between that ancient picture of the martyred saint and my neighbor's beautiful first wife—and, come to that, it was not dissimilar, really, even to his present wife, Carla. I mentioned this in an offhand way, and the principal nodded.

"Yes, I have thought that myself," he agreed. "I don't know if you are familiar with the history of our town, but that is the saint in whose name Usti once set out to invade Tal. Of course, they failed—"

He hesitated, then made up his mind. "One moment," he said. He opened a closet in a corner and took out an old print, which he displayed to me.

"Do you notice anything about this?" he asked.

He was making me quite uneasy. "Of course," I said. "It is another picture of the saint."

"But it is not," he said, shaking his head. "This is the Sorceress herself. The one my house is named after. Look behind her in the print; you will see the interior of our church, empty except for the altar and cross, just as it was two hundred years ago . . . when the Sorceress was stretched and whipped there on the rack."

I said, "It is quite a close resemblance."

He looked at me gloomily. "A resemblance? Yes. Of course. One would not say that it was the same woman, of course; that would be impossible. But it is curious, all the same, that these women should look so much alike, almost as though it were only a woman of a certain sort who could—"

He stopped there. "Yes?" I asked. "Who could what?"

But he only shook his head again. "They say the Sorceress spoke in a strange voice," he mused. "She spoke Czech. The baroque saint spoke German. The armies they tried to lead included Protestants and Catholics, Czechs and Saxons, even the Swedes and the Spaniards were involved, all fighting over this town and the precious metal mines nearby."

"And all directed by a sorceress?" I ventured.

"Sorceress?" He drew himself up and looked at me indignantly. "One cannot believe in sorceresses! Or even saints. No, no. It was hysteria that drove them all, to be sure, simple hysteria!" He said all this triumphantly, as though by saying "hysteria," as he might have said "tonsillitis," he had diagnosed a disease which I, as a doctor, would certainly know how to cure.

I tested him. "My assistant spoke of a galactic intelligence," I ventured.

My neighbor laughed, a bitter kind of laugh. "We are never free of the vestiges of old superstition," he declared, "even if now they give it new names. Oh, Doctor, I am so grateful to you! Now, this evening, for the first time I feel I am beginning to live like a rational human being, with the help of your medical science."

I managed finally to make my excuses and leave him, quite disturbed in my mind. It sounded as though my village of Usti had suffered quite a large number of cases of split personality, and over rather a long period of time. There was nothing in the medical literature to suggest any previous situation of that sort, I was sure. Yet that was not in itself a bad thing, at least as far as my personal interests were concerned. It occurred to me quite quickly that to discover something really new in psychiatry could be very rewarding to me, even at this late date in my career. To describe it in a professional journal would make me famous, even in the West. It could be illustrated with Kork's prints and paintings; I could see it clearly in my mind's eye.

As I was contemplating this attractive prospect, I was hurrying to the patient who formed its subject matter.

She was not in her cell. The cell itself was no longer functional; the iron bars of its door had been twisted open to let her escape. And in the cell itself, sitting quietly, was my trustworthy male nurse, Frantisek.

"What's happened?" I cried, imagining all sorts of things. Mrs. Kork was not a large woman and certainly not strong enough to have bent those bars, although it was true that hysterics sometimes displayed strength far beyond the normal. Could that be true here? And was such a phenomenon typical of the split personality? I thought happily of how this would add another dimension to my paper, once I had made a literature search to verify the uniqueness of this symptom.

But it had not been Mrs. Kork who bent the bars. "It was your assistant," explained Frantisek placidly. "He was talking with the patient through the bars, and then he decided to release her. As he had no key, he simply bent the bars—he is a weight lifter, you know."

"But he lost his strength!"

"He has it back now," said Frantisek. "I believe he's out in the back yard now, exercising."

When I hurried out of the building and into the little courtyard, there he was. He wore only his underwear, with his belly protruding, and he was indeed practicing his weight lifting again. He had no proper bars and disks, of course, but he had taken some folded metal beds from the storeroom. He was lifting two of the things in each hand, an expression of great pleasure on his face.

"Mrs. Kork?" he said, pausing only briefly to speak to me. "Yes, of course I released her. It was very important. She explained it all to me; she is here to stop the conflicts over Tal. They've decided to talk things out at some island in the Pacific Ocean—no more fights, a fair share for everyone—"

"What fights?" I exploded. "What are you talking about?"

He said severely, "You must not lose your temper, Doctor. What Mrs. Kork is doing is far more important than our work here. Can't you see that she has fixed my spine? I will return to active sport at once. Already I've carried that old car our neighbor left here over to his house! Eighteen hundred kilograms, at least!" He set the folding beds down and began to look around for something heavier to lift. Over his shoulder he went on, "You must believe in Carla

Kork, Doctor, because she is bringing us a whole new world. Even the ambulance driver saw that at once."

"The ambulance driver? What about him?"

"Why," said my assistant, studying some huge barrels of spent oil, "she told him she needed to go to Geneva, so of course he agreed to drive her there."

"To Geneva! I don't believe it!"

My assistant shrugged and began lifting the huge barrels. "Oh, he had doubts at first," he said, puffing slightly with the effort. "Then he had a telephone call from his mother-in-law. She has decided to leave his home and return to her own apartment in the city—just what he has been praying for all these months! It was his greatest secret wish . . . so he started the ambulance at once and they drove off."

I lost my temper completely. "Such behavior in a mental institution!" I cried. "You should all be inmates, not staff. As to you, you are fired. Take your things and get out of here at once."

I heard him calling something after me as I marched away, but I didn't listen—it was only more foolishness, about the things Carla had told him. I was wrong, he was saying, because I didn't believe in the whole brain; I was right-brain-dominated; right was not righteous; Mrs. Kork had freed him of that tyranny. . . . Real madness. I could not concern myself with it. I had to decide what to do next.

Certainly, the logical thing to do now was to notify the police of an escaped patient. I hesitated to do it, though. In the first place, it would be embarrassing to Kork to have his wife pursued like a common criminal. It would also jeopardize my wonderful paper on her case, since premature publicity, before I had had a chance to complete my research, would mean other psychiatrists would learn of it, and perhaps come here to study her. . . .

Fortunately, I was saved the necessity of picking up the phone to the police. I heard the sound of sirens outside and hurried out to find our old ambulance slowly returning, escorted by two leather-coated policemen on motorcycles, their sirens going.

Carla had gotten as far as the border but, of course, she didn't have the necessary exit papers. They had brought her back. "To you, Doctor," said one of the policemen. "She insisted on that, not to her husband, and that woman really is used to giving orders. . . . By the way," he added, looking embarrassed, "is it true that she can grant wishes?"

I looked at him in amazement. "Are policemen so superstitious?" I demanded. "No one can grant wishes!"

He looked both uncertain and a little resentful. "It's just that she gave me a tip for the Sunday soccer match. Before I bet on it I'd like to know if it's worthwhile." He hesitated, then his training took over. "In any case," he finished, "I am leaving her in your custody. Naturally, we will file complete reports on this incident with the authorities."

"Naturally," I said, and promised to give him a short medical account of the case for his report. Then I turned to Carla Kork.

As the policemen got back on their cycles and left—this time with the sirens still—she walked quietly into the building. I followed with some concern, but she merely went back to her restraining cell and sat down once more on the cushion, her legs crossed and her handsome knees displayed. She looked me directly in the eye.

"You are the person of authority here, I see," she said, still in that deep contralto voice, filled with self-confidence and authority. "Therefore you must arrange for me to leave here as soon as possible. In Geneva there is an agency which will transport me to Hawaii, or, if it is simpler, I could fly directly there. It is to your advantage that this happen as soon as possible, because your mines have been a source of trouble for a long time."

"I see," I said, not very truthfully. I studied her carefully. "Can you tell me what is so important about our silver?"

"Silver!" she said with contempt. "The silver is trash. Your mines contain a great deal of uranium—you people used to use it to color glass green, until the Curies began to study it."

"Ah, yes. It is the uranium you want. I understand."

"No, no! Uranium is as common as dirt. It only happens that there is a rare form of it, quite scarce everywhere in the galaxy, which your ore has in very worthwhile quantity. Many races would like to have it, and I am afraid that that has caused a certain amount of inconvenience for your people here—wars, revolutions, even what you call religion or sorcery. As soon as I can reach the conference in Hawaii I can submit this question to orderly decision, and you will have peace here. Do you understand how important my errand is?"

"I see," I said again, trying to be calm. The woman was quite motionless on her pillow, but her posture, the way she held herself, looked like a heavy hen that would like to fly away. I walked over to the window, pulled down the net, and sat on the sill.

"Mrs. Kork," I said, maintaining an air of professional confidence, "I think we should discuss your case in some detail. Split personality is not uncommon. We can treat it; it is only necessary to get at the root causes. Generally speaking, patients with your complaint are responding to severe childhood trauma. They retreat into daydreams, because their real lives are painful. Sometimes their parents are physically cruel to them, beating them, starving them, mistreating them in many ways, and this resentment against their parents causes this personality dissociation later on."

She said, frowning, "But we do not know our parents. We are hatched out of communal clusters of eggs."

"Now really, Mrs. Kork!" I remonstrated. "I have your records available; the names of your parents are easy to find. Please cooperate for the sake of your own mental health."

"But I am cooperating," she said in surprise. "Haven't I given you one reward already? And another is due very shortly."

It was obvious that I could not reach the core of sanity within her delusion at this time. I bid her a curt good-night and left her, promising nothing.

Frantisek was standing at the main gate of the building. I ordered him to lock it and keep his eye on it, from outside, all through the night, to make sure Mrs. Kork did not depart again.

"Very well," he said. "But you have a guest waiting for you."

A guest? I could only suppose that it was some higher police official, prepared to keep me from my sleep by asking a great many annoying questions about this puzzling case; but in this I was wrong. When I went out to the courtyard I saw my wife's little sports car parked there, and she had taken the liberty of going up by herself to my little room, where I found her sitting on the bed, waiting for me.

"Good evening, Barbara," I said politely.

She looked at me with concern. My wife is a handsome woman at any time, and now, in her attractive travel costume, she looked even better than usual. I wished, not for the first time, that I were not so much older than she. Our marriage could have been quite different.

She said, "You sounded so strange, I thought I should come at once." And then, with some astonishment, "Have you been dying your hair?"

"Of course not," I said, surprised. Then I glanced into the little mirror next to my fridge. Actually, my hair had become quite dark again, even around my temples.

"You've done something," she declared. "Maybe you've had your teeth fixed, too?" There was a tremor in her voice, which I didn't understand until she said suddenly, "Are you doing all this for someone else?"

It took me a moment to understand what she meant. My wife suspected that there was another woman!

The idea was so bizarre that I couldn't find any words to answer her. She hardly gave me a chance. She pulled me down to the bed beside her, almost weeping, and said, "Oh, my dear! This is why you've left me! Why you've made yourself look young again! But she can't have you. I'll fight for you, my dearest. . . ."

And so she did, in the ways that she knew well. After all our years of marriage, she knew exactly what touches, what little movements of her body, what expressions of her face were most effective.

I have not been entirely candid, and so I must now say that my retreat to Usti was not caused solely by my need to concentrate on my big book. It was more personal than that. Perhaps it was more noble than that, in a sense, because my increasing age had become more evident to both of us and I had decided to liberate my younger wife. I did not dislike her. On the contrary, I looked forward to our twice-a-month encounters with anticipation, and left them with regret. But they were not always satisfactory to either of us, and I could not accept the humiliation of advancing age.

Of course, if I had been my own patient I might have given myself quite different advice. Mature and harmonious sexual life is as natural and necessary as bread: so I instructed the audiences at my lectures. But even bread was no longer as sweet to me, once my teeth began to make chewing a chore. I was too proud to have a silent witness watching the sadder times of our lives that are called "growing old." Usti was my solution to the problem.

But the problem no longer seemed so grave. It was not only my teeth that seemed miraculously restored to health. Some time later, as we lay naked under the single blanket, my wife raised herself on one elbow to look at me. "I thought you didn't love me anymore," she murmured.

I could not answer, at least not with words. I did find a better way, though, and when we were through she lay back and declared, "My wishes have been answered."

I kissed her fondly, hardly listening to her words . . . and then I froze.

Wishes that were answered! And not just Barbara's: my teeth; my assistant's spine; the ambulance driver's mother-in-law; the policeman's desire to win a football bet. . . .

I leaped out of bed. "Where are you going?" Barbara cried, frightened. I couldn't tell her.

"A patient," I said—it was only half a lie, after all. "I'll be back as soon as I can." And I threw a coat over my naked body and staggered barefoot down the stairs and to the home of my neighbor Kork.

He answered the door fully dressed, almost as though he had expected me. His face was drawn and weary, and as I talked he nodded almost as though in despair. "Miracles?" he said heavily. "Yes, there have been miracles, if you must call them that. And I see that you have shared them."

"What do you mean?" I demanded.

"Your face. Your hair," he said. "You're looking younger, aren't you? And haven't I looked the same now for twenty years—no aging, no illness, not even the loss of my hair? But rational man cannot believe in miracles, don't you see? So I had to—"

He fell silent, looking suddenly fearful.

"She didn't fall from the organ loft," I guessed, shocked.

He muttered, "No one can prove that! But what would you

have had me do? Me, a man whose life has been devoted to reason and science? Those are the foundations of our whole society; I could not let them be destroyed by a single person!'' He glared at me, with blazing eyes. "I can do no more! Someone else must take the responsibility now!"

"What do you mean?" I whispered. He didn't answer.

But I knew.

In my room my wife was full of questions to which I could give her no answers. "There is something I must do," I said heavily, dressing rapidly and taking from my fridge a syringe and an ampoule of morphine. I walked away from her. I could hear her calling after me—begging me to stay, to return to the capital with her, to live together once more as man and wife. "Is it money?" she called. "But we can live on my salary. Don't you understand? I love you!"

And so she did . . . but was it for myself that she loved me? Or was she compelled to it by another "miracle"?

My pride would not let me test the answer to that question.

Carla was no longer in the padded room. The building gate was wide open and no one was around. "Frantisek!" I shouted. When he didn't answer, I went looking for him. I had a pretty good idea where he would be.

Although Frantisek was a conscientious male nurse, there were a few rules he chose to break. One was to gamble with some of the patients. They had no money, of course; they played for matchsticks, but all of them, nurse and patients alike, played as hard and seriously as though the stakes had been millions. I had long been aware of this and let it go, reasoning that the attitudes of the patients toward gambling might help in diagnosis, and in any case were not bad therapy for some of their symptoms. And, although Frantisek was devoted to the game, he seldom won.

He was indeed where I had expected him to be, in the common room of the patients' quarters, and indeed there were two patients with him around the table. What was different was that this night Frantisek's face wore a broad smile, and the heap of matchsticks before him was huge. He barely looked up when I came in. "Oh, Mrs. Kork?" he said, shuffling the cards. "She said she had to go to the church. I suppose she's there now."

There was no time to discipline him properly. Truth to tell, I didn't have the appetite to do it, either; too much had happened, and what I had to do transcended any simple impertinence. I went at once to the old church, pushed the creaking door open, and peered inside.

The sound of weeping told me where she was, even in the nearly total darkness of the old building. But it was another Carla who hung from the balustrade of the organ loft, between two great portraits of baroque saints, with woolly clouds of marble under her feet. "Get me out of here, please!" she begged, in her human voice, hoarse with crying. "I'm so frightened! I flew up here—but now it's just me, and I'm afraid to come down by myself."

I said, as calmly as I could, "Yes, Carla. I will get you out of here." I climbed slowly up to the loft, speaking reassuringly to her. "You need a rest," I said. "You need to sleep. I have something here that will help you. . . ."

And I pulled up the sleeve of her arm.

An intravenous injection of morphine is the most humane way to kill a person. The patient will lose consciousness long before he loses his capacity to breathe. There would be no more pain. No more sorcery. No more fear . . .

As I walked out of the church, it was almost daylight and Frantisek was coming off duty. He was whistling happily, clutching a great bundle of matchsticks. "A fine day, Doctor!" he called. "Where are you going now?"

"To my new home," I answered. I went to the padded cell and pulled the twisted, barred door closed behind me. Frantisek followed, the smile disappearing from his face.

"But what are you doing, Doctor?" he asked. "You should be getting ready for your morning rounds in a little while."

I said, "I am no longer a doctor. There is no doctor here, only one more patient. I shall write my case history myself, but that is all. Summon someone to treat me, Frantisek. I am insane."

Now that I have completed my report, there is nothing more to say.

Oh, to be sure, there have been some strange things since. It was less than an hour after I entered the cell that I saw Carla herself, seeming quite unharmed, lightly entering a government helicopter, escorted by a pair of diplomats bowing deferentially to her . . . or so, in my madness, I thought I saw these things happening. I even thought that a few minutes later my former assistant came to my cell.

"I am sorry you are unwell," he said, quite civilly. "The government will send some specialists to help you very soon; Carla made them promise."

"Carla is dead," I told him.

"Dead? Certainly not! Oh, you mean that little injection you gave her? But you must realize such a thing could not affect a person with her powers! No, her message got through. She is on her way to the conference in Hawaii, and the cosmic intelligences will settle their differences. Usti will no longer be troubled by their squabbles over our ores! So you can come out of that cell, Doctor, and go back to your wife in a normal world."

A normal world!

I would not answer him. I lay on the padded floor with my eyes closed and my head turned away. How real my delusions were! I thought wistfully of how much I would have enjoyed writing up this case history, if only it had not been my own.

"I am going now to catch my train," my assistant called, looking at his watch. "I'm sorry to leave you like this. Don't you understand? You are not mad. The sorceress, the saint, the so-called 'miracles'—above all the galactic intelligences that are behind all the rest—they are real, Doctor!"

I remained obstinately silent until I heard him sigh, and then the sound of his footsteps going away.

My delusions real?

I thought of that, examining it carefully, like any datum in a scientific study. Could they really be factual, rather than the figments of a disordered brain? Could my youth actually have been given back to me? My wife love me as she had twenty years before? The woman I thought I had murdered come back to life?

I lay there for a long time, analyzing the case from all its aspects. Then I got up and returned to my case history of myself, quickly outlining the latest developments. And at the end I wrote:

"If I am insane, I must remain in this cell until treatment can be obtained, and in my professional opinion the prognosis is not good. But if I am not insane, then still I must remain here. For then it is the world that has gone mad, and for its own sake the one sane person must be confined."

And then I sat with the pen still in my hand, staring into space. Either I was insane, or the world was.

And how could I ever tell which?

The View From the Top of the Tower

BY HARRY HARRISON

Stately, plump Sean Mulligan came from the stairhead, bearing a
bowl of lather on which a mirror and a razor lay crossed. A yellow
dressing gown, ungirdled, was sustained gently behind him by the
mild morning air. He held the bowl aloft just as a voice shrilled up
the stairwell behind him.

"You'll catch your death," Molly sirened, her penetrating voice
in full volume capable of cracking a Guinness bottle at twenty paces.
"But you would live in a Martello Tower, saving money you said, but
no jacks and damp as a Kerry bog, then shaving on the battlements,
Jeezus you'll be struck by lightning. . . ."

Sean tuned out the meaning from her words but the breakers
of sound still crashed over him like waves of snotgreen sea. He
shaved too fast, nicking out bits of skin until the lather in the bowl
turned roseate, whisker-speckled. With a swish and a grunt he hurled
the foamed water from the gunport, then hurried back below. Yet
still the voice broke over him, yet still he did not hear as he pulled
leg into trouser, draped tie about neck, speckled bits of toilet paper
on bloodspotted skin, fled downward, earthward, drinkward. Past the
Forty Foot and pantingly past Bullock Castle toward sanctuary *Sanc-
tus sanctorum.* The Arches beckoned and he obeyed.

With the genius of years the door was unlocked at the precise moment he pressed against it, pushed through, stumbled forward, leaned stout elbow on stouter bar and breathed the blessing into the stout expectant air.

"A pint of the black."

"You've cut yourself shaving?" Noel said in tones of utmost gloom, the only melody that ever issued from his barrel chest, as he filled full the glass, bright yellow above brown.

"I have that and lucky not to have done myself from ear to ear with herself in full spate this morning. The voice of her, it only improves with age."

"Aye. They'll hear her in Wexford next."

"Say Ballina and be done."

Last wipe of strigil, passed over and down, raised high and admired, first touch on tongue, first gorgeous glottis gorging, first sigh of life returned. *Pax vobiscum, pox humanum.*

For Portakal, Earth was a flowing font of language. He had been the first student on his home world, dark planet of an ice-blue star on the far side of the galactic lens, to master the difficult art of mental projection. The tachyon source could only be grasped, understood, utilized by force of will alone. And his will was strong, driven by his need to communicate in other than the muffled tones of his race. Sluggish and thick they oozed along at the bottom of their dense, chill atmosphere, where liquid and gas merged and changed, speaking only with the greatest effort against the pressure of the thousands of miles of gas above. For this reason their language was stripped and truncated, bare and unadorned, brief and brutal. He was the only linguist, self-taught and lonely, for who needs linguists when the language contains only one hundred and twelve words?

What paradise this green warm world of Earth! Twice before Portakal had journeyed here, entered the mind of Earth-dwellers, to speak and revel in the richness of language, to learn and remember. It did not bother him that he had to walk with two legs instead of twenty, lacked tentacles and extra eyes on his fingertips, nor did he even miss the pingle-organs that made copulation so intriguing. No sacrifice was too great when it aided his linguistic research.

It bothered him slightly that his first research attempt had ended almost as quickly as it had begun. His spoken Zulu was quite primitive since the unfortunate body he had controlled had been burned as a witch soon after his arrival. His second occupation, in Japan, had been more successful since extraplanetary mental-possession was known there. His reluctant host, a geisha girl, had lived long enough for him to completely master her language, until he had thoughtlessly walked her in front of a Bullet Train while preoccupied with sister-brother, *shimai-kyoodai* interrelationships.

Now he was ready to research again. His mnemonic notes on Japanese had been scratched into steel-hard ice by his ventral claw. He clacked ten or eleven sets of teeth with pleasure as he took up the tachyon source, reached out with his mind, envisioned once again the blue-green sphere of Earth. . . .

Sean Mulligan felt dizzy—after only six pints?—and closed his eyes for an instant. When he opened them again Portakal looked out.

"Sean me old darlin'," Patsy Kelly said, "sure and you're not dozing off in the middle of the afternoon, sure and you're not?"

Sean blinked blurrily in his direction across the sea of pints, smacked his lips, and said, *"Biru nihong, kudusai."*

"None of that now," Seamus said, shaking an admonitory finger as thick as another man's wrist, for he was a great oak of a man hard-strengthened by a life on the building sites, "none of that. You know that I am ill-educated and don't have the Irish, so none of your stout-fueled priest-trained attempts at superiority."

Portakal rustled around in the synapses of the alcohol-dulled brain he now possessed. Oh foolish error, he was speaking Japanese, not the local language. What did they speak here? Yes, here it was. He sighed as he sank into the linguistic pool, splashed about a bit with pleasure, seized the correct words—then spoke.

"I am Portakal from a distant world across the galaxy. I bring you greetings."

"Jayzus, he's pissed already," Patsy Kelly said with some amazement. "He's been into the whisky at home, that's what he has been doing."

"You will obey my orders and will speak as I order you to if you value your drinking companion's continued existence."

He was dimly aware of pain on posterior and extremities as he struck the hard surface.

"And don't come back until you're sober," Noel called after him. "Shameful a man of your age, not to say education, in his cups this hour of the day."

The pub door closed and Portakal pulled himself up from among the tattered crisppackets, fagends and dogturds. He cursed, in Japanese because that came easiest at the moment. What kind of people were these that didn't know the difference between host and occupier? Disgraceful. Perhaps it was only the occupants of the saki-parlor who thought that way, for he knew that strong drink did strange things to these soft bodies. He would seek one of superior intelligence to converse with.

With slow pace he went along the street, using his newfound skills to spell out the words that swarmed on all sides. A glass window, THE JOLLY FRYER—FISH AND CHIPS, a locked door below, CLOSED FOR LUNCH. Interesting.

Another establishment, a signboard. PUNCTURES REPAIRED. On the other side it read PUNTURES REPAIRED. He made a mental note of the interesting spelling variations.

Then a larger building, made of dressed stone, set back from the road, coming to a point on top, door opened invitingly into the dark interior. He entered, saw rows of flickering flames, a man all in dark approached.

"I salute you, son of a distant world," Portakal said, "and bring you greetings from the other side of the galaxy."

Father Flynn glowered along the length of his impressive nose. "Drinking again, Sean Mulligan, the curse of the Irish it is. And you not to Mass since the Battle of the Boyne. You'll die unshriven, man, you will plunge straight through the bottom of purgatory and into hell before you even know you're dead. . . ."

"I bid silence and order attention," Portakal said testily. Things had been far better in Japan. "My name is Portakal. You cannot see the sun of my planet from here, yet I assure you—"

"The only assurances I want from you, you blackguard, is

a confession of your sins—long overdue. You are the burden that your poor wife must bear, the shame of her coming alone here on Sunday. . . ."

"Will you listen to me?"

"I will not! But I will pray for you, miserable sinner that you are."

This was unbearable, unbelievable. Portakal turned the body on its heel and stamped out into the spring sunshine again. But the sun had vanished suddenly and chill rain came down, drenching him in an instant. He shivered and paid it no heed. There was obviously something wrong with these people. They could not all be hard of hearing. Perhaps he had picked the wrong host for his operations. He slumped against the wall and looked at those who hurried by in the driving rain. Could he make the effort of will to leave this host and find another? He had never done it before. He could only try. He waited until there were a knot of people close by, then willed it. Strongly . . .

Nothing happened. He would have to make the most of it. This creature would have to do. He would return to the first place of drinking and attempt communication again.

Yet when he ordered the body forward it did not move. Impossible! His was the will that had spanned light-years, the strength that manipulated tachyons. This miserable earthling, he was aware of it lurking unhappily in a far corner of the cerebellum, could not fight against his strength of purpose. Then why couldn't he move? He spoke aloud, the only way he could communicate with the subject mind.

"Desist—I order it. We will return to The Arches."

"We will go to the center of regional government," he said in a deep and resonant voice.

Portakal was astonished. Those were not his words—or even those of his host. Then what . . . ?

"Who are you?" he shouted. "I see you there, lurking in a twisted whorl of the medulla oblongata, step forward and present yourself."

An old woman stumbled by, clinging to her umbrella. Took one look at Sean Mulligan, crossed herself and tottered even faster.

"I am Mntkl of the *.^..>, oh Earthman, I bring you greetings from beyond the stars. . . ."

"Get out of this brain," Portakal ordered. "I was here first."

Sean's eyes crossed as each of the aliens controlled one eye to look at the other.

"It cannot be true," Mntkl wailed in stentorian tones. "My mentor grew old and died teaching me the astral projection technique. I have expanded all of my energy to occupy this mind. You must leave."

"Tough-titty," Portakal growled. "Finders keepers, losers weepers. Now crawl away, alien sod, because I have important linguistic research to do."

Sean Mulligan danced in circles, limbs flopping, as the two alien presences battled for control, then splashed down into a puddle.

"I care not a *pisple* for your research," Mntkl thundered. "Mine is a dying world, beset by accelerated entropy. Our fuel is running out. Unless a cargo of U-235 is shipped out to us soonest we go down the galactic plughole."

"Good-by," Portakal sneered unfeelingly. "No one has ever heard of your backward planet in any case—so no one will miss it."

Sean's voice cracked with rage as Mntkl snarled his answer. Then he gargled incoherently as both aliens struggled for verbal control. As this mental battle raged, Sean found that he could see dimly, as through a heavy fog, and when he tried to walk he began to stumble forward. In their urge to speak the alien presences had abandoned control of his body. With shuffling feet he turned in a circle—there would be no welcome at The Arches today!—and started towards Mulrooney's. Walking slowly, talking to himself with high-pitched squeals and rattling gurgles, through the door and to the bar.

"That's a wicked cough you have there," Mulrooney said, setting one before him. "It's that Martello Tower and all the dampness. Put in the central heating, that's what you must do, though I see difficulties in drilling through the granite walls surely twenty feet thick."

Sean raised the pint slowly, then half-drained it. Talking all the time, quite splashily as the stout gurgled past his vocal cords.

Mulrooney went off to serve another customer as Mntkl spoke in dark tones. "A compromise then, give me leave to speak. You would not wish the death of a planet upon your conscience, would you?"

"I have no conscience. Most impractical at the great pressures under which we live."

"Then I appeal to your intelligence—and curiosity. Merely let me go to the national dictator or other qualified government official and make my arrangements for the U-235. This creature will undoubtedly speak the local language better than our host so your studies will quicken."

"What's in it for me?" Portakal asked, intrigued.

"The gratitude of an entire world."

"With that and a *strtzl* I can buy a *krtzl*. You've got to do better than that."

"I have nothing else to offer."

"What about your own language? Might be interesting. How would you say 'Breasts all perfume yes and his heart was going like mad and yes I said yes I will Yes.'"

"N*^ /py # # **.*89."

"Forget it. That's not a language, it's a throat disease."

While they talked Sean raised a shaky finger to Mulrooney, fumbled pound notes to the sticky bar, downed the fresh pint and reached for an even fresher one.

"You are so unjust," Mntkl whimpered, "and selfish. Would you have an entire world die because of your neglect?"

"Damn right," Portakal responded dimly. "Galaxies like grains of sands, stars like dust—or holes in a blanket. Couldn't care less . . ."

His voice trickled away—then returned with an effort. "I find it almost impossible to talk—what is happening?"

"I'll tell you what is happening," Mntkl answered, his fear forcing the words through the cloying blanket of incomprehension. "While we have been distracted this host-creature has been purchasing large amounts of biological poison. The deadly liquid has seeped into the synapses of his brain and is disconnecting them one by one. I am losing control. It will drive us out!"

"It will kill itself at the same time," Portakal squeaked. "We must stop it."

They each took one arm and clamped the hands tight upon the bar. Sean stared glassily ahead as they battled for control.

"So you've stopped talking to yourself at last," Mulrooney said, carefully polishing a glass. "Drunk yourself sober you have. Would you like one for the road?"

"I want," Mntkl said deeply, "no more," squeaked Portakal.

"Your voice changing? Not at your age. Must be your cold. Better get into bed before it turns into the flu."

Legs spread wide, hands clamped to bar, Sean stood there breathing like a locomotive. His alien occupiers would stop him from buying more drink—but could not stop the gallons of Guinness in his gut from seeping through into his blood. Drop by drop the ethyl alcohol oozed until his plasma could have been bottled and sold for gin. His eyes popped with the battle for control.

A battle lost. There was a tiny scream, vanishing into nothingness, accompanied by a small popping sound as Mntkl's grip slipped and his thought patterns vanished back among the stars. Portakal, the more experienced, fought on. But it was a losing battle, a defeat, an alcoholic Armageddon. As the synapses popped open he slipped away, vanished cursing, back to his gunk-atmosphered home among the stars.

"Ahh," Sean said, letting go of the bar and rubbing his sore hands one against the other. Experience counted. The amount of alcohol he had consumed would have killed a teetotaler in twelve seconds, would have preserved intact an entire family of Hooded Rats in a glass jar for centuries. But years of alcoholic overkill had won. What matter that his liver looked as though an entire regiment of the Black Watch had marched over it with hobnailed boots? It was of little importance that millions of his brain cells had been dissolved into jelly so that his IQ had dropped by twenty points. None of this mattered. What did count was that the aliens had been repulsed and he had won. He drew himself up and for the first time in hours spoke with his own voice, through vocal cords tired by the alien battle.

"It's quite a thirst I have. A pint if you please."

"Good man. You had me worried there for a while."

"Had me worried as well, I assure you." He blinked away the alcoholic haze and glanced at the headline in *The Mirror* that lay on the bar top beside him.

"ALIEN OCCUPIERS MEET IN HAWAII," he read aloud. "That's it, by Jaysuz, that's what happened to me. I've been occupied."

"You've been drunk," Mulrooney said, putting the darkpint down.

"I've been both—but no one will believe me." He sighed and drank. "There were two of them. One nasty one, thick as two planks. Wouldn't listen to the other's pleading that his whole planet would be destroyed. Laughed he did. Nasty, pressurized little bugger."

"Sounds like a science fiction story to me. Why don't you write it down before you forget it? Sell it to someone."

"Not me. I'll leave the story telling to the lads who don't drink. A sober, teetotaling, serious lot those science fiction writers I hear. Set them up again, Mulrooney, and one for yourself this time, for I'm beginning to disbelieve what happened myself."

At this moment, as the pint filled full, far across the galaxy a solid creature brooded unhappily at the bottom of a thickening sea, while still further away entropy ran out and a dim star vanished with a tiny stellar scream.

FROM AUSTRALIA:

Don't Knock the Rock

BY A. BERTRAM CHANDLER

The Uluru Grand Motel was not an unusual site for a convention, though the convention itself was. Apart from anything else, it had been going on for a very long time, weeks rather than days. Too, the conventioneers were such a mixed bunch—academics and mining engineers, hardheaded businessmen and two journalists, one of whom was myself. The other was Maridee. It was not altogether coincidental that the name of her host was Mary Dee. She had insisted that the First Surveyors find for her somebody with a name as close as possible to her own, sex likewise. Others had not been so fussy. B'na's Terran host was Sir Gregory Wilcox, one of the giants in the field of international banking, while B'na herself was, as nearly as her title can be translated into my own language, Chief Madam of the House of Many Delights in P'laisir, one of the major cities on her home world C'tus. Both Sir Gregory and B'na were very astute businesspersons, however. They had that much in common.

We had been well briefed, of course, before our real bodies, on our respective worlds, space cities and whatever, had been placed in stasis and our essential essences beamed into the minds of those selected to be our Terran hosts. (And some of those essences had to be recalled, hastily. That belonging to Brix, for example. The being whose title was Reverend Father and name Madigan fought hard, believing that he had been possessed by a devil, went through the ritual of exorcism by a fellow priest and, when that failed, cut his own throat.)

We were only one of the teams. Our mission was to obtain some object of religious/cultural significance, fit it with inertial drive and robot pilot and ship it off to the Galactic Museum on Coloron, where it could take its place among such wonders as the Sea Temple of Phlyxa—an intricately labyrinthed structure formed from a gigantic cultured pearl—and the Hallidoran Colossus. We made our own survey. We were specialists and we took over the bodies—and the minds and the memories and the expertise—of those whose specialties matched our own. B'na—or Sir Gregory—saw to it that we had ample funds for our travels. Costonwas—acting as and through Professor Manning of the Cavendish Laboratory—was able to construct an easily portable solar-powered matter transmuter. As only one element—gold—was required to be produced (from anything at all), the device did not need to be especially large. Dr. Scrivener, a man often referred to as the shuttle diplomat, still functioned as such under the control of Coordinator Gitra, whom you must have heard of as the Peacemaker of the Seven Star System. It was Scrivener who negotiated with the various national and local authorities—but, at first, with little success. The being who sold peace to the Seven Stars just wasn't as good a buyer as he was a seller.

Maridee and myself were the reporters, recording everything for the Galactic Museum, the Interstellar News Syndicate—you name it. Our stories, transmitted by tachyon telepathy, would be promulgated almost immediately by the media on a million or so civilized planets. Perhaps you watched or read or listened to them. Probably most of you didn't. Although culture vultures are by no means a dying breed, they are not a wildly proliferating one.

I must confess that it was a marvelous holiday for the pair of us, in our borrowed bodies. Had we met in our true forms on either of our home worlds, we should never have dreamed of close physical contact. What could a steely carapaced being, all jaws and claws, do to a blob of sentient jelly—except to eat her, of course. But now that the mission is over we still correspond, by tachyon telepathy, and are still good friends. She could, of course, arrange for a male acquaintance of hers to allow my essence into his body, or I could arrange for one of my sex mates to do the same for her, but it wouldn't be the same. Those human bodies, not overly hard and not overly soft, were an ideal compromise.

(I wonder if Mary Dee and John Teague, as my host was named, are still compromising. . . . I rather hope so, although I have my doubts.)

Well, we flitted around the planet, traveling most of the time in those primitive winged contraptions that the Terrans use for rapid (by their standards) transport. Castonwas became more and more irked. He wanted to leak into his host's mind all the knowledge necessary for him to "invent" the Porschon Matter Displacer a century or so before its time, but Gitra opposed this. We were not to interfere, he said, with Earth's normal development. Our orders, as he construed them, were very definite on this point.

(And why, you may ask at this juncture, was our selected monument or whatever to be shipped to its destination by inertial drive, a voyage taking hundreds of years, *anybody's* years? I asked the same question and was told that for a matter displacer to work there must be a continuous supply of matter to be displaced. A planetary atmosphere is such matter and although Space is not a *real* vacuum, matter is in decidedly short supply.)

During our journeyings we saw quite a few things that would have looked really good in the Galactic Museum. There was a sort of sacred mountain, Fujiyama, in a country called Japan. But the diplomatic problems were even greater than the engineering ones, and they were bad enough. (I still think, myself, that the job would have been quite impossible.) Everything had to be done legally, you see. Whatever we took we should have to pay an agreed price for.

In the United States of America we saw a few things that we should really have liked. In the capital city, Washington, there was a tall obelisk, a monument to the country's first president. The engineering side of it would have been simple enough and the reigning president, with whom Gitra had some *very* secret talks, was tempted and even considered the feasibility of extending the vaults at Fort Knox to accommodate the thousands of tons of gold that Castonwas would be able to produce for him. He was on the point of signing on the dotted line when he declared, "I can't do it. I won't do it. What good will all that gold be? If you people are such super-scientists why can't you let me have some super-weapons in exchange for the Monument?" So Gitra had to wipe his memory— luckily Castonwas had cooked up a neuronic eraser for him, disguised as a writing instrument—and that was that. Castonwas felt rather guilty about it, saying that from now on the president would be functioning with only half a brain. Gitra said, "Who'll notice, anyhow?"

In New York we considered three sacred artifacts. The removal of Miss Liberty from her island site—*if* we could have bought her, that is—would have caused no great dislocation to the life of the city, but the old lady herself was in no condition to undertake a prolonged interstellar voyage. The Empire State Building we could have bought, and Brooklyn Bridge, but would they have arrived intact? The engineers among us could make no guarantees as to that.

The other teams were having far greater success than we were. Historical research, Terran art in all its forms . . . They didn't have *our* problems. There was very little that could not be committed to the memories of the researchers and beamed back to the Museum by tachyon telepathy. And as for the occasional paintings and such, there were no problems. Just purchases by some anonymous millionaire collector, all quite legal. S.O.P., as the Terrans put it. Of course, quite a few people would have gotten very uptight if they had learned that such a masterpiece as the Mona Lisa was going to finish up in a gallery about 153 light-years from Earth.

But, as I have said, we were having our problems. Legal, engineering, and, above all, the superstitious sentimentality, the sentimental superstition of the Terrans. In England, for example, there was an old wooden battleship, *Victory*, which had been the flagship of an Admiral Nelson, a figure of some great historical importance. Our engineers assured us that *Victory* would be capable of making her final voyage without sustaining more than minor, easily rectifiable damage. And there was Stonehenge—which, as its name implies, is no more than a collection of stones. But insofar as *Victory* was concerned there was the stubborn sentimentality and, with Stonehenge, sentimentality, superstition, and the fear that the news of its sale and removal might spark off a rising by some people calling themselves Welsh Nationalists. No, Stonehenge isn't in Wales, a subdivision of the British Isles. It is in England, itself a subdivision, but it is regarded by the Welsh as a sacred site. Life, as we all know, can be complicated, but the Terrans have an absolute genius for making it even more complicated than it need be.

Anyhow, the neuronic eraser had to be used again. Shortly thereafter, England's fortunes took a turn for the better. This may have been merely coincidental.

Then we went to France. To Paris especially. There was the Eiffel Tower. With very little modification, with the addition of inertial drive units and life-support capsules, it would have made quite a good interplanetary spaceship. The interstellar voyage would have presented no problems.

But . . .

But Paris just wouldn't be Paris without the Eiffel Tower, and once again there had to be mnemonic erasure after our initial negotiations broke down.

So it went on. Italy, with St. Peter's Cathedral in Rome and the Leaning Tower of Pisa, among other monuments, and the engineering problems such that Gitra never got to the negotiating stage. India and the Taj Mahal . . . Burma and the Shwe Dagon Pagoda . . . stubborn people, sentimental people, superstitious people . . . rickety constructions that would fall apart once they were lifted clear of the supporting ground . . .

Gitra called a meeting.

He said, "The problems are these. First of all, we want something *big*. Even that statue we saw in New York, Miss Liberty, would look rather small in the museum. Second, we want something *solid*. That mountain in Japan might have been ideal, although it's rather too big to shift. Third, we want something whose owners or custodians are amenable to persuasion. Fourth, we would prefer something well away from large centers of population. . . ."

Maridee said, "I am Australian. Or my host body is."

B'na, through Sir Gregory, said, "I have been to Australia. What is there of interest but the Sydney Harbour Bridge and the Sydney Opera House?"

"From the engineering viewpoint," put in Castonwas, "both quite unsuitable."

"There were sacred places and things, in Australia," said Maridee (or Mary Dee), "long before the white man came. One of those places, those sites, has been handed back to the original inhabitants. They hoped to operate it as a tourist attraction, to their profit. But the enterprise has not been so successful as hoped. As a people they are not suitable for employment in service industries. I intend no denigration. How many of us here, on our own worlds, in our true forms, are so suitable? B'na, perhaps, but who else?"

"Come to the point, Maridee," said Gitra.

"The site of which I am talking," went on Maridee, "is the Uluru National Park, in Central Australia. In this park is the great monolith called Ayers Rock by the white men, Uluru by the aborigines. It is believed to be the peak of a great, sandstone mountain, the bulk of which is buried in the desert. If we could work undisturbed with the equipment that Castonwas could fabricate for us or which B'na could buy for us—some Terran mining machinery is quite sophisticated—we could cut it off below ground level and install the necessary inertial drive units. . . ."

"And the legalities?" asked Gitra.

"I know—or Mary Dee knows—an official in the Park Administration," said Maridee. "He is like many people in Australia these days; he claims to be an Aborigine, because it suits him to do so, but he could easily pass for white. He does, of course, have some aboriginal blood in his veins but it is very dilute. He is well educated. *And* he is an opportunistic bastard."

"The legalities," insisted Gitra.

"Patrick Collins—that is his name—is well qualified to handle those. He is a lawyer, and a good one. I do not use the word 'good' in its ethical sense but to refer to his competence."

"You think that he can be bought. . . ." murmured Gitra. "I do not like it. But we have a mission to complete and I, for one, shall not be sorry to return to my own body on Septagna. I am still not used to having to look down to the ground from a considerable height instead of having it, with all its various and fascinating aromas, right under my smelling aperture.

"So, B'na, will you start to organize matters? Travel arrangements and so on. The transfer of money: We have found we need that, no matter where we go." He was warming up. "It may be possible for us to take over the entire Park area. We shall be working as a group so we shall need a cover name."

"The Planetary Archaeological Society," suggested Maridee. "Holding its first annual convention. As Mary Dee I've covered quite a few conventions in my time. This one should be more interesting than most."

So there we were, the hundred of us—we had borrowed or conscripted people from some of the other teams, mainly because Gitra wanted to justify our taking over the entire motel—members of the Planetary Archaeological Society. More and more I was sharing my mind with my host, John Teague. (I felt that I owed him something and as he had ambitions to become a novelist I was feeding him quite a few ideas.) John was not impressed by the Uluru Grand Motel. It was flashy but (and) tawdry. The service was deplorable. The kitchen staff had revived the lost Australian culinary art of murdering such simple cookery as eggs and bacon or steak done any way. If you were lucky your bed got made sometime during the day.

If we didn't think much of the motel staff, the motel staff was regarding us with growing fear and suspicion. There were no other guests, that was the trouble, and Patrick Collins had succeeded in having the entire park put temporarily off limits to normal tourists, blowing up some minor ambiguity in the original contract made with the Pitjandjara tribe out of all proportion. (Oddly enough, we never met any of the Pitjandjara people; the maids, cooks, receptionists, and such had been recruited in Sydney.)

We had the place to ourselves, apart from the hired help. There was a growing tendency for at least some of us to take over the human bodies completely. I resisted it, and so did Maridee. (As far as she was concerned the reverse may have been the case.) B'na had to keep his/her wits about him/her. So did Castonwas and his technical assistants. And Gitra, and one or two more. But there was really no excuse for a respectable, middle-aged physician, whose human body was only approximately similar to the one that was waiting for her back home, to run naked by moonlight with the kangaroos, or for that other lady, whose borrowed body was that of an opera singer and who, on her own planet, was a professor of musicology, to go out, also at night, to join her voice to the dingo chorus.

(Have you ever heard a dingo howl?)

There were mutterings among the staff. City-bred they were, but the old beliefs of their people still persisted. There was whispering of spirits from the Dream Time returned in human form.

Maridee and I were present at most of the talks that Patrick Collins had with B'na, Gitra, and Castonwas. At the first one he was suspicious, although he had already seen the color of our money when the initial arrangements had been made. Nuts we might be, but we were wealthy nuts. He was shown the miniature matter transmuter that we had been carrying with us, watched as it converted soap and towels from the bathroom into what was indubitably a small heap of gold dust. He was told that a larger machine would be assembled from parts that we should have flown in and a sizable area of otherwise worthless desert similarly converted. I could see the cupidity gleaming in his eyes as he said, "If you are telling me the truth, such wealth could do much for my people . . . but Ayers Rock . . . Uluru, I mean. It has been sacred to us ever since the Dream Time."

Gitra had his arguments ready and said, "It will still be sacred in legend when it has returned to its true place among the stars, even more sacred, it may well be."

Collins said hopefully, "You will leave your matter converter behind, of course, Professor Manning. . . ."

"No," Gitra answered for Castonwas. "Your world is not ready for such a device."

"Not even in my hands?" asked Collins in a hurt voice.

Especially not in your *hands,* I thought.

From the start I didn't like Collins. He was too . . . smooth. He was clever and made sure that everybody knew it. He was handsome, with regular features, and his complexion was no darker than that of many an Australian of European ancestry. But, cashing in on some long-ago miscegenation, he had made a lucrative profession of being an Aborigine and a Land Rights activist.

I didn't like Collins and neither did my host, John Teague. Our hitherto warm—one might say torrid—relationship with Maridee/ Mary Dee seemed to be cooling off. Mary Dee, claiming that she was writing a piece on the famous Patrick Collins, was spending far too much time with him in his caravan, a quite luxurious mobile home, which was parked a little distance from the motel. On rather too many nights she was not coming to my room and, as I soon discovered, she was not returning to hers until some early hour in the morning.

But I was on Earth to observe, to record, not for the gratification of my fleshly lusts. (But fleshly lusts are so much more fleshly when you aren't encased in home-grown armor plating.) So I observed. I got the essential feel of the place. I rose early in the morning to watch the first rays of the rising sun strike that great, brooding Rock, sitting there on the desert like a huge, sullenly glowing red ember. I watched it at sunset as its color slowly shifted to a deeper and deeper purple until, at last, it was no more than a black, ominous hulk against the star-powdered sky. It seemed alive, an enormous, slumbering beast. I could understand how the first human inhabitants of this island continent had regarded it as sacred, how many of their descendants still did so.

During the daylight hours I walked around the Rock. I did not pay much attention to the machinery of various kinds that been set up, to the shafts that had been sunk. I made my way into the caves, where I could feel rather than hear the vibrations as the . . . the surgery was performed far below my feet. I knew what was being done. Finally, the Rock would be resting upon a number of stone pillars, connecting it to the parent mountain. The great inertial drive units would be installed in the base, together with the robot pilot. At last, when all was ready, Castonwas would push a button on the control panel, demolition charges would destroy the pillars, the inertial drive units would go into operation and all the machinery that we had been using, including the matter transmuter, would self-destruct.

And those few of us who had stayed for the final stage of the operation would board the waiting aircraft, crewed by fellow changelings, and get the hell out of there, shortly thereafter to be recalled to our own bodies on our own worlds.

At last it was Zero Hour—midnight, local time, aptly enough. We stood there outside the motel, the twenty remaining members of the Planetary Archaeological Society. Collins—he had insisted that he be allowed to watch—was with us. He was standing far too close to Mary Dee for my taste. The members of the motel staff were all sleeping. Collins—that cunning swine!—had made sure of that by throwing a party for them, playing the big, generous boss, and seeing to it that there was more in the beer and wine than mere alcohol.

It was a calm night but cold, bitterly cold. I looked up into the clear sky and tried to find the star around which Kraklit revolves. I couldn't find it—but I'm no astronomer. No matter, I should be back there very shortly, awakening in my familiar, stiff, clickety-clackety body, leaving John Teague, on this planet, to his odd half-memories, and to Mary Dee.

Mary Dee?

What could any female, in whatever form, see in a male like Collins?

Castonwas, on a folding stool, sat hunched over his control panel with its flicker of dim lights, ruby and amethyst and emerald, their polychromatic illumination making faintly visible his thin, serious face, the face of Professor Manning. (And what would Manning remember of all this?)

"Now!" he whispered.

A long finger made a stabbing motion.

Would it work? I suddenly wondered. Would all the pillars be shattered? Would the inertial drive units start? I had a ludicrous vision of Ayers Rock becoming a sort of Leaning Tower of Pisa on an enormous scale.

But I needn't have worried. Carrying clearly through the still air came the arrhythmic beat of the inertial drive and, a fractional second later, the dull thud of the explosions, sounding as one. There was smoke, and there was dust, and an eerie blue flickering illumination from one of the shaft-sinking machines that was taking its time about self-destructing.

And the summit of the rock, in black silhouette against the darkly luminous sky, was surely higher, was eclipsing a couple of faint stars, then a brighter one. And more, and more . . . And below the base, the amazingly even base of the Rock, there was sky and there were stars and the beat of the drive was loud, and louder, and then diminishing as the sacred monolith was well and truly launched on its long voyage to its final resting place in the sky.

At last it was gone and there was silence.

Castonwas broke it. "That's that. Now we can all go home."

Collins seemed suddenly to realize the enormity of what, with his connivance, had been perpetrated.

"It's all right for *you,*" he almost whimpered.

"*You'll* be all right," said B'na contemptuously.

But, as Castonwas had said, that was that. We made a last inspection of the site. There was the crater, with its vitreous floor. There were other glassy patches around it, where various pieces of equipment, machinery and so forth, had been. Some distance away, hidden among rocks in a position known only to Collins (as well as to ourselves, of course), was that enormous deposit of pure gold, and another patch of glass to mark where the matter transmuter had been. Castonwas amused himself by advancing theories—each of which, of course, he could easily have knocked down—to account for the vanishment of Uluru. His favorite was the descent to Earth of a miniature black hole.

Collins, having made sure that his tribespeople's gold (they might get some of it) was intact, retired to his caravan, there to sleep. He, of course, would have seen nothing. His story would be that he had been overtaken by the same strange lethargy that had overcome the motel staff. The rest of us boarded the waiting jet for the flight to Melbourne. From there we should go our separate ways, finally to abandon our borrowed bodies and to return to our home worlds. Only Mary Dee and John Teague would be staying in Australia. I had been hoping for one last night together, but it didn't work out.

As I said earlier, I hope that John Teague and Mary Dee are still together. But, somehow, I doubt it. I have stayed in touch with Maridee and she, of course, knew Mary Dee far better than I did. She has confirmed things that I, that John Teague, only suspected. And I still possess the sum total of John Teague's knowledge at the time of my possession of him. I know about Swiss bank accounts.

I strongly suspect that even as I, on Kraklit, in my cell in the cave city of Kribble, am feeding these words into my recorder—and even as John Teague, in his little flat in the city of Sydney, is typing what he hopes will be *the* Australian science fiction novel—Mary Dee and the unspeakable Collins are living it up in one of the playgrounds of the very rich on Earth.

I'm sorry about Mary but, of course, I can't be sure. For all I know she and John did get together again and are now living happily ever afterwards.

And there's another thing that I'm sorry about, and of this I can be sure. Long-lived as my race may be, there's no way that I can be around to watch Uluru make its landing on the Great Red Desert of Coloron, to take its honored place among wonders from the myriad worlds.

The Owl of Bear Island

BY JON BING

The landscape outside the window was black and white, with the ocean like gray metal beneath a dark sky. The cliffs were bare and steep, ribboned by bird droppings, the beaches stony and empty with off-white trimmings of dried foam and salt.

It was a lifeless landscape, even this far into "spring." The polar night had lost its grip on day and let it slide into twilight along the horizon in the south. I looked toward the metallic reflection of sunlight and felt invisible feathers rise around my neck. I blinked my eyes.

Why were they this far north?

I thought of my boss as an owl. A great, white snow-owl with a cloud of light feathers. With big, yellow eyes in a round head. With a sharp and cynical beak. With spastic movements. I felt like that when the Owl took me over, I discovered such movements in my own body when the Owl left me.

What did he really want from me? Why was not I, like the others of whom I had heard, guided to the ghetto on Hawaii? What was an extraterrestrial doing on Bear Island, 74 degrees north?

Bear Island is the southernmost of the Spitsbergen Islands. Its area is approximately 180 square kilometers. Its shape is triangular, with the famous Bird's Mountain on the southernmost point. It was discovered by the Dutch polar explorer Willem Barents in 1596, and fishermen were attracted to the island by huge populations of sea elephant and whale. The climate is quite mild: In the warmest month the average temperature is not more than 4° Centigrade, but the average drops in the coldest month to −7°, quite mild for a latitude halfway between the North Pole and the northernmost point of Alaska.

Bear Island was placed under Norwegian sovereignty in 1925. Since 1918, Norway has maintained a station on the island, partly to keep radio contact with the fisheries fleet, partly for meteorological observations. The station was destroyed when the Allies withdrew in 1941, to make it useless for the Germans. A new station was constructed in 1947 at Herwig Port, a few kilometers from the old.

The station was my closest neighbor. I could in principle visit there, either in the boat if there was not too much ice along the coast, or in the small but efficient helicopter in the tin hangar outside the buried bunker in which the Institute was housed. It would take just a little while to fly north and west from Cape Levin to Herwig Port. But I did not fly.

Of course.

After I was possessed, I did not do such things.

I blinked my great yellow eyes, flexed my clawlike fingers over the keyboard of my computer, and did not remember anything . . . until I later shuddered and blinked in front of the screen.

My eyes were sore and staring. More than eleven hours had passed. I got back to the bunk I had made up in the terminal room just before being overwhelmed by deep sleep.

It was, of course, contrary to normal procedure to let one man live through the polar night on his own. There should have been two of us.

Normally, there were, both specialists, experts on the analysis of geotechnical data from sonar probes. We were rather good friends, Norway being small enough to make most people within the same field acquaintances. His name was Johannes Hansen; he was from the small town Mo in northern Norway and was used to long and sunless winters. I was from the south, but I needed the bonus which a winter would bring. We had rather looked forward to a quiet winter of routine work—and a computer, which we could use in our spare time to process the material we had both collected for a paper, perhaps a thesis.

It was not many nights after equinox before the white and dark wings closed over my thoughts and my boss took power.

A few days later Johannes Hansen became seriously ill. I am sure that my boss induced the illness, though I do not know in what way.

Johannes Hansen was collected by a helicopter from a coast guard vessel. He died before he reached the mainland.

The doctors had problems in determining the cause of death, and no replacement was sent out. I remained alone in the bunker of the Institute on the east coast of Bear Island. People from the meteorological station did not visit. Nor did I visit them, though I talked to them by radio from time to time in order to reassure them. It was important that they should not grow suspicious, important to my boss.

My boss knew why he was there. I did not. I did not know what the Owl wanted from me and the bunker of the Institute at Bear Island. I only knew that in this bunker for the better part of the winter a possessed person lived, a person who flapped invisible wings and hooted like an owl toward the night lying across the snow, and the ice outside the windows.

Institute for Polar Geology is the official name. It may sound rather academic. Formally, the Institute is part of the University of Tromsø—the world's northernmost university—but in reality it is financed by the government. Norway had for many years conducted quite sensitive negotiations with the Soviet Union over possible economic exploitation of the Barents Sea; that is, the ocean north of Norway and the Kola peninsula which stretches between Spitsbergen and Novaya Zemlya toward the Pole.

The negotiations were difficult for several reasons. First, the Soviets had considerable military activity on the Kola peninsula—for instance, its largest navy base. Second, preliminary surveys indicated major natural resources on the continental shelf, especially in oil. The coal mines of Spitsbergen were an obvious sign of what might lie hidden by the cold sea. In the summer of 1984 the Soviets made the first major find of natural gas and oil, midway between the Norwegian coast and Novaya Zemlya.

The two countries had not arrived at a final agreement. There was still a contested sector midway between the two countries, popularly known as "the gray zone." In 1984 it was discovered that one of the important members of the Norwegian delegation during the negotiations had been in contact with the KGB and was probably a Soviet agent. All these factors had combined to block the final solution of the gray-zone problem.

Soviet mining ships had made test drillings as close to the gray zone as possible, seeking information on which natural resources it might hide. Norway was too occupied with exploration and development of promising oil fields in the North Sea to start more than symbolic test drills farther north. The northernmost samples were taken at Tromsøflaket, a fishing bank off the shore of North Troms at a depth of 2,300 meters.

The Institute for Polar Geology was founded to furnish more information about the structures underneath the sea bottom in the north, and the sea bottom itself. An installation was constructed at Bear Island, approximately midway between the mainland and Spitsbergen proper. This installation was equipped with a computer system for analysis of data collected by sonar probes. The system was quite powerful. There was a sturdy minicomputer, data bases with all available geological information on the northern seas, programs for analysis developed on the basis of experiments made in the North Sea, plotters and graphic screens for projection of maps and graphs.

The system received data through a radio link with the sonar probes. Some probes were anchored to the sea bottom, while others could be piloted—almost like unmanned mini-subs—by the computer system, into areas from which data was desirable.

The system had no permanent link to those on the mainland. However, through a disk antenna one of the polar orbiting satellite systems could be accessed for computer communication. There was also a link to the mainland by the way of the meteorological station at Herwig Port.

It was a rather fancy computer system. But it was a considerably less expensive way of collecting information than test drilling. Perhaps the Soviets also would have chosen this alternative if it had been open to them, but the system in the bunker at Cape Levin was certainly on the embargo list of the U.S. Department of Commerce. It was not possible for the Soviets to establish something similar.

And this well-equipped bunker was the place where the invisible owl had arrived, from a planet beyond the curtain of northern lights.

Obviously, it was to use this equipment that the Owl had chosen the bunker. It must be information possible for the equipment to squeeze out of the sonar probes. I did not know what it might be, except in rough outlines.

When the Owl had ridden me throughout days of polar night, I came to in an exhausted body. My tongue was dry and thick like a stopper in my throat, my eyes were red and swollen. The Owl showed little consideration for the fact that static electricity in the terminal screen gathered dust from the atmosphere of the electrically heated bunker, and that this concentration of dust irritated the mucous membranes in the eyes and prompted symptoms of allergy. The Owl used my body as long as necessary. It rode me, day after day, and let me recover only sufficiently to endure another ride— impatient with me, irritated by my bodily needs.

Perhaps I was too exhausted to revolt. I nursed myself back to some semblance of health time after time, though I knew that as soon as I became strong, the claws would grip my thoughts and I would be ridden through a new unconscious period.

I noticed the evidence of what had been done, read the log from the computer, and knew that new programs had been written, probes activated, new data collected. Several of the mobile probes frequently went into the gray zone. From time to time they crossed the territorial border to the Soviets. It was probably not out of respect for human agreements or the danger of creating an international incident that the Owl refrained from penetrating deeper into Soviet territory—but rather just because the radio signals became too weak to be received so far from the installation.

I tried to read the programs. They were, of course, written in

FORTRAN or SIMULA—the Owl had to make do with what to him would seem naive languages. But I did not understand the programs, though I was a passable programmer myself.

It could not be oil resources that interested the Owl. I could only guess what he—and I, in my unconscious and feverish working periods—really was looking for. I guessed it would have something to do with the nodules, the bulbs of manganese covering great areas of the sea bottom.

And, of course, even manganese could not be the interesting thing. Next to iron, it is the heavy metal most common in the Earth's crust, though the fraction is no higher than 0.77 percent. Manganese is also identified in metorites and in the spectrum of stars, so it could not be the scarcity of this metal that made an extraterrestrial interested in the cold sea far in the north of the Earth.

But laboratory analysis of nodules show that they contain a profusion of other minerals, among these at least forty different metals, for instance iron, copper, nickel, and cobalt. I thought it might be a trace element that the Owl looked for. Perhaps his search related to the fact that the nodules were so far north, where temperature, magnetic fields, or the strong cosmic radiation had acted to catalyze an unknown process. Or perhaps the solution was to be found in some prehistoric volcanic catastrophe creating the core of the bulbs.

An unknown trace element . . . or an alloy, a chemical compound . . .

It was not the only riddle of the Owl.

I did not understand why it operated in secrecy. The other reported incidents of "possession" of which I had heard, had taken the host directly to Hawaii, where the bosses haggled among themselves in some sort of stock exchange of Babel, where terrestrial goods and services were traded on behalf of clients light-years away —who probably would not be able to enjoy the goods or services for many slow decades. In some way the Owl participated in this game, perhaps collecting secret information on natural resources.

I believed he operated outside the rules of the game. That's why

he had selected the lonely Bear Island, therefore had selected me
. . . a lonely man in a wintery bunker at the shore of the Barents Sea.

I believed there might also be another reason.

My boss hated sunlight. It was perhaps for that reason I had
dubbed him the Owl. He worked only at night. The long polar night
allowed him to work without being disturbed by daylight—until my
body failed.

From time to time I thought of his home planet. A waste-
world, at the edge of a solar system. Perhaps the white wings of the
Owl slid through an atmosphere of methane? Or perhaps his planet
was covered by eternal clouds? Or perhaps it was tied in rotation to
its sun, where the Owl and his kind inhabited the night side?

In my nightmares the Owl became a figure from fairy tales, and
his home planet a magic forest. It felt nearly logical that he should
share the predilection of the trolls from Norwegian fairy tales, by
hiding from the Sun.

And soon the polar night would be at an end.

There were long periods each day when I was free of the Owl.
At last there were only a few hours each night when it dared to sink
its claws into my subconscious.

But I understood that it had done something to me. I did not
fully have free will. I contacted the meteorological station and declared that I would like to stay another winter. And that I did not
really need a summer holiday.

They grew very concerned. I could count on a visit from a
psychologist—at least a radio interview with one on the mainland.
I would have liked to break my isolation—but I was controlled,
guided by the rules the Owl had constructed in my subconscious.

But the polar night has its reflection in the polar summer. From
April 30 till August 12, the Sun never sets over Bear Island. The
midnight sun burns in the north each night, and the shadows pivot
like the pointers of a watch across the whole dial. The landscape
explodes in seductive colors under melting snow. The air is light and
transparent in white sunshine.

And for the whole of this period, more than three months, the
Owl would stay away from me—though it still controlled my sub-

conscious. During this period I must take countermeasures to break out of my psychological jail. In the May sun I looked for the key to the barred door.

I found it. At least I thought so then.

The computer system at the bunker was quite advanced. It had access to, among other programs, a version of PROSPECTOR, one of the most successful examples of expert systems constructed. PROSPECTOR exploits the results of research in artificial intelligence and the knowledge from a large number of experts in geology and petrochemistry. This knowledge is structured in a large set of rules. And this rule system could assist another expert—for instance, myself. The results of analyses could be presented to PROSPECTOR, which at once would suggest that supplementing information should be collected, until it arrived at a conclusion on whether the geological structure described by the information was promising or not.

PROSPECTOR could become the key.

The version of PROSPECTOR to which I had access was a self-instructing program. Through use, the program learned more about the one using it, and about what it was being used for. It automatically constructed supplementing rules, constantly refining its expertise.

Of course, the Owl would not himself start using PROSPECTOR, or my special version, the OWLECTOR. I used the summer to hide the program in the operating system to the computer. It was a sort of extra layer in the program, rather like a hawk floating in the air and keeping an eye on what was happening below. This is how I saw OWLECTOR, like a hunting hawk programmed with a taste in owls. The more the Owl used the system, the more OWLECTOR would learn of the Owl. It would learn enough to take control from the Owl, fight the Owl. And the more the Owl fought to keep in control, the more OWLECTOR would learn of its opponent.

There was a fascinating justice in the scheme. Neither I nor any other human could fight the Owl or any of his galactic colleagues. We had not sufficient knowledge, nor capacity in a brief human life to learn what we needed. But a computer does not have our limitations. It can learn as long as there is somebody to teach. It can learn until it knows as much as the teacher.

It can tap knowledge from the Owl until it becomes an owl itself.

And the computerized owl is loyal to humans. That is the way I have programmed it. And this loyalty will last as long as the program.

There will not be much time. Perhaps only a few hours, a few days. Who knows how soon the Owl will discover the hunting hawk somewhere above, like a dot against the sky?

But perhaps it does not expect such an attack. Perhaps the Owl is arrogant and impatient with weak humans, who fail from thirst and exhaustion. And then it will perhaps not search the sky for a hunting hawk in the form of a computer program, which studies the Owl as prey until it is ready to strike the bustling white bird and liberate me for all future time. . . .

I do not know whether to believe in this or not. But I no longer dream of spectral owls in strange dark forests, but of white owls in snow, owls killed by birds of prey, blood splashing the snow. In my sleep I hear the sea birds cry: They dive and circle through the sunny nights, and I seem to hear the owls hoot.

It will soon be August 12. The sun already touches the horizon at midnight. Soon the Owl will be back, and I will know the answer. . . .

FROM BULGARIA:

Contacts of a Fourth Kind

BY LJUBEN DILOV
Translated by Svetlana Voutova

The International Lunar Base construction team had nearly finished
its work, and its members were gathered in the assembly hall to hear
themselves congratulated by the construction managers. Because the
team came from many countries of Earth, there were several managers, every one of whom intended to speak. The first told of what
a wonderful thing it was that their various nations had been able to
cooperate on this project, and he was handsomely applauded by all.
The second reminded them how difficult the work had been; the
third complimented them on completing the task nearly on time and
almost within budget, and they were applauded too. By the time the
fifth manager rose to speak, there was little left to say, and he elected
to talk about a flight of fancy. "When we are at work out on the
hostile surface of the Moon," he said, "we all wear our spacesuits
and look very much alike. Suppose some more advanced civilization
from another part of the Galaxy should observe us at our labors.
They could hardly guess that the people inside those suits belong to
many different nationalities and races. Such galactic intelligences
would probably be led to think that our entire planet is inhabited
by a single race of peace-loving human beings, united by great and
good ideas."

He paused. The audience knew what was expected of them,
and clapped heartily at the prospect of great and good ideas uniting
the human race. Although they were of many nationalities, they

applauded in the same way, by striking the palms of their hands together, and for the same reasons—the speaker was, after all, a project manager. Of course, none of them suspected that any beings from an advanced civilization were actually quite close to them on the Moon. The speaker beamed and finished:

"Such an idea might be false at present, but, true to our own dreams, we sincerely hope to be truly peace-loving by the day when, at long last, we do get in touch with such intelligences. And we hope they will be pleased with us!"

The speaker accepted his final round of applause with pleasure and sat down (gently in the light lunar gravity) to give way to the final project manager. For him there was even less left to say.

Rather than attempting any further flights of fancy, the last project manager said only, "All that my colleagues have said is true, and I share their congratulations and their hopes for the future. Nevertheless, I must point out that we have certain problems. In particular, some important pieces of electronic equipment are missing. Certainly no one would have stolen them; what would be the point? But it is also certain that they are gone, and I ask every one of you to exercise more care so that nothing more is lost as we complete our task."

It was not a very inspiring speech, but he, too, was dutifully applauded. After all, he was the manager in charge of matériel and supplies, and was only doing his job.

It did not occur to any of the team, as they rose and proceeded to their ceremonial dinner, that the missing equipment was quite close at hand—in a nearby crater full of dust and broken stone, like all the lunar craters—along with a few of those "fanciful" intelligences from other stars.

The intergalactic community of supercivilizations had for some time been keeping an eye on the fledgling culture developing on the third planet of our Sun. Some of these beings intended to help the Earthlings join its united family when the time was ripe, but the project was difficult. The vast distances between stars were not easy to cross. Living creatures could not cross them at all in a single lifetime, because of the limiting velocity of light itself.

Packets of mental energy, however, could travel far more rapidly. A creature from another star willing to allow himself to be transformed into mind-energy could cross the space to Earth in hours, instead of many years. The difficulty was that once he had arrived, he was still only mind-energy. In order to accomplish anything he needed physical existence as well, usually attained by occupying the body of one of the dominant Earth species, the "humans." There was, however, another possibility. An electronic device could be constructed that would allow these bodiless minds to interact at least with each other.

It was also considered advisable, by some of the members of the community, to have a private place to meet and discuss their experiences on Earth, away from any possible human eavesdropping. So when they discovered the construction project on the Moon, it was no trouble at all for them to cause some of the workers to purloin a few small bits of equipment and install them in an adjacent crater . . . and there some of them were meeting.

Since they were nonmaterial, each had to identify itself as soon as it started to speak. Therefore, when the chairman of the disembodied intelligences spoke, he said: "I am First Observer of Planet 1407-Why. I thank the observer of Planet 1113-Warum for his report, and now call on Second Observer of Planet 038-Pourquoi." Through the workings of their electronic interface it was possible for even the thoughts of disembodied entities to take on tones of approval or reproof, and there was a distinct note of the latter in the chairman's thoughts as he went on. "However, Second Observer from Planet 038-Pourquoi, I must say that your previous reports have contained little objective information. You deal mostly with regional natural scenery, and superficially at that. You said everything was beautiful; that the inhabitants of Earth were wonderful, and so on. The general impression, I remind you, is far less favorable. I suspect that you chose an unsuitable human to take over as an observation vehicle."

The being addressed responded at once. "I, Second Observer of 038-Pourquoi, do not think the body I chose was in any way unsuitable. It was a standard specimen of the type 'human,' being male and of average age. However, I agree that there is a problem. My presence within it affected its behavior. It was often surprised at some of its own actions, some of which pleased it, others made it angry. I fear our presence deforms the consciousness of the bodies we choose, and therefore reliable data will be hard to obtain."

There was a quick discussion of this point among several of the intellects present, after which the chairman ruled that Second Observer of 038-Pourquoi should continue with his report in full. The observer did so:

"I took over the body of my subject at an interesting point. It was a designer of machines, and it was totally absorbed in creating plans for a new device. Because this task was arduous, the subject body went to the refreshment counter of the industrial plant where it functions and ordered a beverage we had not previously been familiar with. It is a transparent liquid with an unpleasantly sharp taste; they call it 'vodka.' This is a very interesting drink, fellow observers. It has an impressively rapid effect on a human body. In small quantities it causes a pleasant warmth. As the quantity increases, it changes one's perceptions of the environment and ultimately produces physical effects of several kinds. It is these effects which I wish to emphasize in my report.

"It must be noted that the human who gave me the 'vodka' was of the other sex, called 'female.' That is to say, the two bodies there present were of the two major human types, which propagate by joining together. I will now tell you what followed. . . ."

The being which gave my body the vodka (continued Second Observer from the Planet 038-Pourquoi) said to my body with a smile, "Isn't it a little early for vodka, comrade engineer?"

"Just a small one to keep my courage up," my body replied. But then it contradicted itself, saying, "One more, please." And it drank that one, too, before leaving the refreshment counter and going to a small office nearby. There were three other humans there, who invited my body to sit down. My body did not do that, however. It was feeling quite warm from the vodka, and said:

"Judging by the looks on your faces, this meeting won't last long." I could detect a conflict within my body at that time; it was regretting that it had said those words, because it judged them too arrogant for the meeting.

"It may take a little longer than you think for you to understand our position," said the being the others called "comrade engineer."

It smiled, too; it is interesting that Earth beings often smile when what they have to say seems to contradict any friendly emotion.

"So," said my body, once again frightening itself by its own words, "you think I'm too dumb to understand you. Well, I understand everything! If you want to introduce my machine, you'll have to manufacture it. Then you must stop the production line, which will disrupt the plant's plan. In order to do that, you will have to convince higher authorities that in the long run production will be tripled with the new machine—but you don't feel like walking your legs off to see the higher authorities, because what you really want is to retire on a pension next year, with all the ceremonies due because you have overfulfilled your plan, and perhaps with a decoration. So the best that will happen here is that you will tell me that my machine is excellent, but because of many important considerations you prefer to wait before introducing it—in other words, let the next director worry about it."

The director continued to smile, but said, "And what if we tell you instead that your machine is simply no good?"

"Then," my body said promptly—but even more frightened inside—"I will tell you that either you are lying, or you don't know the first thing about modern technology."

There were no longer any smiles on the faces of the beings in the room, especially not on my body's. It pulled a piece of paper out of its pocket and thrust it at the others. "This is my request for dismissal from the plant," it cried. "My machine is patented. If you don't want it, others will, comrade director!"

The director's face was now quite angry. He tore the sheet of paper in half and dropped it on the floor. "I do not consent to your leaving," he said. "As to the machine, it was developed here, and therefore it is ours by right. What's come over you, comrade? You've always been a good, sensible fellow. You're simply overexcited for some reason. Let's postpone this conversation for a few days."

"We will postpone it forever!" shouted my body. "I am sick and tired of being a good, sensible fellow. I give notice!" And with that he stormed out, slamming the door behind him.

This whole situation (continued Second Observer from 038-Pourquoi) continues to be very puzzling to me. If any of my fellow observers have discovered anything similar, I would be grateful to hear about it when I have finished. I simply can't make it out.

What is more, it got worse. For some weeks now, my body has failed to report to its place of employment. According to their law, the comrade director should have discharged him for unjustified absence. Not only has the director not done that, he has even signed an order stating that my body has been given leave of absence for purposes of research. This is of course quite false. There are other contradictions as well: The director obviously can't stand my body and does not care to employ his machine, and yet the director will not agree to let either of them go. How can such things be with rational creatures?

But there is more. I must now narrate to you what my body did after leaving the office of the comrade director.

My body returned to the refreshment counter and ingested two more glasses—larger ones—of the substance vodka. While doing so, it shouted abuse of the comrade director at the top of its voice. Then it left the building and entered one of their primitive motor cars, driving away at what is for these beings a high rate of speed.

The center of the town in which all this happened contains streets which are quite narrow and heavily congested with vehicles and humans on foot. Several times my body's vehicle narrowly missed others. Then a body of the other sex suddenly rushed out into the street ahead of him.

Calculating the relative speeds and the braking coefficients of the vehicle, I was quite certain that my body's car would impact upon the female, with probably serious results. However, that did not happen. The female being suddenly sprang into the air, flew across the street, and fell on the opposite pavement.

At that moment I experienced two feelings. The first was regret that my body's vehicle had not struck and killed the female, since this would undoubtedly have produced a complex emotional situation which I would have been able to study. The second was astonishment, since I had not previously seen any indication that a human female body was capable of such acrobatics.

However, the emotional situation that did result was quite interesting. Several dozen of the other humans in the street immediately gathered around the stopped car and the woman on the sidewalk, who now seemed unconscious; the crowd was shouting and threatening, and caused my body to experience several emotions. The most prominent one seemed to be fear of certain other human bodies, not yet present, who might soon arrive and take my body away to be punished for operating the vehicle after ingesting the vodka. To avert that, my body sprang out of its car and cried, "Stand aside! This girl is injured! I will take her to the hospital at once!"

In a moment, my body had seized the female and dragged it into his car. He drove away. I observed at once that the car was not going in the direction of the hospital—yet another puzzling contradiction—but, in fact, that did not seem necessary. In just a moment the female body stirred on the seat beside my body and opened its eyes. "Where are you taking me?" it asked.

"To the First Aid Center," said my body at once, although this was untrue.

"No, no," said the female. "I'm all right; I just fainted. But I've torn my stockings."

"I'll get you some new ones—there's a stand just across the street. What's your size?"

The female shook her head. "You don't have to buy me new stockings. It was my fault; that's no way to cross the street."

My body was delighted to hear this. It exclaimed in complimentary tones, "But the way you did it was wonderful! You don't happen to be a broad-jump champion, do you?"

"I don't know how it happened myself. I think that's why I fainted, out of fright at what I had just done."

"Well, then," said my body, beginning to feel the warmth again, "why don't we go somewhere and have a drink on it? I was just as frightened."

The female said, "We'll probably have an argument about who is to stand the drinks." Since it wasn't a refusal, my body said in delight:

"You're wonderful! I can talk with you." Then he said, in a burst of confidence, "Listen, I should admit that I've already had one drink today—actually, more than one. So I must not drive my car for a while, and the best place for me to leave it is in front of my house."

The female looked at him in an odd way. "Are you inviting me to your house?" she asked.

"Have no fear! I am a respectable citizen. In fact, I am quite shy with women—although," he added, "I don't quite know why I'm behaving like this . . . any more than you know how you came to jump across a whole street."

The female did not quite agree to go to my body's house, but on the other hand she didn't jump out of the car when he turned in that direction, and even allowed him to conduct her inside. There she glanced around. She said, in a rather strange tone, "I believe nothing here has been touched by a woman's hand."

"Is it so untidy?" my body asked. "But you're right. My home is as virginal as the Amazon jungle."

"Oh, I don't think it's quite as virginal as all that," said the female, and allowed him to pour her a drink. She fingered the two dusty circles in her stocking in an embarrassed way and tried to hide them with her coat. "That looks so terrible," she sighed. "I'm sorry I gave you so much trouble."

"Trouble?" my body cried. "Why, what could be pleasanter than having a drink with such a charming girl?"

"Hey," said the female, though not at all angrily. "You're supposed to be bashful with women, not ready to make a pass so quickly."

For reasons I have not been able to establish, this caused my body's circulatory system to send a flush of blood as far up as its ears, which made the female laugh.

"Speaking of passes," she said, "I'd better pass into your bathroom and do something about these stockings. Where is it?"

While she was absent, my body surreptitiously refilled both glasses. Perhaps he was trying to put the female at ease by providing her with some of that warming, soothing effect of the vodka, although I could not understand why he did it in such a furtive manner. But when she came out it evidently worked. The female no longer tried to hide her knees. She had removed her coat, as well as the torn stockings, and now her legs appeared quite clearly, smooth and very white.

I observed that my body liked them, but at the same time they made it feel uneasy in a strange way—another contradiction I couldn't figure out. It began to make conversation. "Let me tell you," said my body, "why I am so agitated today; perhaps it will excuse some of my behavior." And it told her the whole story of its machine, its interview with the comrade director, and its desire to leave that place of employment forever.

The female listened not only with attention but even with admiration, and did not refuse when my body poured her another drink. "Why, you're wonderful!" she exclaimed. "I didn't know there still were people who shouted at their directors and gave notice."

My body felt a glow at the praise, but admitted, "I'm not like that usually, unfortunately. I don't know what came over me. It was a sudden leap—like your own across the street." And then it said, "Why don't you try that again? Let's see if you can do as well now. Stand over there against the wall. The room is five meters long; that should be enough, but I'll stand here to stop you if you go farther."

"Oh, no," said the female. "I couldn't do that. Fear gives one wings, you know, and I'm not afraid now. On the other hand," she said, correcting herself, "the saying is that love gives one wings, too. But in our time such love is nonexistent."

"Just try," breathed my body and, laughing, the female hesitantly moved over to the far wall. When she jumped she easily cleared the five meters and wound up in the arms of my body, in amazement. My body instinctively joined its arms behind her back. Their faces breathed quite close to each other. "Why, you were simply flying," my body's lips whispered.

"But that's impossible," her lips responded, close to his ear.

"But here we are. Unless we are both dreaming, you're now in my arms."

"That's also quite impossible," said the female, very illogically. She drew back, though not very far. "You must let me go," she said.

"After I give you a kiss," said my body, and then, shocked at its own boldness, added, "Simply out of gratitude that you saved me from going to prison, do you see?"

"Go to a church and kiss the icons," said the female, still trying to free herself, though still not very hard.

"Well, then," said my body, reluctantly releasing her, "then at least let's repeat the experiment. Go back to the far wall, why don't you?"

And so the female did, with the same result. In a moment she was in my body's arms again. "But I can fly! I can really fly!" she cried, and began blindly kissing my body's face. However, she did that for only a short time. Then she broke away and sat down on the couch, her own blood supply obviously rising to her face and neck. My body followed her.

"But this is wonderful," said my body. "Can't you see what a stir it will make if you do this in public?"

"Oh, I couldn't!" cried the female. She was obviously quite upset. To calm her, my body began caressing the white legs, now bent on the couch, and speaking rapidly.

"But leaps," he said, "are quite common in our time! We've experienced so many—political, economic, the sexual revolution— why, according to the laws of the gradual accumulation and transformation of quantity into quality—"

"What a dialectician you are," she remarked, pushing his hand away as it crept above her knee. "You're making fun of me."

"No, no," my body said earnestly, returning his hand. "Don't you see, they leap so beautifully they deserve to be stroked and caressed."

But the female stood up and declared she must leave. However, she did promise to meet him the next day, so that they could try the leaping experiment again out of doors, where there would be more room.

Fellow observers—continued Second Observer from 038-Pourquoi—there now occurred some events which are very difficult to interpret. To begin with, that night my body did not go to sleep for a long time. It kept remembering the feel of those smooth, white legs as it caressed them, and then imagining some other things whose full meaning I did not then understand. However, its mind was drowsy and rather confused, and at one time it found itself imagining caressing not the girl (whose name was Deena), but the male body called comrade director. This caused my body to jump out of bed and pace back and forth. It seemed quite agitated. At times it would break out into another of those storms of abuse against the director, at others it would feel quite warm and jolly—almost as though it had ingested some of the vodka, although in fact it was drinking nothing but water. This confirms our impression of the nature of the human intellect, which has a natural inclination toward illogical behavior and the absurd. Outwardly, the human restrains his thinking and actions within certain social norms—up to a point. But he makes use of moments of privacy, especially in bed, to engage in absurdities.

Absurd behavior is not limited to the bedroom, however. The next day my body took the female, Deena, in his car to a little river and looked for a meadow for their leaping experiments. This was not odd, but my body had developed a new obsession. Deena had now hidden those white, smooth legs in a pair of trousers of thin material, and my body seemed to desire to have those trousers for itself. Its eyes were glued to them as Deena walked before him to the meadow.

As the purpose of this expedition was nominally to test Deena's leaping ability, she did in fact make several quite respectable jumps —across the little river and back, and then at a number of places, here and there, around the little meadow. This caused my body to be quite excited. It had brought a metal builder's tape for the purpose of measuring Deena's leaps, and found many opportunities to touch the desired trousers while doing so. At the same time it began to speak quite irrationally, addressing the female by inappropriate nouns: "You're a dragonfly! A gazelle!" and the like. It also called her "my magic butterfly," "my gazelle," "dear grasshopper," and so on. She did not appear to mind this, although I should have supposed it would be unflattering for a reasoning being to be compared to lower animals in this way. She even allowed my body to kiss her, and to draw her down onto the grass of the meadow, where it began to try to remove the trousers. I was hoping it would succeed, as I was curious to see what my body would do with the trousers once secured, but Deena objected that people might come. This meant that what my body wished to do with the trousers was socially unacceptable. My body then loudly announced that it looked as though it might rain, which did not seem accurate on meteorological grounds. However, Deena did not object when it led her back into its car and drove them to its flat.

On the way the two humans engaged in some confusing conversation. My body told Deena she should go in for athletics, as she would surely become a world record-holder for the broad jump. Deena replied, "But that would be unfair! I didn't achieve this ability through labor and practice but as a sudden gift. At most," she went on, "I might join a circus. I could get a costume like a beautiful butterfly and flit around the arena. That would earn a lot of money. . . . But really," she said, "I much prefer my present job as the little librarian at the Academy. If I am to fly sometimes, it will be our poetic little secret—after all, I only flew the first time because of you! And then, when I feel like flying, you and I will go secretly to the meadow——"

"Why secretly?" my body interrupted.

"Because I wouldn't want my husband to know about it," Deena responded.

This caused my body to be saddened for reasons not clear to me. It seemed quite subdued for the rest of their trip, not even touching the trousers when they stopped for traffic lights.

However, when they were in my body's flat its mood changed again. They flung themselves on the bed and my body went after the trousers with such determination that it soon had them off. To my surprise, it did nothing with them at all. It simply threw them on the floor and began to attempt to remove Deena's blouse.

"No, please," Deena begged. "I don't want you to look at me. I'm not beautiful—my behind is getting bigger and my breasts are disappearing."

These "breasts" are the glands by which the human females suckle their young. However, they must have additional functions not known to our researchers, because there was quite a long discussion between my body and Deena as to whether or not to uncover them.

There was a good deal more of such discussion, accompanied by a certain amount of struggling as, one by one, the garments of the female were removed. However, the truly amazing part came later. In brief, fellow observers, I was privileged to perceive, and even in a sense to participate in, the reproductive process of the beings from the planet Earth.

I did not at first realize that was what was going on, until the female, Deena, whispered, "Say, be careful you don't get me pregnant—I wouldn't be able to fly with a baby!" At first this only added to the puzzle, for I could not understand why these beings would go through the rather strenuous activities of procreation if, as was implied, they did not in fact wish to procreate. As Deena also said various other things, which were at variance with logic and fact— e.g., "What are you doing to me, my dear?" when it was of course quite obvious what my body was doing—I at first thought the request to avoid pregnancy, too, was not meant to be interpreted in a literal fashion.

However, I have changed my view on that. Fellow observers, I must tell you that this human method of procreation is an astonishing experience. Since few of us have more than one sex, and procreation is merely a routine and automatic biological function, it will be hard for anyone who has not been through it to comprehend what an overwhelming experience it is for humans of both sexes. My body was totally absorbed in it, not only during the actual commission of the act but in its reveries for some time thereafter. Indeed, one could almost say that for a period of days or even weeks my body thought of little else.

This sort of thing continued—went on the observer from Planet 038-Pourquoi—for some little time, during which I gained a deep insight into the motivations and obsessions of the beings from Planet Earth. My body's interest remained focused sharply on the female, Deena, and apparently hers on his. It developed that her "husband" (a term given to the member of the opposite sex who has the principal duty of procreating with a female) was gone on a prolonged trip in relation to his work, and so Deena took a leave of absence from her own employment. They spent all their days together. At night each returned to his own domicile, where my body engaged in reveries, mostly about Deena, but frequently about the comrade director. These reveries differed sharply in content. When the comrade director was the subject of my body's thoughts, the activities envisioned included shouting, berating, and even striking with fists and other objects, while when it was Deena the activities almost always involved some form of procreative activity.

I really feel, fellow observers, that I should not be reprimanded for spending so much time in this single body. It is true that I derived a certain amount of enjoyment from these activities. However, I assure you my purposes were entirely scientific. I would go even farther. I think I would have been quite justified in remaining in that body for a much longer period of time. Indeed, I would have done so, if it had not been for certain events that suggested to me it was time to return here to report.

My body and Deena, as was their custom, had gone to the meadow for another experiment in flying, and in other activities. They then walked through the woods. My body, espying a placard with the words NO HUNTING affixed to a tree, took it down and on the other side wrote an injunction of his own:

The Earth is beautiful!
But for people to see its beauty, they must love one another.
Hey, people! Love each other!

When my body tacked the new orders up on the tree, Deena flung her arms around him and they kissed many more times, both assuring the other that they were happy. But then my body said, "Deena, I have had some strange dreams."

"What sort of dreams, dearest?" the female asked.

"Well," said my body, "when I got home last night, I found a letter waiting for me from my director. It was quite a civil letter, asking me to come in and have a talk with him—'for the purpose of reexamining the question of your machine,' he said."

"But that's wonderful," cried the female.

"Yes," said my body, "but then I dreamed of the director. I dreamed that I was meeting with him. But I didn't look like me. I looked like some sort of monstrous bug! With green feelers and great compound eyes, and jaws that kept moving sideways with a strange clicking noise."

"Oh, my dear," said Deena fondly, "how terrible for you. But of course it was only a dream. Dreams don't mean anything. . . ."

But, of course, in this she was wrong. For those of you who have ever been to my planet of 038-Pourquoi, it will at once be obvious that what my body was describing was, in fact, one of us, the dominant race of that planet! Indeed, my body was describing me!

You will realize, fellow observers, that it is clear that I had allowed some leakage of my own personality into that of my body. I realize the gravity of this. It meant that at least a certain portion of my observations were no longer to be considered entirely objective and valid. This caused me to reflect, with great concentration, on the implications of this unfortunate turn of events, so that I paid very little attention to what my body and the female were doing for some time. I did not fully engage myself with my body again for some hours, until it was already in its flat, preparing to go to sleep.

The telephone rang. It was Deena, sounding very agitated. "My dear," she whispered, as though fearing being overheard. "We can't meet tomorrow. We can't meet ever again, in fact, because my husband has come home."

"But Deena!" my body moaned. "We were so happy together!"

"No," she whispered, "it can't go on. And there's more. I tried to show my husband how I flew and—I couldn't! I was simply unable to get off the ground! It's all gone, my dearest. Forgive me—"

And she hung up.

It was then, fellow observers, that I decided to leave that body and return here to report. It might be alleged that I stayed with that body as long as its experiences were pleasurable, and only left when they ceased to be. That is an unjust accusation, however. I carried out my duties fully and faithfully, and I wish to state that when this meeting is over I will return to that same body for further investigations, whether it is still practicing procreation with the female or not. That concludes my report, Chairman First Observer of Planet 1407-Why.

The packets of energy that swarmed around the electronic device in the lunar crater were silent for a moment. Then the chairman said, "I, First Observer of Planet 1407-Why, must ask a question. You state that the female, Deena, flew through the air. Yet this is not known to be an ability possessed by human females. How do you explain that?"

"I, Second Observer from Planet 038-Pourquoi, have no explanation, Chairman. I can't explain it at all."

"I can," said another voice, speaking up from the cloud of disembodied entities without identifying himself. The chairman said angrily:

"I, First Observer from Planet 1407-Why, request that the being who just spoke follow proper forms and explain himself."

"I am Second Observer from Planet 2311-Perche," said the voice. "I was I who was in the female body, Second Observer from 038-Pourquoi. That is how she was able to levitate."

"What?" roared the chairman, then hastily identified himself according to protocol. "I, First Observer from Planet 1407-Why, as chairman, ask why you didn't stop the experiment at once when you saw your presence was interfering with its reliability?"

"Because I too was enjoying it," said the voice. Once again it failed to identify itself. But no one in the cloud of intellects was in any doubt as to who it was.

The revelations of Second Observer from 2311-Perche created such a stir in the cloud of intelligences that floated inside the lunar crater that it was some time before they realized that Second Observer from 038-Pourquoi was no longer with them.

That observer, in fact, remained absent for some time. The chairman succeeded in restoring order and the cloud proceeded with its exchange of information. But nothing was heard of Second Observer from 038-Pourquoi until a burst of data reached the crater and, when decoded, turned out to be a report from the missing observer.

I wish to announce—reported the observer from 038-Pourquoi —that I have come to the conclusion that I should no longer occupy that same body on a permanent basis, so that now I am in that respect in compliance with the wishes of our chairman. In other respects, however, I am not sure he will approve of what I have been doing. Let me give you a brief outline of the events since I returned to the planet Earth.

I went first to my former body's flat and found it empty. It did not seem to have been occupied for some time, so I went then to the industrial plant where I had first encountered it. My body was not there either. In order to secure information about it, I temporarily entered the body of one of the other employees, a draftsman, and by indirect pressure succeeded in causing it to discuss the absent colleague. "What a pity he's gone," said the draftsman, as though at his own idle inspiration, to the woman at the drawing board next to his. She responded at once.

"A pity! You may well say it is a pity—he was a kind, rather subdued person. All he wanted was for people to respect each other —and to think that he's now in a lunatic asylum!"

"Shocking," said the male body I was inhabiting. "And a waste. After all, the comrade director has now agreed to put his machine into service. He'll be getting a good payment for that, though much good it will do him in the asylum the director drove him to."

"Drove him to?" asked the draftswoman, glaring at him. "That's how much you know about it. There was a woman involved in it, I happen to know." She sighed, admiringly. "Yes," she said wistfully, "you still come across a man now and then who is capable of really suffering for love."

Even after all my experience with Earth beings, I found it a fresh puzzle that they should admire my former body for exactly the same things that caused them to put it in a "lunatic asylum." In order to research this question, I learned the coordinates of the asylum and proceeded there.

It appears that Earth civilizations are incapable of coping readily with cases of ailing consciousness. They are isolated in special hospitals, where doors open only on the outside and windows have special bars. The reason for this must be that such patients are considered dangerous. Yet when I located my former body and entered it, it did not seem to me that either it or the other bodies in the same room could do much harm. The others lay on their beds and looked at the ceiling without speaking. My own body stood at the barred window, staring helplessly out into the yard of the asylum.

It appeared to me that my former body would not be of much

use to me in further explorations, since it was confined to this room. Also my tenancy of it was quite unsatisfactory in other ways, for within its mind was such a storm of memories and painful sensations that I could hardly grasp any of them before it was whirled away and replaced with something new and equally uncomfortable.

Fortunately, at that moment the door opened and two new bodies entered, one of each sex, dressed in white clothing. My body's consciousness defined them as "doctor" and "nurse." It turned abruptly away from the window and complained to the male body:

"Doctor, I've run out of paper again."

"I'll get you some more," the doctor replied. "Are there any other complaints in this room?" None of the other bodies answered, so he added, "In that case, let us just bid each other a peaceful good-night. I'll be on duty and you can call me at any time."

But as he turned to go, my body picked up some scraps of paper from the little table by his bed and handed a few to each of the white-clad bodies. The doctor and nurse took them with only a casual glance, but I was able to make out the writing. It was the same on all of them:

The Earth is beautiful!
But for people to see its beauty, they must love one another.
Hey, people! Love each other!

"Same old thing," commented the doctor in a smiling, good-humored way. "Won't you write something different sometime for a change?"

"No!" cried my body. "That's what matters most. Please hand them round to other people for me."

"Of course," said the doctor, though I observed that the nurse gave him a skeptical look. "It is the most important thing, after all!"

As they were leaving, I transferred into the doctor's body, since it seemed to have more mobility. I was curious to see what it would do with the scraps of paper from my former body, but all it did was drop them in a wastepaper basket.

However, it then put its arm around the body called "nurse" and whispered, "Don't you agree that that is what matters most?"

And then, as the two of them looked up and down the empty asylum hall, it gently led the nurse body into an empty room.

So, fellow observers, as you can see, my researches continue without interruption into these fascinating customs of the Earth people. If any fellow observer would like to research this subject for himself, the nurse body is untenanted . . . and I can promise you a most remarkable experience!

FROM ENGLAND:

Infestation

BY BRIAN W. ALDISS

This is what Marigold Amery did, that morning when the Amery family's *jaskiferianni* returned.

She got breakfast for her bedridden mother, Doris Meszoly, before presiding over the breakfast table downstairs, at which her husband, Hector Amery, and her widowed younger sister, Viola Parkinson-Hill, were present. It was Saturday, so neither Hector nor Viola was at work. Marigold met and kissed Hector when he came in from the garden pool. She then went shopping in the village supermarket, taking the Porsche and joining her friend Mary-Rose Cargill for coffee. She returned home, phoned her son in Manchester, and sat in the garden in the sunshine reading Hesse's *Steppenwolf* for the fifth time.

She had read the novel first some years back, in a Spanish translation in Buenos Aires; Marigold was then living with a musician older than she who had taught her many things. Hesse's book was one of the musician's heritages. Marigold read again of the steppenwolf and its indifference to the life of the bourgeois, and of that "last extremity of loneliness which rarefies the atmosphere of the bourgeois world." She thought, How true, and wondered why this bitter knowledge comforted her. It was then that the *jaskiferianni* materialized inside her, almost knocking her out of her lounger with a cold dose of surprise.

"Enter, you vile poison," she said, as if uttering whatever kind of welcome took off somewhat from the violation of her privacy. By this time, Marigold was more intrigued by it than frightened.

She put a hand over her eyes as cold parts of the thing slipped in among her consciousness. The alien made her get up and walk about the garden, staring at plants, before it flung her back into the chair again. It held her motionless for half an hour while she tried to hum Mozart's 39th at it. But was it listening?

Marigold lay there with the book beside her. The *jaskiferianni* left with no signal of departure beyond a cryptic picture of endless, coiled, piled, gray things. What were they? The thing itself? Its world? There was no clue to scale. Perhaps she looked down momentarily on a mighty structure within which it lived. Perhaps she had glimpsed only a small area of its skin—if it had a skin. The glimpse was wonderful in its very mystery.

She put aside both her repulsion and her attraction, to marvel at life: not simply here, but also somewhere unreachable . . . at the galactic heart, beyond even the flight of Hermann Hesse's thought.

And because the *jaskiferianni* were so unimaginable, every government on Earth was uniting clumsily to think of ways of destroying them. And probably destroying the Amery family too, if necessary.

At twelve-thirty, Marigold heard the sound of her sister's Toyota in the drive. No doubt Viola was returning from a drive to see her latest friend, a creative older man; Marigold approved of the liaison. Jeremy had proved a stabilizing influence on poor Viola.

Marigold was wearing a green-and-gold caftan. She picked up her book and sailed indoors. The two sisters went into Marigold's conservatory-studio, where her latest painting stood unfinished on an easel. They talked inconsequentially while Marigold drank vodka and Viola Perrier water. Hector emerged from his study and called; they went to greet him. He stood smiling from one to the other on the threshold, nervously fingering the wart under his right ear. Preparations for lunch got under way. Marigold's mother's bell sounded, and she took herself slowly upstairs to see what the old lady wanted.

Marigold Amery was a sturdy person with a wide, honest face. Her color was in general golden, including her freckles. She was generally admired, and had many acquaintances, though few close friends. She liked to dress grandly. Her father, now dead, was Hungarian by birth. She had celebrated her fortieth birthday the previous week. Her name as a painter was not well known, although the Tate Gallery had recently bought a painting from her.

She felt the *jaskiferianni* beginning to work in her again, even as she sat with her dying mother.

This is what Viola Parkinson-Hill did, that morning when the Amery family's *jaskiferianni* returned.

She woke with a start at five in the morning, aware that the alien was back and tunneling away inside her, drinking up her every experience as a cat laps milk. Viola lay there naked in her bed, stuck between revulsion and a kind of pleasure that transcended any she had known.

The *jaskiferianni* drove her out of bed and made her put on some clothes. Viola did not choose the clothes. She was powerless to do anything but the alien's bidding. On some matters—some trivial matters, even, like which pair of shoes she should put on—it was firm; on other matters, it seemed vague or indifferent.

Morning light was still milk-dim. The Regency house was wrapped in silence and birdsong. A Siamese cat sat watchful on the landing; even it had been infested.

She went down through the house, and got her car from the garage, and drove recklessly to the coast. The sea was only twenty miles away. All the while, she wrestled in her mind with the cold thing there, saying to it, No, she would not go in the sea, No, she could not swim, No, she hated the sea and would probably drown. To no effect. The *jaskiferianni* drove her just as she drove the Toyota, without consultation, often crashing gears.

And there was the humiliation of having to undress on the public beach, to strip nude, and to plunge into the water. Fortunately, only two distant diggers for lugworms shared the gleaming sand with her.

The *jaskiferianni* loved water. It loved big waves. She had to sport in and out of the breakers, almost drowned, for half an hour. With the alien in her, she swam perfectly. The North Sea was chilly, gray, salty, restless.

Finally, she was allowed to dry herself, dress, and drive home.

The *jaskiferianni* disappeared when she was only a mile along the road, as if impatient at such slow means of travel. It left a nugget of blackness in her mind. Viola called it blackness, although she knew it was something different. Perhaps it was a gift the alien wanted to give her.

She steered the Toyota into a lay-by, and sat back to recover from her experience. It had been fun in a way, the bastard. Perhaps it fancied her. My Ardent Lover from the Stars. When the *jaskiferianni* had first invaded the family and the government had placed the Amerys under surveillance, a scientist—himself showing some interest in Viola—had propounded the theory that the *jaskiferianni* had evolved, over millions of years, away from consciousness into a form of higher automatism, much as the human fetus makes its journey upwards from molecular levels. It could be that the aliens were rediscovering in humanity something they had lost long ago.

Viola thought, Maybe we should try staging some sort of big spectacular show for them, instead of hoping to drive them away. Magic Theater—For Madmen Only. Maybe they're just bored like the rest of us, the bastards. She longed for a drink. A tumblerful of a rough whisky would do the trick. . . .

It was a relief to see Marigold's house again, standing among its pine trees. The hour was still early, but her sister was worrying about her. They comforted each other. Hector appeared in a toweling robe, unshaven, and the three of them sat down to breakfast. Viola poured herself a strong black coffee.

After a shower and change of clothes, she drove over to visit her current lover, a senior producer at the BBC. He was attractive and loneliness had coaxed her to him. They had recently collaborated on a successful triptych of plays, and were hatching a sequel. The *jaskiferianni* returned when they were in mid-discussion. Jeremy was sympathetic and envious—he would have liked to leap into Viola's little psyche himself.

Back home, she went upstairs to sit with her mother, with whom she had never got on as well as had her stronger-minded sister. She passed an hour with Marigold in her studio until it was time for lunch and Hector emerged from his study. Viola could not think how she had once fancied Hector, even allowing for her drink problem. The *jaskiferianni* ferreted out all the details of that involvement. She imagined that aliens of this breed used asexual reproduction and were forever croggled by the human way of doing it . . . the bastards.

Viola Parkinson-Hill was of more slender build than her older sister, more like her Hungarian father, and with something of his dash. She had a wide face, the family face, with golden eyes that had got her a long way in life. Otherwise, she was as dark as her sister was marigold-colored. She suffered from a devouring loneliness. It was a year since her husband had been killed, when the *jaskiferianni* made him drive his car straight over a cliff; it suited her to live temporarily with Hector and Marigold. They got on well; but getting on well was one of Viola's specialties. She was thirty-five.

Even as they ate lunch, she could feel that infernal thing inside her, tasting each mouthful. Viola knew that when it disappeared she would want it back . . . the bastard.

This is what Doris Meszoly did, that morning when the Amery family's *jaskiferianni* returned.

She awoke feeling very ill as usual, and imagined that someone was standing beside the bed. Slowly bringing her head round on the pillow, she discovered that it was not a personage but the curtain, which Marigold had drawn back slightly last thing on the previous night. She dimly remembered moonlight. The curtain hung from pelmet to floor. The old lady admired its graceful folds, trying to think what it reminded her of.

Her ormolu clock, bought by her husband in prewar Vienna, chimed nine from the mantelpiece.

When Marigold entered with a tray, Doris gulped down her medicines greedily. They tasted neither good or bad. The noise was in her ears again. The alien, when it came, seemed a familiar presence, more intimate than the doctor, and she had no fear of it. It was funny to think that only two years ago the aliens had not been known on Earth; now they were a part of everyone's environment, although only six families in England had been infested—and those on and off, at unpredictable intervals.

The *jaskiferianni* was rather like a visitation from Death.

The teaspoon rattled harshly in the saucer as she sipped at her tea.

Doris lay back when she had sampled the breakfast Marigold bought. The alien was tunneling into the decaying storehouse of her memories—perhaps making better sense of them than she could, the old woman reflected.

"Is it with you, Mother?" Marigold asked.

"Death it likes," Doris said faintly, gazing up at her golden daughter. "It's excited. I feel that it's excited by my . . ." After a while, she said, "Perhaps where it comes from, they don't die."

"Then they're lucky."

The old woman mustered her strength to reply. "No, that's not lucky. Aging, that's the trouble. Not death."

She lay back after Marigold had washed her, staring out of the window, barely able to see a distant church spire, bright in summer sun. Her thoughts drifted. Perhaps she would get up for an hour, to sit in the chair by the window.

"Why don't you speak to me?" she said aloud once, twice. No reply.

Viola came up before lunch and talked about her writing plans. Doris had secretly been shocked by the sexual explicitness of Viola's previous plays, and let her thoughts wander while her younger daughter talked. Both she and Marigold were so creative. . . .

She wondered what it must be like out in the heart of the galaxy, unimaginable distances away, where all those varieties of strange life-forms went on incredible journeys. Did they basically make anything *more* of life than humble Earth people, who had traveled no farther than Mars? Was the texture of their lives richer, more intricate?

Occasionally, she thought, the *jaskiferianni* told her something, as it did not do with the other members of its chosen family. Not that it liked her in any way—she remained certain of that—it communicated only to draw on her response. It had told her once, she felt sure, that it was on a long journey between two distant star clusters. Its infestation of the Amery family was its way of passing time until it reached its destination. The Amerys were merely parts of its soap opera. It had no belief in their reality.

Doris could not remember if she had rung her bell for Marigold. But lunch came up just the same, served on a familiar tray.

She did not want it. After tasting the celery soup, she lay back and closed her eyes. Doris tried to remember what celery looked like, growing, but was unable to do so.

Doris Meszoly was the daughter of an actress once famous for her roles in musical comedy, a soubrette who had broken many hearts in her time, before being ruined by her third husband, a horse-racing Scot. Doris was the only fruit of the first marriage, a neglected child who grew into a difficult adolescent. She followed her mother onto the stage, had one success, and then married a romantic Hungarian who might have stepped out of her mother's musicals, except that he was not a count and was broke. Meszoly, however, won the confidence of some London backers, and went into films in a big way, with successes like *He Who Thinks* and *The Passionate Pretenders*, in which his wife played the female lead. They had two daughters, Marigold and Viola, both strong-willed and pretty girls.

Doris, in the last year of her life, was seventy-nine.

This is what Hector Amery did, that morning when the Amery family's *jaskiferianni* returned.

Waking to find that his wife Marigold was already up, he sauntered down into the garden in his bathing shorts. He swam ten lengths of the pool slowly, then took a net and executed his daily ten minutes' maintenance of the pool, scooping the water surface free of drowned insects. The contact with a large silent body of water always refreshed him; it did so even this morning, when he had the worry of the company closure hanging over him.

Hector was returning the net to the filter room when the filthy thing arrived inside him again. It took him and flung him back into the pool. He wrestled with it, and surfaced nearly drowned. The *jaskiferianni* seemed to relish the fear in his mind. Or did it simply play with him, like a cat with a bird? He understood the thing even less than he understood women.

"Get to hell out of there," Hector said. He signaled unnecessarily to one of the scanners that watched over all the Amery estate. Like the other five English families irregularly possessed by these particular aliens, all the activities of the Amerys were subject to international scrutiny. They had long become used to it.

Yet Hector felt profoundly depressed. *Angry* and depressed. The Amerys had been free of the invader for a month, ever since it had forced his brother to step into a busy road and be struck by a passing motorcycle. His brother was still in a nursing home, learning to walk with a prosthetic leg.

Hector ate a perfunctory breakfast with Marigold and Viola, the golden sister and the dark. There was no need to announce that the *jaskiferianni* was back. They knew. You could smell *jaskiferianni*. Well, not smell exactly, but detect their proximity by some interior nose the humans had not known they possessed.

"They flung me into the pool just now," he told his wife.

"Are you all right?"

"Some day we'll get those fuckers."

Once Marigold disappeared on her shopping expedition to the village, Hector tried to talk to Viola, but without much luck. When Viola had come to live with them after her husband had died, she had been practically alcoholic. Hector had got himself into bed with her. It was hard to resist that slender body, that vulnerable smile. Now that she was on the wagon, she would not look his way. As aloof as her sister.

Hector was sure Viola still wanted him, and that only her scruples towards Marigold kept them apart. All the same, he suspected she was having an affair with the boring BBC chap who helped her with her plays.

He deliberately wasted his morning, shutting himself in his study, studying the company reports on his computer terminal—they looked worse every time—and making a long phone call to the company secretary.

Just four years earlier, Hector had taken a daring decision, selling all but a small interest in his own company and investing the capital in his brother's mushrooming firm, which was assembling and marketing ESRSs. They had made a fortune between them; everyone wanted to receive pictures from the Mars station and to own a better communications system into the bargain. The infestation of people all over the world by galactic aliens had changed the picture abruptly. Sales were now approaching zero. The arrival of the visitors from another part of the galaxy had driven them all back to their native hearth.

It looked as if the company would have to be wound up while Hector's brother was still immobilized.

Hector sat slumped for a long while, glaring at the figures in his Video Display Unit.

He did not emerge from his study even when he heard the chink of glasses, and Marigold and Viola talking together.

The *jaskiferianni* visited him once more. This time he was forced to play a videocassette of Viola's first TV play, *The Yearning Fox-Trot*, forced to turn the volume high, forced to watch once more. It was his theory that this alien thing, from whatever awful utilitarian culture it came, could not distinguish between fact and fiction. Inevitably, its view of life would be bizarre in the extreme: like vision without perspective.

But when one gave it thought, how curious was the human obsession with fantasies, lies, and fictions of all kinds. Perhaps you had to come to Earth to savor such richness.

Hector heard Marigold's mother's bell ring for attention as the *jaskiferianni* left him. He remained where he was in the study, doing nothing until lunch, brooding.

Hector Amery had been a well-known athlete, strong in swimming and running. His lean, tanned face was youthful, his fair hair did not show its gray. After breaking an ankle at the age of twenty-three, he'd gone into the marketing of sports clothes, rejigging his father's aging shirt business. By thirty, he was able to bring in a younger partner and to travel. At a party for expatriate British given by the Parkinson-Hills in Buenos Aires—Sir Kendal Parkinson-Hill was in the diplomatic service—Hector had met the post-Expressionist painter Marigold Meszoly. She was his miracle. Hector lured her away from the Swedish musician she was living with and married her.

He was now forty-three. The marriage, like life itself, had not given Hector all he expected. That, he told himself, was because he had expected too much. And then the *jaskiferianni* had arrived unexpectedly, and fouled up his life.

Marigold, Viola, and Hector gathered for lunch. Hector took a luncheon tray up to his mother-in-law and then poured glasses of

Rioja wine for his wife and himself; his sister-in-law kept to Perrier. He switched off the wall screen, which, this being Saturday, was mainly occupied by sports he no longer wished to know about.

The scanners that covered them from different points of the room could not be turned off. The lens watched as Marigold sliced a pizza in three.

"Well, they're back all right," Hector said, lifting his glass. "And I take it that we were all occupied in turn?" The *jaskiferianni* were always "they." "The bastards nearly drowned me."

"They nearly drowned me in the sea," Viola said. "They like to play rough."

Hector said, "They're back, we don't know for how long. I hate those accursed things as I've never hated anything else in my life. I would willingly blow my brains out when they are in there, if anyone thought that that would rid us of the things." He thumped his fist on the table so that the cutlery rattled.

"Oh, they're rather amusing in their way," Viola said, driven into one of her teasing fits by Hector's solemn, flushed face. "They certainly make solitude easy. You could advertise the *jaskiferianni* as complete substitutes for all forms of sociability. They scare you sometimes, but it is rather a thrill to have something so completely intimate with one, knowing all one's naughtiest secrets."

"It disgusts me," Hector said. "I simply feel infested."

"Perhaps your secrets are naughtier than mine," Viola said, with a laugh, hoping it was not so.

He hit the table again. "These things are just having a holiday and using us for their fun. They killed your husband, Viola, they nearly killed my brother, they have bankrupted us, they made you an alcoholic—we're all under threat of death from their whims. How can you take it so lightly? It's unbearable, degrading."

"They used to enjoy my alcoholic bouts. They lead very dull teetotal lives. Adultery and circuses are not known among them. It must be incredibly boring, having to travel through space. What are they, exponents of a super-civilization or some sort of glorified commercial travelers?"

Marigold finished a mouthful of salad and said, "It's true that our lives are in danger. I suppose I am terrified of the *jaskiferianni*, yet I'm more curious than terrified. For all their powers, they seem simple and brutal things—almost elemental. As subtle as a brick. Yet they show a fascination with art."

"I don't think they know what art is," Hector said. "They come from some horrible authoritarian culture in the stars—perhaps the galactic center is just a kind of gigantic anthill—and they cannot distinguish between what is real and what is imaginary. That's why they want to run *The Yearning Fox-Trot* so often. They can't make it out."

"Those unbearable journeys among the stars," Viola exclaimed. "One light-year must be terribly like another. It sounds to me as if they are longing to escape from the unendurable quality of their own existence, and they find the life of an ordinary family like ours endlessly fascinating. As Mother suggested, they may be immortal —that's another kind of burdensome journey. After all, one year's much like another."

"Immortal or not, some day we're going to get those fuckers," Hector said.

At that moment, as if on cue, Doris's bell rang. The meal broke up. Afterwards, Viola served coffee.

Hector took his cup from her and wandered to the window to glare moodily out at the sunlit garden. He would have to go and see his brother this afternoon. This house would probably have to be sold up. What a disgrace!

The fact had to be faced. No one wanted to buy the company's ESRSs. One common factor among the six English families infested by the *jaskiferianni* was that each owned an Earth Satellite Receiving Station. Not that that proved anything. But people were frightened. *He* was frightened. And when you suddenly learned that there were almost magical ways of communicating—really communicating—then you were not going to invest in an expensive chunk of home technology like a receiving station.

If only he had stayed in sports gear. . . .

Those fuckers!

Marigold took her coffee alone in her studio. She contemplated the Picasso sketch on her wall. She switched on her personal stereo, and her head was filled with the music of Mozart's *Don Giovanni*, the passage heralding the approach of the guest of stone.

She spoke into the room, confident that her face, her words, were being picked up in the *Jaskiferianni* Information Center in Birmingham.

"I know you are all thinking like Hector. You would love to blow all these aliens to kingdom come. Yet they are visitors, here voluntarily, and the *jaskiferianni* at least seem less malevolent than curious. They do not even require rare metals, like some of the other galactic species infesting people elsewhere. I want to suggest to you a different approach to the problem, one involving no bloodshed."

She was silent a moment, letting the music flow. After all—but one could hardly say that aloud, certainly not to the uniformed men in Birmingham—was there any great difference between human and *jaskiferianni* loneliness? Did they not offer a unique, priceless way to communicate, if it could be understood? Weren't all human art forms infestations of the material world, designed to overcome it?

The *jaskiferianni* must be trapped.

She said into the flowered silence of her studio, "I presume you are prepared to give the Amerys financial aid on a large scale, if we arrive at a bright idea?"

She knew the answer. The Controller's face would be up on her wall-screen soon enough. She said, "Viola and I will create a complex work of art—with a little help from our friends. The work will be a marathon play, showing in minutest detail the complexity of relationships in an ordinary family like ours; but that family will be in communication with a galactic culture, which will be depicted as immense, crushingly powerful, philistine, bleak, sexless, deathless—and therefore lifeless. . . . The very opposite of our vulnerable and transitory little family groupings . . . permanent but without hope of joy . . ." She was improvising as she talked. "Perhaps these galactic races are the descendants of insect communities, worms, wasps, ants, internal parasites. I don't know. I tend to visualize them as hot-rodding maggots tunneling through the cheese of hyperspace. They have a power of singlemindedness beyond our comprehension. But we have something beyond their comprehension, and there's the trap by which we catch them: a sort of super science-fiction epic so finely imagined and portrayed that they will not be able to tell if it is real or not. *Then* perhaps a real dialogue will begin.

"I believe they need our help and we theirs."

Marigold trembled as she spoke. There was no race on Earth without its art. But to take art to an entire species—maybe dozens of species—without art . . . perhaps it would destroy them. At the least it would alter them entirely.

Maybe Mozart would be more effective than nuclear warheads. She thought of how English culture had enriched the globe—and of how England depended for its enrichment on contributions from all over the globe. Perhaps the galaxy might become dependent on Earth in the same way.

Her thoughts made her dizzy. She sat down in her favorite creaking rattan chair.

Then the *jaskiferianni* was back, suddenly in place, like chill coins dropping into her interior. She gripped the arms of the chair. *Don Giovanni* still washed over her.

Maybe it could read her plan. Yet these galactic conquerors were, and she knew it intuitively, stupid in all sorts of human ways she was not. She was not to be defeated by a worm.

Even if they killed her, Pablo was waiting, and Mozart too.

They stole something they could never have.

They could be caught.

And civilized.

In the Blink of an Eye

BY CARLOS M. FEDERICI
Translated by Joe F. Randolph

Minsky's behavior was what first tipped me off.

"What's with that bald-headed guy?" I had to ask.

Loureiro laughed. He was a thin, good-humored provincial whose legs, a while back, had carried him across three streams to arrive at the capital and get his wish. His laugh was filled with innate mischief.

"The same as usual," he replied. "Galloping craziness."

I shook my head. After taking off my coat and scarf, I hung them on the coatrack and proceeded to get settled for the workday. Not without the customary grumbling, I turned on the ceiling light. Even at midday, our bureaucratic burrow got about the same amount of sunlight as a standard catacomb. Typical of the public administration in my city, I suppose. . . .

"No," I disagreed. "What's happening now has nothing to do with the type of manias afflicting Minsky! I tell you it's something—"

"Oh, come on, buddy! Don't you know him, after living side by side with him for almost twenty years in this dungeon? Does he still surprise you? Or did you forget that he was committed a couple of times to get his brains rearranged?"

My look was more anxious than I intended.

"I keep telling you it's something else. What I just saw—"

"Huh?"

I waited, but he made no comment.

"You're not gonna laugh at me?"

On the contrary, Loureiro was very quiet. He got up with a certain rigidity, took off his glasses, looked first at one and then another pane in the light coming through the window, and then turned his eyes to me without a word. In the same pose, he put his glasses back on and walked out. The waves of his resentment were distastefully left hovering in the air.

That figured, I told myself. At least from his viewpoint. I had just violated an unwritten law of social convention. Since I was classified as the most serious individual on this bureaucratic team, I certainly had no right to act out of character without forewarning, much less to crack jokes of that sort. It was not appropriate for a specialized department head.

I shrugged. It was relatively early. The atmosphere in the Municipal Archives Department would still be peaceful for another hour and a half, until the rest of our skeleton crew wandered back in from lunch. Conditions were more than favorable; I was glad.

So I could hardly complain about anything, and I had to use such intimate moments whenever they came along. That is why, I suppose, I mused over the dreams and chimeras of youth, illusions of a brilliant writing career, and an altogether unique kind of faith that disappeared along with the hair on my head. (It is my belief that you have to face it. We are well on the way to becoming a country up exclusively of government workers . . . the children of constant crisis and chronic underdevelopment, a little like puppets superficially animated, provided with the orifices and limbs necessary for doing necessary duties. Supervisor spreads and flabby muscles, a vacant look with gray matter the consistency of Jell-O. Maybe it is an insidious form of social, although painful, equalization based on a single fundamental model.)

At first, I only tried to temporize with the suffocating atmosphere. I counted on a definite opportunity, any month now, for the purposes of building my expectations on foundations more stable than my orphaned juvenile enthusiasm. But so much time had passed!

Concession after concession, retreat after retreat, the process became irreversible. The toad would never be turned into a prince.

Unless . . .

If these rumors had some basis . . . If Minsky's . . .

I pursed my lips. I could not allow myself to engage in conversations with myself. Self-control—that had become my permanent slogan.

Rumors.

Gossip.

And all those articles published in fringe magazines . . .

Intelligences living in distant galaxies thousands of light-years from our earth. Mental waves, dynamic energy . . . And the total possession of human bodies and minds to be used for mysterious purposes.

Were they fantasies . . . or was there some possibility that they were real? Apparently, there were reliable reports. Reports that spoke of a certain irresistible force no one was immune to. And also some specific process of sudden effectiveness that overrode the occasional victim's will with astounding speed.

In the . . . blink of an eye, so to speak.

I got away from them . . . by losing myself among the others, I avoided detection.

They don't know my plans! Otherwise, they would never let . . . They denounced me. Nobody heeded my appeal! They did not want to understand . . . They look down upon all those like us. They don't believe we have a right to fquh! Of course, they don't know . . . They have no way of knowing what it feels like when . . .

They mutilated me! To keep me from doing it, they . . .

Oh, Multipotents! If they ever discover—

"Hi, there, sweetie."

I was back again. There was no doubt that she thought of herself as the ultimate femme fatale. With just a couple of bats of her eyelashes, she twisted young men around her little finger. It was one of the fastest ways to make a meteoric rise in our city hall. Obviously, one needed certain basic endowments, and I am not talking about trifles like words per minute or impeccable spelling.

"How's it going with you, you plump thing?" she smiled, more syrup than question in her greeting. Leaning across the desk separating us, she offered me her demanding cheek. "A little kiss, a little kiss!"

Only out of necessary courtesy did I do as she requested. At one time, that was a while back, I had viewed Lucy in a different light, but . . . For the time being, she had become the property of management (second floor, air conditioning, and plush wall-to-wall carpeting), with more overtime on the payroll than required for mere bureaucratic duties.

"My, how serious you look, chubby!"

"I was just meditating," I replied.

"Aw! And you wouldn't let me in on it?" Her lips curved into routine innuendo.

"Nothing would make me happier. Maybe you could explain several difficult points to me!"

Of course, there were no personal digs in all this give-and-take. The fruit that Lucy coveted was on higher branches than mine. She was merely practicing her general tactics on me—after all, I was a man, was I not?

"Oh, I'm sorry. Duties call." I pointed to papers covering my desk. "I can't delay these files anymore, or I'll be on the carpet."

With feigned interest, Lucy got close to me in order to look over my shoulder, the soft parts of her anatomy pressing against me. "What about Julio?"

"I wish I knew where that one's gone off to!" I said, shrugging. Rubbing right against her produced some pleasant animal friction. "It's no use waiting for him. I learned my lesson about that."

In fact, Julio Argüeli, theoretically under me, was the eternal escapee from the administrative yoke. He had a whole life beyond these four walls—wife, kids, mistresses, a couple of moonlighting jobs that were much more lucrative though less stable. He was still young, of course.

"Your underling's a shameless scoundrel," Lucy laughed.

"Did you come by for some special reason?" I asked.

"No, I just wanted to say hello! Bye, dear. I'll let you get on with your work."

She took a little sunlight with her when she left. I gave a near sigh. Julio Argüeli, that joker Loureiro, Lucy—they all had a few sparks of life left in them. Burning life, that was consuming each one in its own way.

Minsky and I, on the other hand . . .

I turned pale. Would that not be just the response? Guys *like him and me.*

Then I wondered how much resistance we would put up to an attack of alien possession (should it happen) if our strength had escaped us, like water running through the cracks in a disintegrating dam.

The routine of daily work took me away at that point. It was completely dark when I finally decided to call it a day and emerged from that bureaucratic swamp.

There was hardly a soul left in the building. The enormous brick-and-cement mass of city hall, however, was still alive, like a drowsy beast. The data-processing people worked virtual round-the-clock shifts, as did the janitors and security guards. But in my stronghold of the archives section, I was completely alone.

The door opened with such force that it cracked the wall it banged against.

"What the hell!" I jumped out of my seat in a flurry of type-written paper.

I was watching the most unusual scene imaginable. I barely managed to make out a feverish, whirling mass of arms and legs. Then a human body, jolted by acrobatic paroxysms, appeared before my dumbfounded sight.

That can't be Minsky!

But it was. Now he was sprawled on top of a cabinet; then he jumped back down on the floor, stretching both arms to the limits of their ligaments or maybe beyond, twisting his neck in an incredible manner, bending his back to the breaking point. Something like a parody of Gene and Fred reunited, only without background music and projected at the wrong speed.

He did not notice my presence. For my part, I felt unable to lift a finger. I thought I had stopped breathing, too. What in the hell was going on? Minsky suffered from depression, not hypereuphoria!

The most impressive thing was that all this was taking place in absolute quiet. You could only hear his shoes slapping against whatever surface, wood or tile; there was also a muffled counterpoint of air forced through clenched teeth. But that was all—if you disregarded the pounding of my heart. It was a real miracle that I got out of that situation without shoe marks all over my body.

As abruptly as it began, the show stopped. Whatever it was, it had taken every last ounce of Minsky's strength. I imagine he had to have a reasonable respite to regain his strength.

"Like a shirt hung up to dry," I mumbled, fascinated.

Limp, stretched out in a chair, Minsky was breathing, though almost imperceptibly.

I bit my lower lip. Then I snorted. The most appropriate thing for me to do, I told myself, would be to get help. On the other hand . . .

Guys like him and me.

Minsky, Ephraim. Son of Jewish immigrants, fugitives from the rigors of Czarist Russia. Racial traumas combined with a personality of characteristics described as the classic manic-depressive condition. Including, certainly, an overprotective mother, beginning with the abandonment of the family unit on the part of the *paterfamilias*. A little more than sixty years of that; then he retreated into a shell, after the death of his overpowering mother.

I felt that my hunch was panning out. If, as might well be the case, the alien invasion was really getting under way, would they not have come to our tiny country, the *Ultima Thule* of the alternative to change, last?

I decided to get help. I had to leave the office, since one of Minsky's superchoreographic numbers had disabled my phone.

I should not have done it. During my short absence, Minsky got up from the chair, walked down the hallway behind me, got— without being seen by anybody—to the elevator, went up to the observation deck, and jumped to the street, twenty-four stories straight down.

Useless. Oh, holy Multipotents! . . . inadequate.
That host in particular wasn't . . . I feel as if I've been split into

*a myriad of individuals. The very fibers of my existence are separating.
Multipotents! Merciful Multipotents! I feel as if I'm going to—*

*I need, I need . . . Oh, veils of the Multipotents, I need to fquh!
. . . I've been mutilated, they've torn off my . . . but I have to do it.*

Through one of these usable forms, I—

Oh, kind Multipotents! If only—

The police report called it an accident. No one seemed greatly concerned. I do not think I saw the notice in more than one newspaper.

Alone in the office, during moments when there was no chance of being disturbed (my wristwatch said 10:45 P.M.), I got to reviewing the facts, two weeks after the sad event.

What had happened to my friend Minsky made me begin to take the whole subject seriously. I dusted off as much material as I could find relating to extraterrestrials, possible space invasions, teleportation of alien minds, etc., and systematized the big pile of information according to the limited intellect God had given me. Discarding sensationalist trash, I retained only that which, in my best judgment, deserved a modicum of credulity. I also got busy recontacting old correspondents, those in Europe that some time ago had me as a corresponding colleague, and I had no qualms about prevailing upon the good offices of old friendships made during the time of my association with several print media to supply me with information.

The upshot of all that seemed to be more than promising. There was a solid basis to suppose that the incredible was true. The rumored alien invasion was really happening . . . and with the shameful complicity of certain governments, and the bribable mass-communication media! That was the conclusion, no matter how much it cost me to get there.

I bent over my well-used typewriter.

There was a ream of 8½-by-11-inch paper beside it, and when the smoking keys finally stopped their frenetic clatter, only three or four sheets were left untouched. The wastepaper basket was overflowing. My attaché case opened to gobble up a fat manuscript. Not too lengthy, certainly nothing professional, but on the other hand quite readable . . . and as explosive as an intercontinental missile!

I leaned back in the chair, furniture and human groaning in unison. Fragments of gray light were slinking through the skimpy skylight; the sounds of an awakening city were now starting to reach me from the street.

When I left, at first light on a chilly Saturday, I went floating on the warm sensation of imminent fame. My day had come . . . finally! This material was my passport to a new life.

Things changed radically, nevertheless, at noon on Monday when I got out of bed. With a bitter taste in my mouth and cobwebs in front of my eyes (not that I went on a drinking binge instead of working on the investigation!), I set about the exploits of a new day.

Where had my dreams of glory gone?

"In reality, I don't have anything extraordinary," I had to admit to my left-handed bidimensional twin, the ubiquitous dweller in mirrors. "How well I know that I lack the key element!"

Motives.

Purposes.

The *why* of it all.

Could it be experimentation? Some prescribed ritual of strange and undecipherable significance? A sort of usefulness that escapes any earthbound logic? I tried to coordinate the rhythm of my deep thinking with the movements of my toothbrush, but immediately fell behind. The hibernation my thinking mechanisms had been exiled to during the course of my extended period of rusting bureaucratic routine had not done my gears any good, I realized.

The next step in the program was obvious. I had to sit down and go over the collated material as much as necessary to clear up the mystery. The office would be the ideal spot. Fortunately, hawk-eyed Loureiro had taken a few days of leave. It was more than likely that my subordinate, Julio, had reverted to his customary absenteeism.

So it went; nevertheless, and in spite of completing the plan point by point, after three hours of concentration I still had not reached the end of the tunnel.

"Undoubtedly, it must be some great event," I mumbled. "But what the hell *is* it?"

According to the documents I studied, there should exist a great number of "technified" civilizations in the universe, confirming the good Dr. Asimov's statement. But incalculable intergalactic distances intervene. No conceivable type of propulsion would be able to reduce them to manageable proportions. The theory of cosmic shortcuts put forth by Sagan and others would apparently remain no more than a nice hypothetical formulation, devoid of any pragmatic worth.

So not many options remained. Discarding the physical plane, one would have to search for the solution in another dimension. Finally, the use of mental projection came to be feasible without the term being defined with due precision, at least for the average intellect—like this writer's.

Anyway, the diverse interpretations proposed were unanimous as far as the onerousness of the technique to use in order to achieve said projection, by which it would be possible to move a body at will (in general, completely different from the creature acting as the medium) to project definite gestures or actions at remote distances. As all the sources consulted agreed, huge amounts of energy were needed to effect the process. It would be impossible to expend it on trifles!

"Therefore," I murmured, "motives such as curiosity and even spying could be ruled out. No doubt their aims would be much broader and higher than all that!"

One account, apparently well-documented, maintained that in the Hawaiian Islands some time ago alien conferences and conventions were held. Through the facilities furnished by a definite number of human beings (whose possession by extraterrestrial entities would turn them into little more than magnificent marionettes for the wishes of beings billions of parsecs away), they could discuss, for instance, border limits between galaxies or acts of aggression on an outerspace scale. The Andromeda Federation versus the United Planets of the Cancer constellation, let us say.

Could be. But if such were the case, how did Minsky fit in? His spasmodic final tap dancing certainly did not seem to bear any relation to any type of convention!

Rrrrrrring.

That managed to wrench me from my thoughts. How did it occur to anyone to call at such an inconvenient time!

"Hello," I barked into the mouthpiece.

'This is the director," a dry voice answered. "Is Lucy there?"

The color of my face became Doppler-effect red. Sitting up in my seat, my voice changed tone according to the dictates of good form.

"Uh . . . Excuse me, sir. I thought it was one of Loureiro's jokes. That guy can call at any moment to pester me!"

"Isn't Loureiro away on leave?"

"Hmm!" I cleared my throat. "Uh . . . yes, certainly, I'm sorry. I forgot. Um . . . Were you asking for Lucy, Director? She hasn't been here!"

"You sure? Because she left for the depository in search of an old file, but since she's been gone so—"

"How long ago did she go down? I realize I was so wrapped up in these, uh, payroll costs," I improvised, "that she might well have gone down the hallway without my noticing. Do you want me to take a look in the depository, just in case?"

"If you'd be so kind. If you don't find her, give me a buzz, please."

I stacked all my papers together as best I could and put them in a drawer that I locked. This was something not to be neglected just to appease my present . . . boss.

As was to be expected, the place was like the Mojave desert in the dry season. Not a soul in sight. To get to the depository, you had to go down the hallway and then down a couple of flights of stairs, steeper than I liked, to the nether regions where Apollo had never thrust his golden daggers.

It was the same either at twelve noon or twelve midnight, like in those old movies that had given me pleasure more than thirty years ago. Gloomy dwellings of shadow, illuminated only by dying light bulbs, tiny animals scurrying around at will, disquieting squeaks. The door to the depository was ajar. As I got closer, I started hearing the sound.

I could not quite place it, but . . .

"What?"

I stopped, cocking my ear. Suddenly, I stopped hearing it. I attributed it to my imagination, mechanically shrugged my shoulders, and went in.

Even before putting on the light, I felt someone's presence, and once again the sound, still indistinct. Like a kind of faint, almost imperceptible buzzing, similar to the wings of a dragonfly flapping . . . or else . . .

The short hairs on my neck were standing on end. Now that my eyes had gotten adjusted to the pervasive darkness, I made out in the faint light filtering in behind me the shape of a human figure sitting next to the spot where the desk should be.

But why had she not said anything . . . or else moved?

"L-Lucy?" I stuttered in a thin voice.

Bzzzzzzzzz . . . bzzzzzzzzz . . . bzzzzzzzzz . . .

I could hear it if I stopped breathing. But I suddenly took a very deep breath. Was it my imagination, or was some peculiar smell floating in the area that was seemingly familiar to me?

I think it was due to reflex action on the part of my arm and hand that the light came on.

"Lucy! What's wrong?"

She was resting in a dusty chair, leaning a little against the beat-up desk where old files were stacked up. She remained motionless. Her features, ordinarily yielding to a thousand emotive impulses, showed a most neutral state of passivity.

I got up close. Would it be all right to touch her . . . shake her, perhaps?

"Are you okay, Lucy?" My fingers were paralyzed scant millimeters from her.

There was something right in front of my eyes . . . something like a very subtle miniature fog. I was slow in realizing what it was.

"Oh, God," I said like a sigh.

It was Lucy's thick eyelashes. They were moving with inhuman rapidity, stirring the air and buzzing.

And that smell! All of a sudden I knew what it was—ozone! The smell that is usually detected after a storm.

Or also, I recalled, under less conventional circumstances. According to the literature on extraterrestrials I had lately been cramming myself with, a certain amount of ozone was released every time an alien took possession of a human body.

Sweet existence. Time without time.
Fquh.
Finally, I can . . . There's no longer any past or future. Nothing matters but my fquhing, fquhing, and fquhing. You know very well . . . almost as if you will again have Subelytra, who my executioners destroyed as a means of discipline . . . did they destroy me? Executioners? Discipline? Everything has dissolved into nothing. My universe is here . . . fquhing, fquhing, and fquhing.

This is the only goal of my existence as well as its recurrent beginning. I am fquhing (bzzzzzzzzz, bzzzzzzzzz, bzzzzzzzzz), and this constitutes the entire whole of totality.

Fquhing (thanks to my host), and fquhing . . . and fquhing.

(They say it's a degrading, infamous, and repugnant vice. I call it heavenly bliss.)

I am here, in front of her. I have no intention of moving. I will try to prevent what happened to Minsky.

Her eyelashes have kept blinking crazily, with brief pauses on two or three occasions, as if to get their strength back. I am trying to determine if there is any rhyme or reason to them, if they are trying to transmit some message.

Several hours have passed.

I need to think. I have to review several of my hypotheses.

Never would it occur to me that Lucy, that nice-looking epitome of vitality, was going to be chosen to house one of those . . . entities. People like Minsky and me . . . As can be seen, such considerations do not count at all.

Maybe they see us as a uniform type of creature. Minsky, brutally abandoned as soon as they had squeezed as much as they could out of him, would no doubt have fallen into the acutest depressive crisis in his life. He was pushed to suicide. Such minor points apparently do not enter the possessor's purview.

Its objectives—I have to find out who they are!

No doubt, their motives have to be . . . eschatological. Certainly valid on an intergalactic level, way beyond our inherently limited intellect.

I have to get to the bottom of this.

This is my big opportunity! I can write the story of the century, the biggest best-seller in history. . . . Say good-by to disappointment! Hello, fame!

The masses will applaud me!

My whole life will be transformed . . . in the blink of an eye. Amen!

FROM POLAND:

Particularly Difficult Territory

BY JANUSZ A. ZAJDEL
Translated by Wiktor Bukato

Standing in front of the Ministry building, Wiktor had a sudden feeling of being alone again: of repossessing his body as a sole owner and disposer. For the first time perhaps in his life, he felt the real taste of personal freedom—in contrast to the total subjugation that he had been experiencing since early that morning.

He made hurried adjustments in his clothes, which had been slightly ruined during the struggle with the security officer and the doorman. He was still conscious of his face, red with shame because of all those incidents with him as the main hero—and because of all the nonsense he uttered that day toward very important officials of state administration.

He looked around uneasily and saw with relief that, apart from a dirty tramp taking a nap on a bench nearby, there were no other witnesses of the comic scene, which had just taken place in front of the building. Wiktor had never before been thrown—or rather carried—out.

He was free from the domination of his internal oppressor, not directed anymore to run along the city streets, Wiktor sat down on the bench beside the sleeping individual. His feet ached. His stomach required seeing to.

The alien force had struck when he had been walking toward his office, looking for a nice place to have breakfast. Against his will and intention he had found himself in the University library. There the mysterious "something" dwelling in his mind had requested the astronomical atlas and then, using the coordinates, had found a star called Megrez in the Ursa Major constellation. After repeating several times—with Wiktor's lips—the name of the star, the unusual visitor had directed the steps of his host to the Ministries of Foreign Affairs and of Culture, as well as to some other government agencies. Everywhere, speaking through Wiktor, the being presented itself as "the delegate of the Megrez System with interpreter."

That was enough to make the officials smile sarcastically. None of them listened to the rest of the Megrezian's story with any real attention; after all, the visitor was not able to present any material evidence of its identity, while its external appearance was that of a fair-haired, mustached, middle-aged man. No wonder that every time the stranger from a far-out world had managed to utter just a few sentences of his oration, all the officials called for a doorman or security officer. So many cranks presented themselves these days as delegates of alien races!

Only the director of the Foreign Affairs Minister's office displayed a bit of diplomatic tact and professional routine. Having listened to a few sentences from the stranger, he looked out of the window and said, "Excuse me, sir, is that your flying saucer standing outside the front door? If so, then kindly move it somewhere else. The doorman will show you the parking site for visitors."

At that point the Megrezian was authentically flustered, as if somehow ashamed to admit that it—a very important delegate of an alien race—traveled around the city on foot. Before it could respond, the summoned doorman showed Wiktor out of the premises.

Thrown out of governmental offices—sometimes by force, for the alien often reacted with violence—Wiktor could not even feel resentment toward the people who had treated him with such disrespect. His incredible visitor had not an ounce of diplomatic talent, not even the most elementary intercultural good manners. It was clear that the Megrez System delegate had not rehearsed its part very well. It had not made any effort to look into the resources of its host's memory. That could have given it an insight into the psychology of an Earthman from the country the alien was supposed to operate in.

Since Wiktor had finally comprehended what had happened to him in the morning, he was anxious to grant the E.T. all possible aid—to assist it in its mission, to help it in working out an effective plan of action.

Alas! The alien appeared to be a peremptory individual, to all possible extents presumptuous about its own abilities. It totally ignored Wiktor. It crowded his personality into a far corner of his mind. It treated the human as a subordinate, using his mind as a portable translating computer. No cooperation was possible.

Wiktor found the situation totally insufferable. There could be no talk of partnership and cooperation when one side reached for all the information accessible in the mind of the other, offering not even a thought of its own in return. . . .

"No! I won't let myself be treated like that!" Wiktor rebelled when he was at last free from alien control. "I can understand that it is faced with a difficult task. No doubt it has a devil of a boss and a lot of problems in an unfamiliar location. But to hell with it! I have my own boss! He is not pleased when someone takes a day off without telling him in advance. Since that Megrezian lug is able to penetrate my mind and find there things I almost forgot myself, that means it knows everything that I know. So why doesn't it bother with such elementary things as breakfast for me, or a phone call to my boss? This is sheer impertinence and contempt. I don't feel like being nice to it!"

It must be admitted here that all the morning Wiktor had honestly tried—from that narrow corner of his mind into which he had been crowded by the rampant personality of the Megrezian— to establish some sort of partnership. He hoped at first to define some mode of cooperation. Wiktor believed some *modus vivendi* was indispensable, in the situation when two personalities shared the same body and the same mind. To no avail! The visitor made itself the sole possessor of both these places. It gave no recognition to any rights of its host. To tell the truth, it didn't once even address Wiktor directly. It never introduced itself properly, never uttered a word of greeting, not to speak of apologies for such a sudden invasion.

"Either this is a particularly rude individual or, even worse, *all* of them are bad-mannered!" thought Wiktor. "One way or another, if it comes back and continues to treat me like this, I'll try to retaliate!"

The empty stomach and pained feet made him feel growing dislike toward his visitor. In the beginning the adventure had seemed to offer fascinating prospects. But after hours of running around the city and making himself an object of jokes, he wished his contact with an alien race would end.

At the same time Wiktor realized that after the possible return to his mind the Megrezian would be able to study in detail all the thoughts he had had during its absence. Thus there was no point in preparing any plots against the visitor. Even the most secret of Wiktor's plans could not remain hidden.

"Impertinent cosmic cad!" he snarled, rising from the bench.

The man reclining against the other end of the bench, who had looked like a napping drunk, was not asleep at all. He had been observing Wiktor for some time, and at the moment of the latter's sudden exclamation he moved suddenly.

"You were saying?" he inquired.

"Not to you," muttered Wiktor, dragging his feet toward the street.

"Just a minute!" The individual from the bench overtook him in one unexpectedly agile leap. "Hang on a sec. You said, 'cosmic cad.' What was that about?"

Wiktor walked on, not looking back at the intruder. But the stranger apparently did not wish to bug off.

"Just a sec, man." He assumed an ingratiating tone. "I saw the watchdog fool kick you out of the Ministry. I've had the same thing happen myself, honest! Ain't that one of yours from Aldebaran, by chance?"

Wiktor stopped to face the man.

"From Aldebaran?" he asked, suspiciously surveying a smallish bald man in crumpled clothes.

"I'm sitting here, waiting . . . and what's worse, I'm sobering up. And when I'm sober, this Aldebaranian son of a bitch'll get me again and make me say that shit again," the drunk eagerly explained. "So when I saw you thrown out, I thought, maybe my Aldebaranian found itself a new sucker and would leave me alone. . . ."

"Tough luck. Mine is from the Megrez System," said Wiktor sympathetically.

"And it goes into you every morning and drives you until the evening, with short breaks for food?"

"I don't know. Today's my first day," muttered Wiktor.

"My sympathies!" The drunk offered him a handshake. "You ain't seen nothing yet. We've got to stick together, you and me; otherwise they'll do us in, those bastards! I'm Adam. See what that son of a bitch did to me? It's been two weeks since I can't get it off my back. I've been sacked, I've spent all my money on liquor and this . . . this mother-fucker comes every day, several times every day and checks to see if maybe I'm sober again. It tried to make me to spill my own liquor down the drain but I've been able to find some guy now and then who'd buy me a drink. You wouldn't have anything of the sort, would you?"

"Maybe I would, at home. So you say it's been two weeks? And I was hoping that my own had gone away and would leave me alone. . . ."

"Don't kid yourself, man. I've been counting on that, too. But it seems, unfortunately, that they can't so easily find such perfect hosts as we are. Very few are easy to control, my Aldebaranian says."

"So he talks to you?"

"In a pig's eye! He treats me like I was an animal. But I can hear what it says with my mouth to other people. Since I had that drinking idea, it had to explain my condition to people it wanted to talk to. It told everybody it couldn't find anybody else who'd be a proper host for its personality. It's good that everything it said was taken as a drunk's mumbo jumbo. This way I get it off my back for longer spells, because when I'm drunk, it runs about looking for someone else. Maybe it will find somebody, someday. . . ."

Wiktor smiled. "A good method, only a bit expensive. And not so healthy, either!"

"Just give me enough to drink and I'll show it!" bragged Adam. "But now I feel dangerously sober."

"All right, let's go," said Wiktor resignedly. "Maybe you are right. Maybe we should stick together. . . ."

"Much obliged, man!" Adam was really glad. "We ain't givin' in to any space bastards!"

"If that Aldebaranian of yours watched you better, you couldn't get drunk," remarked Wiktor when both men were walking to a taxi stand.

"They have to take a nap themselves. It's a good thing they do. They can't stay awake all the time; sometimes they disappear from inside their hosts."

"Maybe they are inside us all the time and listen to what we say about them?"

"So let 'em, bastards! Anyway, it's we who are at home, and they who are the intruders. And if they want to hear what I think of them, I can do it right away! I've never made it a secret." Adam snorted with contempt.

"Shut up, will you? We'll talk later." Wiktor hushed him while helping him into the taxi. "Someone could overhear you and mistake that 'they' for someone else—and we'll be in trouble! Our visitors know our thoughts, so there's no need to say anything aloud."

Agabaar could control Adam's drunk mind only with the greatest effort. When it managed to merge into him, it was too late: The empty bottle stood on the table between two boozed-up men. Through Adam's blurred eyes the Aldebaranian surveyed Wiktor's face.

"Who is it?" he inquired hesitantly. "Are you Wiktor, or . . . my Megrezian counterpart?"

The man on the other side of the table gave Agabaar a long, cool, sober glance.

"What do you think?" he asked at last, with a sarcastic smile. "For the past half hour I have been drinking with your host. Or rather making him drunk. Deliberately, I admit."

"Where are you from?"

"You know that. From Megrez."

"The hell if that means anything to me! How can I know the human names of stars and such like?"

"Find some time to go into a library, when you are sober. Check in the Galactic Atlas. I do not feel like giving long explanations. Your barely conscious mind will not remember it anyway. I feel sorry for you; to find such a poor host. . . ."

"So I did, hell! But I can't find anyone more suitable. The people living here are absolutely hopeless as hosts."

"That is correct; this is a particularly difficult territory. I had a stroke of luck: I found myself an intelligent individual, almost an abstainer, and quite susceptible to control, I think. You cannot find many like him here. You will have to settle for your drunkard, and it is even better for me; I shall be better off when establishing trade contacts here. I believe some of our targets are similar. Whoever is faster, wins."

"You aren't a particularly nice partner," said Agaabar with disgust.

"We are not partners, we are competitors, my friend from a distant star," corrected the Megrezian.

"You win this time. But I'll find myself a native ready to submit to my will."

"Not very likely. The people here are particularly averse to submission. Both as individuals and as a nation. If you had studied their history, you would have understood that better."

"It isn't easy to learn history from a drunk who wasn't perhaps a good student, anyway."

"You can believe me, I have checked. You must have seen yourself what methods your Adam uses to stop you from manipulating him."

"Sure, he always finds some guy to buy him a drink. Or he gets the liquor somewhere, even if I let him have only a little money for food."

"Mine is not perfect, either," sighed the Megrezian. "Whenever I leave him for a while, he schemes against me, devises plans to free himself from subjugation. Naturally, he can never succeed because every time I come back and look into his mind, I always know everything."

"As for me, I can't even get a good look at what my drunkard did and thought during my absence. Whenever he gets drunk, he doesn't remember anything afterwards. Sometimes I can't even find my way around in that whole mess inside his head."

"You know what? Better go back to Aldebaran. I shall have more freedom of action and you will ask for another assignment. You can never cope with them here."

"Why?"

"Because you Aldebaranians are known in the Galaxy for your —uh—not very bright minds."

"What? Who says so?"

"Everybody; don't act as if you have never heard that! There is a saying: dumb as an Aldebaranian."

Agabaar jumped from his seat, but the drunken body he was using staggered dangerously.

"Listen, you!" he snarled, sitting down. "On our planet you could have your proboscis beaten off for that!"

"No, I could not. We do not have probosces, only decent cephalopodia, like all highly developed intelligent species should. I suspect that you are absolutely unable to cooperate with the people of this planet because you are on a much lower level of development than they are."

Agabaar's thoughts meandered with difficulty through Adam's ganglions, still buzzing with alcohol. It tried to find some retort in answer to that insult from that impertinent individual from some galactic Podunk, but its boiling rage dulled its wit.

"Why don't you consider my suggestion?" said the Megrezian in the end. "Just get out of here! This territory is really too difficult for you. The people simply, physically detest any alien domination. Their whole nation, with only few exceptions, values independence and personal freedom higher than advantages from contacts with powerful alien powers. I am very doubtful whether you can find anyone who would not try to get you off his back when you were trying to drive him. . . . Well, I shall be going for a while."

"Go to hell," grunted Agabaar.

"That being has offended you, esteemed sir from Aldebaran," said Wiktor with respect. "If I were you, I wouldn't let it pass."

"What can I do?" Agabaar shrugged. "I could batter you, for instance. That wouldn't hurt the Megrezian physically, but at least it wouldn't be able to use you."

"Why should you beat me at all?" smiled Wiktor slyly. "We are both fed up with that lout. You have trouble with Adam. And I am ready to cooperate with someone as civilized and nice as you, Mr. . . ."

"My name is Agabaar."

"So?"

"Do I understand that you suggest, Wiktor . . . ?"

"This will be an easy switch. I am susceptible to control. I guess I have a favorable psychological disposition."

"But I can't do that! Professional ethics, you know! The code of behavior . . ." Agabaar resisted weakly.

"My dear sir! After what this being has said about you? If I were you, I wouldn't hesitate for a moment!"

"Well, that could be some retaliation for all the insults—"

"That's it, my dear visitor! I will also profit from this change. And your opponent will be left with that drunkard. So what do you say? Leave Adam alone, he has to sleep it off, anyway—and welcome to my mind."

"Okay. I'll be with you in a moment." The Aldebaranian had disposed of all its misgivings.

"Now stop thinking, don't think at all!" Wiktor reminded himself, while reaching under the table and taking a hefty swig from another bottle he had left there for this very occasion.

He succeeded with his plan at the very last moment: the *real* Megrezian he had been impersonating appeared from the transmission channel. It was trying in vain to penetrate Wiktor's mind, just taken over by Agabaar of Aldebaran, thus blocking access for any other personality.

Not being able to understand what had happened, the visitor from Megrez started circling the room. Finding a controllable but completely drunken body of Adam, it entered him, woke him up, and managed, though not without difficulty, to reconstruct from his memory a blurred outline of the recent events. It was full of obscurities. One thing was certain, however: Some galactic vagabond dared to seize the individual the Megrezian had selected for itself that morning. The object had been marked. So the theft was not by mistake, but undoubtedly a deliberate act.

"Just you wait, you Aldebaranian stinker!" The Megrezian

furiously expressed his opinion of the representative of a friendly system. "The Galactic Tribunal will not let it pass unnoticed!"

It edged away from Adam to the transmission channel and came back to its planet, where it at once filed a complaint against the Aldebaranian Union of Planets.

"I still can't fully understand how come they'd left," said Adam. "How did you manage to deceive them both?"

"Well, in fact it was only one, the Aldebaranian. The Megrezian acted logically, as I expected. The most important thing was not to plan anything in advance. I had to play by ear, by the spur of the moment. The situation developed itself. I had a stroke of luck and managed to create a conflict between both visitors. As a result of the Megrezian's complaint, the Aldebaranian was recalled from Earth. . . ."

"How do you know?"

"From my Megrezian, who used to visit me here until not so long ago. It looks as if I taught him a lesson of good manners and proper behavior, which he needed very much," smiled Wiktor. "But I don't need its company. It must have given me up anyway. To say the truth, I had expected them to come to grips and make such a row that their authorities would have had to recall both. But one happened to be clever and did not let itself be provoked. Well, it can't be helped, I told myself, there is no other way out. My alien visitor could not understand afterwards why I had done that. It swore at me and questioned me by turns, trying to understand my motives. And I simply hate it when some alien tells me what to do, where to go, what to say, what to think, what to believe in. I'd rather stay here until it goes away or finds another sucker. So this is why I wrote that subversive slogan on a wall."

"End of visit to the prisoners!" shouted the screw.

FROM SWEDEN:

Time Everlasting

BY SAM J. LUNDWALL

After I had been rejected I tried to stay on; but of course they wouldn't let me. I had done my part, or not done it, as it were, now I was merely an inconvenience, a problem to discard as quickly and painlessly as possible. Also, I might have learned something.

Indeed, I hinted I had learned something; I thought it would force them to return me to the base where the aliens could let me live on or kill me, as it pleased them. Instead, I forced them to move me elsewhere, up to the north of Sweden, far away from the air force base outside Stockholm where I and the two other Contacts had been kept. There was a good side to it; they flew up my daughter, whom I had never hoped to see again. And there was a bad side to it; I would never be a Contact again. The door was totally, inevitably closed.

Another air base, a wartime airfield, hardly more than a widened strip of highway and a few inconspicuous buildings in the middle of never-ending woods. My daughter spent her days down by the lake, chaperoned by a long-haired conscript or watching Norwegian, Swedish, Finnish, and Russian children's programs on TV. I walked in the woods with affable men and women, all of them much younger than I, who came for a day or two, even for a week, then departed to wherever results were compared and sums added. I never cared very much for anything of all that. The north of Sweden is an enormous country, largely uninhabited, you can travel for hundreds of miles without seeing signs of human habitation. It is easy to get lost in this enormous wilderness where the night is as light as the day, where days pass away without one being aware of it, where one never seems to sleep. I was already lost in time; I never noticed it.

"I took her over," I said to a more than usually affable young woman who stayed there for some time. She was small and round, with a big smile and rotten breath, and she bravely walked with me for miles, trying to pretend she enjoyed it. Of course, she knew I had taken her over instead of the other way around, that's what made me so interesting. "I took her over," I said, "and I killed her."

"Yes."

"I think they winked at that," I said. "I don't think it mattered so much to them that I killed her. I don't think it matters so much to them, this one person." I glanced at her. She smiled back. "Her," I said, "or him, or it, whatever."

"Yes."

We stood on a rise overlooking the lake. My daughter was out there in a rowboat with the bored conscript. She had quickly found out that she could order him around and have him obey, and she made him run errands like a schoolboy. He didn't seem to mind very much. "I've lost her too," I said, "that's really the only thing that hurts."

She didn't understand. "Yes," she said and smiled.

"You don't say very much." I looked down at the lake. The boat was slowly returning to the shore.

"I'm listening."

I looked at her. "You're afraid of me."

She smiled again. "No."

"You don't like me."

"You don't like yourself," she said with a voice that suggested she understood and shared my opinion.

"I do, but I don't think I understand myself."

"No one understands you."

"You understand me."

"That's true."

"It isn't true at all," I said. "You humor me, that's something entirely different."

"It's an old habit, I have always humored you."

"Everyone humors me."

"It's an old habit with everyone."

I laughed. "What do you want?"

"How did you do it?"

"I loved her," I said and went down the trail to where my daughter was jumping out of the boat, showing her catch. The fish died slowly. When it hung still, she threw it back into the water again.

I tried to explain it to the psychiatrist, but without much success. I had no words to explain with, not even images to explain. I had been brought to the air force base outside Stockholm, together with the two other Swedish Contacts, contact was established, and I was rejected. That would have been the end of it, only it became known I had taken control over the contacting alien, which made me very interesting. I had also killed her, but that was not known then.

"That's what I did," I said. "I took her over, but I didn't know I had. I was scared, I was somewhere in a place I had never seen before and didn't know anything about, I was terrified, and I did something. . . ."

She said: "What did you do?"

I said, "Nothing that would make any sense to you. It doesn't even make sense to me. It was something that isn't done there, something so vile they couldn't even think about it, so shameful they don't have a name for it, or even a punishment. It's simply not done, ever."

She said, "What?"

I had her there, she was interested, it could be a break, a means of getting to the aliens, maybe a weapon of sorts. If it hurt them, it could be useful. I said, "I don't know." She said I must know, surely I must know, and I said I thought maybe we could say it was a sort of unnatural act, as they perceived it. She said, A sexual act? I said, No, I don't think so, not sexual, nothing that has anything to do with reproduction, just something that simply isn't done. I hurt them.

"Yes," she said. "Yes."

"They have a very strong sense of individuality," I said, "the aliens, these aliens I got into contact with. They are self-contained beings, they perceive the world differently from us, they have a different sense of time. . . ."

She watched me. My daughter was out on the lake again, at two o'clock in the morning—catching fish, watching them die, and throwing them back. I looked out through the window.

"They don't perceive the before, during, or after as we do," I said. "They do recognize the difference, but it is a difference that doesn't mean much to them, everything takes place more or less simultaneously. . . . The law of causality would mean nothing to them, cause and effect could follow each other in any order." I rose. "I was there forever," I said, "right there, inside her, a rape that went on for ever, I shared everything she ever had known and ever would know or experience, all of it simultaneously. There's no time with these beings," I said, "no time at all, and all time, all eternity, all past and future compressed in a single present." I stood by the window, looking out.

"You killed her?" she said.

"I stayed with her for all her life," I said. "It's the same thing." I turned back to her. "I don't have time anymore," I said, "that's why I must get back to them if they don't come for me." I smiled at her. "I don't belong here anymore. That's why you are afraid of me—I have lost you all, even the girl out there." I sat down. "I'm waiting," I said. "I don't have time anymore, I can wait forever."

I sat there smiling at her until she went out.

I waited. For the alien, no time existed. These weeks and months could be a moment for her, or an eternity. She could return any time, and she would not have changed at all. I had killed her; but for a species that doesn't know time, death is just another experience among others, she'd be back.

In the eternal night at the bottom of the great oceans, innumerable metal nodules are spread over the never-ending deep sea plains. During millions of years, heavy metals in the water enriched into pebbles on the ocean floors and in time created these billions and billions of metal stones in the bottom sediment. Most of them are very small, less than a millimeter, but some are old even in geological terms and have grown to respectable size.

These great nodules wander.

Many forces interact to make these dead nodules the only things that move in this unchanging world on the deepest ocean floors. The movement is small but perpetual. In a million years, a nodule can cross its ocean. If all factors cooperate in exactly the right moment, it can climb the continental precipice and in time rise to the water level and a new continent's sun. Species and races have appeared and disappeared again during its million-year-long journey between continents, and species and races shall come and go while with eternal patience it rests just above or beneath the water. At one time the continent will sink, and the nodule resume its journey over the deep-sea plains, toward its starting point. In this way the nodule, like Oberon, can girdle the globe with a speed that is incredibly slow only for the fleeting and transitory shadow life we represent.

The stones wander in the eternal night without caring about the passing and transitory world, maybe thinking their stone thoughts, which we cannot comprehend. As long as they move and grow, the Earth is not dead.

I watched my daughter playing on the beach, and I thought of the stones that started wandering long before life emerged on Earth and that will continue wandering long after it has disappeared. During the days and months that followed, I walked in the woods, pursued by shadows without names. I defended myself like when I was a kid, by walking certain trails without ever touching tree roots, or stepping over every second stone. Always a new way of bribing unknown and maybe nonexistent forces. The past pursued me, it had followed me from these places without time and reached out after me with an unbearable gray sorrow, which I couldn't defend myself against but which still never quite reached me.

It was like winters in the country long ago, when I ran up the hill with white meadows behind me and the village somewhere ahead beyond the spruce trees, the village road and the red chapel and the village blacksmith's big red iron-hot workshop where the snow was always black with soot, and there, right in the middle of the slope, the yellow sign with the village name in black letters,

RÖKSTA, which I must run past because behind me was something that came closer and closer with every second, and when I passed the sign, breathless and hot and with the wind ice-cold in my face, turned around, and there was nothing. There was never anything behind me, there was only myself running after me, reaching out arms in a mute and futile sorrow from a past that wants its due but never can have it. The universe is great and black, something threatening behind my back that is pushing me on so I must run, although I don't know why, or how, not toward anything anymore, but away from. I was here, now, and simultaneously I was and would be doing what I had always been doing, just as if I had never done it before, as if I understood it and found it meaningful. I walked in the woods, thinking of the things I experienced somewhere else, which I called love for lack of a better word, although it had nothing to do with love as we understand it, the shameful thing for which these aliens have no name, not even a punishment. I thought about it, or rather about the memory of it, and I thought about the patient, ancient stones, thinking their slow stone thoughts without caring about anything. Nothing changes. All goes on.

FROM THE PEOPLE'S REPUBLIC OF CHINA:

The Middle Kingdom

BY TONG ENZHENG
Translated by Dingbo Wu
Adapted by Elizabeth Anne Hull

My dear and honored Mother's Older Sister,

Thank you so very much for the bundle of sweets you sent at very great expense. I have tried to share them, as you always taught me, with some of the other members of the interstellar delegation, but I'm afraid the clods from Betelgeuse are just being polite, and no one except us—the elite of the northern hemisphere of Tau Ceti V—consider candied seaweed to be such a tasty treat as we know it is. I hate to waste all my treasures on those who really can't appreciate them.

Otherwise, all the members of the delegation that I've met so far are quite nice people, even the strange ones from Aldebaran. Even they are superior company, of course, to the natives of Earth, strange creatures at their very best and sometimes totally illogical. But we're here to study and not to make our judgments—yet.

We representatives of the Inter-Stellar Alliance of Civilizations are once again going to gather this afternoon in the luxurious Lili-uokalani Ballroom at the Makele Motel. This time, however, we are not to settle the interstellar trade balance, not to divide up the natural resources lately procured from Earth. Instead, five of us have just returned from a large continent called China and are going to brief the whole delegation of star travelers on our experiences there and warn the others that we highly intelligent starborn creatures should agree to make that area off limits, because it seems to be more trouble than it's worth.

Our first troubles on Earth, you will remember from my last letter, came when we killed all of our initial possessed humans, by overestimating their emotional stability. Poor Ben, the first body I used, was really a pretty nice guy, but he committed suicide because he couldn't bear being controlled. That was a pity—he was really quite handsome according to Earth standards. (We're all getting more accustomed to their standards in viewing Earth and its inhabitants now.) Anyway, Ben drank so much alcohol that he poisoned his liver and died of violent convulsions. And Elsa, the slim beauty who had been on her honeymoon when she was possessed and recruited to Maui—she hanged herself with her husband's belt from a banyan tree. The other humans said she died of a broken heart at being separated from her husband. I really felt for her, since I'm so far from my own husband, and I hope you are remembering to visit him regularly and reminding him how much I miss him. I do wish he could have had this opportunity to come to Earth with me, and I'm still working on getting council approval for him while I'm here.

But I digress. Greg and Julio, two others of the first lot of possessed humans, didn't commit suicide, but they both suffered from schizophrenia simultaneously and so became unusable—well, there's no need to give the whole list of examples. It's a great pity, but humans should be grateful and willing to pay some price for the opportunity we're providing them to catch up with our higher civilization.

Anyway, I was going to tell you all about my trip to China. It's hard to believe, I know, but on Earth we've been depicted in their newspapers, magazines, radio, and television news stories as brutal alien intruders, instead of the envoys of civilization that we truly are. How else could we be so good at summing up our experiences and making self-examination! Well, having drawn good lessons from the deaths of Ben and Elsa and the others, we overcame our impetuosity. When we first reached Earth, we took over anyone suitable to our individual needs—and you know we are so diverse, even among us civilized races, that it's not terribly easy to find Earthlings who are mentally and biologically suitable for us. But we've learned that it's better in the long run to try our best to persuade humans to cooperate with us, and we offer them all kinds of benefits so that they'll allow us to use their bodies of their own accord. This strategy has proven so successful with many of them that even after we leave them they remain our loyal, faithful agents. Of course, if persuasion should fail, we do still resort to compulsion, sometimes. The cause of ISAC stands above all else!

But back to China. As you must remember from what I've written to you before, in comparison with Tau Ceti V, Earth is very small. However, it has a population of over four billion humans, their most mentally developed species—a great many, indeed, even considering their short stature. After all, they still take up nearly as much space on the ground as we do, and so they are crowded together. And they eat a surprising volume of food, which requires vast areas of agricultural space. Once we teach them our ways of extracting nutrient directly from their primary star, they may be able to enjoy a better life, if they control their population numbers and don't just go and breed up to the very utmost limits of production capacity, like the lower animals. But, as I said, it's not always easy for us to find compatible host bodies, so we go to different countries to recruit our appliances among various nations for the summit meeting on Maui Island. Besides, this way we can discover people of different talents and obtain a more thorough understanding of the various cultures on Earth.

Four other ISAC citizens and I were directed to go to China, a picturesque country with a vast territory and a huge population, in fact, about a quarter of the whole population of Earth. In the countryside it seems that everyone is working very hard and the crops are doing quite well, considering the primitive methods of food production that they use.

In the cities, streets swarm with bicycles and people busy from morning till night. You can hardly find the dazzling facilities for entertainment which are commonly seen in great numbers in the cities of other countries, nor can you find so many idlers there who have nothing to do. Judging from the quality of her architecture, from her transport facilities and from her equipment and installations in agriculture and industry, this is a very poor country, especially in comparison to the opulence of, say, Maui, where I'm sitting on my lanai, sipping coconut milk and munching on a cool slice of papaya, treats to rival any from Tau Ceti V.

When we came to Beijing, the capital city of that vast country, I parted with my other comrades there, each of us going to look for a suitable body compatible with our own specific physiology and psychology. I soon found mine: Wu Li, an engineer working on the production of radionuclides.

I arrived at his residence in the evening, just before dark. He lived in a tiny place with only two pigeonholes of rooms, one for his two children and the other for him and his wife. I was shocked at the meagerness of his furnishings, especially considering the importance of his work. There were only one desk with a dim lamp, a stove with just one oil burner, a short shelf that served as a food cupboard, a table only big enough for two to eat at one time, and one bed in his tiny room.

Wu's wife, Wang Hong, was a teacher. She sat at the desk for hours before and after dinner, correcting pupils' papers—piles and piles of them! They occupied half of the desk. Neither of them really had adequate space to work.

The engineer huddled on a low stool, writing with a board on the bed, with blueprints, books, and other materials piled up all about. Glancing over his shoulder at those computation formulae and technological processes, I could hardly believe my good fortune! He was working on a draft for the production of a certain radioactive raw material—I can't be more specific for security reasons, you understand, Auntie. But even judging by our standards, this was an entirely new and streamlined project which could bring about a revolutionary change in the methods of processing that raw material. It's hard to conceive how such a brilliant talent could be nurtured under such poor conditions. I decided that the potential of the human race may be far greater than we had ever previously imagined. Well, I could not help rejoicing over my good fortune because the material he was going to produce was just the thing most deficient on Tau Ceti V!

I entered his body cautiously so I could use his sensory receptors, but I did not take him over immediately. I figured it would be better to gather more information about him so that I could work out proper ways to persuade him to cooperate with me. It certainly wouldn't do to destroy or even risk injuring this specimen, especially considering the leanness of his body. He seemed to be strong enough, but without any added margin of fat to lose, should I stress him too much.

After a tasty but meager meal of rice, steamed buns, and stir-fried cabbages and onions, he and his wife retired early to save electricity. There was no heat in their house, and since I was sharing his sensations, I was glad when he clung to Wang Hong for warmth during the night.

The next morning he rose early also, and after taking only a thin soup and some more steamed buns, he bicycled off to his factory, arriving before anyone else. This was the very day he was to make his presentation at the factory, and there was to be a deliberative session on his draft plan. I won't bore you, honored Auntie, with all the details of the presentation, but it was clear that those "comrades" who held real sway over the session knew little about technology and even showed obvious disliking of technology. Isn't it puzzling that so important a project should be examined and approved by them!

To my mind, those comrades did have something in common. With their faces all ruddy, they seemed to take rather good care of their health. I was pretty certain they'd had a better breakfast than Wu. They were all so fond of tea that they all carried their own teacups in their portfolios. They never seemed pressed for time and behaved leisurely. They spoke slowly with a habitual lingering echo at the end of each sentence.

With the aid of his blueprints and charts hung on the wall, engineer Wu reported his plan to the session and outlined some moderate conditions indispensable for its materialization. As soon as he put an end to his elaboration, a rosy-cheeked comrade took the floor.

"Don't you mean to switch over to new products?" The cut and material of his clothing suggested to my trained and subtle eye that this was a high-ranking cadre.

"Yes, Comrade Xi," said Wu. He shifted nervously from one foot to the other before he continued. "Because those factories which use our present products are now considering switching their products to goods that are more in demand, and very soon they won't need the same raw and processed materials from us anymore."

"But so far we have never had any problem about the sale of our goods," sneered another comrade, clapping a lid on his teacup for emphasis.

"That's because the state takes them all," Wu said without hesitation. "The storehouses are about bursting with them now." Wu was a good man, not easily intimidated, thought I.

"That's none of our business," said a third comrade. "If we should decide for ourselves to change over to new products and establish direct contact with the customers, who would bear responsibility just in case there might be no guarantee for our marketing? Then we would neither fulfill our quota assigned from above nor give bonuses to the workers down below. Eh?" This one showed tobacco-stained teeth in a sort of smile that didn't really look very friendly at all.

While Wu was still considering how to reply, the second comrade put in again: "How will we build up the funds if you are going to reform the production line?"

Wu was ready with his answer: "I'll get a bank loan."

"Can you provide any documents to back you up for it?" asked the first comrade.

"If not, I won't affix my signature. Phew!" agreed the second.

The third comrade added, "Didn't you say that the new production line needs only one-third of our workers?" This time he showed his teeth again, but it was definitely not a smile now.

"Yes, that will cut down a great amount of labor," said Wu, but the others didn't seem to think this was good news at all, for their frowns furrowed deeper.

"Are you giving me a hard nut to crack on purpose? Where can I dispose of the surplus labor? Pooh!" said Xi, the man in the superior coat.

While Wu sat speechless for another moment, a fourth comrade now joined in. "Do I understand correctly that you want to transfer Engineer Zhang to work as your assistant?"

"Oh, yes," said Wu. "Zhang has studied the subject extensively with me in our spare time after work and is extremely interested in it. However, he now works in the library, in charge of the distribution of newspapers and books. This simply hinders him from giving full play to his professional knowledge."

By this time I was really impressed by Wu's courage as well as his intelligence. But I hadn't counted on the quick answer from Xi. "To do revolutionary work, if your ideology is on the right track, where can't you play your role?" He rubbed his hands along his fine lapels.

"The transfer of personnel is not that easy!" said the second comrade. But Wu was looking patient, so he added, somewhat nervously, I thought, "Well, suppose you write an application for it, and so does Mr. Zhang and so does your section leader. Then we'll consult with all the quarters concerned. Aha?" He shot sidelong glances toward Xi, who had withdrawn from the center of the circle, purposefully turning his back on Wu and the others.

Several other workers standing around and listening were taking detailed notes all the while this previous conversation was going on. For a while I thought some of them wanted to speak also, but they looked from one to another in blank dismay as the inquisition proceeded and ultimately decided to remain silent. These men and women were all comparatively younger than the ones who did speak.

It seemed as if the meeting would now close without any action being taken on Wu's revolutionary new plan, but finally the factory director, a middle-aged man with spectacles, opened his mouth. "Comrades, we all know the problems in our factory quite clearly." He pushed his glasses up on his nose and looked significantly around at everyone, both the speakers and the younger nonspeakers. "Outdated technology, outdated machines, outdated products, without the slightest changes for twenty years. According to our accounts, revenue and expenditure are balanced annually, but we are curing our boil by cutting out pieces of meat from the state's large canteen caldron. Now that everything is undergoing reform, the state won't allow us to eat from its canteen caldron anymore. Our factory will collapse if we don't find a way out in renewing our products and raising our labor productivity. Engineer Wu's project is the key for us to get rid of our present passive position. I suggest you comrades give it some further thought."

I was happy to hear at last a voice of sanity, even if it was so timidly expressed. Xi certainly didn't want to agree, but even he was pushed to admit that they could not just dismiss the proposition, when all the reasonable evidence was on the other side from his stubborn position. "All right," he finally agreed. "Let's have an inner-leadership consultation about it then."

I could hardly believe how quickly nearly everyone there left the room on hearing these words, including Wu. I found myself carried along with him back to the production lines. Once again, you can well imagine how perplexed I was. Why must the person concerned leave while his plan was under deliberation? Only three others besides the four who had spoken in the meeting were left in the meeting room.

As Wu walked back to his work station, he slumped and his face darkened. I knew he was terribly upset. The other people who had walked out of the meeting room together with him were trying to soothe him with encouraging pats on the shoulder. They all seemed quite sincere, but I couldn't understand why they hadn't taken the floor and supported him at the crucial moment. Humans are very confusing creatures.

When they got to the workshop, a big crowd of workers surrounded them. They were all eager to put in a word. This time they were all dressed so identically in white shirts and dark blue cotton pants that I really couldn't distinguish any of them from the others.

"What's the result of all their deliberation, Engineer Wu?" asked one.

Another pressed, "Aren't we going to be allowed to carry out such a good project?"

"We don't want to be carried along on the socialist stretcher. We have two legs of our own," joined still another voice.

And "We can certainly break new paths of our own."

However, Wu shook his head without a word. Now everything was clear to the workers. They all held their tongues as the younger men in the meeting had done before.

All of a sudden, a young man shouted at the top of his voice:

"If someone makes a show of officialdom, let's appeal to the authorities higher up!"

Grievance and fury ran high among the workers. "Right! In the name of all our workers we support Engineer Wu's plan!"

Out of curiosity, I left Wu's body in the workshop for a few minutes and went back to the meeting room. Heated discussion was going on there, too. Those comrades who had spoken earlier were now adding more points to their views.

Xi had unbuttoned his good cloth coat, and was warming up to his topic: "We must no doubt support all reforms, but being leading cadres, we must also consider: Is it a genuine reform? What is the motivation of the reformer? Eh?"

The yellow-toothed one joined in, "We must no doubt go ahead boldly and fully with the proper use of intellectuals, but while making use of them we must also pay attention to their ideological remolding! Engineer Wu's plan stresses his personal role only. Doesn't he get a bit cocky? Whew!"

"We must no doubt act in accordance with the policies," Xi agreed solemnly and nodded with a frown as if to say, go on.

And the one who always looked at Xi out of the corner of his eye added, "Engineer Wu has very complicated social connections. He has relatives living abroad and he himself keeps in personal contact with the chemical societies in the United States, Germany, Britain, Japan, and other countries. What kind of organizations are they? What kind of people are their members? Who has made investigations about these? These questions have yet to be set straight! Hmm?"

"One point just between you, me, and the gatepost," said Xi's other toady. "A story is going around that Engineer Wu misconducts himself. It is said that he took a stroll with a *woman* last night. The two got quite close to each other. See?"

Although I am more intelligent than any Earthman, I found myself utterly at a loss. Of course, I knew that the charges against Wu were lies. I was with Wu and his dear sweet wife all night long myself. But even if there were any personal indiscretion on his part, what did that have to do with the merits of the plans he proposed?

Poor Engineer Wu! If he attempted nothing and accomplished

nothing at all, he would be probably thought of as a good guy; at least he would be inconspicuous. But now that he tried to do something significant, he at once became a person to be examined and, sadly, if nothing could be found wrong, it was to be invented! What kind of logic was it? Odd logic!

The middle-aged, bespectacled director seemed to lack experience in dealing with such problems. He simply did not know how to cope with those oblique insinuations. The education he had received hadn't prepared him for this. Yet he was a good man, and not ready to give up. "So far as your suspicions against Engineer Wu are concerned," he began again, "we can no doubt make investigation and find out the real situation. For all that, I still suggest you all give some further thought to the positive factors of his plan. As our meeting today can't come to any decision about it, I'm going to report the case to the municipal Party Committee right now and ask our superior to examine it."

For all the director's tactful and mild wording, those comrades still pulled long faces while walking out of the meeting room. The one in the good coat hunched his shoulders on his way out as if he suddenly felt the coldness, despite the wool cloth. And the fine tailoring didn't help in the slightest!

That was enough. So far as I was concerned, I knew all I needed to know about Engineer Wu now. He was talented but poor; he cherished high ambitions but suffered wrongs. I could satisfy all his needs and desires. According to the study of human psychology that I'd made in the United States in the past few months, I was sure I could easily win him over and make him serve us.

I waited with patience for another three days. I wanted to give him enough time to introspect, to call the whole situation to mind and ponder it over, to feel disappointed and suffer torments. I wanted to offer him a cup of the sweet spring water of happiness at the moment when he felt most depressed. I knew the common nature of mankind who will usually go to either of two extremes at such a moment: confine himself to bed at his last gasp or fly into a rage and give vent to it by drinking heavily.

I was surprised to find that Engineer Wu was an exception.

Anguished as he was, he didn't eat very much for three days, so that he appeared quite emaciated; but he worked in the factory every day as usual and bent over his bed improving his plan at night all the same. What a freak he was!

I finally could restrain myself no longer. Things didn't seem to be working out as I had anticipated, so I saw no other course than to take Wu over. Although he was still concentrating on his work, he sensed my existence at once. I knew how grossly violated he felt when I took over his body and mind. He tried to resist as hard as any of the others ever did, as all the Earthmen and women do, but he had no choice.

I ordered him to stand up and go out of the room with me. He toddled along with odd steps. As a matter of fact, he moved the way I move at home. Remember, Auntie, the gravity here is only one third of ours at home. I suppose the expression on his face and his uncustomary gait caught the attention of his wife and children. They gathered around him and asked all sorts of questions: What was the matter? Was he ill? Where was he going? What should they do to help him? For, of course, they only imagined that he might be ill, not that he was possessed.

But I forbade him to reply. I made him struggle to get free from them and walk out into the night. Now that I had full control over his mind, even his paternal protective love for his children couldn't prevent him from abandoning them when I commanded.

We climbed to the roof garden of a luxurious hotel. This was a very quiet place, spacious and open on all sides. After I persuaded him, I planned to send him to the Makele Motel on Maui directly via "Dimension Five Drive." But, as you realize, I had to have his cooperation to transport him via the fifth dimension, or we'd risk losing his brilliant mind to "jet lag" for an unpredictable amount of time. Some humans that we've transported against their will have never recovered. His was too valuable a mind to risk.

First, I made clear who I was and what I had come for, and then we began our dialogue, which went on in his brain by means of a stream of consciousness, of course.

"Now come along with me."

"Where to?"

"Maui, Hawaii, the United States."

"What for?"

"We, the Inter-Stellar Alliance of Civilizations, need your knowledge."

"My country is going ahead with construction and my nation is revitalizing herself. In duty bound to my motherland, I won't leave her."

"That's just an empty dogma."

"No, it's not an empty dogma. It is the faith mixed in my flesh and blood. It is the principle of my life. It is my sublime spirit."

"But you are in straitened circumstances and your plan is slighted. If you go to Hawaii, you can have a suite of rooms, beautiful girls, sumptuous food and live like a king."

"But I love my wife and family."

"Bring them along then. What's more, we'll build a factory specially for you to materialize your plan of production."

"I'll contribute my knowledge to my motherland only. Riches of any kind in the world can't tempt me to betray her."

"Who appreciates patriotism? Don't forget that you are now under examination, under slander, and under general suspicion!"

"More and more people will understand and support me."

You know how patient I usually am, Auntie. I will scratch your back for hours if you ask me to do it nicely. Without complaint, I will hold a fan for my father's elder brother while he sings off key and I never let him believe he's less than fascinating as a performer. But Engineer Wu was just plain exasperating!

"I'm your boss now! You can't refuse to do whatever I order you to. If you don't believe me, I order you—three steps forward!"

He took three steps forward outside the low balustrade of the roof garden where he stood, and reached a very dangerous edge. Half a step more, and he would fall down from that sixteen-story building.

"Don't you see? You have to obey even if I order you to meet your end!"

"Even if you take my life, you can never make me betray my motherland!"

What use would his corpse be to me?

Just then I heard a shout from behind. "Old Wu! Old Wu!"

I—or I guess I should say *he*—turned around and saw the spectacled, middle-aged factory director and Engineer Wu's wife running over. Gasping for breath, they did not notice the tense atmosphere in the dark.

The director grasped his hands and pulled him back inside the balustrade.

"Why, you're here! You make us search high and low for you. Now, the leading cadres concerned in the municipal Party Committee and the Chemical Industry Bureau have examined your plan and reached the unanimous opinion that yours is a pioneering work of great value. At the meeting this afternoon, the bureau leaders made an official decision: Your project is to be carried out without delay and you are commissioned deputy director of our factory in charge of this project."

As I did not allow him to open his mouth, he was unable to give any answer. However, shivers came from the bottom of his heart, and big tears slid down his cheeks.

The director, mistaking the cause for the tears and shivers, rattled on: "Moreover, Zhang will be your assistant, just as you wished. Do not cry, gentle Wu. All will be well."

Needless to say, things now looked hopeless for me. I felt like crying myself and so I made Wu cry all the harder, but I could feel that his tears were of joy and triumph over me, even as I still made his body obey my rule. I know we may need to negotiate with Wu again in the coming months, but for the present I felt I could do nothing more, without actually destroying the poor man, for whom I could not help feeling affection as well as admiration.

At this point, I decided to leave Wu to his destiny (for the moment) and seek out my four comrades from the stars. Imagine my surprise to find that I was not the only one of us who had met with unexpected resistance. They all had chosen their respective appliances: a soldier, a peasant, a worker. However, when it came to the critical juncture, each of the others met as firm a resistance as I did. The worst defeat was suffered by the fifth of my star-traveling comrades, who had selected a ragged pupil with a red scarf around his neck as his only ornament. When my comrade tried to persuade him to leave school, to abandon all those disgusting studies and to go to Hawaii's golden beaches for a good time, the kid clasped the leg of a school desk desperately and would not let go. He finally lost consciousness in the struggle between "order" and "will power." After his teacher—who turned out to be Wang Hong herself—sent him to a hospital, the boy even asked the doctor to bind him to the bed for fear of losing control of himself in a coma. In the face of such a staunch nation, we experienced and knowledgeable representatives of the ISAC were at our wit's end.

After considerable sharing of our experiences, we agreed that we should return to the meeting at Maui and consult with the full delegation before proceeding further in China. I tell you, Auntie, China is an unusual country where poverty and affluence, absurdity and science, vulgarity and sublimity, past and present, real and ideal, are all interwoven intricately. This can hardly be observed to the same degree in any other country in the world. Although I have returned with temporarily clipped wings, China has aroused my great interest. I hope that some day I can go there again and make a long-term study of this nation and this country. Everything that happens there now may complement the conception of the "cosmic civilization" that we respect and revere above all else.

Glancing at the clock I see that time grows short, honored replacement for my own dear discorporated mother, and I must go to make my report. I promise I'll finish this letter immediately after I return.

Well, Auntie, I told them as I told you. After my speech, the Liliuokalani Ballroom resounded with hissing, screaming, yelling, squawking, clacking, and twittering. My comrades were discussing the causes of our failure in the trip to China.

Some wondered whether the physiological structure of the Chinese was so abnormal that they can defy natural laws. But it isn't! Humans are all composed of carbohydrates, fats, proteins, RNA, DNA, and what not. And the Chinese are surely human flesh and blood.

But I think I know the answer now. Our control over Earthmen can only reach the limit of their physical lives. If someone adheres to a certain principle above his own life, our control will come to an end. The Chinese are unusual. We must study these human beings further to see if they are unique.

What an unfathomable enigma the Chinese nation is!

On the Inside Track (Umkreisungen)

BY KARL MICHAEL ARMER
Translated by Joe F. Randolph with Karl Michael Armer

July 9, 6:00 P.M. As always on beautiful summer days, Robert Förster's heart was burdened with bitterness. Colors were too bright. People were too carefree. On days like this he felt the weight of his seventy years painfully bearing down. New layers of depression and brooding anger formed on the shell that separated him from the outside world.

Today it was worse than ever. The weather and scenery had the unreal perfection of a picture postcard that you get in the mail just when you do not want it. The sky was so high, the blue so deep that life seemed to hold nothing but promise. Every hope, no matter how elusive, seemed to be within the realm of possibility. If you were young enough. White yachts were leisurely skimming over the waters of the Chiemsee under an afternoon breeze, almost as weightlessly as clouds scudding across the sky. The multihued sails of wind surfers, vivid specks reminiscent of impressionist paintings, slipped in and out between the yachts. Cattle were grazing on a peninsula jutting out into the lake. The tinny tinkling of cowbells provided an unobtrusive but constant score for the travelogue unfolding before Förster's eyes. In the background, snow-capped peaks crowning the

Bavarian Alps glistened beneath the sun in bold relief. That was the kind of day it was.

"Shit," Förster said.

He liked the way it sounded so much that he repeated it, "What a load of Goddamned shit."

The young woman sitting next to him on the lakeside bench looked at him askance. He glared back at her. Why should he care what she thought? To her he was nothing but an eccentric old coot, anyway.

"Don't you like people talking to themselves?" He chuckled. "I do. At least that way I'm talking to someone I like."

She got up and left. She had good-looking legs and a nice little ass. Like Barbara, when they were young, oh, so many, many years ago. They had been in a tiny cove on one of those secluded Greek islands. She came out of the turquoise-colored water of the Aegean sea, her svelte body covered with beads of water sparkling in the sun, Aphrodite reborn, goddess of love, priestess of their secret honeymoon rites. She seemed immortal in her glorious youth. Thirty years later she committed suicide. What had gone wrong? And why, for heaven's sake, why?

Förster's hand tightened around his cane while he tried to blink away the mist from his eyes. Look at yourself. What a sentimental old fool you have become. No style or dignity. Just lounging around insulting other people.

He was wrenched from his reverie by Samson's deep-throated growling. The big St. Bernard had woken up and was looking around bleary-eyed. He seemed to be confused. After a couple of seconds he let out a startlingly human sigh and put his head back down on his paws.

"Well, big fella, dreaming of the good old days again?" He patted the dog on the back, surprised at the degree of affection welling up in him. How thin Samson's coat had gotten. And his face was almost white. The St. Bernard was more than eleven years old, which was tantamount to seventy-seven human years. *The poor guy is even older than I am,* Förster thought. They were two oldsters in a world filled with smart young people who never gave a thought to the fact that they too would one day be stooped and tired.

"Relics, that's what we are, Samson," he said. "Relics of the worst type. Of no interest to historians or learned biographers, only something for file thirteen. Let's go before they sweep us up and away."

When he reached for the leash he had wrapped around a metal leg on the bench, the St. Bernard suddenly jumped up and started barking as if possessed. With legs trembling, he stood in front of Förster as if confronting a dangerous enemy, his bloodshot eyes wide-open.

Förster staggered to his feet, frightened and thoroughly confused. All of a sudden he felt seasick. It was weird. What was going on here? Something was pulling and tugging at his body as if forces were operating on him without anesthesia. So this is what it is like when you die! How strange! His knees gave way. He sank back down on the bench.

Suddenly, everything was as before.

"Easy," Förster told the dog automatically, "easy"—he hesitated for a fraction of a second, trying to remember—"Samson."

A spastically bent hand moved across his field of vision. He experienced a moment of pure, intense horror when he realized that it was his own hand moving of its own accord. He watched his hand perform strangely intricate gestures as if doing some Thai temple dance. It seemed to him that this was not real, he was merely watching it on a monitor. Watching it with detached scientific interest.

Have I lost my mind? Förster wondered in the unnatural calm accompanying a state of shock.

"No," answered an alien voice inside his head.

So Förster's first contact with the extraterrestrial was cut extremely short, because he passed out right then and there.

July 9, 6:20 P.M. After a few minutes Förster came to. His eyes were riveted to a small white cloud hanging motionless in the sky, like the enigmatic remains of a smoke signal. There was that thundering stillness in his head that occurs after an explosion, or after the last passionate crescendo of a symphony when so many feelings are competing in your chest that you cannot tell them apart. The shock of being overwhelmed.

He tried to remember everything the voice had said to him in the last few minutes.

"So you're an extraterrestrial," he said slowly. "An E.T. in my brain." He chuckled in his usual fashion. "That's truly amazing. Science fiction in a live performance, in every sense of the word."

As he got no answer, he shrugged and turned his attention back to the lakeside idyll he hated so. It was an alien landscape populated by young healthy humanoids. He had nothing in common with them —had not had for many years now.

"Well then," he said. "Welcome to the brotherhood of aliens." He felt a twinge of bewilderment.

"Aren't you an Earth person?" the voice asked.

"I was for many years," Förster replied. "But now I'm old. Old people are the extraterrestrial aliens in this world. We're so isolated that we might as well be living on another planet. Other people know that we are out there somewhere, but they couldn't care less. Life goes on without us. We have no more say about what happens. We're just onlookers, outcasts on our own world. That's why we're both aliens on this planet."

"I see," said the voice after a short pause.

"The only difference between us," said Förster, working himself into a rage, "is this. Meeting up with an extraterrestrial is usually a first-contact story, but growing older is more often than not a last-contact story."

"You are bitter."

"Yeah, that I am. Growing old's no fun."

"But you can get a lot of mileage out of these years. You're well-off, you're educated, you live in beautiful surroundings. You should be happy."

"Yeah, I should be, but I'm not. And that drives me up the wall. I'd like to be happy, but I'm not succeeding. Something's out of whack with me. I'm such an asshole that I can't be happy, even once." He started crying. "Here, look at me," he said in despair while wiping his face with a big blue handkerchief. "I never used to cry, but nowadays I get all watery-eyed whenever I see a young couple with a baby, because they remind me of my younger days." He folded his handkerchief very slowly, very precisely. "I'm sorry."

"That's all right," the alien said.

July 10, 9:30 A.M. Although it was still pretty early in the day, heat was already beating down on the Café Panorama lakeside terrace, where Förster was having breakfast. Every few seconds a refreshing breeze cooled him off. Förster, nevertheless, was sweating. The beach umbrellas were badly arranged, casting shadows on the aisles while tables stood in blazing sunlight.

Förster was sitting alone at his table, as usual. He had tried to push the umbrella into a better position, but he was too weak. The shade had not budged. Nobody made a move to help him.

When he went to pick up his coffee cup, he noticed his hand violently shaking. He made an effort to steady it. After all, he was being watched.

"Don't mind me," the voice said.

Förster thought about it. "But I know you're there," he said. "You're inside me. You're using my brain like a reference book. You can make a marionette out of my body. No matter what I do, you're watching me over my shoulder. That's where your 'Don't mind me' is a bunch of bullshit."

"I don't take that kind of crap from some country bumpkin like you!" The voice suddenly got loud and forceful. "Watch what you say." Förster's hand shook and sloshed the hot coffee out of the cup and on his other hand. It hurt. "You're under my control, get it? So behave yourself. Just look at your dog. It knows how to obey."

You damned bastard! Förster thought, filled with seething hate. *You damned outerspace bastard. I'm not a St. Bernard. I'm not your dog. I won't be treated like that!*

"Bow-wow," the alien retorted mockingly and clammed up.

July 10, 9:50 A.M. "All right," Förster directed his message inward. "I flew off the handle a little. I didn't mean it. Let's be on speaking terms again."

He got no answer.

"Hey, you . . ." Förster suddenly realized that he did not know the name of the entity possessing him. "Come on."

The alien remained mute.

"Aw, the galactic superbrain's pouting. How atavistic. I thought you were smarter and more objective than that."

Förster sensed a weak emotion he could not classify, even though it seemed familiar to him. But that was the only response from the alien.

Förster felt an astonishing touch of regret. He missed the voice of the furious invader. Arguing was still better than no communication whatsoever.

He listened attentively. After several minutes he finally gave up. All alone once again.

"Well, kiss my ass then," he mumbled. He motioned to the waiter, who seemed not to notice—as usual. Everything was back to normal.

He dropped his hand that had been sticking awkwardly up in the air and laid it on his other hand. It was a very stable position, his hands did not shake that way. He leaned back and looked out over the lake where a swan was gliding by. The two straight lines forming its V-shaped wake sparkled on the calm green water. The swan acted very proud. It was a young swan.

July 10, 7:30 P.M. Förster was exhausted. All day long he, rather the alien controlling him, had been calling, conferring, wheeling and dealing. Hour after hour, Förster heard himself talking in some foreign language he did not understand. It was frightening. He thought he was schizophrenic.

Now he was sitting in his comfortable easy chair by an open window, trying to relax. He felt as if he had undergone major surgery, weak, jittery, old, more dead than alive. The only sounds in the room were those of birds chirping in the garden and the regular ticking of the grandfather clock. How loud it sounded! Förster closed his eyes.

"It was a hard day today," the alien's voice said softly.

Förster did not move a muscle. "Leave me alone," he babbled. "I'm bushed."

"Me too."

Taken aback, Förster blinked. Somehow it had never occurred to him that the extraterrestrial could get tired. He acted so all-powerful. He was certainly young, a thoroughly tested specialist in interstellar contact. And he had no body, he was just a mind.

But minds can get tired. Nobody knew that better than Förster.

"Being tired serves you quite right," he said with the last trace of anger he could muster in his exhausted state. "Nobody asked you to come here and make weird deals. Why are you really doing it?"

" 'Cause it's my duty. There aren't many people on my planet who can bridge big voids between the stars by thought projection. There are only a few of us, and the work's very stressful. But somebody has to do it."

"Doesn't sound very heroic."

For the first time the alien let out something like a laugh, but there was no humor in it. "It's anything but heroic. It's very tiring and duller than dull. What's so special about being a member of an interplanetary field service?"

"Interplanetary field service?" Förster repeated disconcerted. "That's . . . I mean—I hadn't considered it from that angle yet."

"Yeah, I know. To you we're what the mythical white gods were to the Incas—powerful beings from another world, with superior knowledge and astounding devices. But we're only a couple of business people trading a few glass beads for valuable raw materials. And that's your good fortune, because instead of salesmen we could be mercenaries who'd rather rip off than pay."

"But—"

"That caught you off guard, didn't it? You pictured us as outerspace brains, scientifically and intellectually advanced, didn't you? I doubt we are. We merely came here to do business. And I have to do it as coolly, quickly, and efficiently as possible so that I get high returns. So don't bellyache to me that you're too old and tired, because it just costs me time."

Coolly, quickly, and efficently, Förster thought. *Strange, this could have come from Berghäuser, his former boss decades ago. Selling's like boxing, Förster. Whoever's faster, more resistant, and more powerful wins. Yes, Mr. Berghäuser. No, Barbara. Not today. I'm too tired. Have fifteen customers I have to call on.*

He noticed that the alien had been quiet for a while.

"I don't want to rub you the wrong way," the alien finally said.

"No, no," Förster said. "That's all right. It was very . . . down to earth." He shook his head and even smiled. "It's unbelievable. You have the salesman's blues. I can spot it a mile away. Too much routine and too far from home. The salesman's blues . . ."

The alien's voice again got hard and authoritarian.

"That'll be enough of that. I'll be in touch tomorrow at seven on the dot. See you then."

"Yep," Förster said. "Good night," he added after a short pause.

July 11, 2:00 P.M. Förster pushed the empty dessert dish aside and belched discreetly.

"That was good." He felt full and satisfied as he had not in a long time. All morning long he had been doing business, partly in the alien's language, partly in German or English. It had been very strenuous, but he had been filled with strange delight. He was busy again, and in a certain way he even had a goal. He had not felt like this in years.

"I'd like a cappuccino," he said to the waiter scurrying past him. He did not say it loudly, but there was a new tone of authority in his voice the waiter responded to.

"Súbito, signore."

"Well, well! Your old self again, old man?"

The overt aggressiveness in the alien's voice shocked Förster so much that he could get out only a feeble, defensive "Well, yes."

"Wow, fantastic!" the extraterrestrial said irritably. Then came a maelstrom of emotion in whose swirling confusion only one feature stood out—hysteria.

Förster paid no attention to it. He was furious. What right did this intruding interloper have to spoil his mood? For the first time in years he had a hint of lust for life, and this bastard was trying to mar it for him!

"Still the salesman's blues?" he taunted.

"You're damned right!" the alien exploded. "My God, how I hate it. Lousy planet, lousy business, lousy people. I can't hack it anymore! Things were never this bad until I teamed up with you. A Sirian neurotic and an Earth neurotic—what a terrific team. Just why do I do it to myself?"

Förster was upset. It was not so much the emotional outburst per se that stirred him up, but rather the vague, almost subliminal knowledge that the alien was a mirror image of his own behavior. The signals were extremely clear—self-pity and aggression. Envious of happy people because you yourself were unhappy. Förster did not like that mirror image.

"It's already tough enough, but you make me a complete outsider on my own team," the alien fumed. "Every Earth person who's been taken over by outerspacers should participate in meetings that are held in their respective countries to coordinate activities. I'm one of the few who couldn't attend because . . ."

He hesitated for a moment, but Förster knew what was coming anyway and instinctively held his breath.

"Because you're too old and decrepit. The long trip's too risky for you to undertake. That's a bad joke. I'm stranded. Stranded in a dying man."

Förster said nothing for a long time. "Why," he finally whispered, "do you say such things? That's malicious and cruel." Acting on a whim, he ordered a bottle of red wine. The alien did not interfere.

When Förster left the restaurant about an hour later, he was pretty drunk and left too big a tip.

July 11, 3:30 P.M. When Förster opened the door, Samson was lying in front of him. There was so much pain in the animal's eyes that it had an effect like ecstasy.

"Samson!" Förster yelled. "What's the matter with you, boy?"

He got on his knees and put his hand on the dog's head. At the same instant, as if the St. Bernard had expended his last ounce of energy to experience one last touch from his master, Samson died.

"This is too much," Förster wheezed. "It can't be true."

Mulling over the next few minutes the following day, he wondered how many tears there were in a wrinkled old man like him.

July 11, 6:00 P.M. The pen jerked across the paper and drew a wavy line resembling mountains with sharp peaks and deep valleys. Another device emitted beeping sounds which were pretty regular, but not completely so. One of the pieces of adhesive tape holding the electrodes to Förster's body itched. An analyzing device in the corner hummed and shook a test tube of Förster's blood, an efficient new-generation Dracula.

Förster submitted to the monthly checkup with stoic indifference. He hardly noticed the humiliating procedures, the poking at and probing in his body. He lay on his back wearing only his underwear. The plastic cover on the examining table sticking to his body seemed to be clutching him tightly like a hungry octopus.

Nobody but Förster was in the room. No doctor or nurse stood watch over routine procedures these days unless something went wrong. You were connected to a multitude of machines, and Dr. Electronix performed the examination.

Everything in the room was white, bright, and clean. If the reports of people who were clinically dead and then revived were true, you seemed to float up at the moment of death and move toward a dazzlingly bright light. From that aspect the examining room with its humming, featureless brightness seemed to be a simulator for death candidates. An anteroom to death.

The thought passed quickly. Förster again stared at the ceiling impassively. He had nothing on his mind, he was just waiting for something. The E.T. did likewise. They were two aliens on Earth, isolated together. Two black holes into which all the sadness and depression in the universe poured.

July 11, 11:00 P.M. It was one of the few privileges of age, Förster thought as he poured himself a second glass of Drambuie, that you require little sleep. Too bad that you could not start on any new enterprises with all your free time.

He was sitting in the living room in his favorite easy chair. He was looking through the window at the trees, swaying silhouettes with silver leaves shimmering in the chalk-white light of a full moon. He was wide-awake, slightly drunk, and up to his knees in memories.

Acting on a whim, he put a record on. Debussy's "Claire de Lune." While the romantic piano sounds permeated the room, Förster's thoughts began to wander. Scenes from his life flashed before his mind's eye and went out again.

A joyless youth in a strict, loveless home. During his school days a long series of puzzling diseases—psychosomatic, as he now knew. An irascible father. Failure, weakling. The first year at college. Complete disorientation, which gradually gave way to a feeling of freedom. Then the outbreak of World War II. Out of the lecture hall and up to the front. Six years in which he stopped thinking. Nothing but fight, advance, retreat. He did not hate anybody, but he killed other men to keep them from killing him. Somehow he stayed alive. He was the only one of his company of 120 men to survive the war.

Sometimes he still dreamed about shells hitting and blowing up foxholes and hurling broken bodies through the air. Bodies without faces, without limbs, but still alive. Cannon fodder for insatiable warlords. He dreamed about the icy cold of the Russian steppes, snow red with blood for kilometers, the leather belts they chewed on because they had nothing to eat. He dreamed about the Siberian POW camp where he spent four years. The Russians treated them badly, but he could not blame them for it at all. When he was finally released and after ten years returned to civilian life, a shadow lay over him. He was not neurotic or psychotic, no, but he seldom laughed and seemed singularly distant. He acted like someone who had been subjected to electroshock therapy too often and who was now waiting for the next jolt with tense anticipation.

Förster's flow of memories was interrupted when the music stopped. He flinched, drifting between reality and memories for an instant. Then he found himself back in reality.

There was a thundering silence in the room—and in his thoughts. The alien was keeping quiet. Nevertheless, Förster was sure that he was listening intently.

"Well, have you obtained any interesting information about life on Earth?" he asked sarcastically.

"Yeah, that I have," the extraterrestrial said. He seemed to want to add something, even though he then fell silent again. "Maybe you should put on another record," he said after a while. "That'll do us some good. That music was very lovely."

Förster nodded. He got up and put on Frederic Chopin's Nocturne No. 2 in E-flat Major. With music came memories. At the beginning of the fifties he got acquainted with Barbara. They got married, and she made him very happy. His climb up the corporate ladder began. He made a good deal of money. The big break kept eluding him, though. He lacked charisma, his bosses said. That did not bother Förster. He was leading a wonderful life with Barbara and the kids. But the shadow still followed him and never left. He was happy, but it was a second-hand happiness because it came from the circumstances and not from the heart. He kept telling himself: You have everything you want. You should be happy. But it did not work. He finally resigned himself to that. At least he was contented.

The record player shut off with a soft click.

"How beautiful," the alien said. "How wonderfully beautiful. I believe music is the best thing this planet has to offer. Please play me some more of it."

The extraterrestrial's voice was so soft and urgent that Förster unhesitatingly pulled another record off the shelf.

"Lonely, huh?" he said.

"Who isn't?" the alien replied.

Förster looked across the dark room to the corner Samson always used to sleep in. "Yeah, who isn't?"

The needle was put on the record. "Strangers in the Night." Barbara had loved that melody. How many times had they danced to its sounds! Förster could not dance, but when he and Barbara were together, he could. "Midnight Cowboy." He had heard this tune for the first time late one night in his hotel room. Oh, those lonely nights in a hotel while he was on the road. Being the last person at the bar. Undecidedly shaking the empty glass in his hand. One more! Sorry, sir, we're closing now. Oh, yeah, well then, good evening. Good evening, sir. Then lying on the bed sweaty and restless in his dark room. Outside it is quiet. Everybody is asleep. But not you. Soft music purred from the radio, comforting all who had no other consolation. Help me make it through the night. Lying in the dark listening to music is nice. Thoughts flow quietly. There is a bitter sweetness in your loneliness. While you are thinking over your life, you slowly fall asleep.

Förster now felt the presence of the extraterrestrial quite clearly. It seemed as if the alien had moved closer.

"Moonlight Serenade." Also one of Barbara's favorite melodies. She had requested it from every hotel orchestra. She was a good dancer. The way she did the tango drove men crazy. Förster enjoyed it the best he could. But that was all in the past now. Barbara was dead and gone. And it takes two to tango.

He felt miserable. And the extraterrestrial felt exactly the same way. Uncertain quaking emotions struck Förster, quite obviously the telepathic equivalent of passionate crying.

Förster did not know what to do. "Now it wasn't all that bad," he said helplessly. No, not really. "Moonlight Serenade" reminded him of his tenth wedding anniversary. They were dancing on the terrace of a luxury hotel on the Côte d'Azur. Stars twinkled in their Mediterranean splendor. The sea was a dark mirror that a phosphorescent wave crest sometimes rippled across. A colorfully illuminated fountain splashed nearby. In the background, the palatial hotel was shimmering in the darkness like a fairy-tale castle. Up there little Sandra was sleeping happily and contentedly in their room. And he danced with Barbara on and on and on. His feet hardly seemed to touch the floor. Tonight he was Cary Grant, and Barbara was Grace Kelly.

Yes.

"It wasn't really all that bad," Förster muttered. "No, not that bad at all," he repeated, rather surprised, and fell asleep.

The ghost of a smile was outlined on his lips.

July 12, 3:00 P.M. The air-conditioning unit in the conference room was set on high. Cold. White walls, white leather and chrome furniture. Cold. A smartly dressed guy in a pinstripe suit with eyes like marbles. Cold.

The negotiations with Dr. Hellman—the name of the smiling businessman enjoying himself—had reached an impasse. Förster had not understood a word of the conversation he had been carrying on in some foreign language, but it was also unmistakably clear to him that it had stopped dead.

He felt anger and desperation rising in him, emotions that were not his own but radiated from the otherwise hermetically sealed mind of the extraterrestrial.

At first, Förster was amused by the helplessness of the all-powerful alien. But then the echo of the alien's frustration got so loud and so similar to his own depression that spontaneous solidarity germinated in him. He wanted to help his extraterrestrial tenant somehow. Nobody should be so humbled.

When the alien lost control over Förster during his emotional crisis, Förster acted without thinking. He simply got up and went to the door.

Two separate things happened.

He heard a kind of hysterical laughter in his head linked to a feeling of release.

Dr. Hellman jumped up and rushed after him, spewing out a stream of words. Obviously, his bargaining position was not so good as he made it appear.

It so happened that the alien was then able to close the deal to his satisfaction. When they left the office building and went into the heat on the street, the extraterrestrial said quite calmly, "Thanks, Robert."

That was the first time the alien had called Förster by name.

July 12, 11:30 P.M. That night, too, Förster played whatever came to mind—Tchaikovsky, Gershwin, medieval madrigals, African tribal chants, and lots of Mozart. The room was almost dark, the problems of the world far away. Everything was pleasant.

As Förster was looking for a new piece of music, he caught sight of a stack of records that were off to one side on the shelf, separate from the others. He smiled.

"Here, this was something different at one time," he said. "The Rolling Stones. '2,000 Light-Years from Home.' That's for you. And there, the Beatles. 'When I'm 64.' That's for me."

Yet when he picked up the record, his hand began trembling, and he realized he had made a bad mistake. Sudden grief flooded out his thoughts. Nothing was pleasant anymore.

"What's wrong?" the alien asked.

"My kids," Förster said. "I must've been thinking about my kids. I bought these records for them back then. My God, how long ago that was. Almost twenty years, Sandra and Richard . . ."

Sandra was their first child. How he had doted on that tiny tot! When her miniature hand closed around his outstretched finger for the first time, that was possibly the loveliest moment in his whole life. Her faint gurgling sounds, which had filled the house with magic harmony. Her first words, her first clumsy steps undeniably ending in a plop on her diaper-cushioned behind. And how fascinating it had been to watch that little kid exploring her world. How she laughed and marveled at things he himself no longer noticed. In those days he had learned a lot from Sandra, a new unpretentiousness, a new openness to the many small wonders in life. How uncomplicated it was to be happy.

In time, Sandra had kids herself. She had married a guy Förster could not stand, who lived in Berlin. I can't come, Dad. Heinz has so much to do. And with the kids it's so hard to get away, and it's such a long trip. Some other time, perhaps. Yeah, some other time, Sandra. Click. I would not mind your telling me lies as long as you were at least happy. But you are not. Oh, Sandra. So much love that will never be returned.

And Richard was stranger still. As a kid, he had always been a bit chubby and awkward, but unbelievably friendly and even-tempered, a chubby-faced angel nobody could say no to. Most of all, Förster recalled two episodes that for some reason had stayed in his mind. They were at the zoo. Richard was three years old. For the first time in his life he had gotten an ice cream cone and paid for it with the money his father had counted out beforehand. He was so proud of his accomplishment that he forgot to eat his ice cream. He stared and stared at it—his very own first ice cream—and the colored balls were melting and dripping and smearing his hands and his blissfully smiling face. A year later, on a bitterly cold Sunday in December, Richard came into his study with his broken toy truck and said, "Put it back together, Daddy. You can do it. You can do anything." Förster saw the blind trust in the boy's face, and sweat broke out on him because he knew he could not fix the toy. It was a moment of both such intense pride and pain that it still moved him deeply after all these years.

Richard was now a successful dental surgeon, slim, suntanned, dynamic. He had a perfect house and a perfect wife. Everything he did was perfect. He was even perfectly unhappy. His birthday and Christmas cards always arrived punctually.

Förster noticed that he was still standing in front of the record player and was holding the album in his hand. "When I'm 64." Life is guaranteed to take the worst of all possible turns. Förster's law of autobiographical flashbacks.

With a hopeless gesture he sat down. A life filled with struggle and striving—for this wretched result? That was a cruel joke.

Suddenly, the alien's voice, which he had completely forgotten about, was in his head again. It was tender and filled with sympathy such as Förster had not experienced for an eternity.

"You're a good man, Robert Förster. I like you a lot." The alien thought for a moment. "Your memories always surprise me over and over. Our lives have so many parallels. Battling against the worst odds, giving your best, and ending up as a winner with a feeling of loss. I'm familiar with that." A kaleidoscope of incomprehensible alien scenes flashed through Förster's mind, memories of a distant planet. "Funny how life in the universe follows universal rules."

Förster felt the sincere warmth in the words of the alien, who did not seem to him as strange now as he once had. The extraterrestrial's concern was as startling as a surprise visit to someone sick in bed and just as comforting.

"Thanks," he said. "Thanks, uh . . ."

"Sassacan," the alien said. "Sassacan's the name."

July 13, 7:00 A.M. An early-morning peace still lay over the land. The sun had just risen over the treetops. Its down-sloping light cast grotesquely long shadows and made dewdrops sparkle. The lake was calm; only a couple of fishermen were rowing across the water through the haze. In the cool, fresh air wafting across the balcony, the rattling of Förster's breakfast dishes sounded louder and happier than usual.

"Now we're friends," Sassacan said. "That happens very rarely on my missions. Generally speaking, I'm regarded as an oppressor, an occupation force. Here on earth it seems to be just the same way. But you're an exception."

"I am?"

"Yeah. Despite your personal problems you've been unusually open-minded. Most people react hysterically when I . . . come to them. From the first second on, you were completely cool, calm, and collected."

"Maybe because I'm old. I've seen a lot in my day. I know nothing's impossible. What could still surprise me?" Förster took another sip of coffee. "You made it easy for me. You respected me —after a while. Most of you outerspace types seem to be very aggressive. Why do you act differently?"

"We're not all cast from the same mold. We come from different planets, so we behave in different ways. You know, we Sirians had a horrible war not too long ago. That experience has made us more peaceful than other races."

"I see. Yes, war changes one." For a moment, Förster's thoughts started wandering. Dying men writhing in blood and mud. Dead children in ruins, their arms torn off like discarded dolls. Small, unimportant bodies, which did not count in the larger scheme of things. Oh, God.

"You dwell a lot on those things, Robert."

"Yeah. They've changed my life."

"You also think about Barbara frequently," Sassacan said, changing the subject.

"I simply can't forget her." Förster stared at his coffee spoon as if it were an exotic insect. "Though she's been dead for ten years now."

"Ten years?" Sassacan said. "I didn't think it had been that long ago. She's so . . . present in your thoughts."

"You didn't think so?" Förster was taken aback. "But you did know that. You can read every last one of my thoughts."

"It's not that simple. To me your mind's like a great big library. I can find any piece of information in it. But I have to scrounge around for it first. There are a lot of unread books standing on the shelves."

"So that's the way it is." Förster chuckled in his distant fashion. "So do I still have my own little secrets from you?"

"Yes, of course." Sassacan was now talking very slowly. "I started to like you when I read your thoughts about Barbara. So much love for a sister from Earth has deeply moved me."

"A sister?" Förster sputtered. "You mean, you mean you're a female?"

"Yes, most of the time, that is."

Förster gulped. "That changes the score. Then we're on the way to an interstellar love affair, aren't we?"

They both laughed a little too loudly about that.

July 13, 6:00 p.m. Last night a thunderstorm had blown up and cleaned and cooled the air. Förster enjoyed his constitutional on the lakeside promenade much more than he had during the last few weeks. The weather was mild, you could see as far as the most distant mountain peaks. And he had a friend.

Förster and Sassacan watched the souvenir vendors dismantle their stands with postcards and silly plastic mementos. Swimmers and surfers were landing on the beach and packing up their things. Handsome young people with well-proportioned bodies so deeply tanned that their lips seemed pale on dark faces. They got into their Broncos, Pajeros, Jeeps, Rabbit convertibles and sped away to some other pressing engagement. Eager hedonists always on the go. To Förster they still seemed more alien than Sassacan, but he did not hate them anymore.

"A beautiful day today," he said.

"Yes," Sassacan said.

Snatches of sound from a carnival drifted across the lake. Förster was listening to the oompahpah of a brass band. "You wanna listen to music again this evening?"

"Oh, yeah," Sassacan said. "Very much."

"How about an organ concert . . ." Förster stopped, irritated somehow. "Anything wrong?"

"I have to go back tomorrow," Sassacan's voice was as emotionless as a vocoder. "The job's finished. The traveling salesman travels on. You know how it is."

"But," Förster stammered, "right now?" He could not talk anymore. Blood roared in his ears. His heart beat like a hammer. *Now that I have had a taste of hope!*

"Life's a sadist," Sassacan said.

Förster said nothing. He plopped down on a bench, older and lonelier than ever before, shivering in the warm sunlight.

July 14, 3:30 P.M. Förster slammed the telephone receiver down on its cradle with intense satisfaction. He had just canceled his weekly doctor's appointment. "Make your money off of some other old idiot, doctor. I'm still not so infirm that I have to sit around in your consulting room all the time. I'll let you know when I need you."

He sniggered. I'll let you know when I need you. That was a good one. Took that smart-ass authority figure down a peg or two.

In every respect it had been a remarkable day. At breakfast in the Café Panorama a slim young man sat down at his table. He seemed bewildered and distressed. Somehow they got to talking. It turned out that the young man had inherited a company that was highly respected, but with the flood of cheap imports from the Far East could not compete anymore. With modern production equipment he would again be able to land contracts, but he did not have enough ready cash, and banks would not extend him any credit. In a few weeks the firm would go bankrupt.

"That's simple, young man," Förster said. "What you need is a sale-and-leaseback contract. It goes like this. You sell your expensive factory buildings to a leasing company. You get a lot of money for them. At the same time, you rent the buildings back from the leasing company. That way you can stay in there and continue production, *and* you turn your hidden reserves into ready money. You invest this money and get your firm on its feet again. When you've made enough profit, you buy back the factory buildings after a couple of years."

The young man choked and panted until his face was dark red. "That's incredible!" he gasped. "That's it! How can I ever thank you?"

"That's all right," Förster said offhandedly. "It was a pleasure for me. From now on, perhaps you'll view old people in a little different light. A lot of years means a lot of experience, you see." He passed his business card across the table. "Just give me a call if you run into problems."

"I most certainly will," the young man said happily and hastily got up.

Förster watched him with amusement. So he was not quite a

doddering old fool yet. The waiter found that out the hard way, and he paid for it when as usual he ignored Förster's signal. Förster went to the business manager, who fired the waiter on the spot. "That's the fifth or sixth complaint this week, Schulz. That's it for me. You're dismissed."

Nice going. Yes, people, Förster is back in the swing of things. Watch out and don't cross me. I'm not gonna let anything happen to me anymore.

The morning was extremely hectic. Sassacan still had a lot to finish before she left Earth. She seemed pretty mad. "Typical. The others stay here quite a while longer, but we Sirians have to wind up our business in record time again. Always the same old thing."

But that did not bother Förster. On the contrary, he even liked the high level of activity. It was better than morosely sitting on some park bench and watching the party from outside.

Perhaps that was why he reacted so quickly to the incident in the Swan Hotel. He had just finished a conversation with one of Sassacan's business associates and was waiting for a taxi in the hotel lobby. Outside, a heavy summer thunderstorm was raging. Rain poured down windows like a waterfall. A woman with a huge Labrador retriever rushed through the door pretty well soaked. At that same moment, lightning struck the office building on the other side of the street. A blinding flash and ear-splitting thunder filled every corner of the room.

The Labrador got loose and ran through the lobby barking and terrified, eyes bulging. He looked as aggressive as a dangerous beast.

Förster was the only one who acted. As the dog sped by him, he grabbed the leash and shouted sharply, "Sit!"

The dog was so well trained that it obeyed instantly in spite of its terror. Förster patted the dog reassuringly. "Easy there, Samson boy, easy. Everything's all right. Take it easy."

Panic gradually faded from the dog's eyes. Meanwhile, his master had walked over beside Förster.

"Thanks," she said calmly.

Förster turned to her and knew at once this was a special moment in his life. Barbara was there again. Of course, it was not

Barbara, but she would have looked like that at sixty. Short, silver-gray, almost-metallic-looking hair in a page-boy cut, gray eyes that reacted with amusement to his stare, a beaming face that hid its years, plus a radiating youthful vitality. Plain expensive clothes.

"That was extraordinarily quick thinking on your part," she said. "I really must thank you, Mr. . . . ."

Förster kept staring at her. The way she looked, the way she talked. It was a miracle. He suddenly realized that all the years he had been weighed down with anger and depression, he had been waiting for just such a moment as this, as a candle waits for the match to light it.

He realized that he had not answered her question. "Förster," he said. "Robert Förster."

"I'm Katharina Erhard." She smiled. "Are you a reporter? You seem to be quite inquisitive."

"Oh, no, excuse me, I—" With mild astonishment he observed how he put his arm on her shoulder and spontaneously said, "You're dripping wet. Take off your coat, and then let's go to the bar. A little whiskey'll warm you up."

She smiled again and said yes, and then they were sitting in the dark wood-paneled bar and talking and talking. There was a faint smell of wood, leather, and tobacco in the air mixed with the fragrance of her expensive perfume.

Förster was happy.

July 14, 9:00 P.M. From the east, night spread across the sky. In the west, the day took its leave with bizarre-looking cloud sculptures scudding across a horizon festooned in gold, red, and purple.

Förster stood on the terrace of the *Herrenchiemsee* Castle and gazed upon the splendor of the park as it slowly slipped into twilight. Water in the big fountain created gracefully dancing, regularly changing figures. Bright light fell on the terrace from the hall of mirrors behind Förster. Hundreds of torches were burning inside there, and expectantly cheerful people in evening clothes waited for the castle concert to begin.

And Katharina was waiting for him. He thought about the trip on the paddle steamer which had brought them across the lake to the island where the *Herrenchiemsee* Castle was located. They stood at the railing, quiet, their heads full of thoughts. The evening wind smelled of algae. Förster listened to the asthmatic chugging of the old steamer. How many things he saw, smelled, and felt that he had not noticed in the past few years.

It was the most natural thing in the world for his hand to close over hers and for him to kiss her. Their lips touched with the soft, wonderful tenderness that you could only find in very small children who have just discovered the grace of giving. Then they went back into the passenger room, where they drank a glass of champagne and celebrated the grand reopening of Förster's life.

"I'm very happy," Sassacan said, "that I can end my stay on Earth on such a lovely day and happy note. I'm leaving you now, Robert."

Förster nodded. This moment had to come. It was a sad moment.

"Sassacan," he said. "I'd like to say so much to you, that I hardly know where to—"

"No need to," Sassacan said. "You know I'm looking through you."

"Oh, sure," Förster laughed. "What an unbelievable story. Of all 'people,' an extraterrestrial helps me get back to the land of the living."

"You've helped yourself," Sassacan said. "All I've done is interrupt your routine just as you've interrupted mine. We've learned a lot from each other."

"Yeah. Too bad you have to go now."

"You do have Katharina now."

"Luckily. I don't know if otherwise I could really bear losing you." A thought flashed through Förster's head. "Hey, wait a minute! Katharina . . . the young man with the bankrupt company . . . Katharina looking like Barbara. A whole bunch of coincidences for a single day. And the fact that just after a few minutes I put my arm around Katharina. That's not my way. You arranged everything and pulled the marionette strings a bit. Right?"

"Maybe, maybe not," Sassacan replied. "No matter. You're happy, and it makes my leaving easier."

"You bastard," Förster said. "I like you. Goddamn it, but I do like you."

"I like you, too, Robert. So long. Keep moving."

"So long, Sassacan. And thanks for everything."

Then Förster was all alone again. Lost in thought, he stared at the park, which now lay in full darkness. His lips moved, mumbling soundless words. Then he turned around and walked to the brightly illuminated hall of mirrors. At the door he cast one more glance over his shoulder up at the sky.

Good luck, Sassacan, wherever you are.

The stars were slowly coming out.

The Legend of the Paper Spaceship

BY TETSU YANO
Translated by Gene Van Troyer and Tomoko Oshiro

Halfway through the Pacific War, I was sent from my unit to a village in the heart of the mountains, and there I lived for some months. I still recall clearly the road leading into that village; and in the grove of bamboo trees beside the road, the endless flight of a paper airplane and a beautiful naked woman running after it. Now, long years later, I cannot shake the feeling that what she was always folding out of paper stood for no earthly airplane, but for a spaceship. Some time long ago, deep in those mountain recesses . . .

I

The paper airplane glides gracefully above the earth; and weaving between the sprouts of new bamboo, stealing over the deep-piled humus of fallen and decaying leaves, a white mist comes blowing, eddying and dancing up high on the back of a subtle breeze, moving on and on.

In the bamboo grove the flowing mist gathers in thick and brooding pools. Twilight comes quickly to this mountain valley. Like a ship sailing a sea of clouds, the paper airplane flies on and on through the mist.

□ 231

> *"One—a stone stairway to the sky*
> *Two—if it doesn't fly*
> *Three—if it does fly, open . . ."*

A woman's voice, singing through the mist. As if pushed onward by that voice, the paper airplane lifts in never-ending flight. A naked woman owns the voice, and white in her nudity she slips quickly between the swaying bamboo of the grove.

(Kill them! Kill them!)

Alarm sirens wove screaming patterns around shrieking voices.

(Kill everyone! That's an order!)

(Don't let any get to the ship! One's escaped!)

(Beamers! Fire, fire!)

A crowd of voices resounding in this mist, but no one else can hear them. These voices echo only in the woman's head.

Tall and leafy and standing like images of charcoal gray against a pale ash background, the bamboo trees appear and disappear and reappear among the gauzy veils of the always folding rolling mist. The fallen leaves whisper as the woman's feet rustle over them. Mist streams around her like something alive as she walks, then flows apart before her to allow the dim shape of what might be a small lake to peek through.

Endworld Mere: the *uba-iri-no-numa*. After they had laughed and danced through the promises and passions of living youth, old people once came often to this place to end the misery of their old age by throwing themselves into the swamp's murky waters.

Superstition holds that Endworld Mere swarms with the spirits of the dead. To placate any of the lingering dead, therefore, these valley folk had heaped numerous mounds of stones in a small open space near the mere. This place they named the *Sai no Kawara*, the earthly shore where the journey over the Great Waters began. They gathered here once a year for memorial services, when they burnt incense and clapped hands and sent their prayers across the Wide Waters to the shore of the nether world.

No matter how many stone towers you erect on the earthly shore of the River of Three Crossings, the myths tell us that demons will destroy them. Whether physical or spectral, here too the "demons" had been about the tireless task of destruction. In the very beginning there had probably been but a few mounds of tombstones to consecrate the unknown dead; but over the years, hundreds of stones had been heaped, and now lay scattered. Throughout most of the year, the place was now little more than a last rest stop where the infrequent person bound on the one-way trip to Endworld Mere paused for a short time before moving on. Because of its deserted silence, men and women seeking a little more excitement in life found the place ideal for secret rendezvous.

Secret meetings were often a singular concern for these simple village folk. They could think of little else but pleasure. "Endworld Mere" is a name that suggests even the old go there with stealth, and possibly the dreadful legends surrounding the place were fabricated by anxious lovers who wished to make it a place more secure for their trystings.

Owing to these frightening stories, the village children gave the mere a wide berth. Round lichen-covered stones, rain-soaked and rotting paper dolls, creaking wooden signs with mysterious, indecipherable characters inscribed on them: For children these things all bespoke the presence of ghosts and ogres and nightmare encounters with demons.

Sometimes, however, the children would unintentionally come close enough to glimpse the dank mere, and on one such occasion they were chasing the madwoman Osen, who was flying a paper airplane.

"Say, guys! Osen's still runnin' aroun' naked!"

"*Hey*, Osen! Doncha wan' any *clothes?*"

All the children jeered Osen. For adult and child alike she is a handy plaything.

But Osen had a toy, too: a paper airplane, as thin, as sharp-pointed as a spear.

> "*One, a white star*
> *Two, a red star* . . ."

In the mist she sings, and dreams: the reason she flies her paper airplane, the hatred that in her burns for human beings.

Osen, whose body is ageless, steps lightly over the grass, reaches the mere where the enfeebled old cast themselves away to die. The paper airplane flies on against the mist before her. No one knows what keeps the plane flying so long. Once Osen lets go of it, the "airplane" flies on seemingly forever. That's all there is to it. . . .

A madwoman, is Osen, going about naked in summer, and in the winter wearing only one thin robe.

2

There is a traditional song that the village children sang while playing ball, of which I vaguely recall one part:

> *I'll wait if it flies,*
> *if it doesn't I won't—*
> *I alone will keep waiting here.*
> *I wonder if I'll ever climb*
> *those weed-grown stairs someday—*
> *One star far and two stars near . . .*

Naked in the summer, and in the winter she wears one thin robe.

Most adults ignored the children who jeered at Osen, but there were a few who scolded them.

"Shame on you! Stop it! You should *pity* poor Osen."

The children just backtalked, often redoubling their jeers to the tune of a local rope-skipping song, or else throwing catcalls back and forth.

"Hey, *Gen!* Ya fall in *love* with Osen? Ya *sleep* with her last night?"

"Don't be an idiot!"

Even if adults reprimanded them like this, the kids kept up exactly the same sort of raillery. After all, everyone knew that last night, or the night before, or the night before that, at least *one* of the village men made love to Osen.

Osen: She must have been close to her forties. Some villagers claimed she was much, *much* older than that, but one look at Osen put the lie to their claims: She was youthful freshness incarnate, her body that of a woman not even twenty.

Osen: community property, harlot to all who came for it, the butt of randy male superiority. Coming to know the secrets of her body was a kind of "rite of passage" for all the young men of the village.

Osen: the village idiot. This was the other reason why the villagers sheltered her.

Osen was the only daughter and survivor of the village's most ancient family. Among those who live deep in the mountains and still pay homage to the Wolf God, the status of a household was regarded as supremely important. That such an imbecile should be the sole survivor of so exalted a household gave everyone a limitless sense of superiority—Osen! Plaything for the village sports!

Her house stood on a knoll, from where you could look down on Endworld Mere. Perhaps it's better to say where her house was *left*, rather than stood. At the bottom of the stone stairs leading up to her door, the openwork gate to her yard didn't know whether to fall down or not. Tiles were ready to drop from the gate roof, and tangled weeds and grass overgrew the ruins of the small room where long ago a servant would hold a brazier for the gatekeeper's warmth in winter.

A step inside the gate and the stone stairs leading up were choked with moss and weeds. The curious thing was, the center of the stairway had not been worn down; rather, both sides were. Nobody ever walked in the middle, say the old stories. According to the oldest man in the village, on New Year's Eve they used to welcome in the new year and send off the old with a Shinto ritual, and in one line of the chant there was a passage about a Gate protected by the Center of a Stone Stairway built by a forgotten Brotherhood; and since no one knew the meaning of that, the old man said, people felt it best to avoid the center of *this* stone stairway whenever they passed up or down it.

The stairway climbed a short way beyond Osen's house to where the ground flattened and widened out and was covered with a profusion of black stones. An old crumbling well with a collapsing roof propped up by four posts was there. Sunk into the summit of this hill, one of the highest points in the valley, the well had never gone dry: Fathoms of water always filled it. If any high mountains had been massed nearby this would have explained such vast quantities of water; but there were no such mountains, and this well defied physical law. Sinner's Hole, they called it. When the men were finished with Osen they came to this wellside to wash.

Once when a shrill group of cackling old women gathered at the well to hold yearly memorial services and pray to the Wolf God, one of them was suddenly stricken with a divination and proclaimed that if Osen were soaked in the well, her madness would abate. This cheered up those who envied Osen's great beauty, so on that day twelve years ago poor Osen was stripped to the raw before the eyes of the assembled women and dunked into the winter-frigid well water. An hour later, her body blushed a livid purple, Osen fainted and was finally hauled out. Sadly her idiocy was not cured. Story has it that the old crone who blurted the augury was drunk on the millet wine being served at the memorial service, and that afterward she fell into Endworld Mere and drowned. Because of the wine?

From then on, once someone undressed her, Osen stayed that way. If someone draped a robe over her, she kept it on. Since someone undressed her nearly every night and left her as she was in the morning, Osen most often went around naked.

Beautiful as the men might find Osen's body, others thought it best to keep the children from seeing her. Therefore, each morning a village woman came around to see that she was dressed. Osen stayed stone-still when being dressed, though sometimes she smiled happily. She went on singing her songs—

> *"Folding one,* dah-dum
> *fold a second one,* tah-tum
> *a third one fold,* tra-lah!
> *Fly on, I say fly!*
> *Fly ever on to my star!"*

—folding her paper airplanes while she murmured and sang. And one day soon, to the stunned amazement of the villagers and eventual focus of their great uproar, Osen's stomach began growing larger.

No one had ever stopped to think that Osen might someday be gotten with child.

The village hens got together and clucked about it, fumbling in their brains for hours to find some way to keep Osen from having the child. Finally they moved en masse to the ramshackle house where Osen lived her isolated life, and they confronted her with their will.

The idiot Osen, however, shocked everyone when for the first time in living memory she explicitly stated her *own* will: She would have this baby.

"Osen! No arguments. We're taking you to the city, and you'll see a doctor."

"Don't be *ridi*culous, Osen. Why, you couldn't raise it if you had it. The poor thing would lead a *pathet*ic life!"

Large tears welled in Osen's eyes and spilled down her cheeks. None of the village women had ever seen Osen weep before.

"Osen . . . baby . . . I *want it born* . . . ." said Osen. She held her swollen stomach, and the tears kept streaming down her face.

How high in spirit and firm in resolve they had come here to drag Osen away! Why it all evaporated so swiftly they would never know. Captured now by the pathos, they too could only weep.

Osen soon dried her tears, and began folding a paper airplane.

"Plane, plane, fly off!" she cried. "Fly off to my father's home!"

The women exchanged glances. Might having a baby put an end to Osen's madness?

And then the paper airplane left Osen's hand. It flew from the parlor and out into the garden, and then came back again. When Osen stood up the airplane circled once around her and flew again into the yard. Osen followed it, singing as she gingerly stepped down the stone stairs, and her figure disappeared in the direction of the bamboo grove.

One old crone, with a gloomy, crestfallen face, took up a sheet of the paper and folded it; but when she gave the plane a toss it dipped, fell to the polished planking of the open-air hallway.

"Why does *Osen's* fly so well?" she grumbled.

Another slightly younger old woman said with a sage nod and her best knowing look, "Even a stupid idiot can do *some* things well, you know."

3

> *First month—red snapper!*
>   hitotsuki—tai
> *Second month—then it's shells!*
>   futatsuki—kai
> *Third, we have reserve, and*
>   mittsu—enryōde
> *Fourth—shall we offer shelter?*
>   yottsu—tomeru ka
> *If we offer shelter, well then,*
>   tomereba itcho
> *Shall we fold up Sixth Day?*
>   itsuyo kasanete muika
> *Sixth Day's star was seen—*
>   muika no hoshi wa mieta
> *Seventh Day's star was too!*
>   nanatsu no hoshi mo mieta
> *Eighth—a chalet daughter*
>   yattsu yamaga no musume
> *Ninth—left crying in her longing*
>   kokonotsu koishiku naitesoro
> *Tenth at last she settled in the small chalet!*
>   tōto yamaga in sumitsukisoro
>
>   *—Rope-skipping song*

Osen kept flying her airplanes, the village men kept up their nightly visits to her bower, the village women never ceased their fretting over her delivery . . . and one moonlit night a village lad came running down her stone stairs yelling: "She's *hav*ing it! Osen's baby's on the way!"

A boy was born and they named him Emon. When he was nearly named Tomo—"common"—because Osen was passed round and round among the village men, the old midwife quickly intervened.

"As the baby was coming out, Osen cried *'ei-mon,'*" the old woman reported. "That's what she said. I wonder what she meant."

"Emon. Hmmm . . ." said one of the other women gathered there.

"Well, try asking."

Addressing the new mother, the midwife said, "Osen, which do you prefer as a name for the baby—Tomo, or Emon?"

"*Emon*," Osen answered clearly.

"That's better, it's related to Osen's entry gate," said an old woman who had memorized the chants for the Year End Rites.

"How do you mean?" a fourth woman said.

"Emon means *ei-mon*, the Guardian Gates," said the old woman. "I've heard that in the old days the New Year's Eve rituals were recited only here, at Osen's house. *Ei-mon* is part of the indecipherable lines . . . let's see . . . ah, yes, 'You must go up the center of Heaven's Stairs, the stone stairs protected by *Ei-mon*, Emon's Gate.' "

At this a fifth woman nodded.

"Yes, that's right," she said, adding, "It's also in one of the songs we sing at the New Year's Eve Festival. Here . . . 'Emon came and died—Emon came and died—Wherever did he come from?—He came from a far-off land—Drink, eat, get high on the wine—You'll think you're flying in the sky. . . .' "

"Hmmm, I see now," said the fourth woman. "I was thinking of the *emon* cloth one wears when they die. But a man named Emon came and died? And protects the gate? I wonder what it all means. . . ."

The women took pity on Osen's child and everyone resolved to lend a hand in raising him. But . . . Emon never responded to it: He had given only that first vigorous cry of the newborn, then remained silent, and would stay so for a long time to come.

"Ah, what a shame," one woman said. "I expect the poor deaf-mute's been cursed by the Wolf God. What else for the child of an idiot?"

"We said she shouldn't have it," another replied with a nod.

Indifferent to the sympathy of these women, Osen crooned a lullaby.

    "Escaped with Emon, who doesn't know,
    flow, flow . . ."

  "Why it's a *Heaven Song*," one of the women said suddenly.
"She just changed the name at the beginning to Emon."

  Moved to tears by the madwoman's lullaby, the women spontaneously began to sing along.

    "Escaped with Emon, who doesn't know,
      shiranu Emon to nigesōro
    flow, flow, and grow old
      nagare nagarete oisōro
    all hopes dashed in this mountainous land.
      kono yama no chide kitai mo koware
    No fuel for the Pilgrim's fires—
      abura mo nakute kōchū shimoyake
    no swaying Heaven's Way.
      seikankōkō obekkanashi
    Emon has died, alone so alone,
      Emon shinimoshi hitori sabishiku
    wept in longing for his distant home."
      furusato koishi to nakisōro

  Everyone so pitied Emon, but as he grew he in no way acknowledged their gestures of concern, and because of this everyone came to think the mother's madness circulated in her silent child's blood.

  Not so. When he was awake Emon could hear everyone's voices, though they weren't voices in the usual sense. He heard them in his head. "Voice" is a vibration passing through the air, sound spoken with a will. What Emon heard was always accompanied by *shapes.* When someone uttered the word "mountain" the syllables *moun-tain* resounded in the air; the shape projected into Emon's mind with the word would differ depending on who spoke it, but always the hazy mirage of a mountain would appear. Listen as you will to the words *Go to the mountain,* it is only possible to distinguish five syllables. But in young Emon's case, overlapping the sound waves he could sense some one thing, a stirring, a *motion* that swept into a dim, mountainous shape.

For the tabula rasa mind of the infant this is an enormous burden. Emon's tiny head was always filled with pain and tremendous commotion. The minds and voices of the people around him tangled like kaleidoscopic shapes, scattering through his head like voices and images on the screen of a continuously jammed television set. It's a miracle that Emon did *not* go mad.

No one knew Emon had this ability, and men kept calling on Osen as usual. In his mind Emon soon began walking with tottering, tentative steps: Along with, oh, say, Sakuzo's or Jimbei's shadowy thoughts would come crystal-clear images, and with them came meanings far beyond those attached to the spoken words.

"Hey there, Emon," they might say. "If you go out and play I'll give you some candy." Or they would say something like: "A *big whale* just came swimming up the river, Emon!"

But Emon's mind was an unseen mirror reflecting what these men were really thinking. It differed only slightly with each man.

And then one day when he was five years old, Emon suddenly spoke to a village woman.

"Why does everyone want to sleep with Osen?" he asked.

Osen, he said; not *Mother*. Perhaps because he kept seeing things through the villagers' minds, Emon was unable to know Osen as anything more than just a woman.

"E-emon-boy, you can *talk?*" the woman replied, eyes wide with surprise.

Shocking. Once Emon's power of speech was known, they couldn't have the poor boy living in the same house with that common whore Osen. . . . So the men hastily convened a general meeting, and it was concluded that Emon should be placed in the care of "the General Store"—the only store in the village.

This automatically meant that Emon must mix with the children's society; but as he knew so many words and their meanings at the same time, the other children were little more than dolts in comparison and could never really be his playmates. And not to be forgotten: Since he was Osen's child the other boys and girls considered him unredeemably inferior, and held him in the utmost contempt. So it was that reading books and other people's minds soon became Emon's only pleasure.

4

I once spoke to Osen while gazing into her beautiful clear eyes.

"You're pretending," I told her. "You're crazy like a fox, right?"

Instead of answering, Osen sang a song, the one she always sang when she flew the paper airplanes, the ballad of a madwoman:

> *"Escaped with Emon, who doesn't know,*
> *flow, flow, and grow old . . ."*

The "Heaven Song," of course. Now, if I substitute some words based on the theory I'm trying to develop, why, what it suggests becomes something far grander:

> *Shilan and Emon fled together,*
> Shiranu to Emon to nigesōro
> *Fly, fly, and they crashed,*
> nagare nagarete ochisōro
> *the ship's hull dashed in this mountainous land.*
> kono yama no chide kitai mo koware
> *No fuel—the star maps have burned,*
> abura mo nakute kōchūzu mo yake
> *interstellar navigation is not possible.*
> seikankōkō obotsukanashi
> *Emon has died, alone so alone,*
> *Wept in longing for his distant home.*

The last two lines of this song remain the same as in the version recorded earlier, but all of the preceding lines have subtly changed. For example: In line one, *shiranu* would normally be taken to mean "doesn't know," but in my reinterpretation it is now seen as the Japanization of a similar-sounding alien name—*Shilan.* In the second line, I am supposing that *oisōro* (meaning "grow old") is a corruption of the word *ochisōro* (meaning "fall" or "crash"); and I am further assuming that *kōchū shimoyake* ("Pilgrim's fires") in line four is a corruption of *kōchūzu mo yake* ("star charts also burned"). In lines three, four, and five, three words have double meanings:

> *kitai* = hope/ship's hull
> *kōchū* = pilgrim/space flight
> *seikankōkō* = heavenly way/interstellar navigation

In the above manner, line three changes its meaning from "all hopes dashed in this mountainous land" to "the ship's hull dashed in this mountainous land," and so forth.

There is more of this sort of thing. . . .

Once a week an ancient truck rattled and wheezed up the steep mountain roads on the forty-kilometer run between the village and the town far below, bearing a load of rice sent up by the prefectural government's wartime Office of Food Rationing. This truck was the village's only physical contact with the outside world. The truck always parked in front of the General Store.

Next door to the store was a small lodging house where the young men and women of the village always congregated. The master of the house was Old Lady Také, a huge figure of a woman, swarthy-skinned and well into her sixties, who was rumored to have once plied her trade in the pleasure quarters of a distant metropolis. She welcomed all the young people to her lodge.

On summer evenings the place was usually a hive of chatter and activity. Even small children managed for a short time to mingle in the company of their youthful elders, dangling their legs from the edge of the open-air hallway. Rope-skipping and the bouncing of balls passed with the dusking day, and the generations changed. Small children were shooed home and girls aged from twelve or thirteen to widows of thirty-five or thirty-six began arriving, hiding in the pooling shadows. They all came seeking the night's promise of excitement and pleasure.

It was an unwritten law that married men and women stay away from the lodge, though the nature of their children's night-play was an open secret. And how marvelously different this play was from the play in larger towns and cities: The people who gathered at Old

Lady Také's lodge doused the lights and immediately explored each other's bodies. This, it must be said, was the only leisure activity they had. In the mountains, where you seldom find other diversions, this is the only amusement. The muffled laughter of young girls as hands slipped beneath their sweat-dampened robes, their coy resistance. . . . And the heady fragrance that soon filled the room drew everyone on to higher delights.

Occasionally one of the local wags would amble by the lodge, and from a safe distance flash a startling light on the activities. Girls squealed, clutching frantically at their bodies, draping their drenched clothes over their thighs. In order to salvage this particular night's mood, someone asked in a loud voice:

"Say, Osato, your son's gonna be coming around here any day now, isn't he?"

"*What?*" said the widow.

"Yeah—he finally made it. I think!"

"Ho!" she laughed. "Ho! You're being nasty, kid. He's *only* twelve. . . ."

"Well, if he hasn't, he'll find out how to pretty soon," the voice continued. "So maybe you should ask Osen as soon as possible . . . ?"

"Hmmm . . . You might be right. Maybe tomorrow. I could get him spruced up, take him on over in his best kimono. . . ."

A young man's voice replying from deep within the room said, "Naw, you're too late, Osato."

"And just what is *that* supposed to mean?"

"For Gen-boy it's too late. He beat you to it. It's been a month already." Laughter. "His mother's the last to know!"

"But *he* never . . . Oh, that *boy*."

As ever, Emon was near them all and listened to their banter. And sometimes, as everyone moved in the dark, he searched their minds.

(There'll be trouble if she gets pregnant. . . .)

(Ohhh, *big*. It'll *hurt*. What should I do if I'm forced too far?)

(I wonder who took my boy to Osen's place? I *know* he didn't go alone. Yard work for that boy tomorrow, lots. I'll teach *him*. And I was waiting *so* patiently. . . .)

Emon's mind-reading powers intensified among them as he roved over their thoughts night after night. He could see so clearly into their thoughts that it was like focusing on bright scenes in a collage. He was therefore all the more puzzled by his mother, Osen. She was different. Didn't the thoughts of a human being exist in the mind of an idiot? The thoughts of the villagers were like clouds drifting in the blue sky, and what they thought was so transparent. But in Osen's mind thick white mist flowed always, hiding everything.

No words, no shapes, just emotion close to fear turning there. . . .

As Emon kept peering into the mist, he began to feel that Osen let the men take her so that she might escape her fear. Emon gave up the search for his mother's mind and returned to the days of his endless reading.

His prodigious appetite for books impressed the villagers.

"What a bookworm!" one of them remarked. "That kid's *crazy* about books."

"You're telling me," another said. "He read all ours, too. Imagine, from Osen, a kid who likes *books.*"

"Wonder who taught him to read. . . ."

Visiting all the houses in the village, Emon would borrow books, and on the way he tried to piece together a picture of his mother's past by looking into everyone's minds. *Was Osen an idiot from the time she was born?* he wanted to know. But no one knew about Osen in any detail, and the only thoughts men entertained were for her beautiful face and body. Her body, perhaps ageless because of her imbecility, was a strangely narcotic necessity for the men.

A plaything for all the men of the village, was Osen, even for the youngest: for all who wished to know her body. Their dark lust Emon could not understand, but this emotion seemed to be all that kept the people living and moving in this lonesome place—a power that kept the village from splitting asunder.

Osen—madwoman, whore: She seized the men, and kept them from deserting the village for the enchantments of far-off cities.

5

A memory from when I was stationed in the village: In front of Old Lady Také's Youth Lodge some children are skipping rope. In my thoughts I hear:

> *First month—red snapper!*
> hitotsuki—tai
> *Second month—then it's shells!*
> futatsuki—kai
> *Third, we have reserve, and*
> mittsu—enryōde
> *Fourth—shall we offer shelter?*
> yottsu—tomeru ka

The rope-skipping song I recorded earlier in this tale. A little more theory: With only a shift in syllabic division the song now seems to mean:

hitotsu	*kitai*
(one)	(ship's hull)
futatsu	*kikai*
(two)	(machines)

and with but a single change of consonants we have:

mittsu	*nenryōde*
(three)	(fuel)

Almost like a checklist . . .

Eventually the day came when Emon entered school. He was given a new uniform and school bag, purchased with money from the village Confraternity of Heaven Special Fund, which had been created long ago to provide for Osen's house and living. Emon went happily to the Extension School, which was at the far end of the village. There, in the school's library, he could read to his heart's content.

Miss Yoshimura, the schoolteacher, was an ugly woman, long years past thirty, who had given up all hope of marriage almost from the time she was old enough to seriously consider it. Skinny as a withered sapling and gifted with a face that couldn't have been funnier, yet she was a kindhearted soul, and of all those in the village she had the richest imagination and most fascinating mind. Having read so many books, she knew about much more than anyone else; and the plots of the uncountable stories she had read and remembered! They merged like twisting roots in her imagination, until they seemed to be the real world, and "reality" a dream. Most importantly, though, where everyone else never let Emon forget his inferiority, only Miss Yoshimura cared about him as equal to the others. Emon readily became attached to her, and was with her from morning until evening.

One day the old master of the General Store came to Miss Yoshimura.

"Ma'am," he began, "Emon's smart as a whip, but there's gonna be trouble if he becomes, you know, grows up too early."

"Ahm, oh, well . . ." Miss Yoshimura said, flustered.

"Since he's got Osen's blood and what not," the old man went on assuringly, "and watches the youngsters get together at Old Lady Také's place . . . well, if he gets like Osen, there'll be trouble. Some girl'll wind up gettin' stuffed by him, sure enough."

Embarrassed, Miss Yoshimura said, "Well, what do you think it best to do then?"

"Now as to that, we was thinkin' since he dotes on you so, it might be better for him to stay at your lodgin' house. Of course, the Confraternity Fund'll pay all his board."

"All right, I don't mind at all," said Miss Yoshimura, perhaps a bit too quickly. "Of course, only if he *wants* to do it. . . . How I *do* pity the poor child. . . ."

And in her thoughts an imaginary future flashed into existence, pulsing with hope—*no I could never marry but now I have a child whom I will raise as my own and days will come when we hesitate to bathe together oh Emon yes I'll be with you as you grow to manhood*—Her face reddened at her thoughts.

Emon came to live in her house, then, and happy days and months passed. Most happily, the other children ceased to make so much fun of him. And the men never came around to sleep with Miss Yoshimura as they did with Osen.

She avoided all men. Her mind shrieked rejection, that all men were nothing more than filthy beasts. Emon quite agreed. But what went on in her mind?

As much as she must hate and avoid men, Miss Yoshimura's thoughts were as burdened as any other's by a dark spinning shadow of lust, and come the night it would often explode, like furnace-hot winds out of hell.

Squeezing little Emon and tasting pain like strange bitter wine, Miss Yoshimura would curl up tightly on the floor with sharp, stifled gasps. The entangled bodies of men and women floated hugely through her thoughts, and while she tried to drive them away with one part of her mind, another part reached greedily for something else, grabbed, embraced, and caressed. Every word she knew related to sex melted throughout her mind.

Miss Yoshimura always sighed long and sadly, and delirious voices chuckled softly in her mind.

(Oh, this will never do. . . .)

Denouements like this were quickly undone, usurped by their opposites, images flocking in her head, expanding like balloons filled with galaxies of sex words that flew to Osen's house. Miss Yoshimura fantasized herself as Osen, and grew sultry holding one of Osen's lovers. Then the lines of her dream converged on Old Lady Také's lodge, and she cried out desperately in the darkness:

"I'm a woman!"

Male and female shapes moved in the night around her. . . .

She returned to her room, where moonlight came in shining against her body. She moaned and hugged Emon fiercely.

"Sensei, you're killing me!"

At the sound of Emon's voice Miss Yoshimura momentarily regained herself—only to tumble yet again into the world of her fantasies.

(Emon, Emon, why don't you grow up . . . ?)

Conviction grew in Emon's mind as the days turned: In everyone's heart, including his dear *sensei's*, there lurked this ugly thing, this abnormal desire to possess another's body. *Why?* Emon did not realize that he saw only what he wished to see.

Everyone's desire. From desire are children born. I already know that. But who's my father?

He kept up his watch on the villagers' minds, that he might unravel that mystery, and he continued to gather what scraps of knowledge there were remaining about his mother. More and more it appeared that she had escaped into her mad world to flee something unspeakably horrible.

In the mind of the General Store's proprietor he found this:

(Osen's house . . . People say it was a ghost house in the old days, and then Osen was always cryin'. No, come to think about it, weren't it her mother? *Her* grandfather was killed or passed on. That's why she went crazy. . . .)

Old Lady Také's thoughts once whispered:

(My dead grandmother used to say that they were hiding some crazy foreign man there, and he abused Osen, so they killed him, or something like that. . . .)

And the murmuring thoughts of Toku the woodcutter gave forth a startling image:

(Granddad saw it. Osen's house was full of blood and everyone was dead, murdered. That household was crazy for generations, anyway. Osen's father—or was it her brother?—was terrible insane. An' in the middle a' all them hacked bodies, Osen was playing with a ball.)

Old Genji knew part of the story, too:

(Heard tell it was a *long* time ago on the hill where the house is that the fiery column fell from the sky. Since around then all the beautiful girls were born in that family, generation after generation, an' couldn't one of 'em speak. That's the legend.)

Long ago, in days forgotten, something terrible happened. Osen alone of the family survived and went mad, and became the village harlot. This was all that was clear to Emon.

6

They say that time weathers memory away: In truth the weight of years bears down on memory, compressing it into hard, jewel-like clarity. A mystery slept in that village, and sleeps there still. Over the years my thoughts have annealed around these puzzling events, but the mystery will remain forever uncovered—unless I go there and investigate in earnest.

I have tried to return many times. A year ago I came to within fifty kilometers of the village and then, for no rational reason I can summon up, I turned aside, went to another, more *amenable* place. Before embarking on these journeys I am always overcome by an unshakable reluctance, almost as if I were under a hypnotic compulsion to stay clear of the place.

Another curious fact:

In all the time I was stationed there, I recall no one else from the "outside" ever staying in the village more than a few hours; and according to the villagers I was the first outsider to be seen at all in ten years. The only villagers who had lived outside those isolated reaches were Old Lady Také and Miss Yoshimura, who left to attend Teacher's College.

If going there I actually managed to come near the village proper, unless the military backed me I feel certain the locals would somehow block my return.

Is there something, some power at work that governs these affairs?

Such a power would have a long reach and strong, to the effect that this village of fewer than two hundred people may exist outside the administration of the Japanese government. I say this because during the Pacific War no man from that village was ever inducted into the Armed Forces.

And who might wield such power? Who mesmerized everyone? Old Lady Také, or the Teacher? And if both of them left the village under another's direction, who then is the person central to the mystery?

The madwoman, Osen?

When summer evenings come, my memories are crowded with the numerous songs the village children sang. It was so queer that everything about those songs was at complete variance with the historical roots that those villagers claimed to have: That the village had been founded centuries earlier by fugitive retainers deserting the Heike Family during their final wars with the Genji in the Heian Period, and that since that time no one had left the village. Yet none of the old stories lingering there were of Heike legends. It is almost as if the village slept in the cradle of its terraced fields, an island in the stream of history, divorced from the world.

Is something still hidden beneath the stone stairs leading up to Osen's house? "Unknown Emon" gave up in despair and abandoned some thing there. A pump to send water up to the well at Sinner's Hole, or something hinted at in the children's handball song:

> I wonder if I'll ever climb
> those weed-grown stairs someday?
> One—a stone stairway in the sky
> Two—if it doesn't fly,
> if it never flies open . . .

When the day of flight comes, will the stairs open? Or must you open them in order to fly?—Questions, questions: It may be that the mystery of "unknown Emon" will sleep forever in that place.

And what became of Osen's child?

After a time Emon once again attempted what he long ago had given up on—a search of his mother's mind. The strange white mist shrouding Osen's thoughts was as thick as ever.

(Begone!)

Emon's thoughts thundered at the mist in a shock wave of telepathic power.

Perhaps the sending of a psychic command and the discharge of its meaning in the receiver's mind can be expressed in terms of physics, vectors of force; then again, it may just be that Emon's telepathic control had improved, and he was far more adept at plucking meaning out of confused backgrounds. Whatever: With his command, the mist in Osen's mind parted as if blown aside by a wind, and Emon peered within for the first time.

Her mind was like immensities of sky. Emon dipped quickly in and out many times, snatching at the fragmented leavings of his mother's past. The quantity was small, with no connecting threads of history: everything scenes in a shattered mosaic.

There was only one coherent vision among it all: A vast machine—or a building—was disintegrating around her, and a mixture of terrible pain and pleasure blazed from her as she was held in a man's embrace.

And that was *odd:* that out of all her many encounters with all the men of the village, only this one experience had been so powerful as to burn itself indelibly into her memory.

The age and face of this man were unclear. His image was like seaweed undulating in currents at the bottom of the sea. The event had occurred on a night when the moon or some other light was shining, for his body was bathed in a glittering blue radiance. All the other men Osen had known, lost forever in the white mist that filled her mind and robbed her will, and only *this* man whom Emon had never seen existed with a force of will and fervency. Joy flooded from the memory, and with it great sorrow.

Why this should be was beyond Emon's understanding.

A vague thought stirred: *This man Osen is remembering is my father. . . .*

While Emon poked tirelessly through the flotsam in the minds of his mother and the villagers, Miss Yoshimura played in a fantasy world where her curiosity focused always on Osen. It was now customary for her to hold Emon at night as they lay down to sleep, and one night her heart was so swollen with the desire to be Osen and lay with any man that it seemed ready to burst.

How could she know that Emon understood her every thought?

How could anyone realize the terrible wealth of pure *fact* that Emon had amassed about their hidden lives?

But his constant buffeting in this storm of venery took its awful toll. Excluding the smallest of children, Emon was of the unswayable opinion that all the villagers were obscene beyond the powers of any description. Especially Osen and himself—they were the worst offenders. Through the minds of the men he was constantly privy to Osen's ceaseless, wanton rut, and the pain that he was Osen's child was heavy upon him. Ever she bared her body to the men, and . . .

Emon hated her. He hated the men who came to her, and in his superlative nine-year-old mind this wretched emotion was transformed into a seething hatred for all the human race.

It was on one of his infrequent visits to his mother that he at last vented his anger, and struck an approaching man with a hurled stone.

"Drop dead, you little bastard!" the man raged. "Don't go makin' any trouble, if you know what's good for you. Who d'ya think's keepin' you *alive!*"

Emon returned to the parlor after the man left and gazed at his silent mother's dazzling, naked body. He shook with unconcealed fury.

(I want to *kill* him! I *will* kill him! *Everybody!*)

Osen reached out to him then.

"My son, try to love them," she murmured. "You *must*, if you are to live. . . ."

Stunned, Emon fell into her arms and clung to her. For the first time in his life he wept, unable to control the flow of tears.

Moments later Osen ended it all by releasing him and standing aimlessly, and that is when Emon began to suspect—to hope!—that her madness might only be a consummate impersonation. But it may have only been one clear moment shining through the chaos. There was no sign that the madness roiling Osen's brain had in the least abated.

Emon little cared to think deeply about the meaning of Osen's words, and his hatred toward the human race still filled his heart. But now he visited his mother far more often. It was during one of these visits, as he sat on the porch beside Osen some days or weeks later, that Emon *heard* a strange voice.

The voice did not come as sound in the air, or as a voice reaching into his mind with shapes and contexts. It was a *calling*, and it was for Emon alone—a tautness to drag him to its source, a thrown rope pulling. Unusually garbed in a neat, plain cotton robe, Osen was staring down the long valley, her mind empty as always.

"Who is it?" Emon called.

Osen turned her head to watch Emon as he scrambled to his feet and shouted the question. The vacuous expression on her face suddenly blanched, frozen for an instant in a look of dread.

"*Where are you!*" Emon shouted.

As if pulled up by Emon's voice, Osen got slowly to her feet and pointed to the mountains massed on the horizon.

"It's over there," she said. "That way . . ."

Emon hardly glanced at her as he started down the stone stairs, and then he was gone. He didn't even try to look back.

Time froze in yellow sunlight for the madwoman, and then melted again. Osen wandered blindly about, wracked with sobs, at some point arriving at the small waterwheel shack that housed the village millstone. The violence of her weeping resounded against the boards. She may have lost her capacity for thought, but she could still feel the agony of this final parting from her only child.

One of the villagers, catching sight of her trembling figure as he passed by, approached her with a broad grin, reached for her body with callused hands.

"Now, now, don't cry, Osen," he said. "Here, you'll feel lots better. . . ."

The look she fixed him with was so hard and venom-filled, the first of its like he had ever seen from her. For a moment he felt a faint rousing of fear shake his heart, then slapped his work clothes with gusto and laughed at his own stupidity.

"Now what in hell . . ." And cursing Osen, he grabbed to force her to the grassy earth.

Osen slapped his hands away.

"Human *filth!*" she shouted clearly, commandingly. Her words echoed and re-echoed in the stony hollows around the water mill: "Be gone and *die!*"

As Emon hurried far off down the road, the witless villager walked placidly into Endworld Mere, a dreamy look transfixing his face as he sank unknown beneath the dark and secret waters.

In the bamboo grove white mist danced again on the back of the air, and a white naked woman-figure ran lightly, lightly, chasing a paper airplane that flew on and on forever.

At the *Sai no Kawara*, the earthly shore where children come to bewail the passing of those who have crossed over the Great Waters, there is a weather-beaten sign of wood inscribed with characters that can only be spottily read:

It seems so easy to wait one thousand—nay, ten thousand years . . . driven mad with longing for the Star of my native home . . .

FROM THE PLANET EARTH:

We Servants of the Stars

BY FREDERIK POHL

And last month I went back to Maui, checked into the Makele Motel, changed into shorts and loafers, slathered myself with sunburn lotion, and strolled out to the pool.

How terribly, unbelievably different it looked! There were no machine-gun posts behind the hibiscus, no American and Soviet jets making contrails overhead as they guarded us. It was just a Hawaiian resort motel again, and when Julio shot up out of the pool, splashing water all over, blowing and gasping as he climbed out to greet me, he didn't slither like a snake. "Allo, Ben!" he cried, his face grinning so wide it showed three gold teeth. "Is good to see you, man! Welcome to the Tenth Anniversary Reunion!"

I shook his hand and let him order me a Mai Tai, though we hadn't been particularly close in those days when the Makele Motel was the conference center for the invaders from the stars.

But that was a long time ago. . . .

See, the terrible thing about what happened to all us unwilling servants of the stars wasn't just that we were—well—*invaded.* I don't mean our countries, I mean *us.* That was bad enough. It was worse than that, because there was nothing in human experience so terrifying and demeaning as to have some slug or fish or carnivore or monster from another star suddenly preempt your body. That only began to scratch the surface, anyway. Then came the wrench of being torn away from your normal life; however dull and unpromising that might have seemed, it was a shocking bereavement to have it all stolen away without warning. When we captives came here to the Makele Motel, we were in a state of terror and disorientation.

It didn't get better. As we were worked past exhaustion in the service of our star lords—as we mourned what we had left behind and found we could not even find new friends or lovers here, because at any moment we would be snatched away from whatever we were doing—as the ordeal wore on we were all in a state as near to psychosis as a human being can be without total breakdown. Probably we would have broken down if we could. But that was not allowed.

But the very worst was that the whole thing had caught our world by surprise. One day we were living our lives, fretting over taxes, worrying about terrorists, wondering if the bombs would fall —living, in other words, a normal twentieth-century human life. And the next day—without warning!—we all discovered that our planet was a target for plundering by creatures who had no interest at all in what we thought about it.

See, it wasn't just us on Maui who were in shock. It was our whole world.

I suppose such agonies were not new for the human race. Powhatan's Indians, the Australian Aborigines, the Zulus, the Indochinese peoples—all of them, long ago, had had the same sort of experience as the Europeans arrived to take over their lands. But that was long ago, and, besides, we weren't *natives*. We were civilized people! That is to say, we were the kind of people more used to doing the taking over than to suffering the taking from.

It is hard to remember just how terrified everyone on Earth was then. . . .

What, finally, made it bearable?

Well, first there was the realization that it wasn't really all that new. Individuals from other stars had been sneaking into Earth minds for centuries. They just hadn't announced themselves so blatantly before.

And then, I suppose, it was just that you can get used to anything.

After the aliens finished dividing up their shares of what they wanted from Earth, and the shuttles began launching their cargoes of tribute into space to start their millennium-long photon-sail voyages to the other stars—why, then they disbanded the conference in the Makele Motel. We were free! We could go back to our lives!

We did.

Of course, there were still aliens popping up all over Earth, whenever they felt like it, wherever they chose. Scientists, I suppose. Possibly even tourists. But they only came to visit for a while, and then they went away again. A nuisance for those whose minds were preempted, of course. But easy enough for the rest of us to bear.

We had come to terms with the notion that we were property, you see. It wasn't hard. Powhatan's Indians and the Aborigines in Australia had learned the same lessons long before.

By dinnertime there were at least twenty of us veterans at the Makele Motel and more checking in every hour.

There was Elsa, who had wept herself to sleep every night, because she was a skinny little newlywed when she was taken and she hadn't had a chance even to kiss her new husband good-by. She wasn't so skinny now; her husband was with her, and so were three kids, ages babe-in-arms to almost-teen-obstreperous. There was Greg, who had tried suicide one night and luckily failed; there was Alice, the demon old gin-rummy player who had seemed too ancient and fragile for our kind of life, but looked healthier and more alert than most of the rest of us now, ten years later.

And then, just as the waiters were serving the Baked Alaska, there was Lois.

Lois . . .

We had been lovers—tried to be—succeeded as often as we could, which wasn't very. It wasn't that she was my kind of gal, and I certainly wasn't her dream. She was black and trendy; I was Orange-County silicon-and-space upright. Even what you might call "conservative." We had not been drawn together by any sharing of interests but one.

We were both scared witless.

She came into the Liliuokalani Room and stood there for a moment. I put down my wine glass and stood up, staring at her. She stared back.

When she came over to the table we politely shook hands.

"Damn, Ben," she said, inspecting my aloha shirt, "are you going beach boy or what?"

"You've put on a little weight," I told her. And I pulled out the chair next to mine for her to join me, and she did.

I dawdled over my Baked Alaska and let it melt while she caught up through soup and shrimp and mahi-mahi with wild rice. We kept looking at each other, sidelong glances that looked away when the other person caught one. I was wondering if we would wind up in bed together again, now that there was nothing to drag us apart.

I was wrong about that.

We did end up in bed together that night, but it wasn't the same at all. When it was over I got up, brushed my teeth with the wrapped spare toothbrush in her bathroom, put my clothes on, and went back to my own room to sleep.

After all, I do have a wife and son back in Malibu.

So our Tenth Reunion wasn't much of a success, socially speaking.

It was pretty good in another way, though. Alice put me onto something pretty good with the Sirians, and Greg and I worked out a co-sponsoring deal with some low-level nuclear wastes from Idaho for the people of Bellatrix 9.

We've all done pretty well at that sort of thing, of course. The star people don't pay us in money. They pay us in information. I made my first million out of a neutral-density foam-metal alloy from my former master; it's very big in ship building, they tell me.

You see, the people from the stars aren't really all that much different from you and me.

They made all their deals and agreed to all their treaties. But when the original delegations went home, the ones who didn't think they'd done as well out of Earth as they hoped began offering bribes —squeeze—little tips, to make sure that the best shipments went to their solar systems and not to those of some competitor.

The big news at the reunion was that Elsa's former master was really hard up for carbon-14. Everybody in the galaxy wanted that, of course; it was part of the basic metabolic needs of some of their half-living, half-computer machines. It was as vital to them as oil had been to the large industrial powers on Earth a generation or so ago, and, like those industrial powers, they wanted it enough to pay very well.

Elsa was nearly sure that if a consortium could be arranged to produce at least ten metric tons of the stuff, what her contacts would pay would be no mere invention or new material. It might even be the secret of interstellar transmission itself.

And then we, too, could start roaming the Galaxy, looking for planets to plunder.

LINO ALDANI. Born in 1926, Aldani is not only one of the leading Italian sf writers today but has made a major contribution to Italian science fiction with his annual *Interplanet* anthology, launched in 1962, the same year he published his critical survey of sf, *La fantascienza* (Science Fiction). Among his other well-known books are the collections *Bonnanote Sofia (Goodnight Sophia)* in 1964 and *Quarta dimensione (Fourth Dimension)* in 1963. He has also used the pseudonym N. L. Janda.

BRIAN W. ALDISS. As a past president (and one of the founders) of World SF, and as an inveterate traveler, Aldiss is known in person in most of the world's quarters, and his writing has made him well known everywhere else. One of the leaders of science fiction's "New Wave" movement of twenty-five years ago, Aldiss has demonstrated mastery in science fiction of all kinds (most recently his notable "Heliconia" trilogy), and as a critic and author of many works outside the field.

KARL MICHAEL ARMER. Born in 1950 in rural Bavaria, Armer studied business administration, psychology, and sociology, finally taking a Master of Business Administration degree from Wurzburg University. He now lives near Munich with his wife and two children. In addition to fiction, he writes non-fiction articles about sf, has edited four anthologies, is a regular contributor to various magazines on music, graphic arts, interior design, and travel, and as a photographer has sold pictures for magazine advertising, travel articles, and record covers. A great admirer of J. G. Ballard, Armer describes himself as a "slow writer." Although his science-fiction output has been relatively slim, his work has been translated and published in more than a dozen countries.

JON BING. Born in 1944 in Tonsberg, Norway, Bing took a law degree in 1969 and earned his doctorate in law in 1982 with a dissertation on the processes of legal communications. He has written extensively on law, communication, and astronomy in both scholarly and popular publications, has held a professorship in the Norwegian Research Center for Computers and Law since 1970, and consults with many prestigious international organizations. Following a pattern not uncommon among science-fiction writers, Jon Bing has collaborated extensively, primarily with Tor Age Bringsvaerd, as well as writing solo. His prolific science-fiction work includes some twenty short-story collections (which have been translated into several languages), beginning in 1967 with *Rundt solen i ring*, as well as both adult and juvenile novels. He has also done several translations from English into Norwegian (Aldiss, Ballard, Le Guin, Pohl, etc.), three sf stage plays, and a number of radio plays and television series, all of which have received numerous awards.

ANDRÉ CARNEIRO. Although perhaps better known as a poet in Brazil, Carneiro is also generally recognized as Brazil's most original sf writer, a label he himself shuns because of the fears and prejudices surrounding science itself. His stories and poems have been translated into English, French, Italian, German, Spanish, Swedish, and Japanese, and he is also well known for his theoretical contribution to the understanding of sf in his essay "Introducao ao Estudo da Science Fiction." His best-known sf works include *The Diary of the Lost Space-Ship* (1963), *The Man Who Divided* (1966), "Darkness" (in Putnam's *Best SF of 1972*), *The Free Swimming Pool* (1978), and *Lovechaos* (1983).

A. BERTRAM CHANDLER. Born in Aldershot, England, on March 28, 1912, Jack Chandler (as he was known by his friends) died June 5, 1984, in Sydney, Australia. Chandler always claimed that for most of his life he served two mistresses, science fiction and the sea. His sea career, from Apprentice to Master, spanned the years 1928–1975. His literary career began with freelance journalism and light verse in 1932; he has published more than forty novels. Many of his works won awards: three Ditmars (the Australian award), the Invisible Little Man award in the United States, and a Japanese award, the Seiunsho.

LJUBEN DILOV. Born in 1927, Dilov is a graduate in philology as well as a writer and editor, and has been active in the Union of Bulgarian Writers, with special duties in developing younger writers. He is editor of Bulgaria's leading literary magazine, *Septemvry*, and co-editor of the science-fiction series "Galaxy." Dilov has published thirty books, including *The Way of Icarus, The Burden of the Space-suit,* and *Unfinished Love Affair of a Girl Student,* all of which have reached prints of 100,000 each—a very high figure for his relatively small country—with another half million copies translated into other languages. He is a member of World SF and of International PEN.

TONG ENZHENG. Enzheng was born in Ningxia, Hunan, in 1935, and is now an archaeologist and associate professor in the History Department of Sichuan University. He spent one academic year in the United States as a visiting scholar in 1980–81. "Dense Fog Over Old Gorge" (1960) was his first sf publication. "Death Ray on a Coral Island" (written in 1963 but not published until after the Cultural Revolution) won China's 1978 Best Short Story Award, and was filmed in 1980, China's first sf film. "The Magic Flute on the Snowy Mountain" (1979) won the second-place prize in China's Second Juvenile *Belles Lettres* Awards. Enzheng's latest work, *The New Pilgrimage to the West,* a delightfully humorous juvenile tale about Monk Xuan Zhuang's tour of the United States with his three disciples, Monkey King, Pigsy, and Sandy, was first serialized in a magazine and then printed in book form in 1985. Enzheng is a member of the Chinese Writers' Association and of World SF.

CARLOS M. FEDERICI. First inspired to enter the sf field by a Wilson Tucker novel *(The Long, Loud Silence,* translated as *El Clamor del Silencio)* at age 15, Federici discovered early that the fantastic was fascinating and he liked to escape from ordinary life, which he regards as a healthy way of expanding his thoughts. Among his favorite writers are Asimov, Bradbury, Dick, Kornbluth, Pohl, Sturgeon, and Wallace. He published his first story (not sf) in 1961, and his sf debut, "Primera Necesidad" ("Prime Needs"), appeared in 1968. Beginning in 1985, and still running as this goes to press, is a new weekly serialization that Federici is publishing in a daily newspaper. It's called "Umbral de las tinieblas" ("Threshold of Darkness"), a sequel to the Lovecraft Mythos. Other current projects in progress include a book compiling several connected nostalgic stories about Hollywood's golden years.

HARRY HARRISON. Harrison was born in Stamford, Connecticut, grew up in New York City—and was promptly drafted in the United States Army when he reached his eighteenth birthday. Some years later, older if not wiser, he returned to civilian life with a sergeant's stripes. After a short term in college and a longer one in art school, he spent the next few years in New York as an artist, art director, and editor, and finally as a freelance writer. Once he started moving he did not stop, and the Harrisons (with son Todd and daughter Moira) have lived in Mexico, England, Italy, Denmark, and Ireland, with briefer stays in twenty-nine other countries. He is the author of thirty-two novels, all of them still in print, has published five collections of his short stories, four juvenile books, and edited countless anthologies—including two textbooks for the teaching of science fiction. His books have been translated into twenty-two languages. He was founding president of World SF. He received the Nebula Award and the Prix Jules Verne for his novel *Make Room! Make Room!,* made into the film *Soylent Green.*

ELIZABETH ANNE HULL. Born in Upper Darby, Pennsylvania, Hull moved frequently as a child, finally settling in and around Chicago for most of her adult life. Married and divorced young (with two daughters to support), she finished her bachelor's degree at

Northwestern University while working in manufacturing, advertising, the travel industry, and publishing. She ultimately earned a doctorate at Loyola University with a cross-disciplinary (English and Psychology) dissertation, "A Transactional Analysis of the Plays of Edward Albee" (1975). Since 1971 she has taught at William Rainey Harper College in Palatine, Illinois, where she developed curriculum for a course in science fiction, which she has taught since 1973. She also teaches creative writing, composition, and several other literature courses, among them Drama and Film and Women in Literature. She has been active professionally in academic organizations, including the Illinois College English Association (president 1976–78), the Midwest Modern Language Association (co-founder of the sf section), the Science Fiction Research Association (editor of the *SFRA Newsletter*, 1980–83), and the Popular Culture Association (co-chair of the sf & Fantasy sessions, 1975–77). Her first sf story, "The Matter of the Midler," was translated and adapted for radio in Munich, Germany, in 1980. Another sf tale, "Second Best Friend," has been sold to *Aboriginal SF.* In 1984 she worked in tandem with Dingbo Wu to translate Yahua Wei's "Conjugal Happiness in the Arms of Morpheus," a Chinese story that stirred much controversy upon its original publication. She has similarly adapted Enzheng Tong's story for *Tales from the Planet Earth.* In 1984 Hull married Frederik Pohl; they now live in Palatine, Illinois, calling their home "Gateway."

SAM J. LUNDWALL. The incredibly prolific Sam Lundwall is not only a mainstay of Swedish science fiction (as author, translator, editor, and publisher) but contributes significantly to Swedish letters in other fields as well—though, to many Swedes now approaching middle age, he was most famous of all as one of Sweden's leading rock singers of the 1960s. He is a former president of World SF and, a polyglot, has maintained familiarity with the literature and contact with the writers of science fiction in many countries worldwide. His classic study of the field, *Science Fiction: What It's All About,* was published in the United States as one of the earliest popular discussions of this genre of writing. He has also done an illustrated history of science fiction and a number of essays on science fiction in the non-English-speaking world. He currently makes his home, with his wife and daughter, in the suburbs of Stockholm.

JOSEPH NESVADBA. Born in 1926, Nesvadba was trained as a psychiatrist, but began writing dramatic sketches and detective stories, as well as satirical sf in the tradition of Karel Capek. He has published numerous sf short stories and novels, several of which have been filmed, as well as a number of mainstream and mystery novels. Subtle irony is his trademark. He has been translated widely throughout the world. In English, his work is available in the Judith Merril and the Harry Harrison/Brian Aldiss volumes of *The Year's Best SF* and Donald Wollheim's *World's Best SF*.

FREDERIK POHL. Another of World SF's past presidents, Pohl has also served as president of the Science Fiction Writers of America and as a Council member (and current Midwest area consultant) for the Authors Guild. He has received five Hugos, two Nebulas, two of the International John W. Campbell Awards, the American Book Award, the annual award of the Popular Culture Association, and numerous other honors. His best-known science-fiction novels are *The Space Merchants* (written in collaboration with the late C. M. Kornbluth), *Gateway, Man Plus,* and *The Years of the City.* He has also written extensively in other areas, including history (he is the Encyclopedia Britannica's authority on the Roman emperor, Tiberius), politics, and science, and has published fiction and poetry outside the science-fiction field. He makes his home in Palatine, Illinois, with his wife, Elizabeth Anne Hull.

SPIDER ROBINSON. One of the best-regarded science-fiction writers to appear in recent years, Spider Robinson has not only won many awards in the science-fiction field but is perhaps even more dearly loved by fans for his incredibly rapid flow of wicked puns. He has collaborated with his wife, Jeanne, on many occasions, both in their award-winning science fiction and in the furtherance of her dance group. The Robinsons live in Nova Scotia, Canada.

SOMTOW SUCHARITKUL. Born in Bangkok in 1952, Sucharit-kul grew up in various European and Asian countries and was edu-cated at Eton and Cambridge, England, before coming to the United States eight years ago. His first career was as an avant-garde composer, and his compositions have been performed, televised, and broadcast on four continents. He was appointed representative of Thailand to the International Music Council of UNESCO in 1979, and began writing science-fiction stories about that time. His first novel, *Starship and Haiku*, won the Locus Award, and he has been twice nominated for the Hugo Award as well as winning the 1981 John W. Campbell Award for best new writer. His works include the satirical *Mallworld*, the galaxy-spanning *Inquestor Tetralogy*, and (under the name S. P. Somtow) the mainstream titles *Vampire Junction* and *The Shattered Horse*.

TETSU YANO. Called the "Mr. Science Fiction" of Japan, Yano has performed notably as fan, writer, translator, and editor of science fiction ever since first discovering the field as a teenager. After Army service in World War II, Yano returned to Japan to work with the U.S. forces, during which time he found American science fiction available for the first time. He won the World SF's annual transla-tor's award, the Karel, in 1985, and has been honored with many other awards for his writing. Yano was one of the organizers of the first International Symposium on Science Fiction in Japan in 1970, which for the first time brought science-fiction writers from Japan, England, and North America together with those from the Soviet Union, and has been active in many such events ever since.

YE YONGLIE. Yonglie was born in Wenzhou, Zhejiang, in 1940, and published his first work, a poem, just eleven years later. Since graduation from Beijing University in 1963, he has directed more than 20 science-fiction films and published about 2,000 articles and more than 90 books. His 1979 volume *On Science Belles Lettres* was the first Chinese book discussing theory of the sf genre. His "Little Know-All Travels to the Future," which won the top prize in China's Second Juvenile *Belles Lettres* Awards, has been adapted into a serial television program; more than 30 episodes have been shown so far by China's Central Television. Yonglie's sf stories and articles have been published in the United States, France, Great Britain, West Germany, Japan, and Switzerland. In West Germany in 1984, he and Dr. Charlotte Dunsing edited and published *SF Aus China,* the first Chinese sf collection published in a foreign language abroad. He is a member of the Chinese Writers' Association and a trustee of World SF.

JANUSZ A. ZAJDEL. Born in Warsaw on August 15, 1938, Zajdel became second only to Stanislas Lem in popularity in Poland until his untimely death in 1985. His writing career, which began in 1965, was marked by many awards, including recognition for the best science-fiction novel of the year in Poland for *Limes Inferior* (1982) and *Paradyzja* (1984). A Trustee of World SF, Zajdel was able to attend the World General Meeting in Fanano, Italy, in May of 1985. But he had been fighting cancer for three years, and two months later, on his return to Warsaw, he passed away.

The Legendary Science Fiction Novel

THE SPACE MERCHANTS

by Frederik Pohl and C. M. Kornbluth

"A novel of the future that the present must inevitably rank as a classic!" —*The New York Times*

_____ 90655-2 $3.50 U.S. _____ 90656-0 $4.50 Can.

And the Brilliant Sequel

THE MERCHANTS' WAR

by Frederik Pohl

"We've waited a long time...and our patience has been well rewarded." —*Best Sellers*

_____ 90240-9 $3.50 U.S. _____ 90241-7 $4.50 Can.

Gripping Science Fiction

CHILDREN OF THE LIGHT Susan B. Weston

Accidentally marooned in a ravaged future, Jeremy Towers is almost literally the last man on earth. He becomes the key to the survival of the species and the principal pawn in a political battle to create a new world. "Ranks with Walter M. Miller's *A Canticle for Leibowitz*..." —*Locus*

____90305-7 $3.50 U.S.   ____90314-6 $4.50 Can.

DEATHHUNTER Ian Watson

They built a cage to trap Death itself...and found more than anyone imagined...."Creative beyond the boundaries of ordinary imagination." —*Best Sellers*

____90033-3 $2.95

SUNDIPPER Paul B. Thompson

Matthew Lawton is the finest Sundipper of all, one of a group of brave men and women who fly their specially-designed ships directly into the sun to tap its devastating energies. But a beautiful woman on the run involves Matthew in a race for his life.

____90706-0 $3.50 U.S.   ____90707-9 $4.50 Can.

I HOPE I SHALL ARRIVE SOON Philip K. Dick

Visit the universe of this master of science fiction. "The most consistently brilliant science fiction writer in the world."

—John Brunner

____90838-5 $3.50 U.S.   ____90839-3 $4.50 Can.